THE
HEART
OF THE
DEAL

D0063250

THE HEART OF THE DEAL

A Novel

LINDSAY MACMILLAN

alcove
press

This is a work of fiction. All of the names, characters, organizations, places and events portrayed in this novel are either products of the author's imagination or are used fictitiously. Any resemblance to real or actual events, locales, or persons, living or dead, is entirely coincidental.

Copyright © 2022 by Lindsay MacMillan

All rights reserved.

Published in the United States by Alcove Press, an imprint of The Quick Brown Fox & Company LLC.

Alcove Press and its logo are trademarks of The Quick Brown Fox & Company LLC.

Library of Congress Catalog-in-Publication data available upon request.

ISBN (hardcover): 978-1-63910-010-1
ISBN (ebook): 978-1-63910-011-8

Cover design by Kristin Solecki

Printed in the United States.

www.alcovepress.com

Alcove Press
34 West 27th St., 10th Floor
New York, NY 10001

First Edition: June 2022

10 9 8 7 6 5 4 3 2 1

For my mom, Amy MacMillan.
You light up my life and so many others' lives every day with your warm, exuberant spirit and extraordinary ability to build people up so that they believe in themselves as much as you believe in them.

PART 1

1,825 DAYS TO GO

CHAPTER ONE

QUARTER-LIFE CRISIS

Returning from a long Sunday in the office, Rae paused at the top of the stairs to catch her breath. She didn't want to show up out of breath to her own birthday party, particularly her quarter-century birthday party.

Dabbing her face with the sleeve of her suit jacket to mop up the sheen, she let herself into her apartment—the Perry Street Penthouse, as she and her roommate Ellen had rebranded their top-floor walk-up.

"Happy birthday!" Ellen shrieked from the kitchenette. She was slicing blocks of cheese with a plastic knife.

"I'm twenty-five, not eighty-five," Rae said. "No need to shout." But she was smiling. "Where's everyone else?"

Everyone else being the two friends from college she'd managed to hang on to through the real-world craze of the past few years. The Scramblettes, the foursome called themselves, after their joint culinary invention—a half omelet, half scrambled egg creation accidentally born from subpar flipping abilities. The spelling was inspired by the Rockettes to give it some New York flair.

"Sarah just texted that she's getting on the subway," Ellen said. "And you know how Mina is . . ."

Rae grunted. She'd hoped that midtwenties would be more punctual than early twenties, but apparently the Scramblettes were still the Scramblettes. "Why aren't you wearing your robe?"

They'd agreed on a bathrobe theme—much more sophisticated than a pajama party, Rae thought, much more adult-ish.

"It's over there," Ellen said, pointing to the undersized couch, where an oversized robe was draped over the armrest. "Snitched it from the hotel during my business trip."

"Very savvy," Rae said, retrieving her own robe from her bedroom. The term *bedroom* was generous. To afford West Village rent, they'd inserted drywall to split the one bedroom into two. The wall stopped a foot short of the ceiling to comply with fire regulations.

Rae removed her bathrobe from one of the plastic hooks that held up most of her belongings, the ones that hadn't already fallen to the floor. The landlord didn't allow nails, and her closet didn't fit anything beyond her black work pants and white collared shirts. In an attempt to mitigate the sexism rampant in investment banking, she dressed identically to the men. She thought the strategy might be working, though perhaps that was only because modern sexism was often too subtle for anyone—including her—to notice.

Online, the bathrobe had looked like a confident white, but it had turned out to be more of an indecisive eggshell. Still, better than the polka-dot one she'd been tempted by. Polka dots were early twenties, not midtwenties, not to mention that robe had been four dollars more expensive.

The glamorous stereotype of Wall Streeters dripping in money didn't exactly apply to Rae. The investment bank she worked for had slashed salaries for junior employees to improve profit margins, and she had big student loans to pay off. Unlike most of her colleagues, she didn't come from wealth and hadn't gotten the job from nepotism. She'd hustled to get in, and she was going to keep hustling until she got out. She made herself put ten percent of her salary into her "Poet's Fund" every month—an idealistic pot that would let her quit her corporate job one day and pursue her writing dreams.

Ellen, too, was money conscious, determined to live frugally now so she could indulge in the lavish lifestyle she was destined for later on. It was one of the things that bonded them—gleefully finding ways to save a few dollars and rolling their eyes at other twenty-somethings who spoke so cavalierly of private helicopter rides to the Hamptons.

Rae shed her corporate costume, slipped on the nearly soft fabric, and rejoined Ellen in the living room.

"Start in on this," Ellen said, pouring her a coffee mug of rosé. The wine glasses were all chipped or sitting in murky sink water.

Rae had specifically requested rosé, as nothing articulated midtwenties elegance more than an accented vowel.

"And look how much cheese we have," Ellen said, pointing to three plates stacked high with Brie, cheddar, Gorgonzola, and a few other varieties Rae didn't even know the names of. "But can you believe it, I forgot crackers, so we'll just have to eat it straight."

If anyone else had forgotten the crackers in the cheese-and-crackers equation, Rae would've been annoyed, but this was just how Ellen was, focusing so much on the details that she overlooked the basics, and Rae loved her more for it. Ellen's whimsy brought wings to Rae's logic-driven life, and Ellen swore that Rae kept her from crashing. They worked like that, filling in each other's gaps.

Rae took a swig of rosé, followed by a goopy chunk of Brie. "It's a pretty good chaser," she said approvingly.

"You don't need a chaser for rosé."

"At my age you do."

Ellen was still only twenty-four.

Rae's phone buzzed. Her heart palpitated—not a fluttering palpitation because a crush had texted but a plummeting palpitation because a boss had.

Decimal points don't match on pg. 62. Send thru updated version ASAP.

As an investment banking analyst in the Mergers & Acquisitions group, Rae's job was to prepare PowerPoints, spreadsheets, and financial models to assist the higher-ups as they wined and dined CEOs of big companies and pitched them on why they should buy other big companies to make even more money. If Rae's bank won the deal and facilitated the acquisition—which involved very little intellectual prowess and a whole lot of extravagant pageantry—they made a disgusting amount of money in fees, none of which trickled down to the sleep-deprived worker bees at the bottom. At its core, Rae's role was just to be everyone's personal bitch, accepting each menial request 24/7 with a cheerful "Will do!"

Rae began replying to the text, but Ellen snatched the phone away. "No work tonight," she said.

"But—"

"The global economy isn't going to collapse if you don't fix a fucking decimal point."

Ellen drowned Rae's protests with the Quarter Century Club playlist she'd made. The first song was well-selected—poppy without the sugar—and stirred a certain optimism in Rae.

Twenty-five was the year she'd finally be promoted, rising from Wall Street's bottom rung to its second-to-bottom rung. And it felt like a more low-key era when she could meet up with the Scramblettes for sushi on a Friday night and then be curled up in bed before the just-out-of-college crowd had even wiggled into their constricting miniskirts and stilettos.

Sure, it was more than a little disconcerting to compare her mid-twenties reality of fifteen-hour workdays and takeout meals for one to the married-with-a-dog-and-kid-on-the-way lifestyles of her friends back in her Indiana hometown, but at least in Manhattan she felt like she was moving. She wasn't exactly sure where all the motion was leading, but there was some sense of *forward*, and on good days, even *upward*.

Turning up the volume on the speaker, she and Ellen pranced around the apartment, twirling their robes for effect.

Many songs later, Sarah arrived, wearing an oversized sweatshirt rather than a robe. "It's basically the same," she said, when Rae asked why she hadn't adhered to the theme.

"No," Rae said, voice clipped. "Sweatshirts say, 'I'm lazy and haven't showered in days.' Bathrobes say, 'I'm effortlessly seductive and smell like fresh peaches.'"

"She's right," Ellen said, as the three of them formed a lopsided triangle on the floor, leaving room for Mina.

The couch wasn't big enough to fit all four of them, even if they squished, and they preferred collectively suffering on the hardwood to relegating just one of them to the floor.

"I think twenty-five is going to be the year Rae meets the great love of her life," Ellen proclaimed, topping off their mugs.

"Definitely," Sarah agreed.

"No," Rae said, bad mood about work spilling now into a bad mood about love. "I'm focusing on my career."

"And you're crushing it," Ellen said, as she often did. "I just think it's time to join the modern age and get a dating app."

"I barely even get to see my friends," Rae said, resenting her job for consuming her life and herself for letting it. "Why do I want to waste my time on complete strangers?"

"Everyone starts out as a stranger," Sarah said.

Rae thought about how, when she'd first met her college boyfriend in that over-capacity, beer-soaked frat basement, he hadn't felt like a stranger. She didn't like it, how she still remembered the untainted beginning. They'd dated for a few years before he'd cheated on Rae with the girl Rae had been living with right after college. He'd spun the blame on her: "You're in an exclusive relationship with your job!"

"It's good to keep working your relationship muscle," Ellen said. "So it doesn't atrophy too much."

"My relationship muscle is very strong, thank you," Rae said, feeling a stab of betrayal at how Ellen was lecturing her about love, on her birthday no less.

"How many dates have you been on since you and Jake broke up?" Ellen asked. Ellen went on first dates just about every week. None of them had stuck yet.

"Plenty," Rae said, though it wasn't true. She hadn't technically been on any dates since her breakup two years ago, not unless you counted the time she'd gotten drinks with a client—a networking event, she'd thought—and he'd ended up hitting on her.

Maybe it was recalling the way his hand had slid assertively up her thigh that night, or maybe it was the way she was now sitting on the floor eating blocks of cheese at her own birthday party, but something made her see her dating life in a new light—a very dim, very dark light that was flickering ominously, as if to warn her it was about to go out altogether.

Reminding herself that she had more important things to focus on than meeting guys, she tried to push back against the angst, but the angst pushed back with a mind of its own, like it was staging a coup on her own brain, a coup it had been planning for a long time now and had chosen tonight to execute, knowing how vulnerable she'd be to a quarter-life crisis.

The anxiety escalated into full-blown panic. She'd completed twenty-five laps around the sun and yet was still at square zero when it came to love. In trying to climb up the corporate ladder, she'd fallen completely off the romantic ladder.

Chugging the rest of her rosé, she reached for an unopened bottle of room-temperature Chardonnay. "Shit," she said, yanking on the cork-screw. She still struggled to open wine bottles. She should've mastered more of these adult things by now, but she hadn't, and in this moment, she was certain she never would. "I'm in a romantic recession."

Ellen and Sarah rattled off a string of supposed-to-be-soothing words, but Rae's screeching escalated as she kept tugging the cork, which was shredding as it stayed stuck in the neck of the bottle. "A romantic recession!" she cried, latching on to the alliteration. "And my dad didn't even send me a birthday card." The negative spiral was all intertwined. "And I hate my mom's boyfriend. And I'm going to be staring at pointless spreadsheets for the rest of my life and never write a single poem. And I'm going to die alone, surrounded by cats!" she concluded in crescendo.

"Well, then that's not really alone, is it?" Sarah asked, trying to lighten the mood. "Since you'll have the cats."

Rae tried to glare, but her eyelids were too tired. The thought of work tomorrow made her want to simultaneously curl into a ball and teleport away, away, *away*.

A serrated blade of clarity woke her up. "I have to meet someone this year or it's all over," Rae announced, pivoting to her no-nonsense business voice.

"What do you mean?" Ellen said. "You're still so young."

"Twenty-five is just a baby in New York," Sarah agreed. "People settle down way later here. There's no rush."

"Well, by Midwest standards I'm basically approaching old-maid territory," Rae said. "And sorry to break it to you, but the biological clock doesn't give a damn about New Yorkers' enlightened lifestyles. Our eggs are still bleeding out every month."

"Don't say that," Ellen said with a shudder as Sarah gagged at the graphic visual.

"It's just the truth," Rae said. "Think about it logically." Usually her analytical mind could talk her out of overreacting, but this time it was doing the opposite. "Let's work backwards with the math. Women's biological clocks expire at thirty-five, so I need to have all my kids before then." She'd seen too many stats about how the probability of pregnancy complications and birth defects increased after thirty-five, and she didn't trust that she'd be one of the lucky ones.

"I want three kids, spaced at least two years apart, so that means I'll have my third kid at thirty-five, my second at thirty-three, and my first at thirty-one." She was determined to create a big, boisterous family, the kind she'd always longed for as an only child.

"And I want to be married for a bit to build a solid foundation with my husband before our offspring take over our lives," she went on. This part was particularly important. She'd done the math to figure out that she'd been conceived on her parents' honeymoon, and she thought this might have been one of the key variables that had doomed them for divorce.

"So that means I've got to tie the knot *before I turn thirty*." The big three-oh, only five years away, loomed large and menacing in her head and in her heart.

She paused for a breath. When it didn't come, she plowed ahead anyway. "So married at twenty-nine, and build in a year for planning the wedding, so let's say I get engaged at twenty-eight. And we'd want to live together for a year before getting engaged to validate compatibility, which puts me at twenty-seven, and we have to date two years before that to make sure we're making rational decisions, not just swept up in the hormones. So that puts me at *twenty-five*."

She shuddered, infuriated with herself because she hadn't thought about this earlier, though she knew she had on some level—she'd just tried her best not to acknowledge it until it came bursting out tonight. "I need to meet my husband ASAP so I can get married before thirty, or it's all over."

Ellen and Sarah looked rattled, like Rae's words struck too close to home, like they too were getting spooked by the cruel truths of womanhood and the shrinking pool of eggs.

"ASAP!" Rae repeated, with the same urgency with which her bosses were always requesting financial models for the deals she worked on.

The penthouse door opened. It was Mina, standing there in jeans and heeled boots, bathrobe nowhere in sight. "So sorry I'm late," she said, panting from the six flights of stairs. "My Uber driver drove like a grandpa." She kicked off her shoes and joined them on the floor. "What'd I miss?"

Rae waited for the others to give away her meltdown, but Ellen just said, very casually, "We're downloading a dating app for Rae to bail her out of her love slump."

Mina clapped, like this was the best of all possible answers. "Scramblettes to the rescue!"

Rae gave up on the cork. She left the damaged bottle on the floor and lay down on the couch, mismatched socks dangling off the edge. She wrapped her robe tighter, sealing herself in. She felt like she'd been stuck in a calamitous scene from someone else's memoir, only to turn the page and find out it was her own story, but someone else had written it for her.

Ellen perched herself on the armrest, stroking Rae's hair. Rae didn't get much physical touch these days, with the exception of firm handshakes at work and pointy elbows to the ribs on the subway, or on a good day, the grazing of a barista's hand as he passed Rae the whipped cream–topped cappuccino that had become her daily breakfast.

"I need to close the marriage deal before I'm thirty," she mumbled so only Ellen could hear. She spent all her time helping close deals at work, locking in mergers and acquisitions. Now it was time to lock in a husband.

"You don't need to worry about marriage right now," Ellen said, patting Rae's head. "You just need to have some fun."

But Rae wasn't going to be dissuaded. It had all become horribly transparent. She could see her own future projected forward, out to three decimal points. If current trends continued, she'd become one of those old, bitter women who stuffed her empty life with expensive handbags . . . a sharp-elbowed, scowl-defaulting New Yorker who wasn't just immune to frivolities like love, but truly above them.

The timeline was expiring fast. Getting married before thirty was an ambitious goal perhaps, but she was an ambitious person.

And it was the only way she could have it all—the stellar job and the stellar family. She couldn't wait until she rose in her career to find a husband. She had to find him now, or it would be too late.

The pressure of it all was paralyzing. She rolled over on the couch, put on her headphones, set a downer indie song on repeat, and handed Ellen her phone, trusting her to know what to do, or at least know more than she did herself.

Sometime later, Ellen tapped her shoulder until Rae took off her headphones.

"Are you okay with your profile?" Ellen asked.

Rae lowered her eyes to the screen Ellen was showing her. She cringed as she saw RAE, 25 on the top of the profile, followed by photos of her smiling stylishly at a party, smiling athletically on a mountaintop, smiling approachably with her golden retriever back in Indiana.

Rae nearly told Ellen to find some other photos—with angles that showed the true width of her nose or how pasty her skin had become from years of rarely seeing the sun except through office windows. But showing her flaws meant losing out to the filtered competition, so she kept quiet.

Underneath the pictures came the quick stats:

Height: 5'4"

Rae experienced another letdown upon realizing she had willfully entered a world so shallow that height was the first attribute listed.

Hometown: Meridian Hills, Indiana

She was technically from Pocksey, but apparently the Scramblettes didn't think that sounded alluring enough, so they'd opted for the town next door.

College: Columbia

That much was true, but she hated its Ivy League attitude. It sounded softer spoken aloud but looked prickly and pretentious written out.

Job: Finance

She was glad, at least, that they'd put "finance" rather than "investment banker." It was slightly less abrasive, though the nuance would probably be lost.

She scrolled to keep reading the rest of her summary, but there was nothing more. Just like that, Rae had boiled herself—all her past achievements and failures, current hobbies and routines, future ambitions and uncertainties—down to just another profile that guys would spend two seconds—three if she was lucky—glancing at before deciding whether to swipe "like" or "next."

It felt even worse than distilling herself into a one-page résumé.

She could hear her Indiana friends: *Come on, Raelynn, you're better than this.* Everyone back home called her Raelynn. The *Lynn* had fallen off once she'd stepped foot on Columbia's campus in New York, seven years ago now. *Rae* was more city chic. But how much more of herself was she leaving behind as time went on?

She didn't have the emotional capacity to debate this now, so she turned the music up and whispered or shouted, she couldn't tell which, "Just publish it."

Publish. The verb she longed to hear in reference to her poetry, now more depressingly affixed to her dating life.

Sprawled horizontal, Rae lifted the mug to her lips. It seemed Ellen had filled it with red wine after cutting their losses on the bottle of white. The wine trickled onto her robe in tacky red polka dots, wiping out all the gains she'd thought she'd made in her adult life. Without sitting up, Rae kept slurping and began swiping for her soul mate.

She had five years—1,825 days, she calculated—to close the husband deal before her thirtieth birthday, and there was no time to procrastinate.

CHAPTER TWO

THE DATING APP BAILOUT

"What do you think of this guy?" Rae asked Ellen, tilting her phone toward Ellen to display the profile of NICK, 29.

They were lounging on the penthouse couch on a Friday night a couple weeks after Rae's birthday. Rae was wearing her bathrobe, now wine stain–free thanks to a trip to the dry cleaner in a concerted midtwenties effort to *invest in myself.*

Ellen was in an oversized T-shirt and boxers. Their heads were at opposite ends of the couch, legs bent at the knees and feet delicately resting beside each other's ears. It was the most space-efficient posture they'd found, and they could hardly even smell each other's reused socks over the lingering odor of the broccoli-and-beet scramblette they'd cooked for dinner. It hadn't been their best egg invention to date, but they still considered it a success, since it hadn't triggered the smoke detector.

Ellen broke eye contact with her own screen to look at Rae's. "Definitely not," she said, within nanoseconds. "No guys making peace signs in their photos. We've been over this."

"But he doesn't have a backwards hat or beer can," Rae said. "Doesn't that make it better?"

"Marginally. Next."

Rae kept swiping suitors with one hand and snacking with the other, reaching into the family-sized bag of popcorn on the coffee table. Snack & Swipe—they'd patented the game, which had taken precedence over a night out with Sarah and Mina.

The dizzyingly large market size of eligible bachelors was addicting, and Rae had missed her subway stop multiple times on her commute to and from the office.

"What about him?" Rae asked Ellen, showing MIKE, 27.

"Next," Ellen said. "He's holding a dead fish."

"What's wrong with fishing?"

"There's nothing wrong with fishing, there's something wrong with using a four-foot-long dead trout to impress girls. It's like he's overcompensating for something."

"You're ruthless," Rae said, taking notes in the spiral pad propped open on her lap. *No dead fish*, she added to the list, below *No shirtless photos* ("ego alert"), *No inflatable swans* ("party boy"), *No tech entrepreneurs* ("code for scam artist"), and the list went on. Rae hadn't come across her ex's profile yet, but if she did, she knew he'd fail on multiple criteria.

"I take my job as your dating app mentor very seriously," Ellen said. She was well qualified for the role, with years of app experience under her belt, though even if Ellen had never swiped a single profile, Rae probably would have still consulted her just as much.

Ellen had had that effect on Rae since the first time they'd met on the street two years ago. Rae had been walking down Tenth Avenue one Saturday to pick up a prescription that had been sitting at the pharmacy for three weeks when she'd spotted a stylish brunette crossing at West Twenty-Ninth. The girl—Rae still thought of herself and her contemporaries as girls rather than women—looked about her age but far more put together, in heels and a camel trench coat with a chic black bag, her shiny dark hair pulled into a chignon, if that was the right word.

Rae had felt a surge of inadequacy at her own sloppy ponytail, sweatpants, and plastic grocery bag that was doubling as a purse.

Then, as Rae was taking in how the girl's heels confidently clicked on the pavement, the girl fell down. A car hit her, not pausing for the pedestrian "walk" signal. Rae called 911, and Ellen was taken to the hospital with a fractured wrist. That afternoon, Rae visited, bringing a dozen bagels in lieu of flowers.

She'd worried that Ellen might be a "no carbs" type, but Ellen gleefully devoured the bagels, looking much less glamorous as she spilled crumbs on her hospital gown.

After the ex-boyfriend-cheating-with-the-roommate scandal, Rae broke her lease and moved in with Ellen, who'd been trying to fill the second bedroom of a "historic West Village penthouse" she'd fallen in love with at first sight. Ellen's roommate search hadn't been going particularly well—most prospects backed out once they realized it was a prewar walk-up building, and the ones who made it up the stairs were put off by the minor detail that the second bedroom didn't actually exist yet. Several tenants had still been interested, given the relatively attractive price point and objectively attractive location, but Ellen vetoed prospect after prospect for "roommate red flags," which included not eating ice cream or being picky about drinking only *chilled* white wine.

"The universe wants us to be there for each other when we're hurting," Ellen had proclaimed as she and Rae cosigned the Perry Street lease. "First the car accident, and now this."

"What about this one?" Rae said now, and showed TIM, 28 to her mentor.

After a full profile review, stretching nearly six seconds, Ellen approved. "Great smile. Very genuine. And I like that he's from North Carolina—southern guys are more chivalrous. And he has dogs in three pictures, so he must have a really kind heart."

"I know," Rae said, wondering what she should wear to Thanksgiving with Tim's family next year. Perhaps a sundress with a light jacket, but she'd pack layers to be safe. "He's perfect."

"Find out if he has a brother, will you? We could double-date."

"I'll ask once we meet in the flesh. I hope he circles back with a cute date idea."

"Rae-bae, you're going to have to overcome your old-fashioned guy-asks-girl-out views if you want to find your diamond in the dating app rough," Ellen said.

Maybe it was a consequence of her Midwest roots, but Rae still wanted to sit back and be courted. In every other part of her life—advocating for herself at work, pushing her way onto the crowded subway, hailing a cab so it didn't whiz right by—she had to be tough and aggressive. When it came to love, she wanted to be quiet and soft and have her perfect man swoop in when she least expected it, like in the romance books she didn't have time to read anymore. But if she waited for that to happen, she'd be waiting forever, well into her thirties, when she'd no doubt look back and curse her idealistic twenty-five-year-old self for not taking more initiative.

"Fine," Rae told Ellen, not feeling very fine at all. "What should I say?"

"Just say, 'Hey, Tim! Want to get drinks next week?'"

Rae typed the phrase verbatim, proofread it three times, and sent it off into cyberspace with a jolt of adrenaline.

She began swiping faster to hedge her heart with more options, and also snacking faster to relieve the correlated anxiety.

"Just remember," Ellen said. "It's not personal if he doesn't reply. Guys ghost me about half the time."

This didn't bode well. If fifty percent of guys were ignoring Ellen, whose profile was an unattainable mesh of glamour-meets-girl-next-door, Rae would be lucky to achieve a ten percent response rate.

"Got it," Rae said, though she knew that of course she would take it personally if Tim ignored her and of course she would devour a pint of ice cream calling him a series of defiling names. "So how's your own pipeline looking?" she asked.

"Can we please not use work jargon to describe our dating lives? It's so unromantic."

"Ellen, we've outsourced our dating pool to an algorithm. The app has removed the romanticism, not me."

"It's okay to be practical," Ellen said. "But not transactional."

"Practical not transactional," Rae repeated, jotting down the acronym PNT. "Got it. Any dates lined up this week?"

"I have a first date tomorrow with Sean." She showed Rae the profile of a thirty-year-old who worked as a corporate-grade bond investor. "We're the same age, once you adjust for gender," Ellen explained. "Since women's brains are three years more mature than their actual age and men's brains are three years less mature."

Rae was intrigued by this numbers-based way to compare compatibility. "So you're twenty-four but have the maturity of a twenty-seven-year-old? And he's thirty but actually twenty-seven?"

"Exactly," Ellen said, looking pleased with her contribution to the science of modern love. "So stay away from anyone under twenty-eight. They're still children."

"Too bad women don't have that luxury of growing up slowly," Rae grumbled. "How unfair is it that men don't have to worry about a biological clock? They can keep playing the field for as long as they want and then have kids in their old age with no negative ramifications. Talk about systemic sexism." This had become her new favorite rant, and she hadn't grown tired of recycling it yet.

"I know," Ellen agreed. "It's a cruel joke from our creator."

"I mean, given how much humans have evolved over thousands of years, you would've thought that *just maybe* women's childbearing years could've been extended to keep up with the increased life-span. But no, that would just be too much equality, wouldn't it?"

"I'm with you," Ellen said, but then switched the conversation back to her dating lineup. "I might go on a second date with Billy."

Rae was still mulling over the biological injustice of being a woman, and it took her a few moments before she remembered to reply. "Which one is Billy again?"

"Law school guy I got tiramisu with last weekend."

"I thought you didn't feel a spark."

"I didn't, but his follow-up was impressive. And I really want to break the third-date curse."

Ellen was convinced she had a curse that prevented her from getting past date three with anyone. Whenever Ellen really liked a guy, he pulled a spectacular disappearing act, and whenever a guy really liked Ellen, she vanished with equal gusto.

"It's not a curse," Rae said, for what must have been the hundredth time. "You're just prudent with your emotional investments."

Rae's phone buzzed. It was the app letting her know she had a new message from Tim.

Heyy! Ya lets do it. U free Tues nite?

"That's the fastest reply I've ever seen," Ellen said. "Told you you'd be a natural."

"I'm not dating someone who texts with bad spelling," Rae said, eyeing Tim's reply with disgust. "Clear deal breaker."

"Don't be so picky," Ellen said. "Guys are rarely this decisive. We can't let this opportunity slip by." She snatched Rae's phone and sent a reply. Sounds great!!! 9pm @ Bathtub Gin?

Rae grabbed the phone back. "What're you doing? You know I'm not a three-exclamation-points person."

"That's just how the game is played. He needs to know you're excited, or he'll choose one of the dozens of other girls he's matched with instead."

"Joy."

"Once he meets you, he'll obviously realize your unrivaled amazingness. If he has a full-sized brain, that is."

"That's a lofty assumption for guys in New York."

"True. But to speak your language—you have to diligence a lot of duds before you find the one. It's a numbers game, really."

Rae had a mind for numbers, but she was a words person at heart, and even the idea of getting rejected left her feeling cold and small. She admired Ellen's persistence, the way she kept putting herself out there again, one letdown or fizzle after another, but she wasn't formed from the same mold.

"It only takes one jackpot," Ellen said. "And who knows? Maybe it's Tim. He seems really great."

"Let's just hope I can recognize him."

"Watch it," Ellen warned.

There had been a recent debacle where Ellen had shown up at a bar and not been able to find her date because she'd been looking for the athletic, thick-haired person from the dating app pictures instead of the rotund bald man waiting for her.

"Just wait," Ellen said. "You're going to have your share of horror stories too."

Rae must have blanched, because Ellen added quickly, "But they'll make for good material for us to laugh over at our bachelorette parties one day. We're in this together, Rae-bae."

The *we* injected Rae with a surge of warmth, or maybe it was just the way Ellen's socks felt like earmuffs. "Promise?"

"Popcorn promise," Ellen said, tossing a kernel of popcorn into the air for Rae to catch with her mouth. Rae missed, and the popcorn fell behind the couch, into a crevice they'd never attempt to reach with the vacuum.

Then they both looked back at their phones and kept sourcing dates with the work ethic of bankers sourcing deals.

CHAPTER THREE
FIRST-ROUND INTERVIEW

"Does natural deodorant actually work for you?" Rae asked Ellen through the phone as she walked, cloaked in sweat, up Ninth Avenue through the bustling streets of Chelsea.

Chelsea was a vibrant cross between West Village charm and Midtown crowds. Quaint three-story brownstones with character-steeped stoops were jammed right next to high-rise glass skyscrapers with edgy hexagonal windows. The mishmash of architecture coexisted with such confidence that it gave the impression it had always been this way, that the city had in fact been designed like this right from the start. A faint garbage-and-sewage scent permeated the air—Manhattan's signature perfume that Rae had been breathing for so long that she hardly noticed it anymore.

The sky was dark, but the streets were bright with light spilling out from offices and apartments, 24/7 diners that oozed grease and grit, jam-packed gyms where impossibly beautiful people sprinted on treadmills in the windows as if determined to evoke envy among the plebian passersby, and from the headlights of bumper-to-bumper traffic where the impatience of being late to something very important was one of the million emotions swirling in the grimy, glorious potion that was the Manhattan night.

Between blocks, Rae could catch a glimpse of the Empire State Building's iconic spire, lit up like a manmade lightning rod and shifting colors like a mood ring. The landmark was something of her north star in New York, helping recenter her when she got disoriented.

She was on her way to meet up with Tim at Bathtub Gin, a speakeasy whose entrance was located through the back of Stone Street Coffee Company, an unobtrusive little spot that was easy to miss if you weren't *in the know* or following explicit directions from Google Maps, like Rae was. It couldn't be more than forty-five degrees out, and on another night, Rae might have found humor in how she was somehow perspiring through goose bumps. But not tonight.

"Natural deodorant works," Ellen assured her. It was a weeknight, and Ellen was away for work on a project in Ohio—"making PowerPoint slides summarizing made-up data and common sense," as she described her management consulting job. She'd sneaked out to take Rae's call from an office bathroom stall. "You just have to put on a couple layers."

"I put on five," Rae said, nerves sharpening her voice.

Ellen had been preaching the perils of regular deodorant—a fast track to cancer with its aluminum toxins, apparently—and Rae had chosen today to try out a natural variety. It had been an elegant idea, ringing in this new *I'm a midtwenties woman who's ready to meet her true love* era with eucalyptus-extract armpits, but the sweaty reality was making her regret not sticking to her trustworthy routine of extra-strength sport gel.

Ellen was not the type of person who had to choose between smelling good and plugging her pores with carcinogens. Rae found it as fitting a metaphor as any for the differences between them.

"I'm sure you smell fine," Ellen said. "You have your exit plan in place?"

As part of the predate coaching lessons, Ellen had told Rae about the importance of limiting the first date to an hour to avoid getting trapped. The key, Ellen said, was to let the guy know ahead of time about the time constraint so he didn't take it personally in the moment.

"Yes," Rae said, proud of her execution. "I told him I have to dial into a conference call in Asia in the evening at ten, our time."

"A conference call?" Ellen said, and Rae could feel her cringing from her toilet seat perch. "You had to pick *that* as your excuse?"

"What was I supposed to say?"

"Literally anything else! A friend's birthday, a furniture delivery . . ."

"A furniture delivery at ten P.M. on a Wednesday? A conference call in China is way more believable."

Ellen sounded like she was about to refute the point, but the toilet flushed beneath her. "Damn automatic flushes," she said. "Just try not to talk about work the whole date, okay?"

"Okay," Rae gulped, mentally reciting the safe topics Ellen had given her. *Family, hobbies, dogs, vacations, roommates.* She'd written the acronym FHDVR on the margins of her work notebook all week. "Can I just have a chip in my ear so you can talk me through it?"

"You'll be great, Rae-bae. My boss is calling me, I have to run. But text me right after! And he's an idiot if he doesn't fall in love with you within the first five minutes, overactive sweat glands and all."

And just like that, Ellen hung up.

New York shuffled around her with its midweek pulse, and Rae felt cripplingly alone. Ellen had helped make her dating app profile, Ellen had lined up the first date, Ellen had coached her on what to say, but now it was just Rae walking to the bar to meet up with a complete stranger.

Her feet felt heavy as they clacked against the cement sidewalk. As if protesting being forced along, one of her heels got stuck between the grills of an iron drainage grate. Yanking herself free, she wanted to turn around and go back to the penthouse, stopping by Percy's

Pizza for some comfort slices, but she soldiered on, determined to make Ellen and the rest of the Scramblettes proud and determined to get one date closer to her wedding day.

Not wanting to arrive early, she did a lap around the block and circled back at 9:03 to wait outside the speakeasy, doing her best to dodge the mystery liquid dripping from the rickety scaffolding overhead. Tim still wasn't there, unless he was the fiftysomething man pacing the sidewalk, ranting about "fucking double standards."

Rae looked down at her phone, willing herself to emanate a *No rush at all, I'm just calmly and coolly catching up on my vibrant social life* vibe.

He's late, she texted the Scramblettes' group chat. What if he doesn't show?

How late?? Mina asked.

3 mins, Rae texted.

Give him 10!

Agreed, Sarah chimed in. Probably just subway delays.

Ellen added, But if he bails, I'll find out where he lives and deliver a gift basket of cockroaches!

Plz take the ones from my apartment? Mina texted.

After I get rid of the clan in my dresser . . . but you've got this, Rae!

We love you!!

Rae felt a smile poke through. She wondered if guys cheered each other on before dates too.

"Rae?"

She looked up, and there he was. Tim. Dressed in a crisp white-collared shirt with meticulously parted blond hair. Her first reaction was that he looked nearly like his profile pictures.

She smiled and automatically stuck out her hand. He shook it.

A handshake? Rae chastised herself as they let go. *This isn't a business meeting!*

She wanted to run to the bathroom to text the Scramblettes about her screw-up, but she heard them in her head.

You can recover from that!

Not nearly as bad as the time I head-butted my date when I went in for the hug . . . almost gave him a concussion!

Just order a couple shots, and you'll loosen up!

Tim held the first door but forgot to do so for the second door, which led into the speakeasy, so Rae followed him inside. The bar was dimly lit, long and narrow with swanky leather booths, striped armchairs, and a real copper bathtub that seemed to have been put there with the hope of a naked flapper lying in it, smoking a sultry cigarette while men looked on with self-righteous lust.

The space was crowded with tweed sport coats and black cocktail dresses. Rae was so accustomed to her work-late-go-home-sleep-and-repeat routine that it always came as a surprise to recall that there was an alternative version of New York City where socializing wasn't confined to the weekend.

A waiter seated them at a table in the back, wedged between the overly ornate wallpaper and another date-night couple. Tim sat across from her, and there was nowhere to look except at each other or down at the candle in the middle of the table. Rae chose the candle.

"Two gin and tonics to start," Tim said to the waiter. Rae didn't even mind that he didn't ask her before ordering. She just wanted a glass to hold so she had something to do with her hands, which were twisting in her lap.

"So, Rae," Tim said, giving her an easy smile. "Tell me about yourself." He seemed to have the small-talk routine down, and Rae wondered which number first date she was for him. She felt like she was on an interview, back in the 1920s when a woman never would've gotten a job on Wall Street.

He folded his hands on the white tablecloth and waited for her to answer.

*   *   *

Forty-six minutes later, Rae was returning alone to the Perry Street Penthouse. She walked down the Highline, an old train track converted into a pedestrian walking path that was lined with exotic-looking trees and shrubs. Perched twenty feet above the street, it provided some respite from the concrete chaos below.

Impossibly posh apartments rimmed the Highline, and most of them had their curtains thrown open, as if inviting people to stare in and drool over the glamorous lives of their occupants. It had the opposite effect on Rae, the grandeur feeling cold and sterile. Looking into the windows of one of the apartments, she saw a man and woman watching the same TV show in separate rooms and drew up a sad little story that they were a married couple who'd grown apart as they'd grown rich.

Depressed by the emptiness of it all, Rae descended back to street level on West Fourteenth and hurried on toward the quieter section of the West Village, where the familiar streets swaddled her close with their cobblestone love and ivy-wall peace. On an overbuilt island where everyone was always in a rush, this was the closest place that felt like home. It was still quite loud and crowded on an absolute basis, but it was relatively calm and quiet, especially in the less desirable, more affordable part where she and Ellen lived—a fifteen-minute walk from the subway but close to the Hudson River and its slow-burning sunsets.

Rae called Ellen on the phone and willed her to pick up with their BFF telepathy.

"What's wrong?" Ellen answered on the second ring. "Did that asshole stand you up?"

"No," Rae said, body and breath slowly unclenching. "We had our date."

"It's already done?"

"It was forty-six minutes," Rae defended. "Rounds up to an hour."

"Well, how was it?"

"It was . . . I survived."

"What did you talk about?"

"Dogs, mostly, and places we wanted to travel. A little about our families. I mostly steered the conversation away from work." It hadn't been easy, as he'd kept probing with questions like *Do you see yourself on Wall Street long-term?*

"Good job," Ellen said. "Was he threshold-level attractive?"

Threshold-level attractive, or TLA, as Rae thought of it, was one of Ellen's dating terms—it meant a guy just had to be a certain level of good-looking, and from there his personality carried the chemistry.

"Yes," Rae said. "Though he definitely lied about his height."

"Why do guys do that? We find out in the first two seconds once we meet them."

"And he made the waitress take back his drink because he didn't think it was strong enough."

"Red flag," Ellen said. "Two red flags in one, actually. High maintenance and potential alcoholic."

"And it was really hard to hear in the bar. When I told him my parents were divorced, he thought I said my parents had a horse. I had to shout it like five times."

"You told him your parents were divorced?"

"Well, yeah," Rae said. "He asked if my family was back in Indiana." He'd actually asked if they were back in Illinois, but she'd been so grateful he'd brought up a topic so that she didn't have to scrounge for one that she hadn't been nearly as offended as she usually was when people mixed up the two.

"I'd maybe wait until a second or third date to bring that up," Ellen cautioned.

"Why?" Rae said, prickling as she turned west onto Perry Street, lined with mostly alive oak trees whose golden leaves had nearly all abandoned the branches by this time of year. She crunched a few of the fallen leaves with her heels to release some anxiety, immediately feeling remorse for breaking them into bits. "I didn't tell him all the gory details, but I'm not going to pretend that my parents are still together."

Ellen had one of those perfect families whose Christmas card photo was an actual representation of their closeness. Rae usually shared in Ellen's happiness and liked knowing that those kinds of families could exist, but she wasn't above the occasional twinge of resentment.

She thought back to Tim's "Oh, that's a bummer" reaction when she'd mentioned her parents were divorced. *Investment risk*, he must've been thinking. Ellen was right. Rae had scared him away.

"He just wasn't my person," Rae said aloud as she chided herself. "It's fine." She was far more compatible with Tim the Character she'd invented in her head than she was with Tim the Real Live Person.

"So how did you leave it?" Ellen asked.

"I think he said nice meeting me and I think I repeated it back. I can't really remember, I was just focused on avoiding a kiss." The verb *avoiding* didn't really fit, as he'd made no attempt, but better safe than sorry.

"Well, I'm proud of you," Ellen said. "I wish I were there to celebrate with you and Ben & Jerry. Best kind of double date."

"I'm just going to write my haiku and go to bed." Rae had decided she'd write a haiku after all of her first dates to highlight key takeaways and help her home in on the right match. A poem was more elegant than bullet points, and a haiku was the most efficient form for the task.

After saying good-bye to Ellen, Rae reached their apartment building, an ugly concrete outlier among the brick and brownstones. The unrefined paintbrush of time had streaked it with yellow and gray, and boxy air-conditioning units protruded from the grilled windows, dripping unclean condensation and threatening to topple out altogether onto the heads of pedestrians below. A precarious-looking metal fire escape zigzagged all the way up to sixth-floor penthouse. In the event of an evacuation, Rae had decided that it would be far more dangerous to trust those stairs to hold her weight than to jump out the window with a bedsheet parachute.

Opening the door with an old-fashioned brass key that got stuck in the moody lock about half the time, she started up the narrow stairs, not even bothering to avoid the vomit stains on the pilled carpet like she usually did.

Sucked in by the dating app, she swiped through a fresh batch of profiles as she finished trudging up the ninety-six steps. Once inside the apartment, she wrapped herself in her robe and sprawled out on the little couch that felt too big without Ellen.

Feet hanging over the armrest, she wrote her first haiku on a pale-yellow Post-it note.

> On date number one
> I learned not to shake his hand
> or mention "divorce."

She stowed it under a stack of student loan paperwork so no one would see it, least of all her, and then checked her phone to see if Tim had texted her. He hadn't. She didn't really want to go out with him again anyway, but she at least wanted him to ask.

After setting her alarm for 5:50 A.M., she turned off the light and jammed in foam earplugs to partially dampen the horns and sirens and errant hollers of drunkards, all competing for attention in this urban circus ring.

CHAPTER FOUR

DATE SUMMARIES

"That's it," Rae said, panting into the penthouse after her tenth fruitless first date. "I'm burned out."

She yanked off knee-high boots and made a beeline for one of the ice cream pints packed into the woefully small freezer.

"What was wrong with this one?" Ellen asked, folding laundry in the living room, or at least clumping the clean clothes into piles.

Ellen was on laundry duty, meaning it was her turn to lug their dirty wardrobes down seven flights to the basement washing machines, infamous for gobbling quarters and socks. They'd problem-solved by buying enough underwear to sustain them four full weeks between washes, but the downside was that when they did do laundry, they had so much that it took between three hours and three days to put away.

"I'll read you the haiku summary," Rae said, taking a sticky note out of her pocket.

> Date ten not bad but
> his all-time favorite book was
> The Wall Street Journal.

"But you like the *Wall Street Journal* too," Ellen pointed out.

"I *tolerate* the *Wall Street Journal*. And it's a newspaper, not a book, for crying out loud."

"I still wouldn't say enjoying business news is a deal breaker."

"But not sharing french fries is?" Rae quipped.

Ellen had just ended things with someone after three dates because he wasn't adequately enthusiastic about her helping herself to his food without asking.

"Generosity is the cornerstone of any good relationship," Ellen asserted.

"As is an ounce of creativity." Rae dug into the ice cream pint with a fork (no spoons to be found) and ate standing up. The couch was draped with still-damp leggings and sweaters.

"Well, I'm still proud of you," Ellen said, sorting their underwear—lacy thongs in Ellen's pile, cotton-blend briefs in Rae's. "You've come a long way in a short time."

It was mid-December now, two grueling months after the great emotional crisis of Rae's twenty-fifth birthday.

"My sweat glands have certainly normalized," Rae said. "Though that's probably just because I stopped using that stupid natural deodorant you recommended."

There had been other cringeworthy moments beyond the sweat and handshakes—spilling red wine on her date's monogrammed shirt cuffs, being hit with a slippery kiss and instinctively wiping it from her mouth, admitting her writing ambitions to a guy who'd audibly scoffed upon finding out she was unpublished.

After her fifth painful date, she'd assembled the Scramblettes for a performance review, soliciting feedback. She'd worked her way up the learning curve—stepping up predate diligence, cross-checking LinkedIn profiles with dating app profiles, screening for matches who were differentiated from the competition, and honing her *About me* pitch.

"At least the percentage of guys who asked me out again improved by a multiple of three in the second cohort of dates," Rae said, congratulating herself with a generous forkful of ice cream. "Sixty percent compared to only twenty percent."

"Drink," Ellen said, pointing to an already-opened wine bottle on the kitchen counter. The Scramblettes had imposed a rule where Rae had to drink every time she used corporate lingo to describe dating. It hadn't curbed her habit yet. She took a swig straight from the bottle.

"But I still haven't found my husband," Rae moped. "The algorithm is flawed. It matches like with like, but I don't want another investment banker whose idea of scintillating conversation is debating whether discounted cash flow analysis or precedent transaction data is a more reliable method of valuing blue-chip corporations."

Ellen snickered. "Are you sure you don't want to go on a second date with any of the guys you've met, though?" she asked. "First dates are good for screening out psychos, but it's hard to actually get to know someone."

"No," Rae said. "The opportunity cost is too high."

"Drink again."

Rae took another swig. "I just mean, why would I choose to suffer through more small talk when I could be meeting someone new or catching up on sleep?"

"That's what toilet naps are for," Ellen said.

The toilet nap was Ellen's newest invention. It went like this: you sat in your office bathroom stall and set your phone alarm for ten minutes, then rested your head on the stall's side wall, touching it with only with your hair, and dozed off. Rae had dismissed it as unthinkably unsophisticated until she'd tried it. She'd been averaging two toilet naps a day from her "banker bunker" stall at work, the one refuge from men breathing down her neck.

"That just proves my point, though," Rae said. "I'd rather be napping on a toilet than going on second dates. And besides, none of the guys passed the arm test."

"What the hell is the arm test?" Ellen asked.

"You know," Rae said, with a certain pride in being able to share dating tips with Ellen now, not just the other way around. "When you're talking to him, do you find a reason to reach out and touch his arm in conversation?"

"I usually just go for the lip test," Ellen said. "Or the dick test."

"The arm test is a better gauge of long-term compatibility," Rae said. "Chemistry can grow over time, but there needs to be a certain baseline of attraction. And the arm test tells you that."

Even the date Rae had half hooked up with hadn't passed the arm test. She'd just been trying to feel *something* other than nerves or numbness.

"The arm test," Ellen said. "Interesting theory."

"Ready to delete our apps?" Rae asked.

She'd pitched Ellen on the benefits of a dating detox heading into the holidays. They'd take a couple weeks off to let the learnings sink in, revise their forward strategy and focus on becoming their best independent selves, then enter the new year refreshed and ready to go. The data showed that taking breaks led to better leadership decisions, so Rae figured it should lead to better love decisions too.

Ellen had been showing signs of cold feet, as she'd always had at least one dating app active since her sophomore year of college, but she grimaced bravely.

Maneuvering through the living room's bra obstacle course (Ellen's were harder to bypass than Rae's), Rae stood beside her best friend in physical and symbolic solidarity. "Three," she counted down.

"Two," Ellen said, reaching for Rae's fork to snitch an inspirational mouthful of ice cream.

"One."

"Delete!" they said together, jabbing at the *Delete* and *Confirm* and *Yes, I'm sure* buttons.

"Let the dating detox begin," Rae said.

They looked at each other, momentarily at a loss as to how to spend their Saturday night without an endless pipeline of potential soul mates to swipe.

"We could still play Snack & Sort," Ellen said, gesturing to the piles and piles of clothes.

"All right," Rae said, setting the ice cream down among the laundry wreckage. "Might as well."

CHAPTER FIVE
REGULATORY LOOPHOLES

"I feel free without the dating app," Ellen said the following Friday night as she and Rae dumped the contents of their refrigerator into the skillet for what they called a "catch-all scramblette"—tonight it was onion, salami, and sweet potatoes. "Like I can actually be present and hear the universe rather than staring at my phone all day, swiping for a needle in a shitstack."

"I know," Rae agreed, though she was starting to miss the swiping. The first few days of the detox had been reasonably successful. She'd gone to the gym two nights in a row, read the first three chapters of a novel her mom had given her last Christmas, and searched the internet for new jobs. Without thousands of romantic options at her fingertips, there was a certain comfort in scrolling through thousands of employment options.

But evaluating jobs wasn't the same as evaluating dates, and Rae hadn't realized how much she'd looked forward to swiping prospects from bathroom stalls, cafeteria lines, and subway trains to break up the long days. She missed trying to correlate photos with personality traits, and she missed the ego boost when guys liked her profile, validating high demand for her.

Dating-app withdrawal, she supposed it would be called. If she hadn't had Ellen staying strong by her side, she would have caved by now and redownloaded the app.

"And the risk of getting hit by another car has declined dramatically," Ellen went on. "Now that I don't have my head buried in my phone when I walk."

"Yes," Rae said, trying to catch Ellen's good mood as she gave the scramblette a half stir, half flip. "I told you a hiatus was a good idea."

* * *

"You're never going to believe what just happened," Ellen said the next morning, bouncing into the penthouse, yoga mat in one hand and green juice in the other.

Rae was horizontal on the couch, slurping caffeinated cereal. She'd been planning on joining Ellen for hot yoga as part of their detox agenda but hadn't gotten to bed until two A.M. after dealing with a late-night "fire drill" at work that involved the life-or-death matter of changing the colors of all the bar charts in a PowerPoint presentation from light gray to dark gray, as the lighter pallet apparently looked "too soft" and would surely be the make-it-or-break-it reason a client chose to do business with them or not.

She had a vague recollection of hissing at Ellen when she'd come in her room this morning. Eventually, she had managed to rouse herself and even made it as far as the kitchenette to scavenge day-old coffee and month-old Cheerios. As she'd been reaching for a mug and bowl, she'd decided it was more efficient just to combine the efforts and add the cereal directly to the coffee. Fewer dishes to wash— or more accurately, fewer dishes to sit in the sink all week. She'd tinkered to get the optimal coffee/cereal ratio and had been feeling rather accomplished until Ellen came in, glowing with post-workout sweat. Ellen was one of the few people for whom the verb *glow* was appropriate when describing sweat.

"Did the yoga studio find out you're not a student anymore?" Rae guessed. They'd given their expired college emails to receive the student discount and were waiting to be discovered.

"No," Ellen said, wedging her rolled-up mat into the closet and giving the door a few kicks until it stayed shut. "I just met the perfect guy. We were making eye contact all through tree pose, and we talked after class and he asked me out to Per Se tonight. Can you believe it? Apparently he knows the owner."

Per Se was a three-Michelin-star restaurant overlooking Central Park that booked up months in advance. It had been high on their aspirational list for years.

Rae clunked down her mug on the coasterless coffee table. "But we're on a dating detox," she said. "Remember?"

"We're on a dating *app* detox," Ellen said. "Not a complete dating detox."

"No," Rae said. "It's a full boy ban."

"He's not a boy," Ellen said. "He's thirty-three."

"He could still be a Peter Pan in men's clothing," Rae cautioned.

"I have a good feeling. Right here." Ellen pointed to her toned abs and hop-skipped into the bathroom to start the shower.

"And it's all thanks to you, Rae-bae," Ellen called out over the running shower. She reappeared in the living room in a towel that barely skimmed the tops of her long legs. "I never would've paid him any attention if I still had the app. I got so used to relying on the matches on my screen that I stopped noticing people I met in real life."

Rae grunted her best contrarian grunt. Even though she'd had the dating app for only eight weeks out of her twenty-five years, she struggled to remember how people ever met organically. Who actually struck up a conversation with a stranger in a coffee shop or yoga studio?

"I'll ask if he has single friends for you," Ellen said.

"No thanks. I'm detoxing." But then, begrudgingly, "You should French braid your hair tonight. It looks very Michelin-star-esque."

"Will you do it?" Ellen asked. "You're way better at it than I am."

It wasn't true. Rae's French braids were always off-center, with flyaway hairs. But a smile split her caffeinated lips. "If you insist."

Ellen grinned and floated around the penthouse, waiting for the shower water to warm up. "What's that?" she asked, peering into Rae's coffee mug.

"Coffee cereal soup."

Ellen took a slurp. "Very innovative," she applauded. "Add it to the list of things we'll patent. Right behind scramblettes and toilet naps."

"And apparently not dating detoxes," Rae said.

"You can own that patent," Ellen declared, brown eyes bright with resurrected fairy tales. "I'll take my tree pose prince."

*　　*　　*

That night, Rae's phone buzzed as she squeezed out one more dab of toothpaste from an empty tube. She considered this one of her more underrated talents and poetically pleasing as well—*extending the life of a toothpaste tube that everyone else would have thrown in the trash days ago.*

Perhaps she'd use it when she made her next dating app profile, under one of those corny *An unusual skill I have is . . .* prompts.

She checked her phone as she brushed her teeth, fearing it was from work and hoping it was from Ellen.

Rae had given Ellen strict instructions to send updates every twenty minutes, but it had been two hours and nothing yet. This indicated things with the Tree Pose Prince were probably going quite well, but Rae still felt left out, craving details to help her vicariously experience the date.

But the text was a number she didn't have saved—a 203 area code.

Hi, Rae—this is Dustin. Sorry for the delay. I've been sick and lying low. Would you like to get tea after work on Wednesday?

Dustin. Her mind rummaged through mnemonic files until it finally landed on the acronym DDST—*Dustin Duke Stock Trader.* Yes, that was it. He'd gone to Duke and worked as a stock trader. That was all she recalled, but apparently she'd been impressed enough to give him her number, perhaps because he used perfect grammar.

She found him quickly from a Google search. The newly honed efficiency of her stalking skills impressed her. From the head shot on his LinkedIn profile, she could tell he was threshold-level attractive—curly black hair and one of those not-even-trying faces.

He was twenty-nine, a point in his favor, since it beat Ellen's man-child cutoff (Rae was still two years his senior based on the gender-years math, but this seemed like a fine age gap). The Wall Street career was two points against him—she must have matched with him before she'd started diversifying her dating app portfolio away from finance bros.

The Greenwich, Connecticut hometown was also a con, given how rich and preppy the suburb was. But he earned two points back for a comment she found from one of his college professors describing him as "a creative visionary."

Halfway down another rabbit hole, she found Dustin's parents' engagement announcement in the *New York Times*, which spurred her to look for proof of her own parents' wedding (no announcement, no photos) and then also their divorce (also nonexistent, according to the internet).

It added to the unpleasant feeling that there wasn't much proof that her dad had really been her dad at all. He'd so easily waltzed off into his new life with a new wife—a woman he'd met on the internet and married a full two weeks after the divorce had been finalized—and twin stepdaughters who'd seemingly replaced Rae overnight. Her dad had invited her to "family Thanksgiving" the first couple years after he'd left, and she'd declined with teenage venom.

That was back when Rae was seventeen. Nowadays they caught up over dinner from time to time when her dad was traveling through

New York on business, but Rae still refused to see his wife, which she figured was probably why he'd ignored Rae's birthday this year. He seemed to be living under a dreamy delusion that sooner or later she would grow up and embrace her new mommy with proper decorum and delight. As this hadn't happened yet, her dad went long and seemingly random spells where he disappeared on her, lashing out by withholding his love.

He always remembered Christmas, though. Every year he sent Rae a glossy card featuring his new family, cozied up on a beach somewhere. Rae wanted to interpret this as a sign that he was thinking of her at the holidays, but her heart felt it as a passive-aggressive message: *Look how happy I am without you. If you weren't so immature, you could be in this photo too.*

Maybe it would be easier to forgive him if her mom were remarried too, but she'd been dating one dud after the next since the divorce, being dragged up and down by middle-aged boys who still hadn't matured into men. Rae blamed her dad for casting her mom out into the murky waters of the fifty-plus dating pool. Nothing was ever black and white, but no matter which way you analyzed it, the divorce was mostly his fault, and Rae couldn't stop resenting him even if she wanted to—which she didn't, not yet.

Rae felt a pang, wishing she were back in Indiana to cook her mom dinner and have long, lazy talks on the back porch as the crickets gave them a private concert. She sometimes felt like a bad daughter for living so far away, especially now that her mom was getting a bit older and was taking care of Rae's grandpa too, but she knew she'd feel stifled if she moved back to Indiana. Her New York chapter wasn't over yet.

Refocusing, she analyzed an article about Dustin's high school soccer team. Dustin had nerdy sports goggles and a bad bowl cut. Apparently he'd assisted the winning goal in the regional semifinals. She liked the trajectory of someone who hadn't peaked in high school, and assisting rather than scoring symbolized a certain selflessness.

If he'd suggested they grab a drink, Rae likely would've ignored the text altogether and waited until January before she had to shout her life story once more in an overcrowded bar. But the well-written suggestion of tea intrigued her with its tranquility. That and the fact that she was home alone on a Saturday night with empty takeout boxes while her best friend was at one of New York's most elegant restaurants with her apparent true love.

Meeting up with Dustin wouldn't technically be breaking the dating detox, since he'd been in the pipeline since before the detox began. It was no more of a loophole than the one Ellen had found.

After spitting out the toothpaste, she texted back. Tea sounds nice.

She didn't feel the need to add an artificial exclamation point.

CHAPTER SIX

ANOTHER FORMULAIC
FIRST DATE

So sorry, stuck at work, don't think I can make it tonight.

Rae drafted the text to Dustin as she left the office on Wednesday. It had been a particularly vapid day—she'd had to get in early to dial into a conference call where she wasn't allowed to speak but was supposed to take detailed notes of what everyone else was saying. Then the bank's holiday party had been canceled in a one-line email blaming "operational efficiency initiatives," which Rae knew translated into "rich people's stinginess."

Though Rae's hours were long, she usually didn't have any real work to do for most of the day, which left her feeling equally useless and exhausted. Due to entrenched inefficiencies of the frat-house hierarchy, the higher-ups were too focused on wooing clients all day to brief the junior team members on their tasks. During these daylight hours, Rae and the other minions were expected to sit at their desks like well-trained dogs, ready to be staffed on a new deal at any time. When the higher-ups went home for the day—or more accurately, when they left to chug beers with more clients—they dumped work on the youngsters' desks and expected them to stay up all night and send through one-hundred-percent-mistake-free deliverables by seven A.M. the next morning.

There was general acceptance on Wall Street that the system was broken but no appetite to fix it. The old white guys who ran the place had all endured brutal hours and sacrificed their happiness and health to get where they were, so damn it, everyone else should too.

Tonight's "urgent" task was putting together a pitch book—a 120-slide presentation packed with fluffy graphs and charts—for a vice president on Rae's team to take to a client meeting with a tech company executive, probably some guy he'd met on the golf course. Naturally, Rae wasn't invited on the business trip, even though she was doing all the work to prepare for it.

The Wall Street life had chosen her far more than she had chosen it. A harmless ten-week internship had somehow become an entire life track.

The day's highlight was her toilet nap and catching up on Scramblette group texts from the safety of the banker bunker, but this afternoon one of her "wannabe bosses"—her name for the dozens of men above her who weren't her manager but ordered her around anyway—had informed her she'd been taking too many bathroom breaks. Rae had thought about telling this middle-aged man that she was having heavy menstrual discharge or perhaps filing a complaint to HR, but she'd just clenched her jaw and told him she would be more cognizant going forward. Bonuses were being decided around now. Once she pocketed the cash in January and paid down more of her loans, she'd strut out of this place with middle fingers raised high. She wasn't in the position to be a full-time writer yet, but she could at least find a job that didn't give her the feeling that her heart was physically hardening every time she walked into the marble lobby of the fifty-story skyscraper.

The only date she felt up to tonight was one she watched on Netflix from the couch. She walked out the revolving office doors, manned by security guards who all knew her name and often fed her inspirational quotes to keep her going through the grind. Tonight, Kenny, the man who worked night shifts, must have seen the exhaustion in her slumped posture. "Now remember, Rae," he said in a paternal sort of way. "A job is just a job."

Rae returned Kenny's fist bump with as much of a smile as she could muster and stepped into the December night.

Cold air barreled through skyscraper wind tunnels, straight into her chest. The prospect of hot tea had new appeal. And Dustin had selected a spot in the West Village, just a few blocks from the penthouse. He was probably already on his way.

Rae shiver-walked toward the Wall Street subway station. The streets down here were narrow and winding, not following the logical grid pattern that governed most of Manhattan. The Financial District, or FiDi, as it was called, was rather ghostly after dark. Rae sometimes joked that it was haunted by all the spirits that had been sucked from Wall Street employees. Their robotic shells stayed hunched over their computers while their human souls drifted through the air, forming misty clouds with the other severed spirits, dampening the Victorian streetlights as if hoping that their earthly bodies might look out the window and wonder why it was so dark. But the bodies never did look. They kept their eyes glued to their computer monitors as if their lives depended on it, fully oblivious to the irony of it all.

FiDi was mostly made up of corporate offices rather than apartment buildings. The only people who actually lived here were young bankers who worked across the street and were trying to scrounge a few extra minutes of sleep by plopping right into bed when they were permitted to head home at three A.M. This proximity made sense in theory, but Rae was glad that she lived in the West Village. It helped keep some semblance of separation between her work life and personal life, however small.

On the subway ride up to Christopher Street, the squeaky train violently lurched to a standstill several times, extending the ten-minute journey into a twenty-minute one. The only explanation given was from the automated recording over the train's loudspeaker, read in an infuriatingly calm voice: "We are being momentarily held by the train's dispatcher." It made Rae and everyone else on the train huff and fume at the incompetence of it all.

Walking fast, she still made it to Té Company on West Tenth, tucked just out of the way of the Seventh Avenue crowds, at nine o'clock on the dot. She felt a rush of gratitude to live in a place that kept its tea shops open so late.

Based on the precedent set by her ten other first dates, she assumed Dustin would be at least five minutes late. Figuring she'd have time to smooth her flyaway hairs and dab the sheen off her nose once she got inside, she didn't look for anyone as she walked through the jingly door and exhaled a shuddery "Brrr."

She'd never actually been in here before, though she'd walked by the tea shop many times. The first thing she noticed was its warmth, hugging her with the same texture as her bathrobe, or perhaps just heating her imagination enough so she could invent a world with cotton air. The second thing she noticed was the pleasing book/human ratio, with bookshelves lining the white brick wall and nearly no one in the matchbox-shaped seating area. The third thing was the sound of her name—a statement rather than a question.

"Rae."

There he was—Dustin, standing up from a chair at a corner table near the lone window.

He was even better looking in person, at least six feet tall, curly black hair longer than in his corporate head shot, bangs grazing green eyes. His bone structure had that *Yup, I could be a model if I wanted* quality. Even if Rae hadn't known he worked on Wall Street, she would've recognized him as a fellow sellout from his white collared shirt. Still, he wasn't wearing a tie and his sleeves were rolled halfway up his forearms, perhaps implying some level of free spirit.

Rae plucked up a smile and sat down across from him. "Sorry to keep you waiting," she told Dustin. "Got held up at the office."

"You're right on time." He spoke slowly, without much change in inflection. His smile lacked charisma, not even showing teeth. "Can I get you some tea?"

He handed her a menu, which had pages of loose-leaf teas, all apparently sourced directly from Taiwan gardens.

Overwhelmed by the options, Rae just said, "Green, please." Immediately she regretted her decision, wishing she'd selected something more exotic, but she didn't want to change her mind now and risk seeming wishy-washy. She wondered if she'd ever go on a first date where she wasn't plagued by self-doubt—maybe that's when she'd know she'd met her soul mate?

As he was fetching their tea from the counter, Rae noticed a book sticking out of his briefcase. She felt a surge of hope before reading the cover: *No Risk, No Reward: How to Find Yield in a Low-Growth Environment.*

It was confirmed. He was just another one-dimensional finance bro. Fatigue pressed in on her from all sides, and she wished she'd gone straight home.

Dustin returned with green tea for both of them, and they sipped in silence. Her hands felt very awkward, and she worried she was going to drop the dainty teacup and smash it to bits. She had a new appreciation for why first dates usually involved alcohol. Tea shop courtship was more romantic in theory than in practice.

"The bookshelves are nice," Rae commented.

Dustin nodded. "They are."

He seemed like one of those guys who was too cool to be bothered with small talk. He'd probably only gotten his job because he was a well-connected white guy who'd reminded his washed-up interviewers of their own heyday.

"So what kind of an investment banker are you?" Dustin finally asked.

The kind who wants to be a poet instead. "I focus on M&A within the software sector," was what she said aloud, knowing he'd understand the mergers and acquisitions acronym. "You work in finance too?" She arranged her face in what she hoped was an authentically unaware expression that didn't reveal how she'd memorized his entire résumé and family tree, out to his great-aunt Carol who had a Twitter account of cat memes.

Dustin nodded. "I'm a macro equities trader, across asset classes."

And so that's what they talked about for the rest of the time—the ins and outs of market volatility and views on when the next recession would hit.

Dustin was the one to wrap it up, before the hour mark, saying he had to wake up early to dial into a conference call in Europe. Rae felt the slap in the face of her own trick being used against her.

They followed the end-of-date template—she halfheartedly offered to pay, Dustin halfheartedly said how nice it was to meet her, and they halfheartedly hugged under the tea shop's flapping awning before fully parting ways.

As she trudged up the stairs of the penthouse, Rae took out a sticky note and scribbled her eleventh haiku:

First date eleven
one more dry finance guy I'll
never see again.

CHAPTER SEVEN
TRENDING UPWARD

"I can't believe you have a *boyfriend*," Rae said to Ellen that Friday as she dusted the penthouse coffee table with an old sorority T-shirt.

They were hurriedly cleaning the apartment before the Tree Pose Prince's inaugural visit. He and Ellen had defined the relationship this week after officially breaking the third-date curse.

"I know," Ellen said, wiping down the bathroom mirror and getting distracted by evaluating whether her eyebrows were even. "Are you paying him under the table?"

"I didn't mean it like that," Rae said. "It's just . . . you've only known each other two weeks."

"Feels like two years," Ellen said. "We just . . . click."

Rae tried not to feel threatened by how quickly this new entrant was gaining market share in Ellen's heart. "I'm still not sure the Tree Pose Prince is worthy of you."

"Don't tell Aaron we call him that, okay?" Ellen warned. "I don't want to come across as too young. He's *thirty-three.*"

"So you've mentioned," Rae said. Ellen kept dropping references about how *mature* and *established* he was.

Personally, Rae hoped she wouldn't be going on dates in sixth-floor walk-ups when she was in her thirties, but Aaron at least seemed to realize Ellen was worth the trek.

"What's that smell?" Rae said, scrunching her nose. It was far different from the typical charred-eggs odor.

"Organic toilet bowl cleaner!" Ellen said proudly. "Lavender scented."

"First you get a boyfriend and then you start using lavender toilet bowl cleaner? My Elle-belle is growing up."

"Had to happen sometime." But Ellen picked up the soap dispenser from the bathroom counter and gave it a squeeze in Rae's direction until bubbles frothed out. They giggled like little girls, at everything and nothing all at once.

*   *   *

"So Ellen tells me you're quite the writer," Aaron said to Rae that evening as they streamed a movie from a laptop—an action film rather than their typical rom-coms. Ellen seemed to be pandering to her new target audience.

The three of them had managed to fit on the couch, but only because Ellen was curled up in Aaron's lap, and Rae was wedged against the armrest.

Aaron didn't seem to have been briefed on their *No talking during movies—and don't you dare sneeze either* policy. Ellen was too lovestruck, and Rae too polite (it was probably shyness, but she liked to think it was manners) to tell him.

"I don't write much now," Rae said. "But one day." There it was, the elusive *one day* plaguing her with potential.

"I know a couple people in publishing, if you want any intros," Aaron said. He had warm, pleasant features, though he wouldn't have cleared Ellen's height filter on the app.

"Thanks," Rae said, trying not to think about how out of reach her writing dreams felt these days. "Maybe when I'm a little further along in my projects."

"Rae leaves sticky note poems on my pillow sometimes," Ellen bragged. "For me to find when I get home from my business trips."

"They're facetious," Rae clarified to Aaron. "Nothing good."

"They're brilliant," Ellen said. "She's the Post-it Poet, and she's going to be a best seller."

Aaron smiled broadly. "Can I reserve an autographed copy of your first book?"

"Sure," Rae mumbled, filled with a crippling sense of failure at how impossibly far a published book was from her smattering of crinkled sticky notes.

She reached into a bag of popcorn while Ellen and Aaron shared another one, finding herself missing how Ellen would snitch more than her fair half.

Ellen began feeding Aaron popcorn, which he nibbled off her fingers. The nibbling turned into kissing, which escalated into full-blown making out.

Rae cleared her throat quietly, and then not so quietly, to remind them she was still there, but to no effect. She was tempted to go into her bedroom, but it felt like she'd be forfeiting more than a couch seat to Aaron, and so she stayed, scooching farther over until she was practically hanging off the edge.

Her phone buzzed. Instinctively her chest tightened in anticipation of an ASAP work request.

But it was Dustin.

Hi, Rae. I had a great time with you on Wednesday. Would you like to come to my friends' Christmas party tomorrow night?

Rae read the text three times. She'd been certain Dustin had been as indifferent about her as she'd been about him—even more indifferent, as he'd been the one to flee before the hour mark. Yet here he was, asking her to a Christmas party with his friends?

Had his conference call excuse been legitimate? Did he actually like her? Had the five other girls he liked better bailed, so she was the backup?

She wasn't sure how he felt, or even how she felt, but she had a desire for something *else*, something other than being a third wheel on a couch that fit only two people.

Sure, that sounds fun.

"Who're you texting?" Ellen asked, having emerged for air from under Aaron's tongue.

"My mom." She couldn't talk about this in front of Aaron. Besides, there was no point in overanalyzing something that wasn't going anywhere.

Great, Dustin replied right away. Text me your address and I'll have my Uber pick you up.

She'd never had a guy offer to pick her up in his Uber before. It wasn't quite a white horse and carriage, but she caught herself smiling as she crunched popcorn, trying to drown out the suction sounds beside her. For the first time in many years, she was going on a second date with someone.

Perhaps Ellen wasn't the only one whose romantic outlook was trending upward.

CHAPTER EIGHT
THE DATE THAT BEAT EXPECTATIONS

"I'm too pale to pull off red lipstick," Rae decided the next evening, frowning at her reflection as she got ready to meet up with Dustin. The bathroom mirror was still clean-ish from yesterday's apartment scrub. "I look like I'm going to a Halloween party, not a Christmas party. Some kind of ghost-meets-clown mash-up."

Rae never wore red lipstick. On Wall Street, red represented lost money, and her wannabe bosses had trained her to avoid it quite literally at all costs—no red pens, no red fonts, no red bar charts.

But she was trying out red lips tonight, figuring it was a nice ode to the holiday theme and relatively subtle compared to the old Santa hat she wore every Christmas, which Ellen had been advocating.

"Stop insulting my best friend," Ellen said, dousing Rae with hair spray so her curls might have a fighting chance. "You look flawless."

"I just don't want Dustin thinking I'm edgier than I am," Rae said. "Don't you think bright-red lips say, 'I'm an effortlessly cool artist'?"

"First of all, you *are* an effortlessly cool artist at heart," Ellen said. "And second, for being so 'not into' Dustin, you certainly care a lot about making a good impression."

After she and Rae had dissected every detail of Aaron's visit—Rae had rated him highly, with a few points docked for "excessive affection"—Rae had listed all the reasons she and Dustin weren't compatible. She'd even written a cost-benefit analysis, which Ellen had discovered and promptly burned over the kitchenette stove.

"I just want to see what a late-twenties party is like and not embarrass myself," Rae said. Twenty-nine rang of robust elegance rather than the tinny elegance twenty-five was turning out to be.

She started wiping off her lipstick, but the resulting smudges were even worse.

Her phone lit up with a text. My Uber is pulling up to your place now—take your time.

"Shit. He's here." She added a hasty layer of fresh lipstick to cover up the damage and then flung on her coat.

Ellen jammed the Santa hat into Rae's pocket. "Just in case," Ellen said, squeezing Rae with a *you've got this* hug.

Rae wanted to ask, *In case what?* but she just stole as much confidence as she could before clunking down the stairs in her not-too-low-not-too-high heels, gripping the railing to keep from falling.

Dustin was standing outside the car, wearing jeans and a forest-green sweater. His hair was less tamed than on their first date, and the look suited him far more than the corporate uniform.

"Merry Christmas," he said as he opened the door for Rae. His smile still didn't part his lips, but in the dim glow of the headlights, the expression looked soft rather than stiff.

"Merry Christmas," Rae echoed, sliding into the back seat.

Getting in after her, he left the middle seat empty between them. He buckled up, and she followed suit. She usually forgot to buckle her seat belt in Ubers, and she liked the feeling of the firm strap against her. Dustin thanked the driver for waiting, and something about the quiet, probing way he said it gave Rae the feeling that Dustin was seeing this driver as a human with a living, breathing story rather than just a servant to get them from point A to point B, like so many people in this city did.

Gridlocked by Saturday evening traffic, the car crawled east along the one-way flow of Perry Street and then up and over to the West Side Highway, picking up speed as they headed north toward the new-money high-rises of the Upper West Side. Out Dustin's window, the Hudson River twinkled with secondhand light, refracting the city's overstimulating electricity into a mellower mosaic. Dustin sat very still, as if he was found in thought rather than lost in it.

Rae started to wish she were next to him in the middle seat. Just to have a better view of the water.

*   *   *

Date is beating expectations!

From the bathroom—bright and clean with the toilet seat down and a mason jar dispenser of peppermint soap—Rae texted the Scramblettes, replying to their twenty-four messages asking how the party was going.

MORE DETAILS! Ellen responded instantaneously. And no banker talk—drink!

What's it like?? Sarah asked. Is everyone old and boring??

Have u kissed?? Mina asked.

Rae smiled to herself. For once, she was enjoying the actual date as much as recounting it with her friends. No kissing . . . yet. Will fill you in at brunch tomorrow.

She snooped in the cabinet to see if the toothpaste tube was full. It was, and it filled her with more inspiration than envy. Before she explored the loo so thoroughly that Dustin might suspect constipation, Rae rejoined him in the kitchen—definitely not a kitchenette.

"Spiked hot chocolate?" he asked.

They'd been here an hour already and hadn't made it to the alcohol yet. Rae had had her hands full of thrilling hors d'oeuvres, including mini quiches she thought of as quichettes, and Dustin had been taking her from room to room, introducing her to his friends and their significant others. Everyone was here as a couple, some even married or engaged. Commitment levels, even more than snack selections, seemed the most statistically significant difference between mid and late twenties. It made her glad that she'd started investing in her love life now rather than scrambling to meet someone in a few years once everyone was already coupled up.

"Yes, please," Rae said to Dustin, feeling an indescribable comfort in the fact that even sophisticated soirees served drinks in mugs, and chocolate-based drinks at that.

"Cheers," Dustin said, and they clinked mugs.

Rae took a sip, smudging the rim with red lipstick.

The apartment was on the ground floor (garden level, New Yorkers called it), and Dustin led them out to the patio, a concrete courtyard encased by fifteen-story buildings. Low flames rose from a portable fire pit, clearing the city air with smoke.

Carols streamed through outdoor speakers. There was only one other couple outside, and Rae and Dustin stood off by themselves, setting their mugs on top of an out-of-season grill.

Rae could smell the fire but couldn't feel it. The air was cold. She found herself liking how it sharpened her senses. "Your friends are great," she said.

"They're good people," Dustin agreed. "Haven't seen most of them in a while."

On their first date, she'd dismissed his even-keeled tone as disinterested, but now she found it refreshingly unhurried. "It's hard to keep up friendships in the real world," she said, thinking about how she'd graduated from college with a smattering of "sisters for life" and yet Sarah and Mina were the only ones she still saw or even texted. She didn't know where she'd be if Ellen hadn't scooped her up.

Dustin didn't answer, and Rae wondered if he had his own stories of shrunken circles. She surveyed the surrounding apartment buildings. A few floors up, a woman's silhouette was standing in a window. Perhaps the woman was staring up at the sky, searching for the moon on a cloudy night, but Rae had the impression she was looking down at the courtyard, maybe angry about the volume of the music, or just lonely and wishing she'd been invited to the party.

"What are you looking at?" Dustin asked, following her gaze.

"That woman in the window."

He evaluated the scene for a moment. "She looks lonely," he said, and waved up at her.

Rae felt something in that wave, in her stomach or her chest, or some optimal ratio of the two, and she too gave a little wave up to the window.

The silhouette did not wave back.

"She probably just doesn't see us," Dustin said, slipping his rebuffed hand into Rae's and giving it a squeeze.

Rae tried to squeeze back, but her fingers remained limp, comfortably stunned by the texture of new skin.

"It reminds me of a William Bellini poem," Rae heard herself say. Her ex was the only guy she'd ever quoted poetry to, and he'd snuffed the habit with enough five-syllable yawns. "*I like to be with people, just not up close.*"

Dustin was quiet, and Rae regretted saying anything. Finally, in a curious voice, he said, "You think she wouldn't like us if she were any closer?"

"No, I just mean—I think there's something nice about watching things from afar like that. She can create whatever story about us she wants—she isn't constrained by facts."

"You don't sound very much like an investment banker."

"I want to be a poet one day." The confession slipped out as easily as the Bellini verse. Perhaps the hot chocolate was stronger than she'd realized.

Dustin didn't laugh or react like she'd just said something crazy. He just nodded, as if he'd expected as much.

"I don't write much now," she added, feeling a rush of embarrassment about the haiku from their date. She vowed to revise it right when she got home tonight. "My excuse is that I can't find the time, but that's a lie, of course."

"Why is that a lie? You're at the office around the clock."

"Sure, but time is made, not found," Rae said, aware of how her face, tilted up, was inches from his own, tilted down. The gap between them had all but disappeared as they'd stared up at the window. They were still holding hands.

Dustin smiled—two parentheses penciled into the edges of his mouth. "That sounds like a line of poetry right there," he said, thumb drawing nameless shapes on her palm.

"Which do you think is worse," Rae asked. She was so tired of going through the motions—playing the corporate character six days a week, and then the dating charade, and to hell with it if the realness backfired. "Deferring dreams or giving up on them?"

After one of his long silences, which Rae already felt herself getting used to, Dustin answered. "Deferring them. Because if you give up on a dream, you can redirect that energy toward a new pursuit. But if you defer it, that energy doesn't go anywhere, except into ballooning the delusion."

Ballooning the delusion.

"Exactly," Rae said, feeling eerily understood. "That's what I'm scared of. That I'll keep deluding myself into thinking that I'll write, until corporate America sucks the last of my soul."

Dustin held her with his eyes, and she hoped he wouldn't let go. "Want my opinion?"

"Yes, please."

"I think you're still in the collecting-stories stage of your life. And eventually, when the time is right, you'll sneeze them out as poems. What's that Bellini quote? *Only do something if it claws at you. . .*"

"*And forces its way out in spite of oh so much,*" Rae finished. She'd been so surprised by everything tonight that Dustin quoting one of her favorite indie writers back to her seemed perfectly natural. Not normal, but natural. There was an important difference.

"You write?" she asked.

"No, I don't have that gene. But I read anything I can get my hands on. Business stuff, sure, but mostly novels. Poetry, too, sometimes—free verse, not the stuff that rhymes for the sake of rhyming. No offense if you like rhymes," he added quickly.

"I don't." She found rhyme schemes offensively trite. "You know," she said, smile flickering with the flames. "I pegged you as a boring finance bro."

"Is that right?" Dustin seemed amused. "Well, since we're being honest, I nearly didn't even ask you out in the first place. I try not to spend my free time with other Wall Streeters. It's not that I hate my job—I actually find stock markets fascinating, how human emotions like fear and insecurity drive all these wildly irrational moves in prices, often at odds with the story of the underlying fundamentals. It's just that finance is only a tiny sliver of the world, and it's so easy to get isolated within it."

Rae had never thought about financial markets like that: a collection of emotions and narratives. It made her like her job a little bit more. "So what made you give my dating-app profile a second look? Was it the irresistible filter of my photos?" she deadpanned.

Dustin's teeth poked through his smile. "Not quite. There was something about the depth of your expressions—3-D even in 2-D." His even tone kept it from sounding sappy, not that Rae would have minded if it had. "I could tell you dreamed about more than money."

Rae let go of his hand just long enough to reach into her coat pocket and pull out the Santa hat, understanding now what Ellen had meant by "just in case." *Just in case you feel free to let him really see you.*

"You've had that the whole time?" Dustin asked as she put it on. "Why didn't you wear it earlier?"

"I don't know," she said, tugging the hat down to her eyebrows. Nobody else was dressed up."

"Rae," Dustin said. They were so close now that Dustin's eyes should have been blurred but weren't. She'd thought his eyes were green but saw now they were hazel, flecked with complexity. "You're too much of a somebody to follow the nobodies."

He wasn't the one who kissed her first, and she wasn't the one who kissed him first, but they met at a halfway point that wasn't the average.

Rae pulled away, aware of how many people could see them—the couple across the patio, the guests inside the apartment, the silhouette in the window.

"Something wrong?" Dustin asked.

Rae didn't want to be the midtwenties girl piling on the PDA at the late-twenties party. But more than that, she didn't want to let other people write her own life.

"No," she said. "Nothing's wrong."

Their lips found each other again as the playlist cut to a new carol and the bonfire crackled beside them, wrapping the memory in a ribbon of smoke.

CHAPTER NINE

LOVE MARKET UNCERTAINTY

"I told you dating apps worked," Mina said the next night, after Rae finished recapping date two with Dustin.

The Scramblettes were on the penthouse floor, exchanging gifts for their annual Secret Santa. Rae had just opened a silk-ish pajama set from Ellen ("two steps up from the bathrobe!"), a GMAT study guide from Sarah ("in case you want to study with me!") and a pink vibrator from Mina ("to help you through your dry spell!"). Rae had gifted them all farmhouse-chic dispensers of peppermint soap, inspired by yesterday's bathroom furnishings. She'd ordered them from her bed this morning and had never been more grateful for same-day delivery.

After her dramatic birthday party, Rae had resolved to ban all future Sunday night celebrations, but this was the only time that had matched up for all four of them before they scattered across the country for the holidays. So here they were, bracing for work tomorrow as they shared a kale scramblette and bottle of red. Last night's late-twenties decor was too fresh in Rae's memory for her to be impressed by the girls' amateur "green eggs and wine" Christmas theme, but she pretended to be.

"You just needed to kiss enough frogs before you found your prince," Mina went on, dabbing peppermint soap on her neck like lotion.

"More like shake enough webbed hands," Sarah teased.

"I really think it's the magic of the detox," Ellen said. "Something about the reverse psychology. How else do you explain that Rae and I both found our dream guys the week after we deleted our dating apps?"

"Is this the first time all four Scramblettes are dating someone at the same time?" Mina asked, reveling at the adult-ish-ness of it. Mina and her latest soul mate had just had the "exclusive" talk.

"Dustin and I aren't dating," Rae said. "I've only seen him twice." She was already regretting oversharing but hadn't been able to help herself from going into every detail of how he'd quoted poetry ("so intellectual!" the Scramblettes had cooed) and waved to the mystery woman in the window ("so kind!") and kissed with exactly the right proportions of tenderness and tenacity ("the spark!") and texted her at 10:34 A.M. this morning saying he'd had a "wonderful time" ("such prompt follow-up!").

Low expectations, high standards, Rae kept telling herself. It was one of the Scramblettes' go-to mottos, but she was already conjuring up next Christmas with Dustin coming to Indiana with her to meet her mom and grandpa. Her mom would like him. She might think he was a little reserved at first, but once she got to know him . . .

Rae reached for her Santa hat, which she'd tossed on the floor when she'd gotten home last night. It still smelled like bonfire. Pulling it on so that it covered her eyes, she tried to relive the patio scene.

The hat was plucked from her head, and she blinked in the stark lighting of the living room. "Back to earth, Rae-bae," Ellen said. "You know the rules. Scramblettes first, suitors second."

"You look hungover," Mina told her. "Only one solution—more drinking." She handed Rae the wine bottle.

Rae took a sip, but she didn't have a hangover, at least not the alcohol-induced headache she was used to. Her heart felt a little hungover from that kiss. Kiss*es*. The plural was important. It had almost gone farther than that, but Dustin had taken a cab with her back to her apartment and said good-bye on her stoop, declining to come up. "I want to do this right," he'd said. *Right* seemed rather subjective, but Rae hadn't debated syntax with him. She'd just kissed him once more, then twice more, and then scampered up all ninety-six stairs, light as a snowflake.

Rae switched into listening mode, rhythmically sipping wine as Ellen and Mina compared notes on their equally perfect boys (they hadn't yet earned the promotion to "men," as far as Rae was concerned) and Sarah prattled on about how dating women was so much more rewarding ("they actually *express* things!"). At some point Rae became liberated enough to text Dustin, I like you a lot!

"Shit," she said, cursing the inability to recall texts like you could recall emails. "He's going to think I'm one of those psycho girls who starts planning the wedding after two dates."

She was that girl, of course, but Dustin didn't need to know that until farther down the line, once he'd fallen in love with her properly.

"If he's the right one, you can't screw it up," Mina proclaimed.

Ten minutes later, Rae clutched her phone, bargaining with the universe: if Dustin texted her back in the next five minutes, she'd donate five percent of her salary—after taxes—to charity. "I've become a crazy person," she announced solemnly. Twenty-five years old, supporting herself in Manhattan, holding it together day in and day out through the long hours and corporate criticism, and yet here she was, coming undone because some guy she barely knew hadn't texted her back.

"Feelings do that," Ellen said. "It can't be helped."

Rae figured it could actually be helped, but she didn't feel like it could be, so she stayed quiet, ears pricked for the soft buzz of a text. She reread his last message several more times—I had a wonderful time last night. The lack of exclamation point had seemed consistent with his usual text pattern, but now it seemed a blatant indication of his indifference. And worse, he hadn't asked a question. The message was clearly just a *Nice knowing you* formality to free him of any guilt of being one of those guys who leads a girl on and then drops off the face of the earth.

After thirty minutes of silence, Rae lobbed her phone onto the couch, out of sight. "It's over," she concluded. "I scared him off."

"Stop that," Ellen said. "He's going to text back."

"There's a chance Rae's right, though," Mina said. "Remember that guy who ghosted me after I sent him a heart emoji?"

Ellen shot Mina a warning look. "That was different," Ellen said, though Rae couldn't help tallying up all the guys who'd ghosted Ellen out of the blue.

"I'm just saying not to take it personally if he *does* ghost you," Mina said. "There's high flight risk with the Lost Boys of New York."

"It should be called *Boy*hattan, not *Man*hattan," Sarah agreed. "Another benefit of dating women."

"It's over," Rae repeated.

"Tell us again how he introduced you at the party," Sarah said.

"He just said, 'This is Rae,'" she recounted. "Is that bad?" It had seemed elegantly vague at the time, but in hindsight it seemed apathetically vague, like he could've been introducing a coworker, or a neighbor he occasionally ran into at the bagel shop.

"But did he say, 'This is Rae' or 'This is *Rae*'?" Mina clarified.

"Or '*This* is Rae'?" Ellen added, unable to keep from jumping in on the analysis.

Rae racked her brain. "Just 'This is Rae,' I think."

"Oh," Mina and Sarah said in unison.

"Let's not jump to conclusions," Ellen cautioned.

But Rae's mind had already leapt to every bad outcome. She'd just been someone to take to a party so Dustin didn't have to show up alone. Maybe his ex-girlfriend had been there with her new boyfriend and Dustin had been trying to make her jealous. He was probably hooking up with her right now.

"I'm moving to London," Rae announced matter-of-factly, as if this was something she had considered prior to ten seconds ago.

Her phone buzzed. She leapt from the floor onto the couch to check it.

It was Dustin.

Still smiling from last night. Can I take you to dinner Tuesday before you fly back to corn country?

Rae hardly even heard Ellen's smug "I told you so" or Mina's "I stand corrected!" She just spewed a few exhales and grinned stupidly at her cracked screen, as if it were to thank for Dustin's reply.

"Time for holiday karaoke," Ellen said, turning on music loud enough that they couldn't hear the couple fighting next door but not so loud that the downstairs neighbors would complain.

Rae joined in on a bouncy rendition of "All I Want for Christmas Is You," telling herself she was directing the lyrics at the Scramblettes, no one else, but she felt the lie in the lightness of her voice as she sang into the wine-bottle microphone and wondered who might see her new silk-ish pajamas.

CHAPTER TEN

LOWS TO HIGHS

"This is a Rockaway Parkway–bound L train," the automated voice announced as the urine-and-pickle-scented subway train jolted to a violent stop, as if on a mission to send as many passengers careening into the walls as possible.

Rae managed to avoid toppling over only because she was sitting down and wedged tightly in a man-sprawler sandwich. Once the temperamental doors finally opened, Rae sped out onto the platform. Two fat rats crossed her path, scraggly tails slithering as they feasted on fast-food wrappers.

She was on her way to Dustin's apartment in Williamsburg. He'd made a reservation at an upscale Mediterranean restaurant near Rae's office, but she'd asked if they could do pizza at his place instead. She was too wiped out to fold a cloth napkin on her lap and yell across the table to be heard.

Rae knew the Scramblettes would disapprove. It was only the third date, and Dustin should still be courting her. But pizza on his couch was exactly what Rae wanted, and what was life at twenty-five if not an exercise in thinking for herself?

She liked the idea of coming to Brooklyn, too, and having a whole body of water between them and her office. The notion had felt less romantic when the rattling subway inexplicably stalled for fifteen minutes somewhere below the East River, but Rae now emerged from the underground into the Williamsburg night, where the air rippled rather than rushed and people shuffled, not shoved, to their own Bohemian beats on streets free of Manhattan's garbage stench.

The nonlinear energy seeped down into her lungs and helped her breathe more deeply. She couldn't help but slow her pace as she scoped out the scene. Even though Williamsburg was just a few subway stops away, she hadn't been here in a long time. Somewhere along the way she'd accidentally adopted the *Why would I ever leave Manhattan?* attitude pervasive among the West Village and Wall Street crowds.

The buildings were low and the sky stretched big and wide, not confined to narrow slivers like in Manhattan. She ambled past free-looking people in denim overalls and corduroy coats smoking pot and strumming ukuleles from fire escape balconies, thrift shops with plaid beanies and high-top Converse shoes in the windows, indie bookstores filled with titles Rae had never heard of, and garages refurbished into coffee shops and craft breweries. Gigantic murals added pops of primary colors to the washed-out brick-and-aluminum-panel siding of refurbished factories.

The neighborhood was an oil-and-water mix of creative and corporate types. It was no secret that the artists resented the recent gentrification that had sent rent skyrocketing and appropriated their hipster culture into a social media hashtag.

Feeling rather ashamed that she was one of the white-collar intruders, Rae pulled her coat more tightly around herself to hide her suit beneath. One day, she vowed, she'd turn her back on capitalism and join Brooklyn's colony of creatives. She just wasn't quite there yet.

Dustin lived on Lorimer Street, a bit farther east where Williamsburg started to get grittier, with more graffiti and abandoned warehouses and weeds growing up through unkempt sidewalk cracks. She felt a pang of compassion for how Lorimer Street seemed a bit overlooked and unloved compared to the glossier blocks near the river. Even before she arrived, Rae dubbed Dustin's apartment the Lorimer Loft, liking how the name rolled off her tongue.

His building was the tallest one on the street—eight stories high, modern and sleek. Rae had the feeling that the locals probably hadn't been too happy when it was built, but she was selfishly delighted to explore such a place. There was an elevator, and though Dustin only lived on the third floor, Rae wasn't able to pass by the elegance of elevator life, so she waited an extra three minutes for it to arrive and lift her grandly to her date. After sniffing her armpits to make sure she didn't need to reapply deodorant, she rapped on the door of apartment 3F.

Dustin opened it and smiled. His hair was wet from the shower, and he'd changed out of his suit. Rae was again struck by his haphazard handsomeness.

"You made it to Brooklyn," Dustin said.

"I made it to Brooklyn," Rae echoed, critiquing herself for not thinking of a wittier reply.

They hugged in the doorway, slightly awkwardly. Rae felt a jolt of doubt. What if the second date had been a blip? What if the third date reverted to the stiffness of the first?

She took off her commuter sneakers and placed them next to Dustin's loafers and running shoes, lined up in a row. After hanging her coat on a peg, she smoothed her black dress, unsexily corporate but at least less masculine than her usual work outfits.

The Lorimer Loft wasn't so much a loft as it was a traditional one-bedroom apartment, but she'd already grown attached to the alliteration and decided to keep it.

The space was large, with a full-sized fridge and its very own washer and dryer. Even more than the sublime amenities, Rae was struck by the cleanliness—the floor free of crumbs and kernels, with dishes drying on a rack beside the sink.

She had new appreciation for why Ellen had purchased lavender toilet bowl cleaner in preparation for Aaron's visit.

Dustin asked if she wanted anything to drink. Rae said she was okay, but Dustin got her water anyway, with three oblong ice cubes. They stood in the kitchen, and Rae continued to look around so she wouldn't stare at Dustin or doodle on the condensation on her glass.

The apartment had that New York minimalistic style, and Rae craved a messy douse of color amid the varying shades of beige.

Dustin asked her how her week was going, and she talked about the deal she'd been grinding on and how she hadn't started packing yet even though her flight to Indianapolis was tomorrow morning. She finally drifted into silence, deciding it was better to be silently boring than noisily boring.

The pizza arrived, and Dustin tipped the delivery man. Rae was impressed he had dollar bills. She rarely carried cash.

They ate on the living room couch, an expensive-looking suede. Dustin rested his feet on the coffee table, but it was a nice table, coasters and all, so Rae kept her feet dangling in front of her, not quite reaching the ground.

She stared straight ahead at the wall—sans TV—as cheese dribbled down her chin. She began to regret her suggestion to order pizza.

"Why're you sitting so far away?" Dustin asked.

Rae played back the question twice before concluding he was inviting her to scooch closer. She did, and on the next slice scooched closer again. By the time they reached the last slice, her legs were draped over Dustin's lap. His pizza-free hand brushed her black-tights-covered kneecaps.

Rae felt impostor syndrome, similar to what she felt at work when she wondered, *Why did they hire me? I don't know anything!* Except now it was, *Why does he like me? I'm so ordinary!*

"Have the last piece," Dustin said.

"No, you have it," Rae said. It was an unsettling feeling, liking someone enough to genuinely want to give him the last pizza slice.

He cut it off-center and gave her the larger half, delivering it with a kiss. Rae was self-conscious about her breath smelling like pepperoni, but at least his did too.

Dustin stood up and walked into his bedroom. "Time for your Christmas present."

Rae felt a rush of panic. The Scramblettes had assured her it was far too early for gifts. She'd spent several hours watching sewing 101 YouTube tutorials so she could stitch Dustin a monogrammed Santa hat and had put an autographed Bellini book in her online shopping cart, but the Scramblettes had vehemently vetoed both, warning against coming on too strong.

When Dustin rejoined her on the couch, he handed her a small parcel, wrapped in red tissue paper. Rae opened it to find a pocket-sized journal with a brown leather cover and parchment-like pages.

"So you can jot down little ideas during your bathroom breaks at work," Dustin explained. "Mucus for the big poetic sneeze one day."

"My very own Stall Street Journal," Rae said, grinning like a kid.

Dustin laughed. He didn't laugh often, so when he did, Rae knew he meant it. Most people had lost that correlation.

Rae cracked the journal open, gently so as not to hurt the spine.

On the first page, in scratchy red pen, Dustin had written a Bellini quote:

If the world feels cold to you,
then at least you know
you're still warm inside.

"Thank you," she whispered, curling against him, her emotional barriers to entry falling away.

"Want to check out the roof?" Dustin said, after more wordless gratitude had taken place.

"I'm fine right here, thanks." Eyes shut in Dustin's arms, she was halfway into a dreamy sleep.

"You've got to see the view," he insisted, scooping her up and standing in one swift motion. "Or I'd be failing in my hosting responsibilities." He carried her into the hall and set her down in the elevator. Rae wondered if she'd ever grow inured to elevator life. They held hands as they rose.

Breathtaking was the word that popped into Rae's head as they walked onto the rooftop, rectangular and empty. Breath*giving*, she corrected, earmarking the word for some future use.

Rae stood at the railing, looking out. Dustin stood behind her, his chin resting on the top of her head so they shared the same view.

If they had been in the thick of Manhattan, they wouldn't have been able to see much from only eight stories up, but here in Brooklyn they had an unobstructed view across the East River. Manhattan shone before them in all its electric glory—Midtown skyscrapers off to the right, with the peak of the Empire State Building plummeting into the lower neighborhoods of Gramercy and the East Village and then rising again, even taller, in the Financial District at the island's southern tip.

The skyline looked like an illuminated line chart of the stock market, jagged ups and downs.

The lights of the Williamsburg Bridge reminded Rae of an elegant beaded necklace draping between the two boroughs. Near and far, the pointy silhouettes of old water towers dotted the city's rooftops like hundreds of rocket ships ready for takeoff.

That old but always fresh feeling hit Rae, the one where she couldn't believe she was really in New York, carving a life for herself. Just an hour ago she'd been trapped in a dark, smelly underground subway tunnel. And now, this . . .

She vowed to write a poem, or at least a poem-ish, about it later, pinpointing Manhattan's magnetism by juxtaposing the *I'm so done with you* subway lows with the *Swear I'm never leaving you* rooftop highs. "My Volatile Man(hattan)," she'd call it.

Dustin kissed her hair, and her impostor syndrome was escorted out by the rooftop wind.

She regretted rolling her eyes when Ellen told her it felt like she'd been dating Aaron for years already. Time wasn't the right metric for measuring relationship depth.

"Isn't it weird," Rae heard herself say, "that we hardly even know each other?"

"We don't know much *about* each other," Dustin said. "That doesn't mean we don't know each other."

It became very clear, looking out at the man-made lights in the God-made night, that she knew Dustin, and he knew her. But she wanted him to know *about* her too.

"My parents are divorced," she said. Then she rephrased it, resenting the passive voice, how it shielded from blame. "My dad left us." The reveal happened so quickly it felt like a post-pizza burp.

"Do you want to tell me the story?" Dustin asked.

"Not tonight. But I will."

He nodded. "You know how I said I hadn't seen my friends in a while? I'll tell you that story soon too."

It didn't matter that they didn't yet know the details. They had shared that there *were* stories and that they wanted to share them, and it felt more intimate than reciting facts and timelines about her dad's affair and the cliché way it had shattered everything she'd thought she'd known.

They settled into one of their silences. The pronoun *their* made Rae smile as it glided through her mind.

"When I first moved to the city," she said, "I hated how the lights squeezed out the stars. But now, on good days, I kind of see the magic in it."

"How so?"

"New York has so much brightness that it doesn't need to rely on distant lights that take thousands of years to reach the earth. We can wish on skyscrapers and taxi headlights and neon dollar-pizza signs, and it's all within our grasp." She paused, then added as a hedge, "And now I realize how corny that sounds, so please disregard."

"Disclaimers belong at the end of legal documents, not poetry."

Rae was about to ask what he meant, then realized she already knew.

"You're a Rae of light," Dustin told her. "Glowing even brighter than a dollar-pizza sign, I'd say."

In that moment, Rae let herself believe in every statistically doomed dream anyone in this city was chasing tonight.

She'd never thought of herself as one of those people who lit up a room. That was Ellen or her mom or the bubbly barista who swirled extra whipped cream on her cappuccinos.

But maybe light didn't always have to be flashing or fluorescent or rely on catching people's eyes. Maybe light could also be soft and shy and snuggle its way into souls through cracked back doors.

"Today was a good day," Dustin said.

"Yes," Rae said, turning into him so that her head rested against his chest, muffling the blaring of fire truck sirens from the street below. "A very good day."

CHAPTER ELEVEN
BULLISH ON LOVE

"The only bad part was I got really sunburnt," Ellen said, peely nosed in the Perry Street kitchenette on the night of New Year's Day.

She and Rae were cooking a "New Year, New York, No Yolk" scramblette extravaganza with wasabi to cleanse the pallet of last year's flavors, "big apples" that were on the dwarfish side, and egg whites to respect their joint resolution to be healthier.

Rae had picked up the overpriced ingredients on the way back from the airport that afternoon. In Indiana, all the stores had been closed for the holiday, but Manhattan establishments refused to forgo even a day of sales. She'd lugged the grocery bag up the stairs, wheezing after a week away from her concrete-jungle hiking regimen.

"Anyway," Ellen said, giving the festive eggs a flip-stir. "Tell me more about your time back home."

"Just the usual," Rae said. "Wore my high school soccer sweats the whole week and played cards with my grandpa while my mom brought out endless trays of food and listed off all of her friends' sons who are 'dropping like flies' getting married. She says I'd better snag a man soon or I'll get 'the leftovers.' It's like she thinks I don't put enough pressure on myself or something."

Rae often felt that that since her mom had wound up without a husband, she was dead set on making sure her daughter never reached the same sorry fate, so she overstepped her boundaries. Every time Rae came home for the holidays, her mom tried to set her up with a roster of fully vetted hometown bachelors, the kind of guys who'd expect her to make them sandwiches and be a stay-at-home mom.

"Sounds like a holly jolly Christmas," Ellen said, cringing. "Did you tell her about Dustin? That should calm her down a bit. He's practically out ring shopping already."

"No he's not," Rae said, but she felt herself blushing on the outside and bubbling on the inside. "I didn't tell my mom—I didn't want to jinx it." She liked the feeling of keeping their relationship private, safe from the harsh judgment of the world and the even harsher judgment of her mom.

"Smart move," Ellen said. "Karma can be cruel like that, punishing people who start flaunting their happiness. I think I'm testing my luck. My whole family FaceTimed Aaron over Christmas."

"Big step," Rae said. "Did they approve?"

"A little too enthusiastically. My dad's ready to give me away. Said if Aaron asked for my hand tomorrow, he'd say yes."

"Because as women we clearly can't be trusted to make our own decisions about who we marry," Rae said dryly. "We need the man of the household to weigh in with his opinion."

"We ladies are far too emotional to make such a big decision," Ellen said, tossing the sarcasm right back.

"Now you're sounding like my grandpa," Rae said. "I tried to explain dating apps to him. He kept referring to my 'virtual boyfriends.'"

"I mean, it's not far from the truth, is it?" Ellen said. "Think of how many guys we 'talked to' on the apps and never actually met in person."

"Fair point."

"So did you and your mom butt heads on all her love-life meddling?"

At midnight, Rae had sent Ellen a dramatic drunk text. Happy New Year Elle-belle my mom hates me and I'm so behind on the marriage and baby train and also I miss you and love you lots and lots.

Rae had gone over to her married friends' house for New Year's Eve, prepared to take notes about the important pillars of a long-term relationship, but they were too exhausted from their baby to contemplate their own love life, let alone help guide hers. Rae had briefly held the baby, a five-month-old boy, and it had been nothing short of terrifying, the way it felt like the little bobble-headed human would roll right out of her arms onto the tile floor.

She felt like she and her high school friends were at completely different life stages. New Yorkers liked to make fun of all the small-town folk who settled down right after college, but Rae was realizing that the joke was on the jokesters—they'd be racing the clock to raise kids before they reached old age.

After her friends had conked out at nine P.M., Rae returned home to sit on the couch with her mom, drinking champagne and watching the Times Square coverage on TV, glad not to be in the crowds while also somehow missing them.

"Our big fight was about something else," Rae said to Ellen now.

"Mr. Non-Right?" Ellen guessed, correctly. Mr. Non-Right was her mom's boyfriend. Rae preferred to leave names out of it, like how she thought of her dad's wife only as That Woman.

Rae had figured Mr. Non-Right would soon exit their lives like the rest of the guys her mom had cycled through after the divorce. But two years in, he seemed a semipermanent fixture, which Rae found even more disagreeable than having him as a fleeting one. The only real value proposition Rae saw in him was that he was simply *there*.

"He's just not good enough for her," Rae said.

"And you told her that?"

"She asked for my opinion," Rae said defensively, though she knew the champagne had made her too honest. "I said she's overcompensating after being cheated on by picking the safe option."

"That's not so bad."

"I think I said a few more things too." Rae winced at the blurry memories. "'You just want a low-risk, low-reward life—no wonder Dad left you!'"

She'd apologized in the morning, and her mom had forgiven her, but their hug at the airport had been short and stiff, and Rae wished she could do it over.

"You'll work it through," Ellen said. "You always do. Did you hear from your dad?"

"He texted me a picture of his family Christmas card," Rae said, showing the heavily filtered beach photo to Ellen. Her dad's arms were wrapped around That Woman's skinny waist, and his two "daughters" were each leaning their head on one of her dad's shoulders. It made Rae very queasy. "Guess he decided I wasn't worth wasting a stamp on this year," she said, trying hard to find some humor in all of it. "And it came with a heartfelt message: *Merry xmas!!* Two exclamation points."

"So juvenile," Ellen said. "Did you text back?"

"I said *U2!!*" She could play his game right back. Not that she was even sure he was playing a game. She was starting to wonder if perhaps he wasn't being calculated, just careless. Maybe his short, sporadic texts weren't passive-aggressive messages to punish Rae for refusing to bond with That Woman. Maybe they were just a sign that he was genuinely so busy and happy in his new life that he didn't have much time to think about her. Rae's cold-shoulder strategy wasn't working nearly as well as she had forecasted. It didn't seem to be accomplishing anything other than helping her dad forget her even more.

Part of her wanted to call him up and try to have a real heart-to-heart talk about how she missed him, how she wanted to work on their relationship, how she wasn't going to think of his wife as her stepmom but maybe they could all get coffee together sometime. But even imagining the conversation exhausted her as much as a long workday—the feeling of walking on eggshells, trying so hard to please, playing the "good girl" character rather than just being able to be her messy self.

And seeking a real reconciliation felt like it would be a betrayal, both to her mom and to her morals. It would mean sending the signal that what he'd done wasn't really that big a deal, when in reality it had been the biggest deal in the world.

"Dustin hasn't replied to my text from this morning," Rae said, switching the subject. "But I'm not worried. Remember how dramatic we were about everything last year?" She said *last year* as if it weren't synonymous with *last night*.

"We've come a long way," Ellen agreed.

Rae had ended up staying over at the Lorimer Loft after date three. It had gotten too late to take the subway, and Uber prices back to the West Village were over forty dollars, so they'd decided a sleepover was the only logical solution. Dustin had bought her a toothbrush from the downstairs pharmacy, and they'd fallen asleep with their clothes on-ish.

She'd forgotten how wonderful it was to be held through the night. Not even forgotten—she'd just never really known what that was like. Her ex had a strict no-cuddling-while-sleeping rule, and her couple of other hookups hadn't exactly been anthropological case studies on intimacy.

She'd rolled away from Dustin at one point, fearing she was crowding his space, but he'd sleep-mumbled, "Where're you going?" and gently guided her back into his arms.

They hadn't talked much while she was in Indiana. She'd kept her phone off as much as she could, unplugging from passive-aggressive work emails during her days off, but she'd texted this morning saying she was on her way back. He hadn't replied yet. Last year she would've filled in the blanks with the assumption that he was hooking up with someone else, but now she just reasoned he was probably building a train set with his nephew, whose picture he'd sent her on Christmas morning.

On her flight back tonight, she'd looked down at the Manhattan skyline and decided there was no more spectacular sight—the sheer scale of the thing, with the Empire State Building welcoming her back like an urban lighthouse.

"I'm going to text him again," Rae said, and drafted a message.

Back in the city . . . want to do something this week? Pizza again or we could (attempt to) cook?

She didn't even have Ellen proofread it. She wasn't scared about double texting him or getting a word wrong, and if that wasn't the feeling of falling in love in the twenty-first century, she didn't know what was.

After sending it, Rae looked up from her phone and caught sight of a spindly plant in the kitchenette's window that they always kept locked so axe murderers wouldn't climb in through the fire escape. "What's that?" she asked.

"Thyme," Ellen said grandly. "The herb!"

"Wow," Rae said solemnly, and plucked some sprigs, not bothering to wash them. "We've become herb people."

"I was going to go with basil, but I thought you'd like the metaphor of fresh thyme."

Rae beamed. "Good choice."

"This is our year," Ellen said, as they sprinkled herbs on their eggs like confetti. "I have a good feeling."

"Yes," Rae agreed. "I'm bullish."

CHAPTER TWELVE

A PLUNGE IN THE HEART CHART

What if he's just like the rest of the Lost Boys in Boyhattan? Rae texted Ellen from her bathroom banker bunker the next day.

The office was buzzing with "a robust pipeline of opportunities," all the wannabe bosses eager to one-up each other at how many deals they could close this year.

Rae had finally been promoted, though the only difference she'd noticed was her title had changed on the company's email server from *analyst* to *associate*. She'd gone to congratulate herself with caffeine, only to find that the free coffee machines had been removed.

Worse, Dustin still hadn't responded to her follow-up text. Her newfound romantic tranquility was proving less durable than she'd hoped.

But he lives in Brooklyn, Ellen replied. Not Boyhattan. And you haven't even had sex yet. There's no way he's going to ghost you before sex.

Ellen had flown to Pittsburgh this morning for a new consulting project to help a steel company reduce operating expenses. If Rae had been in a better mood, she'd suggest Ellen look into how much eliminating coffee machines would save, but she just stared at the last text she'd gotten from Dustin, 8:42 P.M. on New Year's Eve. Wish you were here for a midnight kiss.

Then he'd gone dark.

He must have met someone else at a New Year's party, someone sample-size skinny who blow-dried her hair and had an elegant career like *advertising*.

Rae opened the Stall Street Journal, which she'd been carrying around in her blazer pocket although she hadn't yet thought of anything good enough to write in it. She closed it again and went back to her desk to put together a valuation model for a new deal.

One of her wannabe bosses hovered over her shoulder. The office had a privacy-thwarting open floor plan with rows and rows of computers squished right beside each other, without any dividers. It was touted as a "modern design to foster collaboration," but the only thing it fostered was a culture of perpetual fear and anxiety where the worker bees felt constantly spied on, with nowhere to go for personal space except the toilet. "Increase revenue growth rates to twenty-five percent for the next ten years," the guy barked.

"Shouldn't we model something more conservative?" Rae asked. She never would've dared to voice her own opinion last year but felt like she owed it to women everywhere to use the power of her new promotion. "Since the top line declined by twelve percent year over year?"

"Don't be such a downer," the wannabe boss said, returning to his desk. "The client likes it when we have confidence in them."

A group chat lit up on her computer screen. It was the COTWSM chat, which stood for Coup of the White, Straight Man. The group had been founded by Rae—the token female on their team of twenty—alongside the token Black man and token gay man.

TB and GQ, the other members of the coup, could nearly be called friends. TB stood for Token Black and GQ was Gay Quota. Rae went by EE—Estrogen Employee. They were all quite proud of the acronyms they'd chosen for themselves.

Though they sat only a few feet away from each other, they couldn't actually talk or they'd be yelled at for being off task, so the instant messenger had become their social lifeline.

Yeah EE, why're you being so cynical? GQ wrote. 100000% growth is extremely realistic.

Don't you know anything about client service? TB added. Treat everyone like a needy narcissist.

Rae tried to eke out a smile, but she just kept scowling at the Excel grid taking up the whole of her computer monitor.

The bigger the number they showed, the bigger the fee the bank would skim. But there was nothing underlying the valuation—just random assumptions, rounded out to four decimal points for the optics of precision.

Maybe there hadn't been anything underlying her relationship with Dustin either. Maybe she'd adopted investment bankers' rose-colored glasses and wrongly applied them to romance. She punched in number after number, begging that the task might numb her heart, not just her brain.

*   *   *

"Are you sure your texts were delivered?" Mina asked for the fifth time.

It was two days later, and still no word from Dustin. Rae had sent a code-red text to the Scramblettes, and they'd all assembled to analyze the situation.

Rae was sprawled on the penthouse couch, while Mina and Sarah sat on either armrest, taking turns feeding Rae ice cream and wine. Rae was farther into the ice cream pint than the wine bottle, but she'd made an impressive dent in both. Ellen was videoconferencing from her Pittsburgh hotel room, her face on the computer on the coffee table.

"They were delivered," Rae confirmed, passing around her phone as evidence. Mina shook her head in confusion and passed it to Sarah, who held it up to the computer for Ellen to verify.

"Maybe he had a death in his family?" Sarah suggested.

"Or he's just really swamped at work," Ellen said, so close to the camera that her face was out of proportion, all eyes and forehead.

"I bet he lost his phone," Mina said.

"Guys are always losing their phones," Sarah agreed.

"No," Rae said. "He's just another man-child who's scared of commitment. But is it that hard to send a text saying you don't see it working out? Is that really too much to ask?"

"I'd still give it another couple days," Mina said. "In case he really did lose his phone."

"He didn't lose his phone," Rae said, close to a shout. "He's just not interested anymore."

The group quieted, seeming to finally accept that this was, unfortunately, the highest-probability scenario. Sarah refilled Rae's coffee mug with wine, and Mina passed her the ice cream pint.

Gratitude poked through Rae's hurt, but not enough to fully emerge.

"Wait," Ellen said ominously. "How many dates did you go on?"

"Three." She'd played each one over in her head so many times that it felt like thirty.

"It's the third-date curse! I passed it to you."

Mina and Sarah gasped, but Rae just dug her spoon into the pint with new fervor. "There's no such thing as a third-date curse," she said, needing the apartment to be empty but not wanting to be alone.

"I think it came at a good time," Ellen said. "Better to know now and cut your losses."

No one commented that Ellen had broken her own rule about not using financial terms to talk about dating. Bleak times called for bleak comparisons.

"And it's a whole new year," Sarah observed. "You'll find someone incredible."

"We can make you a new dating app profile," Mina gushed.

Rae felt ill at the prospect. She just wanted to sit on the couch with someone and eat pizza and talk about poetry and deep shit and be held through the night. And she'd found that, or she'd thought she had, but it turned out that no, she hadn't, and the joke was on her. She'd plunged from pristine rooftop to polluted gutter runoff in a matter of days.

When she'd been with Dustin, she'd let her emotions take the reins, no longer consumed by crunching the numbers on the marriage math. Their time together hadn't felt like counting down to her thirtieth birthday. It had felt like counting up from zero to something.

But the something had flipped back to nothing, and with it, the panic from her birthday returned in full force. She was nearly a hundred days closer to thirty and had nothing to show for it. Somehow she'd have to bounce back from this, even though she didn't feel like she had an ounce of elasticity left in her brittle bones. Somehow she'd have to put on lipstick again—not red this time—and rev herself up for new dates. Somehow she'd have to hunt down her husband in these urban wastelands and close the deal before the cruel clock ran out and froze her in an irrevocable state of gloom.

Not able to stand drinking from a mug anymore, she went to the kitchenette and washed out a real wine glass, then transferred the contents.

"He's a fool," Sarah said.

"Biggest mistake of his life," Mina agreed. "Though I still think he'll resurface."

Rae didn't like how this made her cling to a new bubble of hope.

"He clearly has problems," Ellen said. "You dodged a bullet."

Feeling more like she'd dodged the rarest of Cupid's arrows, Rae deleted Dustin's number, then chased it with wine. She wasn't wearing any lipstick, so she left no mark on the glass—no smudge, but also no proof that her lips had ever touched the rim at all.

CHAPTER THIRTEEN
EMOTIONAL INFLECTION POINT

How have you been?

The text came on a Thursday morning in late January. Rae was slouched at her desk, staring at a cash flow statement on her computer with a canned look of concentration. She was nursing a hangover with a half-gallon jug of water.

Bonuses had hit their bank accounts yesterday, and her team had celebrated with bottle service at a Lower East Side club. It had almost been fun until Rae was hit with that bone-deep, shallow feeling as she looked around at all the bodies drunkenly swaying to lyricless house music, celebrating the creative ways they'd managed to siphon money for themselves to fund their mansions in the Hamptons. She'd stepped off to the side for some air when a fortysomething guy from another firm had sauntered over and tried to buy her a drink, assuring her she was "too pretty" to be an investment banker.

Rae had Irish exited and overpaid for a cab back to the penthouse.

It had been a disappointing regression to early-twenties life, but she was trying to forgive herself, since the bonus would allow her to pay off a big chunk of student loans. Her coworkers were always grumbling that bonuses weren't what they used to be. She had a hunch that her bonus was smaller than the guys', but she still felt like it was far more than she deserved for sitting in an air-conditioned office, formatting pie charts. She made substantially more than her mom, who was a public school teacher and objectively had a much harder, more important career.

At least now she could start looking for a new job.

Even before she Googled the area code, she knew the text was from Dustin.

She hated the text, but more than she hated it, she loved it, and even more than she loved it, she hated that she loved it.

She shuffled to the bathroom, where she texted the Scramblettes, soliciting advice for next steps.

Typical guys circling back on their own timelines, Sarah replied. Ignore him!!!

You should def reply!! Mina said. He probably has a good reason!

Low expectations, high standards, Ellen reminded her. But maybe respond to get closure?

In the end, Rae decided she'd reply but wait until the following day. There was something so petty yet powerful about not being the last one to text. She'd hoped she was done with these games.

There in the bathroom, she began swiping through the dating app she'd redownloaded. Determined to stay on track to finding her future husband, she'd been pulling late nights to go on more first dates and even a couple second dates, but each left her lonelier than the one before.

Her thumb tired of swiping and her heart tired of trying, she rested her head on the wall of the stall, but just as she was drifting off for a nap, the automatic toilet flushed beneath her, insensitively loud, and everything hurt again.

* * *

"Does my hair look messy enough?" Rae asked Ellen from the penthouse living room. It was Saturday afternoon, and she was preparing for her coffee closure catch-up with Dustin. She'd spent the last thirty minutes perfecting her *I spent thirty seconds getting ready* look.

"Yes," Ellen said, impatient. "I've told you that five times. Now just go downstairs, get closure, and then come back so we can get ready for our double date."

Ellen had recently uncovered that Aaron had a friend who was single and liked to read, and she'd taken it upon herself to declare that he and Rae were made for each other.

"I have to make sure I'm a few minutes late," Rae said, pacing the penthouse. She refused to be prompt for someone who was about to formalize their breakup. Not that they had ever technically been together, so it couldn't really qualify as a breakup, but still . . .

She'd replied to Dustin's text the following morning—in line for a cappuccino, sans whipped cream. She'd already reverted to eating egg yolks, but she'd been staying strong in abstaining from dessert, at least before ten A.M. She'd typed and retyped her reply to strike the proper tone—aloof but not bitter.

I'm well, thanks was the iteration she'd settled on.

Dustin had replied eight minutes later. I'm sorry I've been MIA. Free for coffee this weekend?

She'd detested the suggestion. Tea was quaint and elegant, but coffee was curt and corporate. But Ellen had been firm that Rae deserved answers, and so, seven hours later, she'd replied, Sounds good.

"Make sure he knows you're seeing other people," Ellen said now. "Just weave it in subtly. It'll be a nice kick in the balls to help him realize what a fool he was."

"Clearly he doesn't give a shit about that," Rae said, but she rehearsed a few phrases in her head to embellish her love life into something much more glamorous than swiping through hundreds of digital profiles a day from her office bathroom stall.

She redid her bun twice more to optimize the careless effect, then changed from one pair of black jeans into another and pulled on her coat, one with a hood that she used as a cocoon on crowded subway trains.

She walked down the stairs and into the late afternoon, toward the Elk, the coffee shop on Charles Street that she'd suggested. She'd wanted Dustin to do the commuting but hadn't wanted to meet at her regular spot at the corner of Perry and Bleeker. No need to taint the space.

The Elk was a small, rustic spot with wood-paneled walls and an old-fashioned menu written on a brown paper scroll. As Rae walked inside, she was immediately reminded of why she rarely came here. The space was too quintessential for its own good and always packed. It felt very squished, and the door closed so slowly that every person who walked in let in several wind gusts.

Dustin was already there, seated at a stool at the window counter. He was as accidentally attractive as ever, hair longer than when she'd seen him last and a shadow of scruff on his face, outlining his jawline. For a horrible half second, her insides leapt.

She sat down beside him, making sure their stools were a safe distance apart. "Hello," she said, cold syllables colliding with the cold draft.

She kept her gaze out the window, at the bare trees that lined Charles Street, somehow growing tall despite being planted in just a small square of soil in the middle of the concrete and cobblestone. Bundled-up people hurried along the sidewalk, many of them couples. Probability would ensure most of them broke up, but the thought didn't comfort Rae as much as she'd hoped.

"I got you green tea," Dustin said, gesturing to a steaming cup beside his own. "Is that all right?"

This perturbed Rae. He'd suggested coffee. "Thanks." She didn't pick up the cup.

She waited for Dustin to launch into whatever lame apology he'd rehearsed, something about how he was juggling so much at work and just didn't have the time to prioritize her like she deserved.

But he just watched Rae watch the passersby.

"So," Rae finally said, forcing herself to meet his gaze. His eyes were no longer a striking hazel mosaic but rather a wishy-washy jumble of muted colors, with dark crescents hanging below. Probably too many late nights partying with lingerie models. "How have you been?" she asked.

In the time it took him to answer, the door clapped in six more gusts of wintry air. "Not great," he said.

Anger jabbed Rae. He was trying to spin the story to elicit sympathy. Her dad had used similar tactics on her mom during those post-affair conversations Rae had eavesdropped on from the top of the staircase all those years ago.

"Why not?" she asked Dustin, trying to hurry him along by staring expectantly. "I have to go soon," she added. She tried to add *to get ready for a date*, but the phrase didn't come out.

Dustin lifted his gaze.

"I spent most of last year living with my parents in Connecticut," he said, speaking as evenly as ever. "Which is why I hadn't seen a lot of my friends in a while until the Christmas party."

It was a departure from the linear narrative she'd crafted. "Why?"

"I was getting treatment."

Rae's stomach scrunched as her heart was punched with regret about every assumption she'd made. When she finally found her voice and ditched her pride, she gritted out, "Not cancer?"

Two women shoved their way onto the stools next to them, and the baristas shouted about macchiatos and matcha and oat milk. Manhattan was intruding, like it did best.

"No," Dustin said, eyes mosaics again. "Just depression."

Rae didn't know what she felt, and she didn't spend time trying to label the emotion. She just let her hand fall to his forearm. "Tell me the story?"

He looked like he was about to say no, but he just said, "Not here."

Rae procured takeout cups, because for some reason, amid everything she'd just found out and was about to find out, it had become very important that they not waste this tea.

Paper cups in hand, they walked outside. Rae followed her feet westward along Charles Street, down West Fourth, over to Washington Place and the spirited heart of Greenwich Village, until they reached Washington Square Park.

The ten-acre park was brown and leafless this time of year, littered with comedy and jazz club pamphlets, orphaned mittens, and cardboard pizza boxes from John's of Bleeker Street. A man in tattered clothes sat in the middle of the walking path, holding an old accordion in his hands but not playing any music. Dustin closed his eyes for a moment, as if he could hear a melancholy song seeping out, and then dropped a couple bills into the man's collection bucket.

They cut through the park's central plaza, where tourists posed by the Roman archway and tossed coins into the large circular fountain. Stifled by the crowds, Rae led them toward a grassy section of the park and chose a bench to sit on, as far out of the way as you could be on an island of five million.

Dustin paused, staring at the bench but not sitting down.

"Do you want to sit somewhere else?" Rae asked.

"This is fine," he said. "I was just reading the inscription."

She noticed a small silver plaque on the center of the bench.

In memory of Tate and Lena Olivares, who found true love in this city of dreams in the summer of '49.

Rae did a rough calculation of how many thousands of park benches she'd walked by in her life without pausing to read the inscriptions.

This was what drew her to Dustin—how he observed and contemplated life rather than just going through the motions. She wasn't sure if she was supposed to let herself think this, but her guardrails had shattered at the word *treatment*.

Dustin left space between them on the bench, but Rae slid toward him.

The stocky brick walk-ups of Greenwich Village bordered Washington Square Park, shielding Midtown's glass skyscrapers. The spire of the Empire State Building poked through, stubborn or defiant, Rae couldn't tell which, or if there was even a difference.

"I've always been prone to it, I guess," Dustin said. "High highs and low lows. My mom said I locked myself in my room as a four-year-old, asking why God created 'pain right here.'" He pointed to his heart.

Rae wrapped her hand around his, like a bandage.

"I was on meds in college, but it felt like they muted my emotions, blocked the deepest human parts of me," he said. "So I went off them and was okay for a while. But last year was a new kind of low. I don't know why."

She could sense how hard he'd tried and failed to complete the $X + Y = Z$ equation.

"I took medical leave at work," he went on. "Went to my parents'. Laid in bed, barely ate. A therapist came every other day, but I didn't talk much. I was so stuck I couldn't even hold a book, let alone read one."

Rae's phone buzzed from her pocket. It would be the Scramblettes asking for updates, or Ellen debating what she should wear to dinner. It felt like another world, irreverently weightless.

"I came back to work in September," Dustin continued. "Thought I was doing better. Thought I could date . . ." He looked apologetically at her, and Rae hated herself for ever thinking he owed her an apology. "But I spiraled again on New Year's Eve. Drinking makes it worse . . ."

Rae wanted to ask about the *it*, what it made him feel and think and not feel and not think. She wanted to ask if he'd ever considered taking his life. She wanted to tell him his unfiltered parts made him exponentially more beautiful.

"What can I do?" she asked instead, mind racing ahead to potential solutions. She could help him find a new therapist and cook him some superfood scramblettes and read books out loud if he wasn't able to himself.

Her whole plan to keep swiping through the dating app until her husband showed up felt so juvenile, so misdirected. Dustin was the only man she wanted to lock down, but even more than that, she wanted and needed to help unlock him from himself.

He smiled weakly, sad stories written in the premature lines around his eyes. "I'm not dragging you into this. It's better if I keep my distance."

Rae's body tightened. She moved away from him on the bench.

"What's wrong?" Dustin asked.

"Don't go," she whispered, just softly enough that if he ignored her, she could almost believe he hadn't heard.

"Rae, I just need to get myself to a better place."

All she heard was *I don't want you.* She pulled her hood up over her eyes. The fabric wasn't as soft as the Santa hat, but it blocked the light better.

"I don't want to hurt you," Dustin said.

"Too late." She was aware that she was making it all about her, but she couldn't stop the habit and she couldn't stop the hurt, so she just kept sitting there in the January air, next to another guy who was about to walk out of her life.

They sat in silence until Rae was certain he'd left. She was so convinced she was alone on the bench that she flinched at the sound of his voice.

"Be my friend?" he asked.

Rae peeked out through her hood. He was still there, right beside her.

A single tear leaked down her cheek. She had no desire to wipe it away. He was asking her to stay. He wanted her in his life, and as a friend. That was even better than a girlfriend, really. You couldn't break up with your friend.

She nodded slowly until her hood shrugged off.

"Good," Dustin said. "Friends." The word turned over on his tongue like he was trying it on for fit or maybe flavor.

He seemed disappointed in himself that he hadn't arced the conversation toward a tidy ending. But they both saw now, in the fading daylight, that there was never going to be anything tidy about the two of them. The question was whether there had to be an ending.

"But you have to promise me something," he said.

"What?" Rae sniffled.

"Don't steal from your own sunshine to keep my soul out of the shade."

A half beat passed, then a whole. Rae had a gnawing yet calming sense that she'd look back at this moment as one of the pivotal emotional inflection points of her life.

"I won't," she said, a hiccup punctuating the poetic promise.

CHAPTER FOURTEEN

BFF BOND RISKS

"It's a recipe for heartbreak," Ellen told Rae the next night as Rae walked into Ellen's bedroom after a full yet empty day in the office.

Ellen was packing for her workweek away, and Rae set a pile of chocolate peanut butter cups and Ben & Jerry's pints on top of her garment bag along with an *I'm sorry* sticky note.

One of the perks of working on Sunday—the only perk, really— was getting a thirty-dollar food stipend. Today Rae had used it to buy Ellen's favorite snacks, even though she'd likely get flagged for violating the corporate expense policy, which mandated that all food be consumed "on premise, while working." Cameras were everywhere, and a database tracked when she swiped her employee ID in and out of the building.

Rae was willing to take the risk to get back on Ellen's good side after bailing on last night's double date.

Ellen had been none too pleased when Rae called to say she wasn't going to make it. "It was a coffee *closure* catch-up," Ellen had hissed. "What part of *closure* didn't you get?"

Rae had explained the situation this morning, assuming that once Ellen heard about everything Dustin was dealing with, she'd understand. She'd reacted quite oppositely, accusing Rae of prioritizing "some guy" over their friendship.

The conversation had been cut short by Rae's phone buzzing with a text from a wannabe boss asking why she wasn't in the office yet.

Rae had hoped that by the time she returned this evening, Ellen would have decided to let the matter rest. This did not seem to be the case.

"You can't gloss this over with chocolate," Ellen said, though she unwrapped a peanut butter cup and pocketed the sticky note. "You're not listening to me."

Rae sat on Ellen's bed, which was always more neatly made than her own. She was tired of sitting but also too tired to stand. "What am I not listening to?"

"How Dustin's going to break your heart."

"We're friends," Rae said, refusing to split up the words with a demeaning *just*.

Ellen tossed an eye roll and four pairs of black tights into her carry-on suitcase. "You met on a dating app. You can't be just friends."

"Yes we can."

Ellen read the resolve on Rae's face. "Fine," she said. "Go ahead. But I think he's manipulating you."

Rae's stiff body stiffened more. "You think he's lying about his depression?"

"No, I just think he wants to keep you a little too close and take advantage of your kindness."

"*I'm* the one who convinced him to let me be his friend," Rae said. "*He* wanted to keep his distance." She felt a jab of fear that she'd guilted him into the agreement. It was less clear from the edge of Ellen's bed than it had been from the park bench.

"Well, he's right," Ellen said, pressing down on her suitcase until it zipped. "Romantic or platonic, feelings are feelings. I know it sounds callous, but he has other people who can support him through this."

The words felt like thieves. "I'm not walking away."

"What about your grand plan to close the deal on marriage before thirty?"

"What about it?" Rae retorted. "It was a dumb idea. You said so yourself."

"I said it was a little rigid to map your life out like that with all those numbers," Ellen admitted. "But the concept of getting married and starting a family isn't dumb. It's what you want."

Rae did still want those things, but they felt very far away, very secondary, compared to more pressing matters at hand. The only timeline in her head right now was the timeline for getting Dustin better. Until that was accomplished, she knew she wouldn't be able to focus on much else, and she didn't want to.

"I'm trying this new thing where I don't overthink things," Rae said, as she silently overthought everything she'd just thought. "I'm just going where I feel like I'm supposed to go."

She knew Ellen wouldn't have much of a rebuttal, as this was very much her own philosophy—that emotions should be allowed to flow out without judgment or censorship—being used against her.

"All right," Ellen finally said, her tone indicating the disagreement was past, if not patched.

Rae's stomach growled. "I'm hungry," she mumbled, and stood up.

"Didn't you eat dinner at work?"

"No. I bought you those instead." She nodded toward the desserts.

"Oh," Ellen said. "Thanks." She tossed a peanut butter cup Rae's way.

Rae walked into the kitchenette, Ellen trailing. "You wouldn't have liked Aaron's friend anyway," Ellen said. "He was more of a Wickham than a Darcy."

The *Pride and Prejudice* reference was as good a peace offering as Rae could think of, next to the chocolate. "Want to split a scram-blette?" she asked.

"Yes, please," Ellen said. "But the thyme is dead."

Rae glanced at the windowsill. The herb had shriveled into a crunchy brown skeleton. Given that Ellen traveled so often, the brunt of the plant-parenting duties fell on Rae. She hardly had the energy to wet her own toothbrush after she got home from work, let alone remember to tend to another living organism. She couldn't fathom caring for something like a goldfish or a cat, forget about a human baby. Once again, she felt a defeated sort of shock that people her age were already having kids.

"We'll get succulents next time," Ellen said, unceremoniously dumping the thyme into the garbage under the sink. "Even we can't kill a cactus."

"Wanna bet?" Rae said, and they laughed a muted Elle-Rae laugh.

"See," Rae said, as she cracked the eggs and jabbed them with a spatula, "our best-friend bond is too high yielding to let men push us towards default."

"You know I don't like finance puns," Ellen said, but her lips quivered, and they ate the thymeless scramblette from the same plate, with separate forks.

CHAPTER FIFTEEN
FRIENDSHIP SYNERGIES

"That flattened cardboard box in the middle of the street," Dustin said, staring out the café window, onto Lorimer Street. "How it's flapping in the wind, like it's trying to fly but keeps getting run over by greasy tires."

"Disheartening," Rae said, sipping an iced matcha latte at the counter seat beside him. "But poignant."

"Your turn," Dustin said. "Find a poem."

Rae's eyes unpacked the scene rather than just scanning over it like she'd grown accustomed to doing. The late-afternoon light slanted onto the street, where crusty snowbanks were blackened by car exhaust. The bagel shop across the street had a line out the door as people queued up for lox-and-cream-cheese sandwiches. It was nearly dinner time by most standards, but Williamsburg hadn't quite wrapped up with Saturday brunch.

"That woman's scarf," Rae said, gesturing to a passerby. "How it's trailing on the sidewalk, trying to break free so it can walk on its own, not realizing it doesn't have legs."

"Lots of literary symbolism," Dustin agreed.

They were playing Poem Spotting, a game they'd coinvented during one of their platonic hangouts in the three weeks since Dustin had opened up about his depression.

They took turns picking out ordinary things that might contain some deeper meaning if woven into verse. Rae was learning, or perhaps remembering, that poetry was less an act of writing and more a way of seeing the world and reflecting on neglected details and textures.

She hoped observing everyday art would lift Dustin farther away from the darkness. And even though she didn't jot down more than the subjects of these poems-to-be (*flapping cardboard*, *dragging scarf*) in the Stall Street Journal, the activity helped her feel like her creative muscles weren't completely wasting away.

"The leftover whipped cream with no croissant left to put it on," Dustin said, gesturing to their empty plate, just a few croissant flakes and the remainder of the whipped-cream side that Rae had requested. "An unrequited-love story."

"You know I'm a sucker for love stories," Rae said, taking a spoonful of straight whipped cream. "Especially edible ones."

Initially, right after finding out about the depression, Rae had only had the bandwidth to think about Dustin's health. She hadn't been focused on dating, or at least she'd been focused on not focusing on it. Now, though, as their time together was developing its own quasi-consistent rhythm, she couldn't help extrapolating forward, imagining the day they'd be sitting at this same counter, hand in hand, painting each other's cheeks with whipped-cream-flavored kisses.

Rae knew it in how all her deepest, deadened parts twitched with new life every time she was within ten feet of him—Dustin was her person, the exquisite combination of mind, body, and soul that she'd been waiting for.

It wasn't fear of ending up alone that made her want to be with him. It was how he made her feel known, like no other guy ever had and, Rae was already sure, like no other guy ever would.

He wasn't just someone to help her close the marriage deal. He was *the* one to help her open up to the mesmeric world, the little moments of magic hidden in plain sight that, before him, she'd seen as mundane, if she'd seen them at all.

And one day, when the depression was gone, they'd reach their inevitable ever-after spelled out in the city-light stars.

For now, though, they were establishing a firm foundation in friendship before he was well enough to move to the next phase of their relationship. It was actually good they hadn't raced into some hot-and-heavy romance, Rae supposed, so they could develop solid platonic fundamentals that would benefit their long-term trajectory.

"I have to say, I think our friendship equity is going up in value every day," Dustin said, looking at Rae in that tender way that made her believe he'd thought about their future, too, and that he wanted it just as much as Rae did—he just had more block-ades in his way.

"Agreed," Rae said, glad she was a misfit between the corporate and creative worlds, since Dustin was a misfit too. "Lots of synergies."

They'd been trying out different tea and coffee shops around Williamsburg, and today they had come here to Poetica Coffee, as Dustin insisted the name had been chosen specifically with Rae in mind. It was a sustainably sourced café just down the street from Dustin's apartment, with potted plants hanging from the ceiling and a greenhouse seating area out back. They were the only two people at the front window counter, but they were seated close together, as if squeezed for space.

A blond-haired guy sauntered by on the sidewalk, dressed in a familiar Barbour jacket. Rae's stomach tumbled before she saw it wasn't her ex after all.

"What is it?" Dustin asked.

"Nothing. Just thought I saw a ghost." She realized how long it had been since she'd thought about him. The guy she'd once expected to exchange *I do*s with was now just a muted memory, a faded feeling, an estranged stranger. Time could sometimes be a little too good at its job, Rae thought—erasing the past like it never happened.

It was sort of like that with her dad. She almost missed the days when she'd missed him so violently that she couldn't breathe. Now, nine years after the divorce, all that was left was a limp sort of sorrow, with occasional jabs of real emotion. It was good how much she'd healed, she supposed, but it made her feel more distant from him, too, like the pain had been their last real attachment point. If he walked by the window now, it would almost be like she was seeing a stranger.

With the angles of his eyes, Dustin asked if she wanted to talk about it.

Rae didn't want to weigh down Dustin's shoulders with any of her baggage. He was carrying more than enough on his own.

"Go again," she said, elbow nudging his, like it was all very casual, like she didn't want to wrap her whole self and then some around him. "Find another poem."

Silence lapsed long enough for Rae's breath to settle back into its Brooklyn cadence.

"The dust on the windowsill," Dustin said. "How, when a ray of sun shines on it, it turns into glitter."

Their eyes tangled, then turned to the street to pluck more poems from sidewalk grates.

*　*　*

"We could fling paint at our wall and get the same effect," Ellen muttered as she and Rae passed an abstract display at a pop-up art fair on Prince Street in SoHo a few weeks later. The road was blocked off to traffic and clogged with dozens of vendors.

Located just south of the West Village, SoHo was an eclectic and ever-shifting shopping district, popular among chic supermodels as well as clumsy tourists. It was a bit too frantic for Rae to want to live here, but she liked having the proximity to be able to pop down into the buzzy streets now and then.

"Let's do it," Rae said. "Though we'd never see our security deposit again."

"I'll use my consulting skills to convince the landlord we've just raised the apartment value hundreds of thousands of dollars," Ellen volunteered.

"And I'll diligence sale prices of comparable penthouses to back up the valuation," Rae added.

"Dream team."

Rae turned over a price tag and flinched. Even now that she technically had enough in her bank account to buy something like this, her mind always compared it to what else the money could go toward—two months of student loan payments, a plane ticket to Thailand, ninety-three pints of ice cream.

"I just don't understand how anyone can charge seven hundred dollars for blobs of color on a canvas," Ellen said.

"Because some people are willing to pay seven hundred dollars for blobs of color on a canvas," Rae replied. "Supply and demand."

"Supply and be-scammed, more like it."

"Trademark that," Rae said. But she walked closer to the print, tilting her head and imagining how it would look in the Lorimer Loft.

She'd been reading up on depression and found a study citing the cognitive benefits of abstract art. That was all the evidence she'd needed to drag Ellen to the art fair. Perhaps *drag* was the wrong verb. Ellen had been very up for going, thinking it a highly sophisticated midtwenties outing. Rae hadn't shared her deeper motive.

"This one sort of looks like a black hole," Rae said, pointing to a black canvas swirled with gray. "Think our résumés are at the bottom of it?"

Rae's job search wasn't off to a roaring start. She'd applied to over a dozen marketing and content-creation jobs at different companies. It wasn't poetry, but it felt like a small step in that direction. *Forward. Upward.* Or even just *Out.* Ellen too was looking for a career switch, something that didn't require living out of a suitcase. Neither of them had heard back from any of their prospects, and they'd begun referring to the online application portals as black holes, sucking their career ambitions into the great cyber abyss.

Getting ghosted by companies felt slightly less personal than getting ghosted by guys, but no more pleasant.

They shoved their way through the crowd to the next booth: oil paintings of European city scenes, heavy on bridges and lampposts.

"Now *this* is art," Ellen said. "I wish Aaron got me one of these prints for our three-month anniversary instead of those crystal earrings. They're way too heavy. I'm going to get old-lady earlobes."

"Listen to yourself, please."

Ellen tossed back her head and laughed. "You're right. I'm enjoying the boyfriend thing a little too much."

"You're allowed," Rae said. "But I draw the line at complaining about crystals."

"Aaron gave me his Netflix password last night too," Ellen said.

"Damn. Must be getting serious."

"Might be," Ellen said, uncharacteristically laconic.

Rae glanced over at her beautiful best friend, bundled up under a knitted hat and scarf. She'd never seen this kind of peace on Ellen's face before when talking about a guy. Envy flickered before rising into shared happiness.

"More kindergarten creations," Ellen grumbled as they passed another stall of splatter paint.

"They're actually more complex than they look," Rae protested. "Abstract art can stimulate a meaningful release of dopamine into the parietal lobes of the brain."

She was pretty sure this held true for all types of art, but the study had mentioned only abstract, and she liked the idea that abstract styles were uniquely effective, that there could be a subconscious benefit to seemingly random and haphazard patterns.

"Where'd you learn that?"

"Saw an article on my news feed," Rae lied.

"Did the article talk about depression?"

She should know by now not to underestimate Ellen's bullshit detector. "Might've been in there," she admitted.

Ellen stopped walking. "Is that what we're doing here?" she asked, voice rising. In another city, the volume might've turned heads, but not in New York. "Art shopping for your boyfriend without benefits?"

Rae looked down at her boots, which were patching up two different cobblestone cracks. "It's not like that."

"You can't try and fix him with your problem-solution framework."

"I'm not trying to fix him," Rae said. "I'm trying to be a good friend."

"You've never bought *me* art."

"I love you enough to *make* you art. New maroon masterpieces on the couch every week."

"Wine stains don't fucking count."

"Ellen, you know you're always going to come first. I just—" Rae squared up and met Ellen's steely gaze as locals and tourists pushed past. "I don't know, I just feel like I'm supposed to be there for Dustin right now." She resisted adding *I'm sorry.*

"You still think he's your Mr. Right, don't you?" Ellen asked, not trying to hide her exasperation.

Rae wanted to deny it so Ellen would get off her back, but she hated lying to her best friend and knew Ellen would see through it anyway. Relenting to the truth, or at least the watered-down version, she said, in a quieter voice, "I just—I guess I think there's still a chance. Never say never and all that."

"*Never,*" Ellen said, with fierce firmness, "get serious with someone with mental health issues. It's the biggest red flag."

"Very empathetic of you," Rae replied coolly, regretting her choice to open up.

"It's one thing if you're only evaluating him as a friend," Ellen said. "But as anything more . . . I mean, why would you knowingly choose to love someone who can't even love himself?"

Rae swallowed the words in one gulp, so she wouldn't have to chew on them, and she felt them drop into her stomach. "You don't choose love," she said, with a defiant sort of pride. "Love chooses you."

The statement felt as firm as fact. Loving Dustin wasn't a choice, not a conscious action but a subliminal attraction. That was what cast such an enchantment over it. She didn't feel like explaining this to Ellen, nor listing off the reasons why she and Dustin would be together in the end. Ellen wouldn't understand the ins and outs and ups and downs of Dustin's days and how it wouldn't always be this way.

Ellen had the same bags under her eyes that Rae felt under her own. They were both exhausted, Ellen from perpetual jet lag from the West Coast project she was staffed on, Rae from working long nights for a deal with an "accelerated timeline," as they were both also searching for new jobs so they could break this tired-stuck-tired-stuck cycle. The prospect of *Saturday* had been the only thing getting them through, and neither one of them wanted to waste it fighting.

"Buy the painting, then," Ellen said, resigned.

"Are you kidding?" Rae said, lowering her voice so the merchant wouldn't hear. "I'm stubborn, not insane. I'll order something from Amazon at a quarter of the price."

Ellen nearly smiled, that smile Rae wasn't seeing enough of these days, between work and Aaron.

"Time for Percy's Pizza?" Rae asked, trying to keep the positive momentum going by making an offer she knew Ellen couldn't refuse.

"Aaron's taking me to dinner in a couple hours," Ellen said.

"So?" Rae said. "Pizza is the perfect predate appetizer. Coat the stomach with carbs before you start drinking."

"All right, let's do it," Ellen grumbled, succumbing to the sense of it or maybe just the soul of it. "I haven't been there in ages—two whole weeks at least."

They walked north to their beloved pizza joint at the corner of Bleeker and MacDougal. Percy's Pizza was a true slice of New York, Rae thought, proud of the pun. It was one of those cash-only hole-in-the-wall family-owned businesses where you could still find a bargain. Famous for its dollar slices, it had recently had to raise prices to keep up with inflation and had painted over the *$1* with a *$2* on the big red sign out front. Rooting for Percy to survive amid all the big corporate chains, Rae considered it a moral imperative to patronize the place whenever she could.

At the counter, she ordered a margherita slice, paying for it in laundry quarters since she hadn't gotten around to withdrawing cash from the ATM. Ellen opted for the four-cheese and proceeded to shake a small mountain of Parmesan on top of her bubbling slice when it came out of the oven.

"Have enough cheese on there?" Rae asked as they grabbed a fistful of napkins.

"Not quite," Ellen said. "But it'll suffice."

The thin-crust, triangular slices were so large they flopped off the edge of their paper plates. There was no space to sit inside, and both of them felt strongly that Percy's Pizza deserved too much respect to be eaten while walking, so they sat down on the curb and ate on the side of MacDougal Street.

"Now this is the glamorous life I always pictured for myself," Ellen said, mopping the grease off her pizza with some napkins as an angry cyclist whizzed by, dinging his bell at them for daring to step a toe into his personal territory.

"It's the authentic New York experience," Rae said with a grin as she wiped stringy cheese from her chin. "Not to be missed."

"All right, let's get home so we don't have to shower under ice water," Ellen said, after they'd devoured every last crumb.

It was always a gamble on weekends if the water at the penthouse would achieve anything higher than lukewarm status after midafternoon.

"You can go in first," Rae said. "Since you're the one with the date later."

"Nah, you can go," Ellen said. "You need it more."

"I'm pretty sure that was an insult."

"Just take the damn offer."

"All right, I'll be quick. It's not like I have to shave my legs or anything."

"Ah, the perks of single life."

"Miss it?"

"Can't say I do. The not shaving, though—yeah, I miss that."

*　　*　　*

"Art and houseplants?" Dustin said after work the next week as he unwrapped Rae's no-special-occasion gifts in the Lorimer Loft kitchen and folded up the boxes for recycling. "Trying to make me into an adult or something?"

"Or something," Rae said. "You'll be thirty in September, after all."

Dustin didn't seem to be dreading the ominous gateway into that decade nearly as much as she was herself. No surprise, given that his fertility would stay strong for decades to come, Rae thought. She resented his male privilege, though she knew it wasn't his fault.

Recently she'd been looking into freezing her eggs. It would give her more flexibility to let life twist and turn, but it was insanely expensive and there wasn't enough research on the long-term consequences for Rae to think seriously about it.

"Thanks for reminding me of my old age," Dustin said. He pulled her into a hug. They were a better height for hugging than for kissing anyway.

Rae didn't mention to Dustin how art and plants were associated with lower levels of anxiety and depression. Vegetables, too, which was why she'd brought over greens along with the usual pizza for one of their post-work platonic catch-ups.

"I brought Command strips to hang it," Rae said, breaking away to fetch her purse. "So your landlord won't charge you for holes in the wall."

"Very thoughtful," Dustin said. "But I actually own the place, so we'll be good." He said it casually, as if announcing that he drank coffee in the morning.

"You *own* it?" She didn't know anyone except the higher-ups at work who owned a place in the city. Not for the first time, she had the feeling that he came from money and tried not to judge him for it.

He set about hanging the print across from the couch, in the space where someone else might put a TV. It was a nice feeling, knowing something was sturdily hanging from the walls rather than resting precariously on plastic and Velcro like everything in the penthouse.

"Looks good," Dustin said when they were done, taking in the dose of primary colors. "But this better not have been expensive."

"It wasn't," Rae told him honestly. "To quote the ever-profound Bellini: *Buying art is a fool's game. Open a tab instead.*"

"Note how he suggested a tab, not a salad," Dustin replied dryly.

"Well, he wasn't exactly the picture of health." She'd read snippets from Bellini's biography and learned he'd been a depressed drunk for most of his life. It had hit on a peculiar kind of fear to know that she and Dustin both gravitated toward the words of such a tortured soul.

Busying herself, she arranged the plant in the kitchen window. She'd transferred it from its original plastic black pot into a red clay one. "This is a philodendron. They date back to the Victorian age, apparently," she said. "Only needs to be watered every eleven days." The instructions had said ten, but she figured eleven would be just fine.

Learning from the thyme debacle, Rae had researched "hardest to kill" plants and selected the philodendron. It showed more ambition than succulents but was still promised to be "failproof for beginners." The heart-shaped leaves were nothing more than a coincidence.

"Does this window get sunlight?" Rae asked. She'd never seen the Lorimer Loft during the day, and though that sounded scandalously romantic, it was just the bleak reality of long days at work and early sunsets. "It's supposed to be somewhere bright but not in direct sunlight."

Dustin moved the clay pot farther from the windowsill. "What should we name it?" he asked.

Rae thought about it. "Phyllis. Phyllis the philodendron."

A weak smile fought its way across Dustin's face. "You and your alliteration."

"Alliteration is one of those little things that never stops being delicious. Like ice-cold lemonade on an August day."

Since she'd been a little girl, she'd planned to have an August wedding and serve giant pitchers of homemade lemonade. The image crashed into her thoughts again now, and she didn't kick it out.

"I like the leaves," Dustin commented, running his hand over the green hearts.

Rae looked away, embarrassed. "Let's eat," she said. "The pizza's getting cold."

"Or the air's getting warm," Dustin said. "Depending on how you look at it."

"I'd rather debate philosophy on full stomachs," Rae said, as she set the pizza and salads on the coffee table. Even though Dustin had a kitchen table, they always ended up on the couch.

Rae could feel a heaviness about Dustin as he sat down beside her, in how he bent one knee and then the other, then reclined vertebra by vertebra.

Rae inhaled her food while Dustin picked at his.

"Not hungry?" Rae asked.

"Not really."

Rae tried not to project what it meant, and she tried not to forecast into the future as they sat side by side but far apart, both staring at the abstract jigsaw print, jarringly out of place amid the beige.

CHAPTER SIXTEEN
MIDTWENTIES BARGAINING POWER

"Your reservation is for two people," the hostess at Carbone, one of Manhattan's most sought-after restaurants, told Rae. "But there are . . . four . . . of you." She eyed the Scramblettes coldly. They were all dressed in sequined flapper dresses and plastic headdresses, standing out just slightly amid the sophisticated cocktail attire of the other diners.

"A table for two will be just fine," Ellen said. "We can squeeze. It's really no inconvenience."

"And double the sales for you," Rae piped in.

"She's turning *twenty-five*," Sarah told the hostess, nodding at Ellen, as if to clear up any doubt about the worthiness of the occasion.

"And we'll post amazing reviews on social media," Mina assured, snapping photos of the trendy interior as she spoke.

Having flashbacks to sitting on the penthouse floor for her own birthday, Rae had called weeks in advance to reserve this A-list Italian spot in Greenwich Village for Ellen's celebration. They'd only had a table for two left, but Ellen had assured her it would all work out.

A middle-aged man walked over. "What's going on over here?" he asked. The glamorous restaurant was very hushed, as if someone had put a candle snuffer over the whole place, so their conversation with the hostess had turned a few scowling heads.

"These girls don't seem to be able to count," the hostess said, but Ellen cut in, talking directly to the man.

"You're not the *manager*?"

The man nodded. "That's right."

Ellen flashed her million-watt smile. "Can you believe it, girls?" she gushed to the Scramblettes, who cooed appropriately. "A culinary icon in our midst!"

The manager appeared delightfully flustered. "Well, I suppose we *have* become something of a celebrity hangout," he said. "What're you ladies celebrating tonight?"

"It's my birthday," Ellen said. "We're having a midtwenties flapper theme—you know, a play on the Roaring Twenties." She chuckled charmingly. "My friend thought of it. She's a poet." She proudly patted Rae's shoulder. "Anyway," Ellen went on, "it just seems there's been a glitch in the reservation system . . . your lovely hostess only has us down for a table of two . . ."

The manager scanned the jam-packed restaurant, apparently seeking a solution.

"The thing is, we're absolutely fine with the small table," Ellen said. "We like sitting on each other's laps. It's so intimate, isn't it? Anyway, I know that's a little unconventional in such an *upscale establishment* as this one, but we promise to be on our absolute *best* behavior." She beamed again.

The manager blinked, but only for a moment. He wasn't the first to have become hopeless under Ellen's persuasive powers. "Well, of course," he said, as the hostess shot daggers their way. "Seems like a very reasonable request for such a special night. Follow me, right this way."

He showed them to a table for two in the corner of a navy-walled room adorned with paintings of the statue of David that showcased several different angles of his chiseled face. Old-world chandeliers dangled delicately from the glass ceiling, and the white tablecloth was set with two candles and a vase of fresh lavender sprigs.

The Scramblettes arranged themselves happily, Ellen on Rae's lap and Mina and Sarah squeezing side by side on the same chair.

"And that," Ellen said in a low voice, once the manager had walked away, "is how it's done."

"You were brilliant," Sarah said.

"So poised," Mina added.

"Midtwenties girls have lots of bargaining power," Rae noted, hugging Ellen from behind.

Thoroughly amused with themselves, the Scramblettes worked to keep their laughs from entering snort territory as the other diners, all glamour and gaunt faces, shot disapproving looks while picking at thirty-six-dollar Caesar salads.

"Order whatever you want," Sarah told Ellen.

"Our treat," Mina agreed.

"Absolutely," Rae agreed, cringing at the prices.

Ellen proposed they split two entrees among the four of them—the lobster ravioli and spicy rigatoni vodka—and Rae loved her more than ever. They splurged on the third-cheapest bottle of champagne.

After they'd scraped their plates clean, Rae flagged down the waitress, who seemed as deliberately miserable as the hostess. "Another round of focaccia, please?" she asked.

"Anything other than . . . bread?" the waitress asked.

Rae disliked how the elegant-sounding *focaccia* was demoted to clunky *bread*. "Just the focaccia for now, thank you," she said.

After another hour had gone by, they ordered one tiramisu for the table, blurting the "Happy Birthday" song as the waitress brought it out.

"I'm scared I'm going to blink and we're all going to be *forty* or something," Ellen said, as the Scramblettes practically licked the petite plate clean. "Time is moving at warp speed."

The champagne bottle was nearly empty. Ellen turned it over and managed to eke out another small glass, which she downed in two sips.

"I have no idea what I want to be when I grow up," Ellen went on. "Except here's the problem—I'm already grown up!"

Rae found it both comforting and concerning that even Ellen wasn't immune to a quarter-century crisis. "You're a fresh twenty-five," Rae consoled. "Lots of time to figure things out. Not like me, closer to twenty-*six*."

She felt no closer to escaping Wall Street than she had half a year ago. The only interviews she'd gotten were with other investment firms. She'd taken a couple phone calls just to feel like she had options, but they'd only reminded her why she wanted to flee the industry.

"I wish I loved something as much as you love words," Ellen said to Rae. "The only things I'm really passionate about are ice cream and sex. Can't exactly make a career from either of those."

"Dessert porn is always an option," Mina said.

"Big monetization opportunity," Sarah agreed.

Ellen scowled. "Grow up."

"Where's Aaron taking you this weekend?" Sarah asked.

Ellen's official birthday was tomorrow, but she'd waived her *You have to celebrate your birthday on the actual day* policy given Aaron was whisking her away for a weekend trip.

"Not sure," Ellen said. "It's a surprise."

"So romantic," Mina sighed. She was between fizzled flings.

"I'm too young to settle down," Ellen said. "Don't you think?"

"Not necessarily," Rae said, rocking Ellen on her lap. "The earlier you meet the right person, the better. Remember the math I presented at my birthday?"

"How could I forget," Ellen said, and Rae regretted bringing it up. She of all people should be more sensitive to the turbulence of emotions caused by turning twenty-five and still feeling like you're eighteen.

"Has Aaron talked about getting married?" Sarah asked.

"Not explicitly," Ellen said. "But he keeps making comments about *next summer* and *our future* and terrifying things like that."

A male waiter came by and deposited another focaccia basket, eliciting a cheer from three-quarters of the Scramblettes. He winked at Ellen, the holdout.

"Is that guy hot?" Ellen asked, eyes trailing him as he walked away. "He is, right?"

"I don't know," Rae said. "I guess he's threshold-level attractive."

"I'd sleep with him," Mina said, as if this were a highly selective benchmark.

"I can't even tell if other people are attractive anymore," Ellen said. "This is a clear red flag."

"It's not a red flag, it's a romantic banner," Rae said. "You're not looking around. That's a good thing."

"I don't even remember how to flirt."

"What're you talking about? You flirted our way in here tonight."

"That wasn't really flirting," Ellen said. "That was just flattering him. Flirting means they ask you out after."

"You want the manager to come over and ask you out?" Rae clarified, trying to soothe Ellen with a practical solution. "Because he will in two seconds flat." She knew that if the manager asked her out, Ellen would immediately decline and run to the bathroom to call Aaron, confessing how completely in love she was with him, how she'd never ever felt this way before and never ever wanted it to end.

"No," Ellen said, looking conflicted. The manager was nowhere to be seen, but she waved the waiter back over. "Any chance you could bring us some"—Ellen wiggled her voice—"olive oil?"

The waiter returned promptly with both olive oil and vinegar.

"See," Sarah said. "You've still got it."

"No, all my allure has dried up," Ellen lamented. "He was clearly making eyes at Rae, not me."

"That's objectively false," Rae said. "You're blocking my face. He can't even see me."

"I actually think Ellen's right," Mina said. "There was definitely some kind of spark. Rae, you should pass him your number."

"Tonight is about *Ellen*," Rae said, peeking out from behind Ellen's shoulder to glare at Mina.

"Yes, and Ellen wants to vicariously experience our complete sexual freedom," Mina said, scribbling her own number on the back of a pink business card she procured from her purse.

Under the table, Rae checked her phone. Dustin had been radio silent the past week, texting only once to say he was "dealing with things." Part of being his friend, the hardest part of it, was respecting his space. All the articles and blog posts and forums she'd read about depression emphasized how important that was. The internet was stuffed with so many stories about people who'd tried too hard to pull someone toward them, only to push them away altogether. The only thing she could do was wait for him to reach back out when he was ready.

Stowing her phone back in her pocket, she drowned the last of the bread in olive oil, then fed it to Ellen.

"Do you have any of those chocolate mints?" Sarah asked the waitress as she deposited the bill, which they split three ways. "It would be such a divine way to end the meal."

Not deigning to answer, the waitress pinched her face and walked away.

"Excuse me," Mina called out. "Could you get a photo of us?"

She didn't turn around, so they settled on a selfie. Ellen's eyes were closed, and the top half of Rae's face was cut off, but Mina seemed pleased. "We look amazing," she said, zooming in on her own face and trying on different filters. "What should I caption it?"

"How about *Focaccia goddesses*?" suggested Sarah.

"Or *Scramblette celebrity sighting*," said Rae. "Let's stop by Percy's Pizza on the way home," she added. "I'm starving."

"Late-night pizza is so juvenile," Ellen said, but Rae could tell she was secretly craving two slices of pepperoni.

"It's not juvenile, it's *timeless*," Rae corrected. "Let us never get too old to appreciate the triangular wonders of carbs, cheese, and sauce."

"Hear, hear," Sarah said, raising her empty champagne flute.

Rising from the table, they escorted a wobbly Ellen out of the restaurant, their feather headdresses flapping in the feisty spring breeze.

"Next stop, Percy's Pizza," Rae announced.

Ellen let out a disgruntled "Humph," but she squeezed Rae's arm three times in gratitude.

CHAPTER SEVENTEEN

BLURRING OF PLATONIC AND ROMANTIC INDUSTRY LINES

"I've never cohosted a real dinner party before," Rae said two weekends later as she heated a pot of water at the Lorimer Loft, waiting for her big moment to dump in the package of pasta. "I'm adding *sous chef* to my résumé."

"I'd hardly call this a real dinner party," Dustin said from his spot beside her at the stove, where he was stirring marinara sauce with one hand and seasoning mushrooms and zucchini with the other. "But I'm not disputing your culinary talents. You make boiling water look easy."

Rae swatted him with the ladle.

It was mid-May now. After weeks of silence, Dustin had texted Rae asking if she wanted to come over for dinner with his friends John and Jenn, one of the engaged couples Rae had met at the Christmas party. Rae had agreed and thought it better to call the gathering a dinner party, which it nearly was, than a double date, which it barely wasn't.

It was just Rae and Dustin right now, plus Phyllis the philodendron, alive and well in the window, sprawling wide but not tall.

Rae had written a list of things she planned to ask him—why he kept shutting her out in long stretches, if he'd still been going to therapy, whether he might reconsider his anti-meds philosophy, how his dark thoughts now compared to what he'd felt last year, what she could do to better support him, etc. The index card was folded in the pocket of her jeans. But now, looking into his hazel eyes, bright tonight, she didn't want to teeter the balance of the evening.

"Close your eyes and open your mouth," Dustin said.

A hopeful fear or fearful hope passed that she would feel his lips on hers. Instead, she tasted marinara.

"You don't like it?" Dustin asked.

"It's good," she said, opening her eyes. "Distinctive."

"My grandmother's recipe," Dustin said. "A dash of cinnamon as the secret ingredient."

"Cinnamon," Rae repeated, wondering how his grandmother had realized this unlikely pairing belonged together.

She set the table, folding the napkins into crisp triangles. Dustin made a batch of margaritas. She remembered how he'd said drinking worsened his depression but stayed quiet as she salted the rims, following instructions she'd found online—turn the glasses upside down and dip them in lemon juice before the salt to make it stick. They drank in the kitchen, taking turns stirring the sauce.

"They're here," Dustin said, when the apartment buzzer rang. As an afterthought, he added, "They might think we're dating."

Rae's margarita sloshed. She hoped she hadn't misheard him. "And why might they think that?"

"I think they just assumed."

Even more than she liked their assumption, she liked that Dustin hadn't debunked it. "Why didn't you set them straight?" she asked in a way that she hoped would open the door to him opening up about his feelings.

Dustin looked down at the rim of his glass, which had already shed most of its salt. "I guess I didn't want to."

The sentence sounded like a full song. Rae tried to temper her expectations and remind herself that Dustin wasn't better yet so they couldn't be together yet, but her expectations soared upward anyway, higher and higher until she was flying in that marshmallow-cloud dreamland she'd thought they wouldn't reach for a while yet.

And just like that, their carefully defined friendship lines blurred into the romantic sector. She wanted to spin him around right there in the kitchen, leap into his arms and kiss him.

Instead, she made herself walk to the door to let in their guests.

* * *

"Your fettuccini was a hit," Dustin said, loading the dishwasher after John and Jenn had left. "You've mastered the art of al dente."

He'd draped his arm around her as the four of them had talked in the kitchen, discussing the short list of wedding venues for John and Jenn's upcoming nuptials, and even as they'd eaten, he'd kept a hand on Rae's knee.

She hadn't put her hand on top of his, but she hadn't moved it, either. It had been easy, delightfully easy, to pretend they were a couple, to picture them following in John and Jenn's footsteps and getting engaged in a couple years, tying the knot at the charming chalet upstate that Jenn had shown photos of, and going on fabulous double dates every week with their married friends, just like a movie.

But as much as Rae held on to hope that this might be their future, she was forced to acknowledge that it wasn't their present or anything close to it. There had been a ruinous whisper in Rae's ear all through the meal, cautioning her that perhaps Dustin wasn't actually professing his love to her at all, that maybe he was just using her as his fake girlfriend so he wouldn't feel left out with his friends.

She willed these fears to be nothing but overdramatic party crashers, but she wanted to hear it straight from him to be reassured. "So we're dating now?" she asked, as nonchalantly as she could, trying to keep him from clamping up.

He clamped up anyway. Rae saw it in the way his whole jaw hardened and his eyes looked cut from the same stone. "You know we're not," he said.

The words scraped her from top to bottom, then bottom to top. She was left with the raw sensation that she was a pawn in a game of chess she didn't know the rules to. "Then why were you acting like it?" she asked.

"I'm sorry," he said, in a disapproving voice that seemed directed inward more than outward. "I just thought it would be easier to go along with it."

"Easier?" Rae asked, sure she'd never done anything harder than preserving this fragile friendship act.

Dustin kept his head down as he answered. "It won't happen again."

She probably wouldn't have been brave enough to say anything more if she hadn't had multiple margaritas, but she had. "You can't ignore my texts and calls and then use me as a prop so your friends think you're living some blissful, coupled-up life," she said, all in one breath so she wouldn't pause and lose her resolve.

"You're not a prop," Dustin said. "That's not what happened."

"Felt like it." The loft was spinning from her drinking too much or maybe just thinking too much. "I need to go to bed."

She thought Dustin might offer to let her crash on the couch, or maybe he'd take the couch and offer up his bed, or perhaps he'd suggest the bed was big enough for them to share it, but all he said was, "Let's get you an Uber."

Dustin took the elevator down with her and waited for the car to arrive. She was drunk enough not to feel the poor economic decision of taking an Uber rather than the subway.

"Text me when you get home," he said.

"Will do," Rae said, closing the door before she tried to pull Dustin in with her.

She thought she might start crying and wondered how many drunk girls had cried in this back seat before. Refusing to be lumped into this statistic, she just stared out the window as the car crossed the Williamsburg Bridge back into Manhattan, blinking at the blurring lights, too tired to wish on them, as she replayed the words Jenn had whispered in her ear as they'd hugged good-bye tonight. *You're really good for him, Rae.*

* * *

"It's a scramblette, not an omelet," Rae corrected, taking control of the spatula and grazing Dustin's hand in the process.

They were wedged into the Perry Street kitchenette on a Saturday afternoon, the first weekend of June. It was the time of year when the city began to stick with humidity and all the heat rose to the top floor. The window air-conditioning unit was wheezing feebly.

"You have to mess up the eggs more," she said.

"Got it," Dustin said, reclaiming the spatula to poke at the contents of the skillet.

"Not *that* much. You still have to preserve an element of omelet elegance."

"Apologies for my irr-egg-erence," Dustin said, suppressing a smile.

His mood was lighter today, and it made Rae want to twirl.

They'd never ended up addressing the events of the double date-ish but had slipped back into friendship just as easily, or uneasily, as they had before.

Even though that night had quickly devolved, Rae figured it was a good sign that he'd been entertaining the idea of romance. She'd pushed him too hard too soon, perhaps, but once the depression lifted just a little more, he'd be ready for more.

This afternoon they'd gone to the Whitney Museum to see a politically themed Mexican mural exhibit, and since it was right in the West Village, they'd come to the penthouse afterward so Dustin could finally get a tour and meet Ellen, who would be returning from yoga any minute.

They ate on the couch, repurposing Ellen's *Vogue* magazines as place mats for the coffee table. "So what's the verdict on the scramblette?" Rae asked.

Dustin took two more bites before answering. "I like how the flavors are intertwined more than in a traditional omelet but there's still greater structure than in a pure scramble. An admirable merger of culinary genres."

Rae happily shoveled in her own eggs. After they finished, she asked, as if walking on the eggshells they'd cracked together, "So how have you been feeling about . . . things?"

"All right," he said. "Getting by."

"Have you still been going to therapy?"

"Yup." He carried their plates to the sink, where he started washing them and the rest of the procrastinated dishes.

Rae held in her hundred follow-up questions, which felt a lot like holding her breath, except without the comfort of knowing she could open her mouth whenever she wanted. Her eyes drooped, and she was lulled half asleep by the sputtering of the sink. The pipes needed fixing, but she was too tired to call the super to report the problem. Between deals and job applications, she'd been averaging only a few hours of sleep.

"Sleepy?" Dustin asked, voice close. The water had stopped, but the pipes were still gurgling.

Eyes closed, she nodded.

He scooped her up, then set her back down on the couch, his lap as her pillow. "I'm not trying to hide anything," Dustin said, tucking a strand of Rae's unwashed hair behind her ear, and then another. "I just have so much rain in my life, I want to keep you as my Rae of sunshine. But that's pretty shitty of me, isn't it?"

She opened her eyes. "No," she said, refusing to succumb to her stormy, selfish tendencies, not when he was the one who was hurting. "You're the antonym of shitty."

He smiled his lyrical smile, and she smiled something back, the other half of the verse she'd been stuck on.

Keys jiggled in the apartment door. Ellen entered, yoga mat in hand. "Rae-bae, I'm home," she sang, stopping midsyllable as she spotted Rae's head on Dustin's lap.

Rae sat up, but not fast enough.

"Hello," Ellen said, voice chilled. "You must be Dustin."

"And you must be the remarkable Ellen."

"I gave Dustin a scramblette tutorial," Rae explained. She tried to point to their dishes as evidence, then remembered Dustin had already washed them.

"That's great, but don't ruin your appetite for our double date tonight," Ellen said, emphasizing the phrase *double date*. Having recovered from her own quarter-life crisis, she and Aaron were sturdier than ever. After Rae had canceled on the first double date attempt, Ellen was set on a redo. "You should really start getting ready."

"Dinner's not until eight thirty," Rae said. "It's barely five."

"Yes, but you'll want to wash and dry your hair and everything."

"Thought I'd just put it in a greasy bun," Rae said. "Authenticity is my whole value proposition."

Ellen did not look amused.

Dustin stood up from the couch. "I should get going. Really nice to finally meet you, Ellen. Hope we'll see each other again soon."

"I'm sure we will," was all Ellen said.

Rae walked Dustin to the door and gave him a quick hug, feeling Ellen's eyes on them. "Have fun tonight," he murmured, and then he was gone, footsteps too soft to hear descending the stairs.

Rae rounded on Ellen. "What the hell was that? The first time you've ever met him and you're cold as a banker? What'd he ever do to you?"

"Other than lead on my best friend?"

"He's not leading me on. We're on the same page."

"If that page is titled 'Delusion,' then yes, I agree." Ellen disappeared into the bathroom.

"That's it?" Rae called out. "That's all you have to say?"

"What do you want from me, Rae?" Ellen shouted over the shower. "To tell you if I think he's in love with you?"

"No," Rae said, burning to know.

Ellen stuck her head out into the living room. "He is. But not as in love with you as you are with him."

"I'm not in love with him," she lied, hoping the neat sentence would hide the messy truth.

"You spend all your nonexistent free time shuttling back and forth on the L train to see him all the way in *Brooklyn*," Ellen said sharply. "If that's not love, I don't fucking know what is."

It was true that the L train was the worst in the city, always over capacity and under construction. Rae couldn't think of anyone else she'd repeatedly endure the journey for, except Ellen.

"You're wasting your time," Ellen muttered, in a tone that indicated that she thought she, too, was wasting her time by pointing this out. "He's never going to be marriage material, and definitely not before you're thirty."

"Yes, he is," Rae said in a loud voice that she hoped would drown out Ellen's doubts and any stray ones of her own. "He's getting better."

"You need to be out there meeting other people," Ellen said. "Get some perspective."

"I already have perspective," Rae shot back. "I must've swiped through at least fifteen thousand dating app profiles, remember?"

"That's not the same."

Rae held in her counterargument about how there wasn't any point in spending her time meeting dozens of other guys when she could be investing it in the one person she knew she'd end up with once Dustin recovered. Ellen wouldn't follow this nuanced logic, Rae knew. Aaron was the embodiment of emotional availability, and Ellen had taken to finding all sorts of ways to drop comments to Rae about how important that was in a relationship.

It was so easy to have the answers when you weren't facing the questions yourself, Rae thought, staying quiet so she wouldn't widen the rift between them.

"Just come on the double date," Ellen said, tone thawing. "We can order appetizers without worrying about paying."

Unwillingly, Rae felt her ears perk up. "And dessert?"

"Desserts. Plural."

"Fine," Rae said, because she wanted things back to normal with Ellen and because she knew where her mind would drift if she were alone on the couch all night. She'd be replaying the double date-ish, berating herself for her thoughtlessness in pushing Dustin into a corner like that just when he'd been getting comfortable with more affection. "But no making out with Aaron at the table," she qualified to Ellen.

"We won't," Ellen said.

"Or *under* the table."

"Damn. Okay."

"Or leaving me stranded while you hook up in the bathroom."

"Someone's been negotiating too many legal agreements."

"These are the conditions. Deal?"

"Deal," Ellen said, clapping the bathroom door shut in lieu of a handshake.

CHAPTER EIGHTEEN
(ALMOST) EXITING THE POSITION

Got final round interview in San Francisco, Rae texted Dustin, then the Scramblettes, from the Starbucks bathroom next door to her office building.

More private than the bathroom at work, but not too far away that she couldn't hustle back at the drop of an email, this Starbucks stall had become her phone booth for calls with recruiters the past few months.

She'd received so many letdowns in this toilet cubicle—companies stringing her along and breaking her heart—that she was unprepared for the encouraging call she'd just received.

Here it was, the long-awaited exit, within reach. A corporate strategy job with an up-and-coming Silicon Valley fintech company that had built a proprietary, highly differentiated market-leading digital platform to help institutional investors better monitor their portfolio risk profile in real time. Those were the buzzwords, at least.

She wasn't riveted by the product, but *strategy* seemed more creative than banking, and she'd gotten a good, human-ish feeling from everyone she'd spoken with, including the woman cofounder. The hours should be better too.

The Scramblettes replied immediately, all-caps strings of CON-GRATS!!! and DON'T LEAVE US!!!!

Ellen had just run into a new job at a start-up that sold chickpea milk in Europe and needed help expanding into the North American market. She'd shown up at the wrong address for an interview at another consulting firm, and by the time she'd walked out, she'd had an offer in hand. Rae had been quietly covetous but now felt a rush of procrastinated pride, trailed by fear at starting from scratch on the West Coast without Ellen squished beside her.

Rae left the stall and ordered a coffee to take back up to justify her absence. She got two extras for the COTWSM members. They'd been getting on her nerves, but now she preemptively missed them.

She texted Dustin a follow-up before he'd gotten back to her on her first message. Should I fly out there and take the interview?

He replied while she was in the crowded elevator up to the forty-second floor. What does your gut say?

More light-headed than lighthearted, Rae delivered the cappuccinos to GQ and TB and sat back down at her desk. A wannabe boss hovered over her shoulder, and Rae braced herself for a scolding for being out of sight for too long.

"Nice job on the cash flow analysis," he told her. "Didn't expect that level of granularity."

Rae waited for the catch, but he just gave a nod and walked away. The COTWSM chat lit up on her computer.

GQ: What was that, EE?? Did the tin man finally get a heart??
TB: I've never gotten that kind of praise in all my years here . . .

Rae replied, They're probably just fattening me up for an all-nighter . . .

But she wondered if perhaps she'd finally passed through the trough of investment banking hell. Her hours had been marginally better since the last deal closed. She hadn't even worked the last two Sundays, and there were rumors of hiring a junior analyst to help with the grunt work.

Did she really want to take a thirty percent pay cut to move to a city where she didn't know anyone except a couple sorority sisters she'd deliberately lost touch with?

And as far as the dating scene went, she'd be starting from scratch in the land of socially incompetent tech nerds, as opposed to her current situation where she'd already sifted through all the coal and found the gold. No, she and Dustin weren't technically together, but they were clearly trending in that direction. She wouldn't be able to be there for him as much—as friends or more than friends—from California.

It was already June. It wouldn't be that bad to stick it out until January bonuses. She could pay off more of her student loans, add to her Poet's Fund, and then be better positioned to take a gamble on something new, something that wouldn't take her away from New York.

Looking again at Dustin's text, she wondered what the difference was between listening to her gut and listening to her heart.

Rae didn't try to figure it out. She just began mentally crafting a breakup email to the San Francisco company, similar to the text template she'd sent guys from her ten first dates, the few who'd asked her out again. I've really enjoyed getting to know you, but . . .

*   *   *

"You can delete cockroaches from the cons," Ellen said that Friday night as they sat on the penthouse couch, color-coded spreadsheet open on Rae's laptop. "We haven't seen one in months."

They were determining whether to renew their lease. Ellen was all for cost-benefit analyses for economic decisions, just not romantic ones. She was advocating that they stay, while Rae craved a new space, something to validate forward motion since she wasn't switching jobs after all.

"I saw a roach in the shower just last week," Rae insisted.

"That was a centipede," Ellen said. "Much less threatening. And you should really move the ninety-six stairs to a pro, not a con. It's keeping our asses in shape."

Ellen's glutes were far more toned than Rae's despite the same climb, but Rae conceded the argument and made the adjustment in the spreadsheet.

"Put high switching costs as a reason to stay too," Ellen said. "Moving is a nightmare."

"The cons are still longer," Rae said, evaluating the list: *Half wall, small fridge, no dishwasher, loud neighbors, cold showers, no A/C, rabid radiator, lost mail/packages, sock-eating basement laundry.*

"But you need to weigh the price and location variables most heavily," Ellen said, well practiced for her new chickpea milk sales job, beginning next week. "Can't beat those. And we've finally invested in chairs, so none of the Scramblettes have to sit on the floor." They now had two plush-ish armchairs across from the couch.

"We could get more space in Brooklyn," Rae said. "Williamsburg, maybe."

Ellen rolled her eyes, then rolled them back again. "We're not moving next to Dustin. If anything, we should think about the Upper East Side. You can get better deals." Aaron lived on the Upper East.

"I'd consider it," Rae said. "If we found the right spot."

Ellen pouted. "But *this* is the right spot. I've become so accustomed to penthouse life, anything else would be too disappointing a letdown to bear."

"Says the one whose bedroom has walls that reach the ceiling."

"We could switch bedrooms," Ellen offered. "I'll be at Aaron's place most nights anyway, since it's walking distance to work. Did I tell you my new office has kombucha on tap? And free snack bins? And a flexible work-from-home policy?"

"So you've mentioned."

Ellen had been talking about little else apart from all the glorious perks of start-up life.

"I don't want to switch bedrooms," Rae said, loyal to her runty room as long as she lived here. "I just think—we can't live like college kids forever."

"Not forever," Ellen said. "Just one more year."

"Fine," Rae relented. "One more year."

"Then we'll find a bigger place uptown and you'll move in with Aaron and me."

"Great," Rae deadpanned. "Third wheeling in an apartment really rings of adulthood."

"Don't worry, we'll get you one of those ocean noise machines to mute the sounds from our bedroom."

"Think I'd need a fire truck siren machine for that."

"Well," Ellen said, holding back a supremely pleased smile, "we have a whole year to figure that out."

And they signed on the dotted line of the lease, committing to another 365 days on Perry Street.

CHAPTER NINETEEN

REAL TALK, NOT DEAL TALK

"Purchase price of thirteen-times recurring revenue. That's a hell of an acquisition outcome we got to, boys," one of Rae's wannabe bosses said, slurping a beer as they celebrated a deal that had just closed. Rae was collectively lumped into the "boys" category, which they probably thought was inclusive of them if they thought about it at all.

They were out at Jimmy at the James, an eighteenth-story cocktail lounge in SoHo with posh modular furniture, glazed tile walls, a working fireplace, and shiny views of Midtown, Wall Street, and the Hudson River. Rae didn't want to be here, but more than that, she hadn't wanted to say no. Women on Wall Street were always grumbling about not being invited for golf or beers, but then when invited, they rarely came.

"Good valuation, sure, but the fee structure fucked us over," another wannabe boss chimed in. "Nothing like we could get away with before the crisis."

"That's why we built an extra fifty thousand dollars into closing costs for the client. Next round's on them!"

The guys hooted and ordered more whiskey and beer.

Rae felt queasy from something more than the drinks.

GQ and TB weren't here, since they hadn't been on this deal team, and Rae had no one to exchange eye rolls with. It had been a few weeks since she'd turned down the San Francisco job, and she felt newly trapped, though she could only blame herself.

She tried to picture these guys around her as little kids, running around on the playground, jumping off swings, building forts in the woods. They must have dreamed of something more than shifting money around and charging drinks to their clients.

She was woozy enough to pose the question to the midforties wannabe boss beside her. "When you were little, what did you want to be when you grew up?" she asked, half shouting to be heard.

"Thought I might be an accountant," he said. "But realized investment banking was the more lucrative path."

"Did you ever want to be . . . an astronaut or something like that?"

"I don't know," he said, like this was all far less interesting than comparing purchase price multiples. "Guess I wanted to be a hockey player, but we all get realistic sometime, don't we?"

"Yes," Rae said glumly. "I guess we do."

Some of the guys were still single, eternal bachelors who hit on college girls for the hell of it, and a couple of them were married to women ten or fifteen years younger, maybe because women their own age were too old to have kids or maybe just because the fresh meat was more fun to parade on their arms at the charity galas they attended to prove they were good people.

One of the married guys handed Rae a beer. She took it to avoid their judgment if she declined. Not for the first time, she wondered if she was making the wrong decision by sticking it out through next bonus season.

She wasn't bro enough to be part of this circle, but she wasn't brave enough to leave it.

No one noticed her exit, and she walked out onto the sleek roof terrace where chaise lounges surrounded a long, skinny swimming pool that felt very *Great Gatsby*–ish. No one was in the pool, but a few people were dangling their toes over the edge while they sipped Aperol spritzes.

Keeping her distance from the other people on the terrace, she looked out over the stainless-steel railing, up toward Midtown and the Empire State Building. Cinematic as the view was, she missed the one from the Lorimer Loft rooftop. The see-and-be-seen vibe in this place left her feeling entirely invisible.

Come rescue me from this work party, Rae texted Dustin.

She tried to mentally prepare for having the text go unanswered, like her prior texts had the past couple weeks. With the sixth sense she'd acquired, she could feel he'd been stuck in a downturn.

But her phone buzzed right away. Where is it? he asked.

Jimmy at the James

Be there soon.

Attempting to temper her hopes, she cracked open the beer and looked around her, at all these people in look-alike suits puffing themselves up with pointless importance to distract from the meaningless vacuum their lives had become. And her, right in the middle of it all.

The best thing that could be said was that she was at least more self-aware, cognizant of how she'd sold out, though perhaps that was actually less forgivable than being someone who didn't realize the choice.

She counted lights in a tall, spindly apartment building a little ways away and did some rough multiplication to estimate how many people were within a three-mile radius of her right now. Often she enjoyed this game, imagining all the parallel and perpendicular stories, but tonight the math felt daunting.

Someone tapped her on the shoulder. Instinctively, she flinched, bracing herself for a wannabe boss to ask why she was being a buzz-kill or requesting that she serve as judge for a beer shotgun contest where they tried to beat their college records.

It was Dustin, dressed just like everyone else in this place, but alive in his eyes in a different way. Not a vibrant alive but a deep one—exactly what she needed.

"You're here," she said.

"'Course I am."

Holding in a reply that might put him on the defensive, she kept her tone light. "Be warned, if you mention the terms *recurring revenue* or *fee structure*, I'm dumping this beer straight on your head."

He smiled beneath his lips. "But those were both of my go-to conversation topics."

"Don't worry, there's still monetary policy to debate," Rae said. "What would you say the odds are of a twenty-five basis point rate cut at the next Fed meeting?"

Dustin groaned, vocalizing the sound that Rae had been feeling for the past two hours. "I was on the phone for ten hours today with clients asking me about that," he said. "I'm all talked out."

"Same here."

They stood in shared silence, staring out over the railing. Rae leaned on Dustin's shoulder, preferring the skyline from this angle. She dropped a kiss on his collarbone.

"Rae," he said, tensing. "We can only be friends."

The words didn't hurt this time. They just reminded her that their *one day* hadn't arrived yet. But they were closer to it tonight than they had been this morning.

"*Only* is for phrases like *only 99 cents* and *one night only*," she replied. "There's nothing *only* about friendship."

"You know what I mean."

She did know what he meant, all too well. He still didn't feel like he was in a solid enough spot to give her what she needed in a relationship. From how he continued to disappear on her without rhyme or reason, she knew he was probably right, even though she felt in her soul that she'd rather take him exactly as he was, beautiful shards of a delicate heart, than wait for the cracks to seal. She wouldn't love him any more or any less once he recovered. But he would love himself more once he beat the depression. He'd be able to see that he was worthy of her love, and that was what mattered. That was why it was so important for her to keep waiting patiently and not pressure him to move faster, not give him any reason to feel like he wasn't enough for her exactly as he was.

"Relax, Dustin," she said, trying to give some levity to the evening, some levity they both needed. "I'm not trying to date you. I'm just trying to love you."

"Oh, is that all?"

She could feel him smiling in the way his breath rose higher than it fell. Their exhales synced.

"Yup," she said. "That's all."

She waited for him to nudge her away, invent some excuse about needing to use the bathroom or get a drink, but after a moment, he rested his head on top of hers. They stared sideways at the straightened city.

"I love you too," he said, almost a regret, and Rae felt more confident than ever that she would always want to be his only, whatever type of only best fought his lonely.

Tonight, only friends was just right.

PART 2

1,215 DAYS TO GO

CHAPTER TWENTY
THE HEART MARKET CRASH

"Dustin?"

Rae turned the lock of the Lorimer Loft. It was the following summer, late on a weekday night. Rae had tripped into twenty-six before she was ready, and her life looked disconcertingly similar to how it had at twenty-five. The same job, the same apartment, the same procrastinated poems, the same L train subway rides after work to see Dustin and try to lift him out of whatever color mood, or colorless mood, was clenching him that night.

Their friendship had deepened with time, in the shape of the crevices made by Dustin's lowest lows. But it hadn't risen in the way Rae pictured it might—that's to say Dustin hadn't been cured and proclaimed he was ready to be with her in every way.

His emotions were still muted, blocked by that invisible wall. Some days the wall stood between the two of them, and other days Dustin let Rae stand on his side of it, so the wall barricaded the two of them from the rest of the world. Those were the good days, Rae thought, though she still hadn't given up on removing the wall or at least transforming it into a gas or a liquid, something penetrable.

Progress wasn't linear, but Rae thought she saw some improvements. When Dustin sank now, he didn't stay sunk for as long, disappearing only for days at a time rather than weeks or months. He always resurfaced as if he'd never vanished at all, and Rae would be too relieved to grill him on where he went, physically and emotionally, during those dark stretches.

But the city had started closing in on him again—too many incompetent people at work, too many gridlocked cars in the streets, too many tacky buildings cluttering the sky. He'd gone back to his parents' house in Connecticut for the past couple weeks to get a breather. Rae had hoped he might invite her up there, but he hadn't. He'd given her a key to the loft to water Phyllis while he was gone, though, so that was something. Through all these months, the little green plant had stayed stubbornly alive. As far as metaphors went, Rae found it an encouraging one.

Phyllis didn't really need watering tonight, since Rae had already come by earlier in the week, but Rae liked being in Brooklyn, farther from her office and closer to Dustin, or at least that's how it felt. And Ellen was out with her coworkers tonight—she'd gotten cultishly close with the other chickpea milk fanatics at her start-up—so Rae was planning to do some reading from Dustin's couch for a while, or just catch up on sleep.

Dustin had said he wouldn't be back until the weekend, but Rae heard music drifting from his bedroom. Her heart leapt. He was home, and he was playing music. He only played music when he felt light enough to let in melodies.

"Dustin?" she called out again.

He didn't answer. Maybe he was sleeping.

Rae went to hang up her jean jacket on her peg. She'd been over here so many times now that she thought of it as *her* peg.

But her peg was already occupied—by a floppy sun hat. That's when Rae noticed the shoes, too, strappy women's sandals scattered on the floor as if they'd been kicked off in a rush.

"Dustin?" she repeated, louder this time.

The bedroom door swung open. Dustin was standing there in boxers, pulling a T-shirt over his head. A woman's voice was behind him, piercing through the music.

Everything was spinning. Rae kept staring.

"Rae," Dustin said again, walking closer.

Ripping her eyes away from him, she strode, shoes on, to the kitchen window. Consumed with the need to save something, she scooped Phyllis into her arms, and soil dribbling onto the floor like bread crumbs, she hurried out the door and down the stairs so Dustin didn't follow her out to the elevator, or more precisely, so she didn't have to notice how he didn't follow her out to the elevator, how he simply shut the door behind her and walked back inside to the girl he'd chosen instead of her.

* * *

"You said you were okay just being friends," Ellen said at the penthouse the next night.

Rae was sprawled on the couch, using her bathrobe as a blanket to cover her eyes. They'd texted all day about The Sun Hat Girl Scandal, but this was the first they were seeing each other in person.

"I know," Rae mumbled from underneath the heavy fabric.

"The writing was on the wall this whole time."

"I know."

"I kept saying it was a bad idea."

Rae yanked the robe down from her face. "I know! So just keep rubbing it in, why don't you?"

Ellen was sitting on one of the armchairs, giving Rae the full couch. "Sorry," Ellen mumbled. "I just always knew he was going to hurt you."

"He didn't hurt me," Rae said, hoping that by saying it aloud it might come true. "We were never even together."

He wasn't hers to lose, but that didn't stop the bottomless, bright-red loss.

"You couldn't have actually thought he was completely celibate?" Ellen asked.

A wounded whine escaped Rae. She didn't know exactly what she'd thought, but it had involved the arrogant assumption that if he was going to date anyone, it would be her. But for whatever reason, probably many, she wasn't what he wanted.

"I doubt he's even dating that girl," Ellen said, as if reading Rae's thoughts. "It was probably just a one-time thing."

Rae wasn't sure if that made her feel better or worse.

Ellen procured a pint of Ben & Jerry's from the freezer, which she attempted to spoon into Rae's mouth. Rae shoved it away. She couldn't remember the last time she'd refused ice cream. That's how deep the hurt was.

"I think this is actually a good thing," Ellen said, eating the rejected spoonful herself. "It makes the boundaries clearer. If you do choose to be his friend now, you'll have your eyes wide open."

Rae's phone buzzed. Dustin had tried calling four times since last night, and now he was texting every thirty minutes, like clockwork. Ironic how reliably he appeared now that she didn't want to hear from him.

"He said he loved me," she squeaked out, wishing she could be back at that SoHo rooftop bar with him, away from the crowd where they'd first professed their untraditional *I love you*s, and also willing herself to forget the scene forever. They'd said it so many times since, always using the phrase in lieu of *Good-bye*.

"I don't think he was lying," Ellen said. "He was just using a different dictionary."

"A shitty dictionary," Rae said.

She was trying, with every broken fiber of her being, to remind herself that this wasn't about her. It was about Dustin and his health. Objectively speaking, it was a good sign that his sex drive was coming back. And as his friend, she'd agreed to be there for him through the highs and lows, the easy times and the impossible times.

What kind of a person turned her back on someone in pain who hadn't done anything wrong and who had, in fact, made it explicitly clear that they were only friends?

Rae tried to make headway with rationality, but the image of those sandals scattered on the floor was too vivid to bear. Ellen had been right all along—Dustin had other people to support him, people who were probably in his bed right now, tangled up in the sheets he'd long since washed after that one night, a year and a half ago now, when she'd stayed over and fallen asleep and woken up in the arms that had felt like an envelope to all the love letters no one had ever written her until then.

"Can you find a home for Phyllis?" she asked Ellen, gesturing to the windowsill, where Rae had set the plant down when she'd gotten home last night.

The leafy symbol of her bond with Dustin was too painful to keep, but tossing it in the trash was out of the question. Understanding the paradox, Ellen took Phyllis into her own bedroom, out of view.

"I'll bring her in to work," Ellen said, returning a moment later. "I've been feeling left out in the *Bring your pet to the office* policy, and I can feed her some of the free seltzer."

Rae gulped gratefully. Then, after glancing at the bare windowsill, she deleted Dustin's number.

She'd stopped going on dates since she'd started being his friend, having no desire and no time, but this now felt like a horrible miscalculation, a sabotage of her overly generous imagination, always expecting that once Dustin got better, he'd start loving her better.

But maybe believing in that healthy, happy version of Dustin was like believing in Santa Claus. It was time to take off the red felt hat she'd been wearing, the hat that had been blocking her view of the truth.

The value of their stock had crashed straight to zero, if there had been any value at all. Perhaps the whole time she'd just been ballooning the delusion that they'd end up together, when he'd clearly never wanted that at all.

She couldn't invest in him any longer.

Her phone buzzed again. Dustin's name no longer showed up, but the 203 area code scraped even more, reminding her that there was a reason she wasn't letting herself look at his name, because the mere arrangement of those six letters had the potential to wreck her and leave her wrecked.

Deleting his number wasn't enough. She blocked it too.

CHAPTER TWENTY-ONE

THE REBOUND

"What're these?" Rae asked, walking into Ellen's room and holding up thin strips of lacy fabric, all brightly colored.

"Thongs," Ellen answered, as she tossed a red bikini into her suitcase.

"Yes, I know what *thongs* are, thank you," Rae said. "What I meant was, how did they end up in my bag?"

"I put them there," Ellen said. "Thought your underwear drawer could use a lake house refresh."

They were packing for an August getaway at Elmer Lake in Indiana, where Rae and her parents had spent every summer when she was a kid, back before the divorce.

Still stinging from The Sun Hat Girl Scandal, Rae needed a change of scenery, something with a water view, and she'd outgrown the over-the-top Hamptons debauchery. Last summer, the Scramblettes had persuaded Rae to join them at a share-house in Montauk with Mina's boyfriend of the moment and his twenty closest friends. Montauk was a seaside village at the eastern point of Long Island, and its cabana-clad beaches and castle-like mansions were something of a New York rite of passage. Getting a glimpse into the life of $15,000-per-night abodes, lobster decks where the pompous prep school crowd in pastel shirts vented about incompetent waiters, and *Are you on the list?* beach bars with a sort-of-famous DJ spinning EDM beats while everyone did coke in plain sight had entranced Rae ever so briefly before exhausting her with its vacuous glamour.

During her bathroom breaks at work, she'd been looking up deals for plane tickets to exotic places from Morocco to New Zealand, but when she'd found a link to that Indiana cottage—"Our Little Yellow House," she'd called it as a kid—she'd gotten such a pang of nostalgia that she'd rented it for all of August, right on the spot.

It was the quietest time of the year on Wall Street, with all the bosses and wannabe bosses at their Southampton palaces or seven-bedroom "cottages" up in Nantucket, and she'd gotten approval to work remotely for three weeks, so long as there wasn't any delay in her responsiveness. It was as close to freedom as she'd come in her four years of work.

Sarah wasn't joining, too busy with business school applications, and Mina wouldn't hear of going to "the literal middle of nowhere" when she could be meeting her next true love at a Montauk beach concert. The Scramblettes were becoming increasingly scattered, it seemed, birthdays and breakups the glue holding them together.

At least Rae still felt inseparably close to Ellen, having talked her ear off about how fine she was cutting Dustin out of her life. Rae hadn't yet grown bored of the plot, but she'd become tired of it, which was at least progress.

Ellen, too, wanted a more low-key vacation, and she and Aaron were tagging along to the lake house. Rae told herself it would be basically the same as if it were just her and Ellen like she'd wanted.

"No one ever sees my underwear," Rae told Ellen now. "So what does it matter what it looks like?"

"No one ever sees your underwear because you don't expect them to see it," Ellen retorted. "It's like the chicken-and-the-egg phenomenon. Which came first, the sex or the thong?"

"Clever," Rae scowled.

"Dress for the boyfriend you want, not the boyfriend you have," Ellen went on.

"If a guy doesn't find me irresistibly seductive in my saggy briefs, he's not the one for me," Rae said.

"Get out of your own way, Rae-bae. I just have this vision of a macho lumberjack across the lake, inviting you over to cook you a steak over the fire that he's built with his bare hands."

Rae rolled her eyes. "We're going to Indiana, not Alaska."

Ellen, who'd grown up in the suburbs of Washington, DC, had never been to the Midwest, except to fly over it in an airplane, but she and Aaron were very excited, a little *too* excited, to see how people lived out there.

"I'm just saying, summer on the lake is a great backdrop for a rebound," Ellen said.

"A rebound from what exactly?" Rae asked. It wasn't like she was fresh out of a relationship, though it felt that way.

"A rebound from anything that's drained your energy," Ellen said, spreading her arms in some yoga pose.

Rae kept her arms folded closed, preferring to stay in her emotional trough, cradled in self-pity and safe from another crash. Every investor knew you couldn't lose anything more when you were already at the bottom.

But she walked back into her room and stashed the thongs in her bag, then zipped it shut.

*　*　*

"Well, look who's back," a voice said, triggering a whole book of memories that Rae had left behind in a lidded box when she'd packed up to leave Our Little Yellow House for the last time, ten years ago now, the summer before her dad filed for divorce.

They'd landed in Indianapolis this afternoon, and after they'd stopped by for lunch with Rae's mom and grandpa, Rae had gotten behind the wheel of her old Ford pickup truck to drive Ellen and Aaron the sixty miles north to Lake Elmer. Fordable Francine, she'd named the truck back in high school, when she'd emptied her baby-sitting earnings to buy the truck fifth-hand for $1,200. Francine couldn't reach much more than forty miles an hour anymore, but she got along just fine on the windy back roads in these parts.

During the drive, past acres and acres of brown-gold farmland dotted with green tractors and red barns, Ellen and Aaron had marveled at the vastness of the open space, the way it felt like they'd been transported back in time a hundred years. Though the landscape captivated them, they couldn't help pointing out every sexist, racist, or homophobic thing they drove by—a catcalling truck driver, an Indian mascot painted onto the scoreboard of a high school football field, an anti-gay-marriage sign in a front lawn.

It was true that, returning here as an adult, Rae noticed how prejudice was rooted as deeply as the oldest trees. She couldn't unsee these things and wouldn't want to but still felt a childish tug to pull the fuzzy blanket back over her head and fall into a deep sleep, uninterrupted by horns or sirens.

They'd unpacked at the cottage, which was half the size Rae remembered, with peeling paint and broken shutters, but as lovable as ever. Now Aaron was borrowing Francine to go hunt for groceries while Rae and Ellen were pulling twin kayaks out from the shed.

The kayaks were covered in cobwebs, like they hadn't been used since Rae and her dad had taken them out all those years ago. It made her want to preserve the white webs or put them in her pocket. Ellen, for her part, was furiously scrubbing down her kayak with sanitizing wipes. She was also wearing white shoes, the first violation of country living. Rae was barefoot, and it finally felt like she could breathe again.

They swiveled their heads to locate the voice. A guy was crossing the yard toward them, and it took only a second for Rae to see the boy right through the man. It was Stu, the hell-raising heartthrob whose family owned the cottage next door. They'd spent many summers together growing up on this lake, and he always used to flip Rae's tube over when their dads were pulling them behind the boat. Then, one star-sprinkled August night when she was sixteen, in the scraggly pine trees dividing the two properties, he'd been her very first kiss.

His body had filled out as much as his buzz cut had grown out. He was wearing an unbuttoned plaid shirt and loose-fitting swim trunks, carrying a six-pack of beer.

Ellen let out a low whistle. "There's your lumberjack," she murmured, like she'd manifested him out of thin air.

Rae dropped her kayak on her foot and tried not to hop in pain. "Stu," she said, walking closer for a better look.

Stu was more than a mirage. He pulled her in for a hug and rubbed his knuckles on the top of her head, mussing up her hair. She used to hate when he did it, but she welcomed it now, finding the old gesture wonderfully comforting. His sturdy frame gave her the notion that if a nasty wind came along, she could stand behind him and be completely sheltered.

The years between them stretched and then condensed. By the time the hug ended, it felt like they'd filled in all the gaps of the past decade, or rather, rewound to a time when there were no gaps at all.

Stu attempted a dramatic courtesy. "The queen of New York City gracing us with her presence?" he said. "To what do we owe the pleasure?"

"Knock it off, Stu-pid," Rae said, using the very mature nickname she'd patented way back when. She briefly introduced Ellen.

Ellen had, of course, heard the story of Rae's first kiss with the boy from the lake house, and Rae could see the dots connecting in Ellen's brain. "What a coincidence you're both back here at the same time," she proclaimed.

"Well, it's not much of a coincidence, if I'm being honest," Stu said. "My mom told me Raelynn was gonna be here, and she made it pretty clear I'd better haul my ass up here if I ever wanted to taste her cooking again. Not that I needed that incentive, for the record."

Rae frowned. "How'd she know I was coming?"

"Apparently your mom told her." Rae's mom and Stu's mom had stayed good friends over the years.

Rae thought back to the little smirk on her mom's face earlier today. She'd figured her mom was just plotting ways to make Rae stay in the Midwest for good, but it all made sense now that she knew a guy was involved.

"You're being parent-trapped," Ellen said, looking perfectly delighted by this plot twist, like small-town life was even more quaint than she could've hoped. "Or kid-trapped, I guess."

Stu's laugh bubbled up like a backwoods creek. "Guess we are," he said, not seeming nearly perturbed enough about the parental intrusion, Rae thought.

Fordable Francine pulled into the driveway, and from the mud splattered across the faded red paint like pastoral art, it looked like Aaron had taken a few dirt-road detours.

"I'll go help him unload the groceries," Ellen said. "I'll let you two . . . catch up." She shot them a devilish look and pranced up to the house, still wearing her life jacket, like it was a prop on a movie set that she was too enchanted by to take off.

By habit, Rae and Stu walked to the dock behind his parents' house and sat down, legs dangling over the edge, feet skimming the gentle water. The lake was a few miles around, the tiny cottages squished right up next to each other with Midwestern friendliness. American flags flew from the docks, and political flags too, the kind that pricked Rae with indignation but also with an understanding that "those people" weren't the depraved "other" the way everyone in New York talked about it from their urban echo chambers. They were her neighbors.

A few small motorboats cruised by, laughter louder than the engines. Bullfrogs were beginning their evening serenade in a synchronous chorus.

"Is your sister around too?" Rae asked Stu.

"Nah, she's married with a baby," Stu said. "Keeps her crazy busy."

It hit a nerve with Rae. Stu's sister was younger than she was, and it made her feel woefully behind. She hadn't let herself dwell on it recently, but now, back here in the zip code of young marriages and young mothers, her fears had nowhere to hide. Here she was, approaching twenty-seven, definitively *late twenties*, with no husband or fiancé or even the prospect of a boyfriend. Ellen had been right—she'd wasted precious time trying to fix a guy who didn't want to be fixed, shoving her love at someone who'd shoved it right back.

She ran the marriage math in her head, finding it equal parts soothing and anxiety inducing. She was two years behind her original forecast, which wasn't ideal, but she could condense the timeline and still be okay. If she met someone soon, she could still date them for two years, skip over the living-together step, then have a six-month engagement and close the marriage deal before her thirtieth birthday to allow enough time to have all her kids before she turned thirty-five.

"Why aren't *you* married yet?" Rae asked Stu. A year older than Rae, he was becoming somewhat of an outlier for not having settled down, and she wondered what his story was. He liked his mischief, but he was the commitment type, nothing like those East Coast Peter Pans.

"Ouch. You've gotten some big-city manners, haven't you?" he joked back.

"I didn't mean it like that," Rae said. "I just meant—I'm sure you've had your pick." Last she'd seen on social media, he'd been going strong with his college sweetheart, but that had been a while ago.

"Yeah, well, I'm sure you have too," Stu said. "Figured one of them city guys would've reeled you in by now."

"Apparently New York guys prefer catch and release," Rae said, trying not to remember the unforgettable sensation of being tossed back, unwanted, into the choppy seas. "Metaphorically," she added quickly.

"Fishing metaphors are the only kind of metaphors I approve of," Stu said with a grin that reminded Rae of how he always used to tease her about the big stack of books she'd cart along to the lake every summer. "Do I have to kick some guy's ass?"

Rae liked the feeling of someone having her back like that, but she couldn't help her protective impulse to shield Dustin from harm. "It's all in the past now," she said, trying to believe her own words but also not liking how stark it sounded. "He just wasn't the right one."

Stu looked sheepishly pleased about Rae's unlucky love life. "Well, you'll find a guy who appreciates you," he said, in a way that made Rae believe him, even though she wasn't trying to. "There's no rush to run to the altar."

"Easy for you to say," Rae grumbled. "You don't have a ticking time bomb in your uterus."

"What?" Stu asked, visibly squirming at the word *uterus*.

"Nothing," Rae said. "I'm just bitter about how guys can have babies as late as they want. Women have to hurry and find a mate before our eggs run out. I mean, how unfair is that?"

"I've never heard anyone say it like that," Stu said, and Rae swallowed a comment about how he probably hadn't been spending much time with career-driven women. "But it's kind of good, isn't it?" he went on. "It's like God's way of reminding you to value family and the important stuff before you wake up one day and realize your life has gone way off course. Right the ship before it's too late."

Rae felt attacked by this analysis, but she kind of agreed with it too.

"And I don't think it's just girls that want to settle down," Stu said. "I'd like to get married soon—I'm just holding out for the one."

Rae bit back a smile that tasted like old times. "Who knew little Stu could be such a romantic."

"Oh come on, don't you remember the handpicked bouquets I'd deliver you?"

"You mean all those dying gray dandelions?"

"Those are the most romantic ones," Stu protested. "They're made for wishing on."

Rae glanced over at the row of pine trees. They'd filled in over the years, and she couldn't help but think how much better they'd hide the two of them now. Stu's sister had spied them kissing and tattled to their parents, and Rae had been so mortified she hadn't spoken to Stu for the rest of the summer. She'd thought they'd have another couple years at the lake together before college, but that had turned out to be the last one. Her mom couldn't afford to rent Our Little Yellow House on her own.

That was probably part of the resentment she still held toward her dad—not just how he'd left her mom out in the cold but how he'd cut her own childhood short and forced her to grow up overnight.

"I know what you're wishing for right now," Stu said, eyeing the pine trees, too, and obviously thinking he was reading her mind about that kiss. His self-confidence was as infuriating as it was endearing.

"That your head will deflate so you can fit through normal-sized doorways?" Rae said dryly. "Damn, you're good."

Stu's eyes flared with laughter. "Shit, you're still trouble for my heart, aren't you?"

Rae didn't feel like she could do much damage to anyone's heart even if she wanted to, but she tried not to bring down the mood with those thoughts.

Stu cracked open two beers and handed one to her. It felt like breaking the rules, like her parents might come out and ground her. The thought was oddly comforting.

"So what're you up to these days?" she asked Stu, swatting a mosquito from his arm. "Working at your dad's dynasty?" Stu's dad owned a chain of Indianapolis-area auto dealerships.

Stu nodded. "The plan is for me to take it over soon so he can live his best retired life and come out here more often. The job suits me, not that it's fancy or anything like Wall Street."

Rae grimaced. "I wouldn't say investment banking is exactly my calling."

"What is?"

Writing went down the wrong pipe. Clearing her throat, she said, "Something else."

"I've been told I'm something else. Though—full disclosure—not sure it's always been meant as a compliment."

A laugh spilled out of Rae, and then another, as if the sound had been uncorked like the bottle of wine they'd sneaked from Stu's parents' house that one Fourth of July.

"Cheers to something else, then," Rae said, and they clinked beer cans. She closed the toast with a wink, mostly to make sure she could still close one eye without the other.

"Come on," Stu said, standing up before things got too sentimental. "I'm taking you on a sunset cruise."

Rae started walking toward the kayaks, but Stu scooped her up and hoisted her onto his shoulder. "On a *real* boat," he clarified, lightly depositing her on a pontoon, a big upgrade from the small motorboat they had whizzed around on as kids.

Ellen and Aaron joined them, cozying up at the front of the boat. Rae sat adjacent to Stu as he revved the engine and backed up from the dock. Country music played over the radio, heavy on banjos and static. They were her old favorite songs that she hadn't heard in ages—the tunes she'd told herself she didn't like anymore but now had to admit she still loved.

"What a dream," Ellen said. "But any chance we could change the station?" Rae could feel her cringing at the twangy melodies that stuck in your head whether you wanted them to or not and all the sexist story lines layered into the lyrics.

Stu grinned. "Sorry, no can do. You're in Indiana now, you've gotta get the full experience."

"Fair enough," Ellen conceded, sitting back and pressing her head into Aaron's chest to mute the sound.

Rae was glad he didn't change the music. Something about it felt like an old lullaby sewing up her unstrung heart. Leaning over the side of the boat, she felt the water spritz her face like it was ready to play, like it had been waiting for her the whole time she was away.

And as they zigzagged across the calm lake, watching the golden sun slip over the horizon, free of jagged skyscrapers or light pollution, Rae felt her love life begin to bounce back.

* * *

"Aren't sand angels more fun than snow angels?" Ellen asked a couple weekends later as they flapped their silhouettes into the strip of beach bordering the lake behind Our Little Yellow House.

"I don't know," Rae said, looking up at the bright-blue sky as her vitamin-D-deficient skin sponged up the sun. "You can't snack on sand the same way you can snow."

"That's true," Ellen said, then switched to the topic she'd clearly been bursting to address. "So, I adore Stu. He's so outgoing and easy to talk to." Rae heard the unspoken comparison to Dustin. "And he brings out your fun side."

"Are you implying I have an unfun side?"

"You can *occasionally* have a little too much artistic angst for your own good."

"Watch it," Rae said, flicking sand Ellen's way. "Or I'll draw devil horns on your sand angel."

"I'm just saying it's nice to see you glowing again."

"I think that's just my sunburn." Despite her best SPF 70 efforts, she was more pink than tan. Ellen, meanwhile, was a shimmery bronze.

"How are *you* feeling about Stu?" Ellen asked.

With the guys always hanging around, there hadn't been much alone time to discuss confidential matters like the rekindled romance between Rae and Stu. Their connection was as easy in adulthood as it had been in adolescence.

He was taking the full month off from work—perks of a family business—and frequently came by to tempt her with coffee breaks and other kinds of breaks. Rae's productivity had been cut in half, but her positivity had increased threefold.

"He feels like home," Rae said, meaning it. "Or at least the home I used to have."

She'd felt a masochistic letdown when they'd kissed—Dustin's lips were no longer the last ones on hers—but had decided that while that might be a poetic way to live, it wasn't a practical or even a pleasant one, so she was focusing very hard on not focusing on the cloud-cloaked *then*, just the sun-drenched *now*.

"This life looks good on you," Ellen said. "Not just good— *radiant*. Would you think about moving back here?"

"Maybe one day," Rae said. "But not now."

"Because . . . ?" Ellen prodded.

"Because of a lot of things. You, first of all. And work. And the Scramblettes. And Percy's Pizza." *And the breathgiving view of Manhattan from a Williamsburg rooftop*, she thought but didn't say.

"Look, you know I'd be crushed if you left New York," Ellen said, taking Rae's sandy hand in hers as they lay side by side. "But you've been wanting to find a new job anyway and have more time to write. And let's face it, the Scramblettes are pretty much fried eggs at this point. And I'm pretty sure Indiana has at least one decent pizza place."

Rae felt like she was sinking into the sand beneath her. Dustin's face flashed through her mind—an errant missile, not a symbol. "Moving back here would be regressing an entire decade, back to my high school self." She shivered at the thought.

"That's not true. Sometimes you have to go backward to go forward," Ellen said in her most Zen voice.

"Don't go all yogi philosopher on me," Rae said. "I'm not moving back to Indiana for some guy."

"Stu isn't some guy," Ellen said. "He's a keeper."

"I know he is," Rae admitted, warmth radiating down to her core as she thought about how cozy the world was from underneath one of his hugs. "Let's not project into the future, okay?" she said. "I'm trying to stay present."

"No projections," Ellen agreed. "I was right about the thongs, though, wasn't I?"

"You're right about everything, Elle-belle," Rae said, and they flapped once more in the sand.

Then, standing up without stepping on their wings, they chased each other into the water, squalling like ocean sea gulls that had accidentally flown to an inland lake and liked it so much they decided to stay.

*   *   *

"What about now?" Stu asked, as they ate cinnamon rolls for breakfast on the back porch of the cottage, which overlooked the lake. The morning light bounced off the water, transforming the blue into gold. It was the last weekend in August, and summer was arcing to an abrupt end. "Will you agree to do long-distance?"

"It just doesn't make sense," Rae said, for probably the eleventh time now. "I mean, I live in *Manhattan*." It might as well have been Mars the way she said it.

"Only a two-hour flight," Stu said. "And you said it yourself—you see yourself coming back to Indy soon."

It was true, she had said it, one night while they were stargazing on the dock, wrapped in argyle blankets she'd found in the closet of her parents' old bedroom. She'd been giving more thought to what Ellen had said. Why was she still trying so hard to make it in a place she'd never belong and didn't think she even wanted to belong? In New York, she was fighting against the world. Here, she was flowing with it.

"I'm not moving back here *yet*, though," Rae said. "I still have this thing called a job back there. Lots more deals to close."

"You can keep working from your NASA control center," Stu said. "And I'll keep delivering whipped-cream coffees."

Rae had set up an elaborate work-from-home office in her cottage bedroom, with multiple computer monitors, noise-canceling headphones, and an ergonomic keyboard.

Stu liked to joke that Rae was secretly directing alien spaceships and that the banker line was just a boring ruse so no one would catch on.

"I need to get back into the real office," she said, though the idea of being suffocated by that misdirected stress made her blood pressure rise. It was like bankers thought they were doctors or something and that lives were on the line every second of the day and night. They freaked out about a mismatched decimal point like a heart surgeon might freak out about the electricity going out in the middle of an operation.

Being physically separated from the rat race had given her more perspective to see it for what it was—a tiny, upside-down snow globe where everyone sprinted around in circles, completely clueless they were trapped inside a glass sphere because they never ventured far enough from their shiny skyscrapers to bump into the wall.

Ellen and Aaron joined them on the back porch. Ellen was getting restless to get back to city life but said she could see herself getting a summer home here down the road. Rae had broken her stay-in-the-moment rule as they let themselves picture it—the two of them sipping chardonnay from elegant wine glasses, their husbands at the grill, their kids chasing each other through the yard, fearlessly leaping off the dock. That outcome felt terrifically, and terrifyingly, in reach from this lake view.

It was easy to envision Stu as the husband in this scene—Rae would slip back into life here, he'd slip a ring on her finger in a couple years, she'd be married by thirty and everything would end up in its place despite her best efforts to run away. She liked this story. It was the kind of movie she'd turn on in the background when she wanted something light and happy that didn't make her think too hard.

"Ellen," Stu appealed. "Tell Rae she'd be crazy not to keep dating me."

"You'd be crazy," Ellen said, reinforcing the message with the look she gave Rae.

The porch was bright and warm. Everything felt a little shallow, a little weightless, but Rae wondered now if those adjectives weren't opponents of love but allies to it. What was so great about deep, heavy things anyway? Depth just gave more space to fall, and weights reminded her of what she couldn't lift.

"All right," Rae conceded. "Let's give long-distance a try."

Stu wrung Rae's hand, then kissed her on the mouth. "And that, ladies and gentlemen," he said, as Aaron and Ellen cheered, "Is how you negotiate with a banker."

"Well done," Rae said, not upset with the outcome.

CHAPTER TWENTY-TWO

AND THE CYCLE BEGINS AGAIN

How's ur day going babe

Stu texted Rae while she was at work a couple weeks after Labor Day. Everyone was back in the office, stressed as ever, and it was as if the August lull had never happened. The long days and nights on Elmer Lake felt a world away, a world Rae wasn't sure she belonged to after all, now that she was back in the hustle and bustle of her metropolitan routine. The pace stimulated her senses in a way the peace didn't.

Stu had texted her earlier too, a good-morning message that she hadn't had time to reply to yet. She felt impatient, and not just because of his poor grammar. She wanted him to *just know* how her day was without having to explain it to him. She wanted him to understand the specific frustration that comes when a decrepit subway turnstile eats your MetroCard for breakfast, the all-consuming dread of going to work that gives way to the adrenaline rush once you get there and strut into a fifty-story office buzzing with worker bees and their bosses, the seething resentment you feel when you have to treat every imaginary deadline like a real one.

But of course there was no way Stu could know these things. He'd never been to New York and didn't know the first thing about the cutthroat finance world. That was one of the reasons they were such a good fit, Rae reminded herself. He balanced her out that way.

I'll call you tonight! she texted him back at her desk—hurriedly, so she wouldn't get scolded for using her phone.

But as she kept sitting there, crunching numbers in Excel, the twitch to text became too intrusive to ignore. Not the twitch to text Stu but the twitch to text Dustin. Today was his thirty-first birthday, as she'd accidentally remembered, or never successfully forgotten. Last year, for his thirtieth, his whole family had gone on a hiking vacation, but Dustin had fallen into a dark patch for weeks afterward, completely shutting her out. She'd bought concert tickets to see one of his favorite bands at Madison Square Garden, but he hadn't been up to going. He'd told her to give away the tickets, but she hadn't. It would have felt too much like surrendering.

The twitching had started in the fidgeting of her feet on the subway this morning and then worked its way up to her fingers as they tapped on her keyboard, adding a sequence of gibberish to the deal summary she was working on. Now the twitching had extended into her limbs and her lungs, and she escaped to her bathroom bunker to ask for help from the Scramblettes.

SOS. Tempted to text Dustin happy birthday.

Ellen texted back right away, and Rae could practically see her pausing her chickpea milk presentation to reply to this mission-critical alarm. DON'T DO IT!!! THINK OF HOW FAR WE'VE COME.

But squatting on the same toilet she'd been using since she was twenty-two years old, Rae didn't feel like she'd come very far at all. Her life was stalled, pun intended. Cutting out Dustin for hooking up with someone when he and Rae hadn't even been dating now seemed embarrassingly childish, the same overdramatic defense mechanism she'd used on her dad and her ex-boyfriend but without a fraction of the justification.

I thought we were #TeamStu? Sarah chimed in.

A bday text isn't cheating, Mina said.

TEAM STU! Ellen said. Gotta get back to meeting but STAY STRONG.

When ur 80, which do you think u will regret more? Mina posed. Texting Dustin or not texting?

Rae found this very profound and felt a surge of affection for Mina despite their months of drifting apart. Ellen could see things as so black and white.

She recalled the Bellini quote Dustin had recited on their second date: Only do something if it claws at you and forces its way out in spite of oh so much . . .

The context had been around writing, but what was texting if not the most modern literary genre? This birthday message was certainly forcing its way out. It wasn't disloyal to Stu, she reasoned. If anything, it showed how much she'd moved on—her ability to reach out in a cordial way rather than pretend he didn't exist because it was too painful to talk to him.

In a matter of seconds, she unblocked, then resaved Dustin's number. Cell phone companies should make the process of retrieving blocked numbers more difficult, she thought, though she was glad they didn't.

She drafted five texts, in decreasing order of emotion, and settled on option three—Happy birthday! How are you celebrating?

Stifled by the bathroom's silence, she shimmied her hips until the toilet sensor flushed. Empowered by the confident sound of rushing water, she sent the text.

A half second of relief was replaced by regret.

Any power she'd had in striding out of the Lorimer Loft, ignoring Dustin's calls, blocking his number—she'd forfeited it all with this single text. Once again, he held all the cards.

He was probably on a Caribbean island with The Sun Hat Girl, phone locked in the safe of the hotel room as they got couple's massages on the beach. When he finally saw the text, he'd misinterpret it as Rae trying to throw herself at him, and he'd explain it away to The Sun Hat Girl as some psycho he'd never actually dated who'd deluded herself into thinking they were soul mates. He'd have no idea how happy Rae was with Stu, how much she appreciated being appreciated, how delightfully simple it was being with someone who wasn't at war with himself.

She thought about adding a *P.S. I'm dating someone, hope you're doing great!* but it seemed like that would make her sound even more desperate if he didn't know she was telling the truth.

Cursing Mina's advice and then triply cursing herself for taking it, Rae returned to her desk and relegated her phone to the drawer where she kept the Stall Street Journal.

The COTWSM chat lit up on her computer.

TB: You look green, EE. Flu??
GQ: If so, plz sneeze on me. Trying to get sick so I can stay home . . .

Just worried about getting staffed on that new deal, Rae replied, dribbling quinoa into the cracks of her keyboard as she scarfed down lunch.

She peeked at her phone, and there it was.

Thank you, Rae. Not doing much, I'm not big on birthdays. How have you been?

Rae read it four times before she began her analysis. The phrase she kept circling around was *not big on birthdays*. Did his introverted personality not like the attention, or was this some deeper commentary indicating that he didn't enjoy celebrating life, that perhaps he didn't even want to be on earth at all?

And then she felt it, the grip of secondhand hurt.

Dustin wasn't off at a Caribbean sex-fest. He was sitting at his desk at work, just a few miles away, alone on a crowded trading floor, staring at a computer and in need of a giant hug.

Another text forced its way out.

Cake on the roof tonight? she asked.

The bubbles appeared right away to show he was typing. She braced herself for rejection.

Yes please.

*   *   *

"I wasn't sure I'd ever see you again," Dustin said, standing beside Rae on the Lorimer Loft rooftop that night. In the backdrop, the shimmering skyline was vying for their attention, but neither of them was looking its way.

He was thinner than she'd seen him last, three months ago now. His cheekbones jutted out of his face like they wanted to escape. Rae had known right away that the pain, the loneliness she'd imagined earlier hadn't been imagined at all.

It was one of the first autumn-esque evenings, humidity-free with just the foreshadowing of a chill.

"Yes, well . . ." Rae said, voice trailing off, as if she didn't quite want her own ears to hear that she was here.

They stood there, looking at each other.

"You don't have any gray hair yet," Rae commented lamely.

"It's dark out," Dustin said. "Wait till you see me in daylight."

Rae tried very hard not to picture waking up beside him in the morning. She was with Stu now, and happily so. She'd already booked a flight back to Indy to see him next month. But that didn't mean she and Dustin couldn't be friends. This was a sign of maturity, the ability to have friends of the other gender. There would be no line-crossing tonight.

"Does this mean you forgive me?" Dustin asked. The lines around his eyes sunk deeper, making him look older than thirty and spelling out the answer to why she'd come here tonight.

"It means I remembered there was nothing to forgive," Rae said as she began lighting all thirty-one candles atop the angel food cake she'd brought.

Using the flu excuse, she'd left work early to shop for decorations and bake a cake from scratch. She'd been caught red-streamer-handed in the penthouse stairwell by an exasperated Ellen, who'd accused her of "being addicted to the art of disappointment." Rae had assured her that celebrating a birthday was a very platonic thing to do and had skirted down the stairs, clutching the cake with both hands as she'd headed off to catch the L train from Eighth Avenue.

"There's a lot to forgive," Dustin countered, and Rae could feel him about to launch into an apology.

"Blow out your candles," Rae said. "Before the wind steals your wishes."

Dustin kept his eyes open, on hers, as his breath extinguished the feeble flames.

Rae set the cake down on the ledge as Dustin looked around the rooftop, seeming to take in the decorations for the first time.

Colored Christmas lights were strung over the railing, plugged into an outlet on the torso-high wall. Streamers looped between light strands, and balloons bobbed in the Brooklyn breeze.

"Why did you do all this for me?" he asked, like he truly couldn't fathom why she, why anyone, would make such an effort.

"I just wanted to see if I could bake a cake without burning it," Rae said. "It did get a little crisp on top, but I flipped it upside down and piled on the whipped-cream frosting, so you can't really tell. A nice metaphor, don't you think?"

Dustin laughed, that soft sound that Manhattan would drown but was safe here in Brooklyn. "Glad to see you're as full of poetic snot as ever."

"And I did it because I love you, obviously. As a friend," she added quickly, resenting the appendix as she said it.

She'd insisted to herself and to Ellen and to the universe that she'd moved on from Dustin, but now she was forced to see, in the reflection of his speckled irises, that she hadn't moved on at all, she'd just moved her feelings for him to a different part of her being, stored them somewhere that wasn't triggered by much . . . except seeing him in person, standing within arm's reach. Everything she'd repressed came rushing back in a torrent of emotion, too raw to be wrong.

His hazel eyes searched her blue ones until they landed on an answer to the question she hadn't known she'd posed. "It will always be you, Rae," Dustin said, and "it" immediately became Rae's favorite piece of abstract art. "I just hate myself for how much I've already hurt you."

"You didn't do anything wrong," Rae jumped in. "I overreacted. That's just what I do."

On some repressed level, she felt like she probably owed a similar apology to her dad, but she wasn't inclined to give it anytime soon, at least not before he offered up an apology himself.

"You didn't overreact," Dustin said. "I treated you horribly. I treat everyone horribly. I don't know if I'm capable of . . . more."

Rae held Dustin with everything she had and everything she'd lost and everything she was finding again. "Of course you are," she said, willing him to feel his worthiness.

Their noses were touching now, eyelashes brushing off symbolic tears and dust and dirt from each other's cheeks.

Rae knew that kissing Dustin would mean bankrupting her relationship with Stu and the future she might have with him. She knew she'd be setting her heart up for another crisis. But without any kind of return-on-investment calculation, she also knew this was a risk worth taking.

So in the kaleidoscope glow of out-of-season Christmas bulbs, their lips met again to restart the emotional cycle.

"I've never had a birthday wish come true so fast," Dustin muttered between breaths.

"Well then," Rae said, gesturing to the lights on the railing and the lights on the Williamsburg Bridge and the hundreds of thousands of other anonymous but not nameless lights dotting their up-and-down-and-up-again skyline "Let's make some new ones, shall we?"

* * *

You know what I feel most guilty about? Rae texted Ellen from the bathroom the next day, between meetings. That I don't even feel guilty. Cheating felt way more right than wrong. I'm a terrible human.

Not you're not, Ellen replied. Love just makes people irrational.

I bet my dad justified it the same way.

This is so much different. You're not married. It's the time of life to figure out what you want.

Still . . . unnerving to know I've inherited that character trait on some level.

Be kind to yourself. The universe has other plans. What did Stu say?

Earlier this morning, Rae had called Stu to tell him that long-distance was just too much for her right now. He hadn't seemed all that surprised or sad, but he had seemed confident that the stars would align down the road. "Call me when you move back to Indy," he'd said. "I've got a feeling the timing will be right by then."

He still thinks we'll end up together eventually.

Personally I hope he's right, Ellen weighed in. But you can't force it.

Rae tried to summon some regrets, but she just flipped back to her conversation with Dustin and reread his text saying that yesterday was the best birthday of his life.

You really think my cheating was just an isolated blip? Rae asked Ellen. Not part of a broader daddy issues trend?

Stop overthinking. You've been in love w/ D for ages. It really can't be helped so at least be honest about it now.

Rae didn't particularly like this answer, but she couldn't deny it either. You'll like him more this time around, I know it.

Double date soon? Also I'm bringing Phyllis home from work tonight. Time for you to take care of her again . . .

Rae swelled at the image of the heart-leafed plant back in the window of the Lorimer Loft.

Thanks, Elle-belle. Gotta get back to a discounted cash flow analysis.

Fun. Staying at A's tonight but girls' night tmrw?

Sarah and Mina invited us to their friend's cousin's party . . .

Oh right. Really don't want to go, doesn't start until 10 . . .

Let's say we're sick?

Used that excuse last time. How about saying the super coming to fix pipes?

Genius.

Do some yoga before you go back to your desk. Self-compassion starts with balance.

Standing in the bathroom stall yoga studio, Rae attempted tree pose but wobbled on her heels, catching herself on the black plastic wall to avoid tipping right into the toilet and having to explain to all the wannabe bosses why her suit was drenched.

CHAPTER TWENTY-THREE
THE GIRLFRIEND PROMOTION

"Aren't subway delays the best way to start the day?" Rae asked Dustin unironically the next Tuesday morning. They were commuting to work together on the L train after spending the night at the Lorimer Loft. "It's like the conductor wants us to have five more minutes together."

With no empty seats, they were standing up, crammed against the door. Rae's arms were wrapped around Dustin's suit jacket instead of the germ-magnet pole, and Dustin was dropping kisses on her forehead, one every three seconds, a more pleasant means of counting time than her usual huffs and grunts.

"Write that in the Stall Street Journal," Dustin said. "The joy a subway delay brings when you're with your true love versus the fury when you're all alone."

"True love?" Rae asked, hoping she wasn't wrongly interpreting a universal *you* as a personal one.

"Sure," Dustin said, with an equal ratio of rationality to romanticism. "That's what we found, didn't we?"

"Guess we did," Rae said, kissing him right on the lips and marvelously amused at how her jaded, jealous former self would be scowling at them, one of *those* subway couples. "All thanks to an algorithm."

"Destiny is never digital," Dustin protested. "The app just helped carry out its work, like one of Santa's elves."

It sounded like something Ellen might say. "Want to get dinner with Ellen and Aaron tonight?"

"I have Jessica after work."

"Right."

Rae was glad that, so far at least, Dustin was keeping her in the loop about his weekly sessions with Jessica, his psychologist. He still refused psychiatrists, as they'd want to put him back on "anti-emotion meds." He didn't want to feel less, he'd told Rae. He just wanted to be able to let all his feelings exist as free-flowing liquids and gasses instead of congealing as solids and sending him into lock-down mode. "Another time, then," Rae said.

"Another time," Dustin agreed. "Jessica thinks it's too early to ask you to be my girlfriend."

"Oh," Rae said, trying very hard not to suspect Jessica of wanting Dustin for herself.

"But I think she's just projecting her insecurities that the woman she's been dating for eight months hasn't introduced her to her pet guinea pig yet," Dustin said.

Rae giggled in that silent way she only did with Dustin. "Could be."

"So will you?" Dustin asked. "Be my girlfriend?"

His eyes were warm against the sterile subway lighting, and Rae found it nothing short of perfect, how he was asking to take this step forward with her while they were stuck in a dark tunnel together. It was far more symbolically sturdy than if he'd posed the question from the rooftop with an unobstructed view.

Her left brain processed a swift sense of victory at getting one step closer to her married-by-thirty vision, but her right brain waved away those forward-looking thoughts, too busy basking in the beauty of this very moment with the person she could finally call her boyfriend.

"Yes, please," Rae said, kissing him again on the lips, aware of but unfazed by all the *Get a fucking room* fuming directed their way in this crowded subway car. "Best promotion I've ever gotten."

* * *

"Fifty-seven dollars a night," Rae said to Dustin as they lay intertwined in his bed, the Monday dawn trying to break their trance. "That's how much rent money I waste every night I stay over here."

In the couple weeks since they'd been boyfriend and girlfriend, Rae had stayed on Perry Street only a couple times.

"You're not *wasting* it," Dustin said. "You're *investing* it in our future."

"Is that what you tell your clients to get them to commit to ten-million-dollar trades?"

"Something like that," he said. "But I can come to the penthouse more if you want."

"No, the loft is ten times nicer. Thicker walls, specifically," Rae said with a wicked grin.

The economic argument held up weakly against the romantic argument.

"You know what they say," Dustin said, drawing abstract shapes on her back, from her neck down to her comfortable underwear. "Investors are as irrational as people in love. That's why there are so many volatile market swings."

"I think investors are actually *more* irrational than lovers," Rae said. "Because at least love is worth losing your mind for. Investors just get worked up about gaining or losing money—such an empty irrationality."

"Which is exactly why we should stay in bed all day."

Rae shook her head as her heart nodded. "We've got to get up." It wasn't even seven A.M., and she could already feel the passive-aggressive emails piling up in her inbox.

Dustin groaned and pulled her closer. This was one of Rae's favorite things about their nights together—how, when it felt like he was already holding her as closely as he could, he somehow pulled her even closer, injecting her body with tactile *I love you*s that squeezed out all her self-consciousness about how parts of her body were too big or not big enough.

"Did you ever think people were exaggerating it?" Dustin asked.

"Exaggerating what?" Rae asked. "How miserable it is to get up on Mondays? Nope, I think that hyperbole is well deserved."

"Not that." He kissed her nose, then her lips. "The love thing. How nothing else matters when you're wrapped up in it."

"Oh," Rae said. "That." She stopped trying to wiggle out of the covers. "I guess I just thought that all the hype around soul mates was more imagination than memoir. That I'd find someone who was good enough and wouldn't leave me and we'd make it work."

"Good enough would never be good enough for a poet like you."

"Well, yes, I realize that now. You've ruined me."

"You're welcome."

"Dustin?" she asked. "Do you think people *have* souls? Or do you think they *are* souls?" She nearly retracted the question, worried it was too deep for this time of day. But the way Dustin tilted his head to consider it made her keep the question there, suspended in the nongap between them.

"I think it depends on how trapped people are by their humanity," he finally said.

Rae waited for him to continue.

"If you get bogged down by all the shallowness and selfishness of being mortal, then I think you're just a person who has a soul," he said. "But occasionally you meet someone who has this lightness about them"—he gave her a squeeze—"like they're free from the human part of living. How does Bellini describe it? *It's not so common to find a soul that's still living in its mortal body. And rarer still, a free soul.* And so I think those people—people like you—well, they *are* souls."

Rae digested the compliment, perhaps the nicest one she'd ever gotten. "You're giving me too much credit."

"No, I'm in your debt."

"Bad finance joke."

"You're smiling."

"Am not."

"So we're playing hooky today, right?"

"I wish . . ."

"Well, why not? It's not like our jobs actually matter."

"Still, we have to go . . ."

"And stare at a computer all day when we could be in bed together instead? Not a compelling pitch."

"We can't put it off forever."

"Better to procrastinate work than to procrastinate love," Dustin said, pulling the sheets over their heads in a homemade tent, blocking them from the corporate chaos pounding on the door.

Rae sank back into Dustin's arms, the only place she really felt big enough to make any kind of difference in the world. "Just five more minutes," she conceded.

CHAPTER TWENTY-FOUR
FRIENDSHIP MARKET FRAGMENTATION

"Two weeks?" Ellen said that Friday night, balking at Sarah. "You're moving away in *two weeks?*"

"Classes don't start until *next August*," Mina said. "Why're you leaving us *already?*"

"I need enough time to travel beforehand," Sarah said. "You know, to mentally prepare."

The Scramblettes were sprawled out in the penthouse. They'd started the evening on the couch and chairs, but nostalgia had brought them all to the floor. They'd even resurrected coffee mug wine glasses as an end-of-an-era tribute.

Earlier today, Sarah had announced in an all-caps group text that she'd been accepted early admission to business school at the University of Austin next fall and had just put in her two weeks' notice at the bank where she worked, a rival of Rae's.

The chart tracking the Scramblettes' get-togethers had exhibited a downward slope over the past couple of years, but the impending fragmentation was still jarring. It was one thing not to see each other often and another to realize you were about to be physically out of Uber range.

"I bet they don't even know what a scramblette is down in Texas," Rae said, feeling several pricks of envy at Sarah's finance escape plan and how her parents were funding it.

"I'll just have to bring it to their menus, then," Sarah said. "Barbecue scramblettes with a side of cornbread."

It sounded pretty good, but Rae scowled anyway.

"Let's go around the circle and share our favorite Scramblette memory," Ellen said, refilling their mugs with a bottle of white wine they'd remembered to chill, even if it had been a last-minute freezer treatment.

Sarah thought about it. "Maybe that time we got kicked out of the ice cream shop for taste-testing too many flavors? Or that concert in the Hamptons when we convinced those guys that the Scramblettes were the opening act."

"Oh yeah," Mina said. "When you autographed that old man's nipples."

"Not his nipples," Sarah corrected. "His *heart.*"

They snickered, reliving the scene.

"My favorite memory," Mina said, "was making Rae's dating app. Or crashing that NBA party." A few years back, they'd taken the wrong elevator to the Gansevoort Hotel's rooftop bar and half accidentally waltzed right into a top-floor suite featuring half of the New York Knicks, their flawless girlfriends, and the world's most elegant cupcake display. "When we got a taste of real penthouse life."

"Shhh!" Ellen said dramatically. "Don't let Perry hear you. She's very sensitive."

"So sorry," Mina said, patting the wooden floorboards affectionately.

"I'm biased," Ellen said, "but I liked my birthday dinner at Carbone when the four of us were crammed around that tiny table, devouring bread rolls. Before the night spiraled and you had to talk me off the ledge from breaking up with Aaron, obviously."

"*Another round of focaccia, please!*" Mina quoted Rae, and they all laughed.

"I don't think it's one specific memory that stands out for me," Rae said. "It's just recurring motifs—passing around ice cream pints, belting into wine-bottle karaoke microphones, texting from toilet stalls, and patenting new scramblette flavors. And sitting on the floor, of course, in an awkward diamond shape that feels like a symmetrical circle."

They were quiet. Apart from the car horn white noise from the street, the only sound was the gargling pipes, which seemed to be clearing their throats in an effort not to leak, just like the rest of them.

"Shit," Mina said. "Who invited the poet?"

"I changed my mind," Sarah said softly. "My favorite Scramblette memory is this one right now."

"No crying," Ellen warned, blinking bravely as she turned the wine bottle on its head and attempted to top off their mugs. Whereas Rae could always squeeze more toothpaste from tubes, Ellen's special talent was shaking wine from empty bottles. But not tonight. There was nothing left.

"Don't leave." It took a moment for Rae to realize she'd been the one to say it.

"We always said New York wasn't forever," Sarah said.

"But couldn't it have been for one more year?" Mina asked. She was reeling most, having been tied at the hip to Sarah since freshman year of college.

"We'll still have the group chat," Sarah said. "And I'll come back and visit all the time."

If they had still been in their early twenties, Rae realized, they would all nod and vow that yes, of course they'd always be this close. But from their late-twenties vantage point, having seen friendships come and go, dissolve and splinter, fizzle and fade, they all knew they'd never be as close as they'd been during these volatile New York years, stumbling side by side from adolescence into adulthood.

They'd clung to each other before finding boyfriends and girl-friends whom they'd started clinging to instead. Maybe that was all most twenties friendships were—training wheels and placehold-ers. The real-world truth was that friendship bonds and relationship stocks were inversely correlated. There was an unspoken acknowledg-ment that in the end, they'd all choose relationships. They had, in fact, already chosen them.

"Here's to the Scramblettes," Ellen said, raising her mug. It looked like she was about to say more, but she ended there before the crack in her voice became a full-blown break.

Sipping cold wine to the wistful line, the four of them clinked coffee mugs one final time.

"The Scramblettes."

CHAPTER TWENTY-FIVE
IN THE RED

Not a good day, Dustin texted Rae the following Thursday. Don't think I'm up for group dinner. I'm sorry.

Rae received the text at work while sitting around waiting for feedback on a model she'd built for a tech company that had been around for only six months and was already being valued at $800 million.

She and Dustin were finally supposed to have a double date with Aaron and Ellen tonight.

Sitting at her desk, she rechecked her Excel formulas while trying to fill in the full story behind *not a good day*. Was he just having a stressful day at work, or was the depression gripping him?

Rae had hoped—naïvely, she now saw—that falling in love might be enough to cure him, to lift him up and keep him there.

She was beginning to feel like she was the third wheel in an exclusive relationship between Dustin and his depression. But it wouldn't always be like this. The therapy would start kicking in soon. For now, she had to be patient.

That's okay! she replied. Want me to come over or would you rather just have a night to yourself?

Come over, Dustin replied. But I'm not at my best.

Amid the losses, it felt like a small win. In time, he would get to know Ellen, but the most important thing was that he wasn't pushing Rae away when he was hurting like he used to. He was inviting her in, and that was enough. It would have to be.

I love you, she replied. Will escape the office as soon as I can.

Then Rae texted Ellen to say that yet again, they wouldn't be able to make it to dinner.

*　*　*

"Dustin?" Rae called out as she sat up in bed the next Monday, panicked that she was late for work.

Rae awoke to clanking from the kitchen. Sunlight was streaming through the Lorimer Loft windows, the thick curtains thrown open.

"Breakfast in bed for the birthday girl," Dustin said, appearing in the doorway dressed in just boxers and an undershirt. He was carrying a plate of whipped-cream-topped pancakes, garnished with one of Phyllis's leaves.

That's when Rae remembered. She was twenty-seven today.

She'd taken the day off work. Dustin had, too, and now he handed her the plate and crawled back into bed beside her.

She ate happily, juxtaposing crackerless cheese on the floor at twenty-five against fluffy pancakes in bed with her boyfriend at twenty-seven. It was a pleasing midtwenties evolution.

Her phone started buzzing on the bedside table.

"It's your dad," Dustin said, handing her the phone with a look formed by all the conversations they'd had about her fractured relationship with her father.

She stared at his name on the screen, debating whether to pick up. By the time she decided she would, it had gone to voice mail.

"I'll listen to the message later," Rae said, infuriatingly pleased that he'd left one. She wanted a few hours to imagine it might be more sentimental than it was.

"Told you he'd remember your birthday," Dustin said, looking relieved.

Rae switched the subject. "Think of all the suckers already at work," she said. "Stressing out about decimal points and tiny moves in the stock market." From this bedroom sanctuary, the manufactured frenzy seemed nothing short of ludicrous, some stand-up comedy skit that had spun out of control into an entire world order.

"Joke's on them," Dustin agreed.

"So what should we do all day?" she asked. It seemed luxuriously rebellious, a whole day stretching before them with no Excel spreadsheets or PowerPoint slides to update.

"I thought we could ride bikes down to Prospect Park and have a picnic," Dustin said. "And try out some new cafés and go poem spotting."

Rae looked at Dustin's face and all the brightness he'd scrounged to plan her perfect birthday and reciprocate the things she'd done for his. But she could see it, too, the fatigue around his eyes, the desire to keep sleeping.

"I think my old age is catching up to me," she said. "How about we just go poem spotting right here?"

"You sure? You love birthdays."

"Yes," she said, thinking about all the future birthdays she'd get to spend with him, how they'd have plenty of time to do all those activities once Dustin got better. "I'm sure."

*　*　*

"I'm not hungry," Dustin mumbled, facedown in bed a couple weeks later.

Rae was sitting on the edge of Dustin's comforter, already dressed for work, offering up what she'd branded an "auspicious omelet" packed with avocados, beets, and organic clovers, all high on the list of depression-fighting foods.

With the Scramblettes officially broken up, Rae had decided it was time to learn how to properly flip omelets and had worked her way up the yolky learning curve through hours of YouTube tutorials.

"Just have a few bites," Rae said, stroking his back with the hand that wasn't holding the plate. "You need your energy."

"For sitting at a desk for twelve hours straight? No, I don't."

She'd tried to correlate his downturns to specific triggers, but they seemed to appear out of thin air—or thick air, rather, through which he could move his limbs only very slowly.

Setting the plate on his bedside table, next to the glass of unsipped ice water she'd gotten him, she crawled into bed beside him, wrinkling her ironed clothes as she wrapped his bare torso with both arms.

"Just three more days to get through at work, and then we have the wedding this weekend," Rae said. John and Jenn were getting married, a vineyard ceremony and reception on the North Fork of Long Island—the Napa Valley of New York, East Coasters called it.

Dustin grunted. Rae wasn't sure if it was a *Yeah, I guess* grunt or an *I don't want to go to that either* grunt. She didn't ask him to clarify, just peppered his shoulder blade with kisses and said, as gently as she could, "We have to go to work."

"You go," Dustin said. "I'll work from home."

Rae's first thought was that she should work remotely today too, but there was a big client pitch later this morning, and she'd finally been invited to be in the room. She wouldn't be the one presenting, of course, but it was progress.

"All right," Rae said reluctantly. "I'll see you this weekend."

Dustin grunted again, a definitively negative grunt this time. He turned his face toward her. His cheeks were too hollow, hazel eyes glazed over.

Rae pressed her cheek against his, not caring if his stubble scraped off her foundation.

"Come over tonight?" he mumbled.

"I can't," she said, nearly changing the words as she spoke so she wouldn't have to disappoint him. "Ellen and I are having a girls' night." She'd bailed the last three times.

Dustin turned his head away.

Rae gave him a final squeeze, attempting energy transfer, and pulled herself out of bed. "I'll put the omelet in the fridge," she said.

She did, then put on her shoes and let herself out. Waiting for the elevator, she checked the stock market app on her phone, catching up on news she'd missed overnight in Asian and European markets.

The stocks were mostly red, posting losses that resonated with Rae's heart. But love wasn't just the days when everything was green and going up. Love was the red days, too, the losses.

She just had to stay invested, and things would come back up. They always did.

CHAPTER TWENTY-SIX
LONG ON LOVE, SHORT ON STOCKS

"I'm going long on love," Rae told Dustin that Saturday after watching Jenn and John walk down the white-rose-petal-strewn aisle as husband and wife. In investing, going long or short meant you were betting for or against something.

"And I'm going short on using stock market terminology at weddings," Dustin said, mouth crinkling with humor.

Two hundred guests had gathered at the Long Island vineyard to watch the happy couple tie the knot under one of those elegant wooden archways Rae had overheard another guest refer to as an *arbor*. She and Dustin had sat hand in hand, exchanging meaningful palm squeezes as they both oozed from their eyes.

Rae found Dustin's crying a reassuring proof point of their compatibility. She couldn't imagine being with someone whose tear ducts were resilient to the power of unconditional love.

They were now ambling through the vineyard, just the two of them, for a quick breather from the cocktail hour commotion. Recently harvested, the leafy vines were bare of grapes, and fallen leaves masked the grass. The sky wore a veil of clouds, thin enough to be aware of the sun's attendance.

Rae was in a rented floor-length satin dress, hemmed with safety pins. Her hair was pulled into a chignon, courtesy of Ellen, who'd helped her get ready at the Lorimer Loft this morning. Ellen and Dustin had bonded more successfully than in past attempts, which was to say that Dustin had offered her coffee, Ellen had accepted, and Dustin had delivered a hot cup that Ellen had deemed "nearly Starbucks quality."

Dustin was in a tux, face newly shaven. He could use another ten pounds on him, but Rae couldn't help staring at his model-esque appearance. Best of all, his mood had risen.

"There's just something about weddings, isn't there," Rae went on, "that injects the most jaded heart with fresh conviction that this couple is going to defy the odds and prove all the dismal divorce statistics wrong?"

As a by-product of a failed marriage, perhaps she was supposed to be a cynic, but it almost had the opposite effect, making her marvel at how reverently so many people still took their vows.

And after watching John and Jenn stare into each other's eyes under the arbor, it was impossible for her to wonder whether they were only getting married because they wanted to have kids before Jenn's eggs ran out. Of course, math had likely factored into their wedding date decision—Jenn was Dustin's age, and she'd hinted to Rae that they wanted one or two kids—but there was so much more to marriage than breathing a sigh of relief at having found a suitable mate to procreate with, so much more to it than all the meticulous math in Rae's married-by-thirty, three-kids-by-thirty-five timeline.

Today had helped Rae realize, in both the third and first person, how walking down the aisle to the right person would feel less like checking off an item on a to-do list and more like pinching yourself to make sure you're not dreaming.

"Take a tissue," Dustin said, producing a pack from his pocket.

Rae realized she was tearing up again. There was just so much love compressed in one space that if she didn't let water out of her eyes, her lungs might burst from the fullness of it. "No thanks," she said. "It goes against my principles."

"Which principle, specifically?" Dustin asked, with an amused expression.

"The principle that love should not be wiped away or hidden," Rae said. "And that's what leaking tears at weddings is—an ode to love in its surest, purest form."

"You're leaking poems, not just tears," Dustin said, his arm around her waist as he shortened his stride to stay in step with her.

"Well, I have a lot of pent-up creative energy after spending all week typing phrases like *undisputed market leader* and *proprietary software stack*."

"Bellini would be proud of you."

"Are *you* proud of me?" Rae asked, voice loosened by bubbly wine and bubbly love.

"Exceptionally. Though *undeserving* would be the better adjective." He gave her a long look that apologized for those mornings he'd pushed her away as she tried to help him out of bed.

Rae stopped walking and wrapped her arms around him to tell him he was more than worth it. Bookended by parallel vines wrapped around perpendicular stakes, they kissed, then kissed again.

She was as hopelessly hopeful as ever that two halves might sum to more than one.

"If a poem leaks in the vineyard and no one hears it," Rae posed, once they started walking again, "does it really make a verse?"

"Do the tears hit the ground?" Dustin asked.

"Yes."

"Then yes. What do you think?"

"I think yes, even if they never touch the ground, because they'll have salted the wind."

Dustin gave her one of those looks that shot straight into her center. "Your wedding vows are going to be the most romantic things the world has ever heard," he said.

"Probably." Rae's laugh got stuck in her chest as she was struck with an overwhelming ache that Dustin be the person beside her at the altar. She knew she wouldn't be able to summon a single verse for someone else.

Dustin's face clouded too. "We should get back," he said, but led them farther away from the white tent, down one more grapevine aisle.

* * *

"What do you like to do in your free time?" Rae asked the college sophomore sitting across from her in the stark conference room. She'd forgotten how young nineteen looked.

Rae's wedding bliss had worn off the moment she'd stepped foot in the office this morning. The least painful part of the day so far was this thirty-minute reprieve interviewing a candidate for a summer internship at the bank.

"I like to follow the stock market," the boy answered. He tugged at his collar, like the tie was restricting him. Sweat stains splotched his gray suit.

"But outside of finance," Rae said, scouring his impossibly perfect résumé for an "interests" section and finding nothing other than *Yale Investment Club President* and *IPO Organization Co-Founder*. "What're you passionate about?"

"Finance is my passion," he said, giving a sharp nod to hammer home the point.

It was painfully obvious that he'd been coached by some upperclassman who'd landed a job at Morgan Stanley and was now milking the role of Wall Street wizard. But it was also obvious Rae wasn't going to make any progress in understanding what actually made this boy tick. Rae was one of "them"—the hallowed, hated gatekeepers.

She remembered the feeling too well. It felt like just yesterday she'd been on the other side of the table, desperately trying to impress her interviewers by regurgitating words she didn't understand.

"Okay," she said, folding up the boy's résumé in what she hoped he would interpret as a symbol of its unimportance. "Do you have any questions for me?"

"How much responsibility were you given as a junior member of the deal team?" he asked. "Did they let you present in client meetings and things like that?"

Rae disguised a snort as a sneeze. "I didn't usually go to client meetings when I first started," she said, as if she'd been invited to any before a couple months ago. Even now, when she did go, she usually stood against the wall because there were never enough chairs at the table. "But the early years helped set a solid foundation."

The boy nodded vigorously. "That's what I want. A solid foundation."

She almost asked what he would build on that foundation, if he could do anything, but there was no need to project her own existential angst onto him, so she just stood up and shook the boy's hand.

He shook too firmly, like Rae used to, overcompensating for his youth.

Rae thought about giving him some kind of warning about how he'd be nothing more than a sleep-deprived cog in a sleepless wheel, but she decided that working on Wall Street was just a mistake you had to make for yourself, like dating flashy frat bros before you could appreciate the depth of a bookworm.

She walked back to her desk and checked the COTWSM chat. TB and GQ had both interviewed the boy before Rae.

TB: What do you think of the fresh blood?
EE: He's very eager
TB: He didn't even know half the line items of a DCF. He'd never survive here.

GQ: He's a straight white guy—that's all the characteristics someone needs

TB: Fair point.

GQ: Never seen someone so excited to build a financial model before. There was literally drool coming out of his mouth

EE: Ah, the endearing innocence of infants

TB: We were like that as interns, too . . . remember??

GQ: And now look at us, three jaded associates

EE: The circle of wall street

GQ: The circle of life

TB: Same thing . . .

Rae closed out of the chat and fidgeted with the width of the bars in a graph she was formatting, then stood up and walked to the bathroom, in need of a nap.

CHAPTER TWENTY-SEVEN
RIDING THE LOVE
BUBBLE UP

"Don't you think it's a little too soon for Dustin to go home with you for Thanksgiving?" Ellen asked Rae from across the table that Saturday. "You've only been together for two months."

The two of them were brunching outdoors at Tartine, a pocket-sized French bistro on the corner of West Eleventh known for its idyllic West Village vibe. The postcard-perfect vision wasn't exactly panning out today. There was no indoor seating available, so they were at one of the sidewalk tables, rocking for warmth on wobbly metal chairs. There was no rain coming from the overcast November sky, but some sort of liquid was leaking from the green awning overhead. At the intersection, construction workers were drilling so loudly that Rae could hardly hear the shrieking toddlers passing by, though she saw their wailing faces as their parents walked them on tight leashes with harnesses. Manhole steam rose from the construction site, stamping the air with a distinctively New York stench and drifting toward their table with a dirty sort of heat. It would not have been Rae's first choice of a radiator.

Her catch-ups with Ellen were sporadic now that they spent so much time with their respective boyfriends, and since the Scramblettes' breakup, cracking eggs in the penthouse kitchenette had felt like staying on too long at a party where everyone was sobering up.

"You were ready to marry me off to Stu after two weeks," Rae reminded her harshly, having to speak very loudly to be heard over the urban background noise. "And Dustin and I have only been *back together* for two months," Rae corrected, surveying the menu. "We've basically been together for nearly two years now, at heart at least."

From their bedsheet tent on Rae's birthday, Dustin had suggested they spend Thanksgiving in Indiana so he could meet her mom and grandpa. Rae had hesitated only long enough to pretend to analyze the situation objectively, and they'd bought tickets on the spot.

"And you're the one who told me that relationship depth isn't correlated with time," Rae reminded.

"I know," Ellen conceded. "But I just . . . I'm worried your love bubble might burst and crash like cryptocurrency stocks." Somewhere along the way she'd stopped reprimanding Rae for using work phrases to describe dating and started adopting it as the most expedient means of persuasion.

"It's not a bubble," Rae said. "Our relationship fundamentals support the high valuation. We have nearly a year of friendship under our belt. His depression isn't gone yet, but it hasn't gotten worse, and he's giving me transparent updates after every therapy session," she said, listing the reasons on her fingers. "The top-line personal growth is trickling down to our bottom line. Cryptocurrencies, on the other hand—"

"Okay," Ellen cut in. "I just . . . I don't want to see you get hurt." She might have added *again* but didn't, which Rae appreciated.

"Better to get hurt from being overinvested than underinvested," Rae said. She wasn't sure if she'd heard that aphorism at the office or if it had sprung to her fresh from this corner table.

The waiter came by for their order. Rae chose the Croque Monsieur, blurting the name quickly to mask poor pronunciation.

When the waiter asked her to clarify, she made one more attempt ("Croak-ee Mon-zoor") before just pointing to the menu in a specific kind of midtwenties defeat. Ellen opted for the eggs Florentine.

"We're splitting, right?" Rae asked, as the waiter walked back to the kitchen and the relentless drilling finally paused.

"I suppose so," Ellen said.

Rae felt relieved. Even now that they could order their own entrées without feeling financially reckless, sharing food was still a key tenet of their friendship strategy.

"How about you and Aaron?" Rae asked. "You've been trending up and to the right for a while now."

Ellen smiled, face radiating both warmth and tranquility. "We're really good," she said. "Very stable. I used to think that meant boring, but now I just see it means secure. Knowing he's always there frees up my energy to focus on my other goals in life, rather than obsessing about guys twenty-four seven. But you probably think I don't have enough love ambition?"

"No," Rae said, though she sort of did. "I just think you're prioritizing what characteristics you want in your romantic portfolio."

Ellen smiled and fiddled with her hands.

"What was that?" Rae asked suspiciously.

"What?"

"You just twisted your left ring finger, like you were imagining a diamond on it."

"Was not," Ellen said, olive complexion splotching with pink.

"You haven't even been together two years. And you're only twenty-six." The numbers didn't sound as ridiculous aloud as she'd hoped. Two years was a pretty typical engagement timeline, and twenty-six was young by New York standards but not a child bride.

"I'm twenty-six and a *half*," Ellen said. "And it's not like we're getting engaged tomorrow or anything . . . we've talked about it is all. He's thirty-five. He wants to settle down soon."

"Do *you* want to settle down?" Rae had pictured that she and Ellen would both get married around the same time and have kids around the same time. The idea of Ellen settling down three whole years before they turned thirty was highly unsettling.

"Honestly, yes," Ellen said. "I've scoured the bachelor market for the past decade, Rae. I'm tired of all the buying and selling and arbitraging of options. I think I've found my unicorn."

Rae wasn't sure if Ellen meant the double entendre of unicorns as start-ups valued at a billion dollars, but her friend's eyes glowed with a billion watts, which was the only key performance indicator that mattered.

"That's great," Rae said, fighting self-pity at having lost stature in Ellen's ranks, though the same could be said for Ellen's place in Rae's life since she had gotten back together with Dustin.

They hadn't let men come between them exactly, but they'd allowed for new entrants that had tipped though not toppled the balance.

The waiter came by. "Could we get one more Croque Monsieur sandwich?" Rae asked, pinching her voice into her best attempt at a French accent.

She wanted to redeem herself by pronouncing it correctly, and more than that, she wanted one more thing to share with Ellen so they could stretch this Saturday brunch for two just a little longer.

* * *

"It should be the day of our first date," Dustin told Rae as they lay in bed forehead to forehead, covers tugged up to their chins. They shared a pillow out of preference rather than necessity. "December fifteenth, in the teahouse."

They were basking in an email-free Sunday morning a couple weeks after Thanksgiving, debating their official anniversary. Through the Lorimer Loft windows, snow was falling in clumps rather than crystals.

The trip back to Indiana had gone reasonably well, even if her mom had made Dustin sleep on the couch and not-so-subtly probed into his family's marriage history (she'd seemed satisfied with what she learned but still showed doubts about Rae being with an East Coaster). Her grandpa had grumbled that Dustin didn't look to be eating enough venison, but he'd poured him his finest whiskey, as sure a sign of approval as any. Mr. Non-Right had blended into the wallpaper as seamlessly as ever.

Dustin hadn't fallen in love with Indiana, but he had fallen in love with the way Indiana had shaped Rae. He'd insisted on riding shotgun in Fordable Francine as Rae gave him a tour of all the sacred spots of her childhood—the old town hall where she'd won her second-grade spelling bee, the friendly tree stump next to her high school that she'd sat on to study during lunch rather than suffer through cafeteria popularity games, the Even Butter Diner where her parents had taken her every Sunday after church, the cornfield running trails she'd put so many miles on after her dad left, trying to sprint so fast and wheeze so hard that her body would be in too much discomfort to pay attention to all the pain underneath, the pain that would still be there when she caught her breath.

They'd gone to the local grocery store, too, to get ingredients for Thanksgiving dinner, and Rae had spontaneously bought marshmallows to make her dad's famous sweet potato marshmallow recipe. It was the first time she'd ever made it without him, and she'd gotten a little carried away stacking the marshmallows high like rainless clouds. Her mom hadn't touched the dish, though she'd looked like she wanted to.

Rae had texted a photo to her dad with a Happy Thanksgiving! message that she mostly meant. Something about being with Dustin made Rae want to try a little harder to repair things with her dad. Dustin's presence gave her a certain confidence—even if her dad ghosted or rejected her, she'd have Dustin's arms to curl up in. And seeing Dustin's pain up close made her wonder more about her dad's demons and the lasting damage that may have been done when his own father had walked out when he was a kid. Though it wasn't yet forgiveness, an uncomfortable sort of empathy was wriggling in through the holes in her heart so that she could start to see him as an aching soul who was emotionally stunted by his shattered past rather than an immoral man who'd so carelessly abandoned his family.

They hadn't made it up to Elmer Lake during the trip. There wasn't much to do there in the fall, and if they went, Dustin would want to hear all about the summers she'd spent there. In her retelling, Rae knew she'd make Stu sound much less attractive, much less wonderful, than he was. She hadn't wanted to lie about Stu or deny the love she'd felt for him—still felt, on some level—she'd just wanted to hang on to the truth that what she'd found with Dustin was another realm of connection, something that couldn't be compared to a summer fling.

"No, our anniversary shouldn't be our first date," Rae said to him now. She was wearing one of Dustin's T-shirts as a nightgown. "It should be the night of our first kiss. December eighteenth, at the Christmas party."

"Or maybe the day we matched on the dating app?" Dustin mused. "If we're being technical about it?"

"If we're being technical, it should be September twenty-third, when you asked me to be your girlfriend."

"But that was only a couple months ago. And we were basically together that whole time we were 'friends' anyway. I was just being difficult and wouldn't call it that."

"Well, at least we agree on something."

"Let's not have an anniversary," Dustin decided. "Drawing attention to one specific day inherently means diminishing the importance of all the other ones."

"With that logic, I'd say the optimal solution is to call every day our anniversary," Rae said, running her hands through Dustin's curly hair, her favorite texture to wake up to.

"You're just looking for an excuse to eat pancakes and whipped cream in bed all the time, aren't you?"

"It might've factored into my thought process."

Dustin laughed, the sound vibrating up from his diaphragm and filling Rae with the feeling that yes, of course they could do this—they could lift Dustin out of the darkness and keep him there. Since the Thanksgiving trip, his ratio of good days to bad days had seemed to be increasing, almost like the Midwest had massaged him with its slowness.

"You make the batter, I make the whipped cream?" Rae said.

"And by 'make the whipped cream,' you mean squirt it from the bottle?" Dustin clarified.

"Don't diminish the artistic prowess needed to create an elegant swirl."

"My mistake. Can I ever redeem myself?" Under Rae's T-shirt nightgown, Dustin ran his hands over her stomach and worked his way up.

"I think you might be able to," Rae said, flipping on top of him to fully seal the gap between their bodies.

"Happy anniversary," he murmured, the words passing from lip to lip without any oxygen dilution.

"Happy anniversary," she said, as the snow continued to fall outside the loft, the dense flakes naïve to their impending asphalt demise.

CHAPTER TWENTY-EIGHT
THE GREAT DEPRESSION

"Are you sure they liked me?" Rae asked Dustin as they sat side by side on the aboveground train from Greenwich, Connecticut, to Grand Central Station. The Hudson River rimmed the railroad tracks, steely gray water merging moodily with splotchy gray sky. Bare-ish trees blurred at an efficient speed.

It was New Year's Day. After going their separate ways for Christmas, Rae had flown back east to join Dustin at his parents' Connecticut estate. It wasn't technically called an estate, but the word had popped into her head when she'd arrived at the magazine-worthy mansion, complete with one of those elegant portico balconies above the front door.

She'd spent two and a half days with his whole family—mom, dad, both of his older brothers, and their wives and toddlers. The highlight had been flipping through old photo albums, catching a glimpse of the boy she would've had a crush on from afar in middle school and only spoken to when he asked to borrow her Sharpie for a class project, which Rae would have interpreted as a declaration of his indelible love (*Now if he'd asked for a pencil, I wouldn't be quite as confident in his unwavering affection—but a Sharpie!* she would've spilled to her diary).

"They loved you," Dustin assured her, for the third time now.

"You don't think they think I'm a workaholic?" Rae asked. She'd spent much of New Year's Eve on the phone with lawyers, hammering out the final points of a purchase agreement for an acquisition she was staffed on. Her firm had been desperate to close one more deal before year-end to boost fourth-quarter profits, and Rae hoped some might trickle into her bonus.

"My family lives and breathes Wall Street," Dustin said, staring out the window as if the disappearing trees were hypnotizing him to sleep. "They all get it."

"I just feel like I wasn't on my A game," Rae said, replaying the error she'd made with his dad, when she'd said she was rooting for the Indianapolis Colts to make the Super Bowl, only to find out they hadn't even made the play-offs. Her scant football knowledge had been acquired reluctantly from office chatter directed around or over—never *to*—her.

"Why do you need everyone to like you so much?" Dustin asked.

"I don't. I just—they're your family. I want them to think I'm good enough for you."

"They don't even think I'm good enough for me."

The comment cut her heart in a jagged kind of pattern.

She missed her talks with Dustin, both verbal and nonverbal. Though they'd been together the past few days, they'd hardly had any alone time. Rae had chosen to stay in her own room. It felt like the proper thing to do to make a good impression, and the estate had more than enough bedrooms.

She felt drained from being "on," balancing girlfriend and employee duties, without reaching her quota of introvert time. "Are you . . . taking any medication?" she asked.

"Did my mom ask you to ask me that?"

"No," Rae said, though his mom had brought up the topic last night as she and Rae prepared deviled eggs for hors d'oeuvres.

"Dustin seems much happier than when I saw him over the summer," his mom had confided in her, a bounce in her suburban step.

Rae wouldn't have chosen the adjective *happy*—Dustin had been silent in most of the group conversations, picking at his plate but draining his glass at meals.

"You're good for him," his mom had continued, delicate features wrinkling gratefully. "And the medicine seems to be working too."

Rae was nearly certain Dustin wasn't taking any medicine, but she'd just nodded and dashed too much paprika over the hard-boiled egg halves.

"No," Rae told Dustin now. "I just . . . got the impression she thinks you're taking something."

"That's because I tell her I am," Dustin said, as if Rae should know this. "Otherwise she worries I'll put a gun to my head or something."

He said it so casually, the way words could be spoken only if they'd marinated long enough in the brain to lose their flavor.

Coldness shot through Rae, as if the January air had shattered the windows. She reached for Dustin's hand, but it was stashed in his coat pocket, so she looped an arm through his limp elbow instead.

Trying to channel Ellen's yoga breathing, she asked, "Do you . . . think about things like that?"

"Not really," Dustin answered, almost bitterly, as if he wished he had the strength to dream up such a plot.

Rae searched for words, but syllables seemed as far away as the spirit of the beautiful, broken man beside her. "I love you."

One river bend later, he answered, eyes still stuck to the windowpane, dirty with raindrop residue. "You're the only one who does."

"How can you say that? Your family loves you."

"They love the parts of me they choose to see," he said. "You're the only one who stares at all of me and doesn't blink or look away."

It sounded like a compliment, but it felt like a cut, and it stuffed Rae's nostrils with a poem fragment.

> they loved him
> in spite of
> she loved him
> because of

"I love you," Rae repeated, falling back on the phrase and hoping it might catch her.

"I'm tired," Dustin said, though he'd gone to bed at nine P.M. last night while Rae had managed to stay up until midnight to clink champagne flutes with the rest of his family.

Rae offered up her shoulder as a pillow, but Dustin leaned his head against the window and put on noise-canceling headphones—a new pair he'd bought himself for Christmas that looked fit for a helicopter pilot. He shut his eyes to the dim daylight.

She tried to let him rest, but she couldn't let it rest.

"Dustin?"

"What?"

"Can we talk?"

He cracked an eye. "About what?"

"What do you need from me right now?"

"I need you to let me sleep."

"But I can't just sit here and . . ."

"Watch a train wreck?" Dustin said wryly.

"You're not a train wreck," Rae said, as their own train screeched along the tracks. "You're getting better."

"Keep telling yourself that," Dustin mumbled, eyes closed again.

Rae thought about giving Dustin's therapist a call. She thought about calling his mom. She thought about dialing one of those depression hotlines in case it was easier to talk to a stranger about this. She thought about texting Ellen, but she knew what her solution would be: walk away.

But love wasn't just the lightness in the air and sunny days with mountain views that stretched for miles. It was the clouds and the weights and the fog that blocked even your own feet sometimes. Real love required finding a way, not walking away.

"Dustin?" she tried again. "Please . . . let me love you at your lows?"

He made no acknowledgment that he heard her except to shift slightly farther away on the hard-cushioned seat.

Rae wanted to say more, but she didn't want to risk having Dustin turn on her, and right now that meant swallowing her heart before it spilled out of her mouth.

"I'm with you," she reminded him, willing the words to be enough.

Keeping one arm looped through Dustin's, hand squeezing his forearm to a reassuring rhythm, Rae caught up on work emails one-handed, resenting the reckless use of *ASAP* for deal summaries and financial models. The only thing needed ASAP was a way to prop up the slumped soul beside her and lift him out of the Great Depression.

*   *   *

"I'm back," Rae called out as she let herself into the Lorimer Loft the following Saturday evening. "Ready to go?"

Dustin had agreed to come to Ellen and Aaron's engagement party tonight. The proposal had come earlier this week, at a seven A.M. yoga class the two went to before work because yes, they were *that* couple. Aaron had gotten on one knee during tree pose, and after singing out her "Yes!" in front of the whole studio, Ellen had called Rae to relive everything thirty times and wag the diamond in her phone camera. The ring was a little too showy for Rae's taste, but Ellen's long fingers carried it gracefully.

It wasn't exactly a surprise—Rae had known it was coming— but seeing the rock on her best friend's hand made it real in a way she hadn't expected, a way that made Rae miss something she hadn't lost yet but now knew she was going to lose very soon.

On one level, the level she was proud of, she was genuinely elated that Ellen had found her life partner, that she'd never be ghosted or taken for granted by any of the dating app fools ever again. But on another level, the shameful one, she felt like someone was taking away the closest thing she'd ever had to a sister, like Ellen wasn't just growing up but actually growing out of her. She was going to be happily married well before thirty, while Rae's own nuptials still seemed very far off. Dustin's pace of recovery seemed to be slowing, even regressing, and she wondered, not for the first time, if she was clinging to false hope.

But then the real Dustin would poke out again, with a hug or a hand or a Bellini verse, and she knew that the hope was real, it was true, and it would win in the end. His depression consumed the majority of her thoughts these days, so there wasn't much space in her mind to sketch out their own wedding, but there was still space in her heart for it, so it stayed safely tucked away as a reverie, loosening her breath when it got stuck on the stress of her not being able to see into the future and verify that it had all worked out.

Dustin had only grunted when Rae recounted the engagement news to him. Rae was learning to understand grunt quite fluently, and she was sure that it was a disapproving grunt, an acrid grunt, but she hoped she was wrong.

Tonight he was lying on the couch, wearing just boxers and headphones, in the same position as when Rae had left to take a long walk across the Williamsburg Bridge and back, in need of fresh air. The only differences were that the window blinds were now drawn and two beer cans had appeared on the coffee table.

"Dustin?" She walked over and sat on the edge of the couch, placing a hand on his bare shoulder.

Slowly he opened his eyes, as if breaking some invisible adhesive seal. His facial scruff was bordering on beard territory. He looked as bearish as the current stock market sentiment.

He slid his headphones down around his neck, not taking them off altogether. "What?"

"Ready to go to the party?"

"Do I look ready?"

She softened her voice the best she could. "It's not for me to say what you should or shouldn't wear."

"But it is for you to say that I have to go?"

"I didn't say you have to go. I said it would mean a lot if you came."

"Word trickery." He wasn't slurring, but his spacing was off. "You're making me go."

"No, I'm not."

"Good. Because I'm not."

Rae tried to count to five before she answered but only made it to two. "Why not?"

"Because I don't want to. Ellen hates me anyway."

"Would it kill you to make an effort?"

She regretted the question immediately. *Kill.* The verb articulating her worst fear. She didn't think things were that bad, but no one who lost someone to suicide ever did. Rae was still pouring over all the online articles, trying to train her eye for hindsight warning signs.

"You could just come for half an hour," she tried. "There's going to be an oyster bar and everything. Just pop in and out."

Dustin's voice hardened even more, bouncing hollowly off all the walls between them. "So I can listen to everyone telling us that we'll be next to get engaged? No thanks."

Rae blinked, then blinked again, with an absurd kind of hope that closing her eyes might change what her ears had heard. "What?" she asked, though she'd understood him with piercing precision.

"Don't insult my intelligence," Dustin said, almost sneering now. "I know you have your little scheme to get married by thirty."

Rae felt like she'd been slapped. She wanted to slap back, but that would just be cruel, hitting someone who was already down, so she turned the fury inward. She must've set some of the marriage pressure on Dustin's sunken shoulders, making him feel like being her boyfriend wasn't enough for her. Or maybe it had been her mom's tactless hints that she wanted to be around to see her grandkids grow up, or even his own mom's comments over New Year's about how it was about time Dustin brought home a nice girl and settled down like his brothers.

It all felt so thoughtless now, like rubbing salt on Dustin's open wounds.

"I don't have a scheme," Rae said, holding one of his hands in both of hers. "I don't care when we get married." She meant it, too, in this moment. The whole timeline of rushing to close the deal felt incredibly misdirected, some kind of banker formula forcing her life into a tiny box when the most beautiful love stories spilled freely in their own shape and time. Her corporate side got the worst of her sometimes, but her creative side always won out in the end. Or at least she wanted it to win out.

"*If* we get married," Dustin corrected.

"If," Rae repeated, nodding fervently to show she believed the word swap, that it wasn't crushing her inside, even though it was. "We aren't following in Aaron and Ellen's footsteps, and that's fine. More than fine. But let's just go over to the party and say a quick hi. It would mean so much to them."

"Rae," Dustin said, and she cringed at how he used her name to end the conversation rather than start it. "I'm not going."

She reminded herself that this wasn't his fault, that his pain was as real as any physical injury. Would she be making him hobble out of the apartment if both his legs were in casts? "Okay. It's okay." She held up the water glass she'd poured for him earlier. The ice cubes had melted, but it appeared untouched.

Through chapped lips, Dustin took a reluctant sip, then another. As he drank, Rae felt herself becoming hydrated too.

"I love you," she said.

"I love you," he echoed, but that's all it was—an echo.

It was getting harder to distinguish where the depression stopped and Dustin started. The demons had such a grip on him that it felt like he was starting to agree with them, starting to prefer their thoughts to his own.

She fought the urge to lie down beside him. She couldn't be late to Ellen's party, and more than that, she couldn't face Dustin's resistance or indifference as she tried and failed and tried again to transfer the balance from her heart into his.

Deep down, she still believed Dustin would never let her go, but she wasn't as sure as she'd once been.

"I'll be back by ten," Rae said. "Don't drink too much."

Dustin put his headphones back on. "Yes, Mom."

CHAPTER TWENTY-NINE
AVOIDING THE CORPORATE BREAKUP

Why didn't you come out last night, EE?

TB instant-messaged Rae at work a few days later.

The guys on her team had gone out to celebrate bonuses. Rae had said she'd join after she finished building a model, but she'd gone straight over to the Lorimer Loft.

Dustin had apologized for skipping Ellen's party, citing that Bellini quote—*I like to be with people, just not up close.* "Except for you," he'd added.

Rae had forgiven him in one fell swoop. She knew he hadn't meant what he'd said. The depression seized him in a full-body take-over sometimes, turning his words into daggers and his eyes into ice.

He'd let her hug him through the night, though Rae wasn't sure if this was because things were better or because he just didn't have the energy to shrug her off.

Wasn't in the mood for a frat party, she messaged TB now.

TB: Fair enough. But you missed a good one. Kevin picked a fight with Sam over who'd brought in more revenue.

EE: Scintillating.
TB: And then GQ quit.
EE: WHAT?
TB: Yeah. Called all the VPs homophobic assholes and wrote his resignation on a bar napkin.
EE: C warning.

Swear words got flagged by the bank's compliance surveillance.

TB: Don't give a shit. I quit, too.

Rae whipped her head to look at TB, slumped in his chair but smiling in a way Rae hadn't seen since their college internship.

"Why're you looking so surprised?" he asked as they walked to the elevator that would take them down to the Starbucks next door. "We've talked about this a million times."

It was true. She, TB, and GQ had repeatedly plotted how they'd quit in a dramatic rage the day they got their bonuses. Her vision included writing *I QUIT* on a Post-it note that she stuck on her boss's door before an eternal Irish exit.

"I guess I just thought . . . one more year, maybe," Rae said.

TB laughed, and the sound ricocheted in the elevator like it was trying to break through the metal walls. "I decided I'd been saying one more year for one too many years."

The sentence struck a depressing chord. "What're you doing next?"

"Middle-market private equity. And GQ's doing late-stage venture capital."

Both these jobs were an extension of the same rat race, just with slightly better hours and slightly higher pay, but Rae didn't point that out. She was too busy feeling disappointed in herself. She'd always thought she'd be the first to quit, and yet here she was, the last one standing. "I need to start recruiting for a new job."

"It's okay if you don't, you know."

"What do you mean?"

"It's okay if you want to stay," TB said. "You've gotten really good, EE. And now with GQ and me leaving, you have more leverage. They can't lose all their diversity hires at once."

Rae deferred the thought, something to contemplate in the long hours without her two allies beside her. "So how did the wannabe bosses respond to your announcement?"

"Drunk yelling, lots of *Fuck yous*. But David, or maybe it was Darren, bought me a fireball shot and said it was good I was getting out while I could."

They walked into Starbucks and joined the line of white men in white collared shirts, faces pinched with proud and perpetual discontent.

Rae took out her wallet to pay, but TB waved her aside. "Coffee's on me. Private equity pays more than investment banking. And besides, you and GQ are the only reasons I'm escaping this place partially sane."

He pulled Rae into a hug, an awkwardly emotional divergence from their handshake status quo.

"One more lap around the building, for old time's sake?" TB suggested after they got their coffees.

Back as interns, before their legs had learned to abandon their restlessness and their eyes had grown accustomed to lightbulb suns, they'd sneaked out to take walks around the building while waiting for more work from the wannabe bosses. At the first buzz of their phones, they'd sprint back inside.

"I hereby appoint you president of the COTWSM," TB said. "It's up to you to carry the coup forward. Don't let them win."

"I won't." But as she said it, she wondered at what point she'd become one of *them*. How long until the diversity of her gender was overshadowed by the homogeny of her thought?

TB held his middle finger high, pointing it up at their forty-second-story window.

"How's it feel?" Rae asked, envy rivaling respect. In a symbolic kind of way, it almost felt like TB and GQ were getting married, moving on to a new life stage and leaving her in the dust, like everyone else in her life.

"Like a fucking dream," TB said.

That was what most dreams on Wall Street were, Rae realized—fantasies of leaving. There were far more wishes made about walking out of doors than into them.

"One more lap?" TB asked, as they approached the entrance again. The lap didn't feel as big as it used to.

Rae felt emails buzzing in her pocket, one arbitrarily urgent request after another. "I've got to get back," she said. TB kept walking as Rae stood in the skyscraper shade and took a couple deep breaths before going back into her pen.

The security guard outside the building looked into her eyes with a touching combination of concern and compassion. "You all right there, Rae?" he asked.

"Yeah," she said, as convincingly as she could. "I'm all right." She forced a smile before letting her face sag as she walked through the revolving door alone.

*   *   *

"Trying to break up with a Wall Street job is like trying to break up with a toxic boyfriend," Ellen told Rae. "They give you a nice present—aka a massive bonus—right before Valentine's Day, and it makes you overlook all the glaring problems in the relationship."

Rae, Ellen, and Mina were getting coffee on a Saturday afternoon in the West Village. None of them had time for brunch. They were at Partners Coffee, an old 1920s artist studio converted into a bougie haunt for slurping down five-dollar cold brews and posting photos on social media of heart-shaped latte art. The floor-to-ceiling windows looked out onto the yellow cab circus of Seventh Avenue and down toward the distant Freedom Tower at the south end of the island. Triangular in shape, with white exposed brick and wooden ceiling beams, Partners was wedged into a crowded street corner, and

Rae didn't like how it felt as if the corners had been sawed off just so it would fit in.

"And you say you want a new job, but something keeps you holding on to the old one, justifying why he'll get better this year," Mina added, holding her iced almond-milk latte in one hand as she swiped through a dating app with the other.

"And he's so clingy and expects you to be there for him twenty-four seven," Ellen added. "And when you do finally get another offer, you get cold feet because you can't even remember who you were without Mr. Wall Street in your life."

"You've got to get out," Mina said, tilting her head to evaluate a digital suitor on her phone.

"It's time," Ellen agreed. "Sarah agrees with us."

Rae felt the panicked sensation of a door that had closed before she'd managed to reach it, but she avoided interpreting their words as truth. She just went into defensive mode, disliking how the rest of the Scramblettes had apparently started a separate group chat to stage an intervention.

"Things have been getting better," Rae said. "I think I'll be able to present my market size analysis to a client at a pitch meeting next week."

"You're doing that thing," Ellen said, "where the shitty boyfriend does one mediocre thing, but relative to everything else he's done it's amazing, and so you think this means he's really changed."

The glare from Ellen's engagement ring felt very bright, and Rae didn't like the sight of it. "But the worst *is* behind me," she said. "And if I stay one more year, I can pay off my student loans."

"I've heard you say that for years now," Ellen said. "You've got to rip the Band-Aid off."

"But with TB and GQ quitting, I'll be on the fast track for the vice president promotion . . . then I'll have a lot more exit options. And I'll start setting more boundaries. No checking emails after ten P.M., things like that."

"You're wearing investment blinders," Ellen said. "You can't see clearly."

Mina looked up from her phone. "It's an emotionally abusive relationship."

Rae got the sense Ellen had coached her on the points to make.

"Physically abusive, too," Ellen said. "You're losing weight."

"No, I'm not." If she was, it was only because she'd been trying to feed Dustin her food. "I'm giving it one more chance. If it doesn't get better, I'll quit."

Mina made a skeptical sound and Ellen made a skeptical face.

"We're just looking out for you," Ellen said. "Sometimes it's hard to see how toxic a relationship is when you're in it."

Rae looked down at her cappuccino, refusing to dwell on the double meaning, or even the single meaning. "I'm twenty-seven," she said, avoiding calculating the exact number of days before her thirtieth birthday but knowing it was now under one thousand. "I'm old enough to make my own decisions."

CHAPTER THIRTY

EMOTIONAL DEPRECIATION

"You know how investors just blindly follow what everyone else is doing?" Rae said to Dustin from the Lorimer Loft rooftop on February 14. "It's the same thing for how people approach Valentine's Day. Everyone buying overvalued roses and cramming into restaurants to overpay for undersized portions."

They were standing at the railing of the vacant roof deck, overlooking the volatile skyline that had begun to feel, for better or worse, like *their* volatile skyline. An open pizza box was propped on the ledge that they'd made into a table.

"I'm glad we're going against the market," Dustin agreed, giving her hand a squeeze. His skin was the only glove she wanted, the only glove she'd ever want. She had a feeling, magnified by the symbolism of this red-hearted holiday, that they were turning a corner together. As much as the depression tried to keep them apart, Rae thought that it just as often brought them closer together as they fought against a common enemy but never against each other.

"Pick up the next slice," she said, nudging Dustin toward the pizza.

They'd agreed on a no-gifts policy, which they'd both breached. Dustin had had potted sunflowers waiting for her when Rae arrived (Rae didn't like the metaphor of gifting cut flowers) as well as freshly made, nonalcoholic hot chocolate.

Rae had brought a framed photo of the two of them from Indiana, along with a poetic pizza. Under each slice, she'd put a Post-it note with a mini poem, all of them Rae originals and all different poetic voices she was trying out to see which fit.

The poems hadn't exactly written themselves, but there had been a certain flow that gave her hope her stories wouldn't always be stuck within her.

Dustin picked up the pizza slice and read the yellow sticky note underneath it.

> when memories of him
> multiply (never divide)
> and make you smile
> even as you stare at
> pointless decimal points
> —yup, that's love.

His mouth penciled in its parenthesis smile. "Is that how you first knew you loved me? When your mind drifted to me instead of decimal points?"

"Might've been," Rae said, relieved his sense of humor was out tonight, a sliver as thin as the new moon above them but even more beautiful. "Or maybe that time I screwed up a gross margin analysis replaying our first kiss."

"Love in twenty-first-century corporate America," Dustin said.

"Love," Rae said, stripping out the qualifiers.

She tugged her hat over her ears. February wasn't really that cold if you knew how to dress for it. "Another one," Rae said, glad to see him eating.

"Read it for me?" Dustin asked, handing her the next Post-it note.

Rae had never read any of her poems aloud before. With only a fraction of the self-consciousness she'd expected, she began.

Spring into the air
and let love
give you life
and be your
remedy of
silver bullets.

She looked up at Dustin, who appeared to be letting the poem sink in, then sink again.

"It's an alternate version of a Bellini poem," Rae explained. "The one about—"

"I know the poem," Dustin cut in, voice hardening out of the blue. "*Stand against the wall and let love murder you with a round of careless bullets.*"

"Yes," Rae said. "Too dark for Valentine's Day, so I put a new spin on it."

Dustin stared at her with a stony expression, which he then turned onto the artificially bright skyline. "You can't rewrite someone's words just because you find them inconvenient."

"I wasn't rewriting," Rae said. "I was reimagining."

"Well, you can't reimagine someone else's thoughts either. That was how Bellini felt—that love should be lethal. And we can either accept that or deny it."

Rae was feeling very cold now, and small, too, a leg-locked ant lost in a supersized, superspeed city. "I accept it," she said, thin voice hitting a thick head wind.

They stood there at the railing for a few more icy gusts.

"I just wanted you to like our first Valentine's Day together," Rae said.

She'd liked the sound of *first* in her thoughts, how it implied more to come. But aloud, *first* felt fragile, without a steady track record of historical data to prop it up.

"I did like it," Dustin said. "Let's go inside."

Rae collected the sticky notes from the ledge but left the Bellini-inspired one behind, wishing on the dim rooftop lamppost that the wind would take this flimsy paper square somewhere else, somewhere its lightness might have a chance to dance in blue-sky breeze.

Then she and Dustin walked back inside, holding each other's hurt but not each other's hands.

* * *

"Is that a scramblette I smell?" Rae asked Ellen the next week, as she trudged into the penthouse after work and thudded her bag onto the floor.

Though they hadn't cooked scramblettes in months now, the meal was exactly what Rae hadn't known she'd been craving. Her nose correlated the burnt-yolk odor with raw camaraderie.

She and Ellen hadn't overlapped much since Dustin had bailed on the engagement party and Ellen had staged the work intervention. Their interactions had been formulaically friendly.

"Not just any scramblette," Ellen said, standing at the stovetop in the hotel bathrobe she'd illicitly acquired for Rae's twenty-fifth birthday. "A Rae-bae scramblette."

Rae felt something lift inside her, something that gave her hope that their tomorrows might resemble yesterdays. "You named a scramblette after me?" she said, entering the kitchenette and peering into the over-capacity skillet. "What's in it?"

"Culinary sunshine—yellow peppers, yellow squash, fresh lemon." Wielding the spatula like a presentation pointer stick, Ellen highlighted each ingredient in the eggy mound. "And then a few bay leaves on top."

Rae changed into her bathrobe too. Over the gap in her bedroom wall, she called out, "What're you trying to butter me up for?" She was the one who should've been cooking an Elle-belle scramblette. "Have I been replaced as maid of honor by Comedian Courtney?"

The couple of times Rae had tried to make plans with Ellen recently, Ellen had been out with a woman from work named Courtney, who was apparently "the most hilarious human in the history of humanity." Rae had mentally tallied the ways in which she was no doubt funnier than Courtney before coming to the conclusion that, given that her core competency was her heart, not her humor, she should lean into her differentiation rather than conforming to the competition's friendship model. Would Courtney wipe Ellen's vomit from the toilet seat or put poems on her pillows? Rae didn't think so.

"Maid-of-honor duties are safe," Ellen said, handing her a plate of Rae-bae scramblette. "It's just . . ."

"What?"

Ellen said the next sentence very quickly, as if it were a single ten-syllable word. "Aaron wants us to move in together."

"Oh," Rae said, settling into the couch and taking a forkful. "Well, I figured you'd move in together when our lease is up. I mean, you are getting *married*."

"But he wants it to happen now," Ellen said. There were still four months left on their lease.

"Now as in . . ."

"*Now*."

"Well," Rae said, looking around the apartment and visualizing how it might accommodate a third person. "I guess we could squeeze him in. It would lower the per-person rent, and I really don't sleep here that often. But he has to keep the toilet seat down. That's a non-negotiable clause."

"Rae," Ellen said, with an oddly sympathetic look. "Aaron wants me to move in with *him*. Into his apartment. It's a one-bedroom, so it just makes more sense . . ."

Rae set down her fork, and then her whole plate. "Right," she said. "Of course. I figured that's what you meant. I was just offering . . ."

"It's a very sweet offer," Ellen said, joining her on the couch. "I just think—it's a new chapter for us, you know?"

By *us*, she meant Aaron and Ellen, and Rae felt herself sink farther into the worn-out seat cushions.

"A new chapter," Rae repeated bravely, trying to see the literary possibility of a blank page rather than the pain of realizing the one prior was finished, scribbled on from margin to margin, unable to accommodate another drop of ink.

"There's a woman at work who's interested in subletting," Ellen said. "Not Courtney—don't worry. I've fully vetted her. The only red flag is that she's one of those inbox-zero people, but that's not really a deal breaker. And," Ellen continued, as if offering up the opportunity of a lifetime, "you could move into my room and get the full wall!"

Rather than exciting Rae, the prospect added to the sensation that things were being closed off.

"And since you practically live at Dustin's anyway now, you'll hardly even miss me," Ellen went on. "And—"

Rae cut her off. "When're you leaving?"

"Aaron's planning to borrow his friend's car this weekend," Ellen said. "If that's okay with you?"

"This weekend as in tomorrow?"

Ellen nodded. "He just found out about the car . . ."

Rae stood up. She wanted to throw out the scramblette, but she just stashed it in the midget refrigerator. "Fine by me."

"You'll still be my best friend, obviously," Ellen said.

"After Aaron." The maturity date of their best-friend bond had finally arrived. Rae shed her robe for her coat. "I'm going to stay at Dustin's."

"You don't want to have a girls' night?" Ellen asked, in a quiet voice. "Play Snack & Swipe and try and catch popcorn in our mouths, like old times?"

Rae paused in the doorway. Their friendship was pivoting, with so much uncertainty in the outlook. "We don't have dating apps anymore. What would we swipe?"

"No swiping. We can rebrand it Snack & Catch," Ellen said. "Bet our kernel-catching percentage will be a lot higher without the distraction from the apps."

A smile squeezed out of Rae like lemon drops in the scramblette Ellen had made. "All right," she said.

She took off her coat as Ellen fetched a bag of popcorn. They met back on the couch in their old, patented Elle-Rae posture, socked feet resting beside each other's heads. Ellen tossed a puffed kernel into the air for Rae to catch. It followed a parabola, up and down again, missing Rae's mouth.

"I think we've actually gotten worse," Rae said after more than a few failed attempts.

"We've passed our popcorn peak," Ellen agreed. "I'll clean out the cushions before I move out."

"That's okay," Rae said, craving something to hold on to from these past few years as roommates, even crumbs. "I'll get around to it. I like cleaning."

"Since when?"

"Since now. New chapters, remember?"

"Yes," Ellen said, her clean, matching socks tickling Rae's ears. "New chapters."

*   *   *

"Which of the therapists do you like best?" Rae asked Dustin, sitting on the edge of his bed. It was a Sunday evening in early March.

He was sprawled facedown on the mattress, shirtless back rising and falling in a lumpy pattern that told Rae he wasn't asleep.

Dustin's therapy attendance percentage had continued to drop as he complained that Jessica "just didn't get it." Rae had done hours of diligence on new options.

"I think Anette is the best one," Rae said, consulting the Stall Street Journal, which she'd repurposed as a research notebook. "Strong credentials, high customer satisfaction ratings, and your healthcare plan will reimburse fifty percent of the costs."

Anette was also very pretty, but the situation was too serious for Rae to dock points for that.

Dustin didn't answer, so Rae presented another therapist. It was a human behavior hack she'd learned at work—executives were more likely to commit to a deal when pitched multiple options.

"There's also this woman named Kim. She has a differentiated approach to recovery—it's very focused on physical movement of the body."

Dustin grunted, which Rae found moderately encouraging, as it at least meant he wanted her to know he was listening.

"Grunt once if you want me to call and make an appointment with Anette, twice if you want Kim," Rae said, trying to lower the barriers to entry.

Silently, Dustin pulled the pillow over his head. The gesture cut to Rae's overcompensating, undercompensated core.

Rae walked to the kitchen to refill his water. He'd been drinking less alcohol lately, but he'd been doing everything else less too. His emotional depreciation seemed to be accelerating, if *accelerate* could describe something attached to so little movement.

The potted sunflowers Dustin had gotten her for Valentine's Day were sitting in the window, droopy from too much water, beside Phyllis, stubbornly green as ever.

Standing at the sink, Rae stared out the window into the eye-level apartment across the street, where a shadow was shifting through translucent blinds.

It reminded her of the second date she'd gone on with Dustin—that Christmas party where they'd stood in the courtyard, looking up at the woman in the window, inventing stories. Imagination had been something winged and feathery back then, lifting her into the freedom of fiction. Now it took the form of a weighty anchor, tugging her to the factual magic of the past.

She thought about Dustin, facedown through the wall.

Then she thought about the dinner she'd gotten with Jenn and John last week that Dustin had bailed on, citing "stock market chaos." Over sticky sushi, Rae had half broached Dustin's emotional downturn.

Neither Jenn nor John seemed surprised. "It's gotten bad before," John had said, and Jenn had added, "We were really worried for a while."

They talked about it like Dustin's emotional trough was far in the past. Rae wanted to believe this, but she figured it more probable that Jenn and John were caught up in the bubble of Manhattan married life, a far cry and a whole river away from any brokenness in Brooklyn.

But perhaps they'd picked up on the undertones, because Jenn had told Rae, with gentle firmness, "It's not your responsibility to take care of him."

Rae had wanted to ask a follow-up—*Then whose responsibility is it?*—but Jenn would say it was Dustin's, and Rae knew that asking him to save himself from depression was like asking a man in the path of a hurricane to lift up his house and carry it on his own back for two hundred miles.

She should probably let Dustin sleep off his mood, but she found herself walking back into his bedroom. The pillow was still over his head, or his head was still under the pillow. She clung to the vision of the long, happy life they'd have together once Dustin got better, and it helped her say the next words, words she knew he wouldn't like. "I think you should consider taking medical leave from work again."

Lurching onto his front, Dustin faced Rae. "Stop," he said. "Just stop it."

Rae was suddenly back in her childhood home, crouching outside her parents' bedroom door, eavesdropping on a fight in the turbulent wake of the affair. "For the love of God, just stop it," her dad had yelled at her mom. "Just fucking stop!"

Rae wanted to crawl out of Dustin's room back to the penthouse, but she didn't want to endure small talk with her new roommate, who was annoyingly nice. She wanted to write or even just read, but her thoughts were stuck in a left-brain loop.

She went into the living room, logged on to her laptop from the couch, and worked on building a financial model for a new deal to show how much the business would be worth after the acquisition. With how impossible it was to forecast even a day ahead in her relationship, there was a certain comfort in projecting revenues ten years into the future.

Too quickly, she finished the model. For a quick dopamine hit, she upwardly adjusted the profit margin assumptions so the valuation rose from $3.3BN to $3.8BN.

Then she brushed her teeth, squeezing toothpaste from an empty tube, and climbed into bed beside Dustin. His breathing had mellowed, and Rae knew he was asleep. The room was dark, except for street light encroaching through the curtains.

Dustin reached out to pull Rae closer.

Rae hugged back, but not too firmly to risk waking him up and letting him realize he'd mistakenly taken her in his arms.

As she watched the angular outline of his face, visible but not illuminated, a verse drifted through her mind, something about how half darkness was more frightening than full darkness because there was just enough light to see the crevices.

Not wanting to untangle herself to write it down, she let the phrase live and die as untethered thought.

CHAPTER THIRTY-ONE
PORTFOLIO ENVY

"I definitely want cupcakes at my wedding," Ellen told Rae one Saturday afternoon in mid-March. "I just don't want to be mistaken for one." Head tilted at an angle, Ellen analyzed her white-ball-gown reflection in the mirror of a SoHo wedding dress boutique.

It was a large, airy space with classical music playing over the speakers on a six-song circuit.

"You look like a princess, not a pastry," Rae assured her from the plush maroon couch she was occupying alone. Her legs were stretched out, black booties dangling just off the side to avoid scuffing the fabric. "But I still like the first one best," Rae added, loyal to the simple lace dress that had enticed them into the store.

They'd only planned on evaluating brunch menus, not wedding dresses, but Ellen had been captivated by a window display and insisted they pop in "for two minutes, just to get a better look."

An hour later, Ellen had tried on half the inventory, discarding dresses at the speed she used to discard dates.

"I think that's my favorite too," Ellen said. "Could I try it on again?" she asked the toothpick-shaped woman named Tina who was helping them.

Tina, whom Rae had resisted labeling Toothpick Tina, despite the alliterative allure, had made a proud fuss over neglecting another bride's appointment to make time for Ellen and her dream figure.

"Your wish is my command," Tina said in her jingly voice. "Though I just *have* to say, I don't think anything can live up to the drama of this one."

Rae shot her a Wall Street scowl, aware of Tina's motive to upsell her on the more expensive dress.

"Ellen doesn't want drama at her wedding," Rae said, and Ellen nodded in agreement.

With sugar in her smile and poison in her eyes, Tina said, "Let's not project our own preferences onto someone else's special day."

"I'm not projecting," Rae said, though she figured she might be.

She tried to imagine the dress she'd wear walking down the aisle toward Dustin one day, but the vision was foggy, like the bathroom mirror after her hot water hog of a new roommate finished her twenty-minute shower.

Ellen waltzed to the fitting room and reemerged one song later in the flowy lace dress, a free-spirited bride-to-be. The veil that Tina put on her—though cluttered with crystals—removed the *to-be* suffix. Ellen was a bride.

A flash of red cut through the fog of her own wedding day illusion. She still couldn't see the dress, but she was wearing a Santa hat. The image should have made her laugh, but it flavored her mouth with melancholy. Perhaps she'd put it in third person and write a poem called "The Bride With the Santa Hat Veil."

"Yes," Ellen said, staring at herself in the angled mirrors. "This is the one."

She spoke with the same clarity as when she'd told Rae about falling in love with Perry Street, and then with Aaron, but her voice was softer now, less concerned about announcing her success in capital letters.

Rae felt a stab of jealousy, the kind she'd credited herself with overcoming years ago. She was experiencing portfolio envy, watching Ellen's basket of investments perform so much better than her own.

Ellen had made the right bets in both the economic and romantic markets. She'd taken a big risk in quitting her large consulting firm and going to a tiny start-up, and it had paid off. And she'd stopped falling for risky romantic options and had instead chosen a reliable, even-keeled boyfriend who was going to make a phenomenal husband.

Rae, on the other hand, was playing it safe at work, stuck in the just-one-more-year cycle. And the risk she'd taken in dating someone with depression wasn't playing out as the best-case scenario, though she knew that, given the option to change her decision, she wouldn't.

After Dustin had shaken her up by telling her so bluntly that he didn't see marriage coming for them anytime soon, she'd had to decide, or rather admit that her heart had already decided, that she'd rather be with Dustin and have her marriage timeline delayed than be with someone else who was ready for that step right now. She still wanted to get married and have kids, and she still wanted Dustin as the husband part of that equation, but she figured maybe it would make sense for them just to have two kids, not three. That would buy them another couple years to focus on getting Dustin better before heading to the altar.

Running through this plan again made her feel a little more confident in her own future, and the jealousy mostly rearranged itself into joy as Rae looked into Ellen's eyes, blurry with clarity.

"Shit," Ellen said. "Anyone have a tissue?"

Tina produced a whole pack from her pocket. "Your wish is my command."

Rae stood up and snatched the tissues away. "Love shouldn't be wiped away."

Ellen took Rae's hand as they stared at their reflections. Ellen looked extra tall on the pedestal, a dark-haired heroine in white. Rae appeared extra short, a fair-haired supporting character in black. They were objective opposites but subjective complements, and Rae felt emotion churning up in her eyes too.

She squeezed Ellen's clammy palm. "You're sweating."

"I need hand deodorant," Ellen said.

"Palm powder," Rae said. "We should patent it."

"There's a large market size of brides who'd buy it. But it has to be all natural."

Tina appeared confused. "Hand deodorant? I'm not sure we have any of that . . ."

"Just an inside joke," Ellen said kindly. And then, to Rae, "Text a photo to the Scramblettes."

The Scramblette group chat had been nearly dormant for a while, but there was nothing like a wedding dress to gather old friends back into its fold. Rae sent three photos of Ellen, all equally perfect.

Mina and Sarah replied right away, as if no time had passed.

Mina: AHHHH WHAT A VISION.

Sarah: CAN'T WAIT FOR THE WEDDING (and for you to meet Nell!!!)

"Sarah's getting a plus-one?" Rae asked.

"Guess she is now," Ellen said with an unconcerned laugh. "I'm not having assigned seating."

"What kind of cupcakes will there be?" Rae asked, cutting to the important questions.

"Not sure yet. Maybe my maid of honor could take the lead on that?"

"Yes, please," Rae said, already dreaming up *Karat Cake* and *S'more Love*. "We'll call them 'couple cakes.'"

Ellen let out an early-twenties squeal, and she and Rae danced around in the spacious wedding shop like they used to dance in the scrunched penthouse living room.

"It's harder to jump up and down in a wedding dress than a bathrobe," Ellen said, seeming to be replaying the same scenes as Rae. "But twirling is more fun." The train of her dress fanned at her feet.

Rae spun her partner around, trying not to spoil the moment with self-indulgent nostalgia. "I get your first dance," she said, carefully selecting the present-tense verb.

"Yes," Ellen said, smiling and crying and flying in white-lace wonder as the song dipped into an instrumental end. "You got my first dance."

CHAPTER THIRTY-TWO
UPWARD REVISIONS

"We need to send a revised term sheet by EOD," Rae's boss—her real manager, not one of the wannabes—said over the phone one Saturday morning in May. "Jim thinks JPMorgan's valuation number is higher, and there's no fucking way we're letting this deal slip through our fingers—it'll be our biggest one of Q2."

"I hear you," Rae said, pacing the white-gold beach of Turks and Caicos, where she and Dustin were spending a long weekend. "I'll connect with Kelly and circle back with an updated model ASAP."

She felt the other beach chair loungers judging her for being one of those New Yorkers who taints vacation with deal talk. It bothered her, but not as much as it would have a year or two ago. There was a certain thrill that came from feeling so needed, even if it was only by her boss.

"Sounds good," her boss said. "Hope you're enjoying your getaway."

"Yes," Rae said, looking out at the turquoise water, willing her boss to hear the irony in his words. "Very relaxing."

After hanging up, she texted Kelly, the junior analyst who'd recently joined the firm—a younger, cheaper replacement for TB and

GQ. They'd hired only one person rather than two, because entry-level salary costs were apparently too much of a drain on billion-dollar profits.

Rae had pushed hard for the new hire to be female, and she felt like her voice might have been heard. Maybe that was why she was taking work calls on vacation, or maybe she was just more invested in winning this deal than she wanted to admit.

Rae had helped present the pitch book at the client meeting, meaning she'd walked through two slides and half of a third with only a handful of interruptions from the higher-ups. The conversation had then slid over to football and golf, the true linchpins of Wall Street deals, but she still hoped this might be a turning point in her career from *cog in wheel* to *chain in wheel*.

Hi Kelly—pls increase EBITDA margins for year 3 and step up 0.25% after that. Need as soon as possible. Thanks!

Rae proudly evaluated the way she'd spelled out "as soon as possible" rather than using the aggressive acronym and how she'd thanked Kelly, even punctuating her gratitude with an exclamation point. She was clearly a much better wannabe boss than the ones who'd hazed her through her early years.

Kelly replied instantaneously. Of course. Will do ASAP. Thanks!

Picturing Kelly hurrying out from brunch with her friends—her only social excursion of the week—to head back to the office, Rae nearly felt guilty before recalling how many Scramblette brunches she'd bailed on for work, and how even now she was working during a romantic weekend away. That was just how investment banking was. Kelly knew what she'd been signing up for.

As Rae walked back to rejoin Dustin on their beach chairs, her phone buzzed with an incoming call. Anticipating her boss calling back, Rae picked up and said, with disguised displeasure, "Hi again."

"Kiddo!"

Rae stopped walking, bare feet slipping in the shifting sand. "Dad?"

"Any chance you're free for dinner tonight?" her dad asked, as if they'd last seen each other weeks ago rather than years ago. "I'm in New York for a conference through tomorrow morning."

The normalcy shocked her nearly as much as it soothed her.

"I'm on vacation," Rae said in a thin voice, the kind that gave cringeworthy flashbacks to her first year of work, when she'd shriveled up anytime she'd been asked a question. "Turks and Caicos with my boyfriend," she added, though he hadn't asked.

Her dad made a cough-humph sound, as if Rae wasn't old enough to have a boyfriend, let alone be flying to a tropical island with him. "Ah," he said. "Too bad. I'm reporting directly to the CFO now. We're putting together our growth plan to expand across the country, and I've told everyone that my daughter is one of Wall Street's rising stars and could help us out. Think you could hook us up with some funds?"

Rae felt the letdown as quickly as she'd felt the lift. He was calling with an ulterior motive. Still, there was a certain triumph that came with picturing him bragging about her and believing she might be valuable. It made her feel like she might be gaining points against his stepdaughters.

The manufacturing company he worked for was too small to gain Wall Street's interest, but she didn't want to disappoint him. "I'd help you if I had any power," she said. "But I'm not exactly running the place."

There was a silence, filled by squawking sea gulls on her side and city sirens on his.

"I could probably make an introduction, though," Rae heard herself say. "To the capital markets team."

"Knew I could count on you," her dad said, in his resonant voice that reminded Rae of the *before* times, the years of shooting baskets together in the driveway and celebrating her straight-A report cards with double-scoop ice cream cones from the dairy farm down the road. "I've got to run to the next meeting now," he said. "But I'll circle back with a text with more info."

"Sounds good."

"I love you, kiddo," her dad said, and Rae thought she might've detected some self-awareness in the way he said it, like he might be shuffling his feet a bit realizing that he shouldn't just be telling her that he loved her now, when he needed something, but that he should be reminding her of this on a regular basis—that unconditional love was, in fact, supposed to be the core gift a father gave his child. And maybe he was acknowledging also that Rae wasn't a kiddo anymore, but he wanted to cling to the past as much as she did, to that undamaged era when Rae had assumed that dads always stayed and her dad had assumed daughters always forgave.

"Love you too," she gritted out, attempting detachment by excluding *I* and tacking on *too*, which made it more of a reply than a declaration. But she still felt the truth of the phrase all the way down to her toes, where sand stuck to un-rubbed-in sunscreen like glitter to Elmer's glue.

Her dad hung up first, and Rae walked back to the chairs she and Dustin had staked out earlier this morning, when the beach had been shaded with elongated palm tree patterns.

Dustin lay shirtless in a bathing suit, a blue-and-white towel draped over his head to block the sun. On the table beside his chair was a bottle of sunscreen, the Stall Street Journal—newly filled with a few tropical fragments—and two iced teas rimmed with lemon wedges.

Dustin had been showing some improvement since seeing Kim, the therapist who advocated physical movement. It had been Kim's idea for them to take a long weekend and change up Dustin's environment. Rae had converted this into action by immediately booking flights.

Rae tapped the top of his towel-draped head, like she was knocking on a door. "Can I come into your cabana, sir?"

He peeked out from under the towel and looked up at her with a clean-shaven face and unlocked eyes. The image was so radiant that Rae had to squint through her sunglasses.

"Are you sure Wall Street can survive without you for five minutes?" he deadpanned with a diaphragm-deep smile.

"It'll be tough, but they'll manage." She tossed her sunglasses onto the sand and draped Dustin's towel over both their heads. It felt like the bedsheet tents they made in the Lorimer Loft but not as dark, and warmer, too, with the sun strumming against their bare legs to an island melody.

"The Great Rae-cession," Dustin said. "I can see the *Wall Street Journal* headline now."

Rae tried to smile, but it snagged on her lips.

"It's just work," Dustin said. "Don't let them get to you."

"It's not that. It's—my dad called and asked me to dinner tonight. Apparently he's on a work trip to New York."

"He didn't give you a heads-up he was coming?"

"No. He didn't. But he asked if I could help his company get some Wall Street money."

"Are you serious?"

Rae started to put on a sarcastic smirk and then remembered she didn't have to hide her emotions around Dustin. "Very serious," she said, letting her hurts and hopes show in plain sight. "But it was sort of nice to talk to him, actually. He's not the villain in the simple little story I've repeated to myself over the years, is he? He's just a hurting, imperfect human like the rest of us—a fifty-something-year-old man who's still a lost boy at heart and doesn't know how to be anything other than what he's seen."

She'd never articulated it quite like this before, to anyone else or even to herself, but she knew she was being fairer to her dad than she'd ever been. Looking back on the divorce a decade later from this newish adult vantage point, she didn't have to grip the black-and-white guardrails for safety anymore. She could venture farther into the grays and try on her dad's shoes for a few steps—contemplating more how the scars from his own father's absence might have stayed etched on his heart like a cruel calligraphy note telling him he wasn't enough, subconsciously compelling him to chase validation from new people and new places to fill the void, ultimately leading him to follow his dad's footsteps right out the door despite all those happy, healing years he'd spent raising a beautiful daughter with a beautiful wife. A sorry sort of softness rose within her as she recalled how he'd swelled with pride at how he was the family man his dad had never been, only to fulfill that wretched destiny in the end because he just couldn't help himself or let himself be helped.

The heavy analysis made Rae feel a bit lighter. Maybe she could find it in herself to extend compassion to her dad without condoning his actions. Maybe forgiveness wasn't so much an offering to the other person as it was an offering to yourself. A precious key to freedom so you didn't give your past the power to lock up your future. An inner antidote to help you heal enough to stay by someone's side your whole life, finally breaking the cycle of brokenness.

Rae picked up the pen and jotted the fragments onto a page of the Stall Street Journal.

Dustin looked at her while she wrote, wincing a bit at the words. "Your dad doesn't deserve you." He paused, then added, "Neither do I."

Rae looked at Dustin through the filtered light. "Don't say that."

"It's true," Dustin said, pressing his face to hers, their eyelashes overlapping. "Your give-to-get ratio has been way too high."

"It's not your fault," Rae said. "Depression isn't something you can control."

Dustin matched her exhale and gave her a squeeze. Even after many months together, Rae constantly craved being closer, closer, closer to him, and there was nothing better than those times, like today, when he seemed to feel that way too. "I wouldn't blame you, you know," he said, "if you—"

"Stop." Rae cut him off. "We're not talking about this."

"You promised you wouldn't steal from your own sunshine to keep my soul out of the shade," he reminded.

"And I'm not." She yanked the towel off, craving metaphorical proof that there was enough sunlight for both of them. In a smaller voice, she added, "Just maybe try . . . not to take things out on me . . . when you're feeling down?"

Dustin pulled her closer as his voice drifted farther away. "I hate myself when I do that," he said. "So damn much."

Rae's chest tightened. He didn't need another reason to be hard on himself. "I love you," she said. "All the time."

True love had no term sheets, no disclaimers, no conditions, no maturity dates.

"I love you," Dustin said. "Forever."

At the word *forever*, Rae braced for the jolt of fear that she'd thought she'd always feel after watching her dad walk out. But the fear didn't come, just a blast of blue-sky freedom.

Dustin reached over and picked up the Stall Street Journal. Carefully, he tore a strip from one of the blank pages and folded it into a thin cylinder that he slipped onto her left hand.

Rae looked at Dustin, then down at the paper ring, then up at Dustin again.

"I didn't mean it, that stuff I said before about not wanting to get married," he said, tone laced with self-hate about the weaponry he'd let slip out as words. "I do want it, more than anything and more than everything. I just need to work on myself more before I can propose for real . . . but I'm yours, for as long as you'll have me."

Rae felt like she was flying. She'd read these words in his eyes before, but to hear them aloud was another thing altogether.

All those things she'd told herself about how fine she was if they stayed boyfriend/girlfriend for a while, all those calculations in her marriage model that she'd pushed back to reflect a new base case—it was nothing but fabricated rationalization, she saw now in the dancing shadows of the island sun. She wanted to marry Dustin, and she wanted to marry him soon, and this was the proof she'd been waiting on to assure herself that the illusion of their future was more than delusion. The paper on her finger felt like the finest diamond, symbolizing that Dustin was every bit as committed as she was. There were still some bumps to smooth over, but they were really going to get there. Together.

"Forever, then," Rae said. She pulled the towel back over their heads to celebrate their symbolic engagement in their cotton cabana, keeping her hand out in the sun so she'd get a tan line in the shape of a ring.

CHAPTER THIRTY-THREE
SUNK COSTS

"You need to cut your losses," Ellen told Rae over brunch a few weeks later, early June.

They were seated in a corner booth at the Madison Avenue location of Sarabeth's, a chic staple of the Manhattan brunch scene near Ellen and Aaron's Upper East Side apartment. The space was rimmed with crown molding and cluttered with baggy-eyed couples and fancy strollers that seemed to have every feature except an efficient way to fold up. Customers pushed their way in the door to stock up on homemade pies, pastries, and marmalades from the bakery at the front of the restaurant. The swinging doors let in muggy heat from the street and gave that feeling that summer was about to stuff its way into the city and refuse to pay rent.

"I've stayed quiet long enough," Ellen continued, reaching for Rae's hand across the table. The waiter had deposited a basket of bread rolls, but they hadn't touched them yet.

Rae pulled her palm away, looking at her ring finger and mourning the way the tan line—or sunburn line, more accurately—had faded, leaving no souvenir except persistent peeling of pasty skin. "I wouldn't exactly say *quiet* is the right adjective," Rae said. "You hated Dustin before you even met him."

What Rae had expected to be a pleasant hour or two discussing Ellen's wedding centerpieces and cupcake selection had turned out to be a hostile relationship takeover, reminiscent of the failed attempt to get Rae to break up with Wall Street.

"I just can't sit by and watch you waste your twenties getting your heart yanked up and down like a volatile tech stock until you end up in a depression, too, with no love left to liquidate," Ellen said.

It was one of her most impressive work-love comparisons, but Rae didn't give her the satisfaction of acknowledging this. "Dustin's getting better," Rae said, though he'd spoken mostly in single sylla-bles this week and had skipped his therapist appointment. The Turks and Caicos trip was proving to have been more of an outlier in his emotional chart than the starting point of a new trend line. "These things take time."

"You've given him time. You'll be twenty-eight this year," Ellen said.

The number loomed there, jarringly close to thirty. Rae attempted to repurpose her napkin into a fan to cool down her neck, but the invention flopped under too-thick fabric.

"Do you really want someone so emotionally unstable to be dad to your kids?" Ellen went on, clearly victim to the biological clock craze as well.

"I'm not even sure if I want kids anymore," Rae said, mostly to punch back against Ellen's anti-Dustin tirade but also to try out how the declaration sounded aloud, so completely opposite what she'd been saying all along. A certain freedom came with the shock factor, but there was an undercurrent of unease.

Though Dustin said he wanted a family one day, Rae was becom-ing less sure that he actually did, or even that he still would when the time came. He didn't want much of anything these days, certainly not himself and sometimes hardly even her. She'd been telling herself that eventually he'd get better and be in the right emotional state to be a dad, but she was starting to wonder, only privately, if perhaps they'd never be completely free from the white-capped waves that swept up and over him out of the deep, blue sea.

As much as she liked picturing having a full house, the image lost its shine when she thought about Dustin giving up his own sleep for their kids, running himself ragged giving them piggyback rides in the pool when he was struggling to stay afloat himself. She was no longer certain that kids were in their future, but this didn't shake her conviction that they still had a future.

In the darker days following Turks and Caicos, Rae had begun to see that she might have gotten ahead of herself, that the paper-ring proposal might not have been much more than a sunny-day whim. But as much as she'd tried to get worked up about needing to know when or if a real proposal was coming, and as much as she'd tried to stress out about the dwindling days of her fertility, she'd found that she was becoming alarmingly unalarmed about her grand married-by-thirty plan going up in dust.

Something about Dustin telling her, in those lucid hours when the demons had been dormant, that he would be hers for as long as she'd have him, had fulfilled Rae's deepest cravings for lifelong commitment and emptied her of her shallowest obsessions to have it fit her analytical plan. It had given her the validation to begin writing herself out of stale narratives and writing herself into fresh ones.

Her new truth was that even if they didn't have kids, even if they never ended up getting married at all, she would still rather be with Dustin, just the two of them, than have all those other things with someone else. The hallowed end goals of being a wife and mom felt hollow if Dustin wasn't there beside her.

"What?" Ellen said, stunned by the bombshell Rae had so casually dropped. "Kids have always been a huge deal for you . . . it's why you came up with all that marriage math crap in the first place, remember? Three kids by thirty-five and all that?"

A baby two tables down shrieked in shrill colic, and Rae took it as a sign that maybe she'd been idealizing kids in her mind. Maybe they weren't all they were cracked up to be.

"Well, things change," Rae muttered, not in the mood to elaborate. "Compromise is a natural part of any relationship."

"You're not compromising, you're forfeiting," Ellen said, looking at her like she was looking at a stranger. Recovering, she appealed to Rae's logical side. "Don't you at least want the *option* to have kids?"

How many times had Rae heard the *Keep options open* argument? Get a job on Wall Street to keep options open for your career. Date lots of people to keep options open in case someone better comes along.

These days, Rae was less concerned with keeping doors open and more concerned with walking through the right one. Every time she stepped into the Lorimer Loft, it was the only place she wanted to be. Even on Dustin's worst days, she never felt like there was an opportunity cost associated with being with him.

Dustin was more important than anything and everything else she'd ever desired, even and perhaps especially that strict deal she'd made with herself to close the marriage deal before she was thirty. Dustin was, in fact, all she'd ever wanted. She just hadn't fully understood her wants until falling in love with him. Now that she *did* understand her deepest desires—to be understood in that abstract, ethereal kind of way that even the most elegant poetry couldn't portray—she was willing to give up just about anything so she wouldn't have to give up Dustin.

"There's more to life than getting married and having kids," Rae said. Whenever she'd heard other women say this, she'd assumed it was just a platitude to make them feel better about their own abysmal fates. But maybe there was some truth to it after all.

"I know that," Ellen said. "But you've always said you've wanted those things."

"Well, maybe I don't anymore," was all Rae said.

Ellen looked very concerned now, like someone else had inhabited her best friend's body. "Rae, look at how much you're changing for him," she said. "I know it's hard to be objective when you're so close to it, but won't you trust me on this?"

"I know I'm changing," Rae admitted, though she had an unshakable feeling that she didn't know exactly how much. She was so far down the rabbit hole that connected her soul and Dustin's that she seemed to have lost her ability to look at herself in the third person. "But that's what you do for love," she went on. "You change with the other person, and sometimes for them."

"Sure, you change to make each other better," Ellen said. "But he's not making you better, he's taking you for granted."

"No he's not," Rae said, though what she meant was, *So what?* Taking people for granted was love's most beautiful luxury—you could show them your splotched and ugly parts and they still stayed. That's what true commitment was.

"Better to get out now than in five years," Ellen said. "I know you've invested a lot already, but it's all sunk costs."

"Stop comparing love to stock markets," Rae snapped.

"Seriously? You're the one who's been commoditizing love with your Wall Street approach since the day I met you."

"Not anymore," Rae said, aware she was an aching contradiction but unaware how to pause the pain or the paradox. "Just stop."

"Fine," Ellen said, looking down to read, or at least stare at, the menu.

Rae evaluated her menu too, counting each word to try to calm herself down, but it just made her feel incompetent to see how these two laminated pages were more of a literary success than anything she'd ever produced.

She looked up at Ellen again, who appeared as tired as the parents next to them. "I appreciate your concern," Rae said. "But I'm not walking away."

Ellen looked like she had another argument on the tip of her tongue, but she swallowed it. "Let's order."

"Want to split the lemon and ricotta pancakes and the Goldie Lox omelet?" Rae asked.

"I'm vegan now, actually," Ellen said.

"*Vegan?*" Rae said, like Ellen had just announced she was joining a nudist colony in the Amazon. "Since when?"

"Aaron and I started last week. It's better for the environment."

Rae humphed, anticipating the blandness of vegan wedding cupcakes. "Well, we could share something else," she offered, scouring the menu for dairy-free, meat-free, flavor-free alternatives.

"I don't think I want to split today," Ellen said.

She didn't say it unkindly, but it felt like ninety-six splinters poking into Rae's heart. "No worries," Rae said. "I'll get both for myself." She'd take half back to Dustin to try to entice him out of bed. To Ellen, she explained, "I worked up an appetite staying upright on the lurchy train over here. Subway surfing really works the muscles, almost as much as penthouse stairs."

"You need to start treating yourself to more Ubers."

"In our thirties," Rae said, trying to give herself something to look forward to about getting older. "That'll be the Uber life stage."

"Then helicopters in our forties?"

"Private limos in our forties," Rae said. "Helicopters in our fifties."

"Makes sense. We wouldn't want to peak too early."

As their smiles nearly scrambled, the waiter arrived to take their separate orders.

CHAPTER THIRTY-FOUR
CUTTING LOSSES

"What're you watching?" Rae asked Dustin as she walked into the Lorimer Loft after work one nondescript weekday toward the end of summer. Her face and hair and suit and sneakers were sticky from her underground commute and that infamous, Manhattan-patented way that subway platforms locked hot air in grimy, rat-guarded vaults.

The stuffy, sticky feeling was pressing on Rae's mind, too, after hours of phone calls with clients who were trying to figure out whether the sudden drop in the S&P 500 meant they should delay their acquisitions. Rae's scripted advice—she felt a self-resentful pride at how she was now allowed to give advice, albeit scripted—had been that no, they should proceed as planned. Asset prices were deflated, making it a favorable time to buy.

Rae took off her sneakers without untying them and hung her blazer on the peg—officially and unequivocally *her peg* now.

She'd moved into the Lorimer Loft after the penthouse lease expired last month. Since she'd effectively been living here anyway, it didn't change much and was definitely the right economic decision and probably the right emotional decision as well.

Rae still didn't feel old enough to be living with a boyfriend, but she felt wise enough for it, so the factors netted out in her mind. Her mom was bearish on the decision ("He'll have no incentive to marry you!") and her grandpa had been kept out of the loop to minimize the chance of a heart attack. In the Scramblette group chat, Mina had unsurprisingly been the most supportive (OMG so exciting!!! BIG STEP).

Ellen had kept silent over text, and Sarah had asked, multiple times, But where will you go if you have a fight?

This risk wasn't relevant for Rae and Dustin. They often went to bed sad, but they never went to bed mad.

Tonight Dustin was slouched on the couch, still dressed in his work shirt, bottoms shed to boxers. A computer was propped open on the coffee table as a TV. He hadn't been in the mood to read lately, or even be read to. Netflix was the only thing he didn't nix.

"*Inevitable*," Dustin answered, as if it were highly uninformed of her to have to ask.

Explosions ricocheted out from the computer speakers. For the past week, Dustin had been watching and rewatching a documentary called *Inevitable* about how all of humanity and seven-eighths of earth's living organisms were going to be destroyed from nuclear warfare within six years.

He went long periods showing no interest in anything and then would latch on to something that Rae found pointless and peripheral—a lost sock, a rude work email, this documentary—as if it were central to his whole identity.

"Come watch it," Dustin said, without rearranging the sprawl of his legs to make room for her on the couch.

"I already watched it," Rae said as she walked into the living room, tights slippery on the hardwood floor. "What good is going to come from watching it again?"

"That's a very defeatist mentality."

Rae bit back a caustic rebuttal. "Can we just talk on the roof? Or watch a movie?"

"This is a movie."

"Another movie?"

"No," Dustin said. "This is important."

Rae joined him on the couch, twining her fingers through his with an *I love you* squeeze. Dustin didn't squeeze back. The colorful abstract art piece she'd bought was still hanging on the opposite wall—watching or mocking, Rae couldn't decide.

Against a canned bombing soundtrack, the man on the screen was explaining how many times more powerful today's nuclear weapons could be—down to the hundredths decimal place—than the ones used in World War II.

Rae felt a crunching feeling, worse than from punching highly specific, highly inaccurate numbers into spreadsheets. She looked down at Dustin's hand, limply joined to hers, and flipped it over to draw reassuring circles across volatile palm lines.

The cuff of his sleeve was unbuttoned, the bottom half of his forearm free from binding. On his wrist lay a thin, fresh scar, the length of an indent on a page and the width of a tea bag string. Beside it was a shorter, fainter replica. Together they formed an inverted V, the faded scar sloped sharply up, the bright one sharply down.

Rae's breath froze as everything else burned. She held Dustin's wrist like she might grip a water bottle, resting her thumb next to, but not on top of, the red marks.

In uneven increments, her mind skipped ahead, past the decision on whether he'd cut himself on purpose, past the punch of her own guilt for pressing away the warning signs, past the analysis of whether he'd used a razor blade or a knife, past the timeline of when it had happened—last night, when she was working late, or if the fainter scar had been there weeks already—past the consideration of whether he had other cuts on his body right at this moment.

Her mind rattled past, but not through, those considerations and lurched to a stop straight in front of the question of how likely it was that this would happen again and that the scars would grow in dimension—the probability that next time she wouldn't find Dustin alert on the couch but passed out in a puddle of his own blood.

She finally spoke, with faux composure. "What're these?"

"What're what?" Dustin asked, keeping his eyes on the screen.

"These," Rae said, avoiding calling the scars by name. "On your wrist."

"Oh," Dustin said, still transfixed on the documentary. "One of the guys at work brought his dog in, and it went crazy on the trading floor. Bit my arm. But I have a tetanus shot, I'm fine."

He said it so smoothly, as if he'd explained it several times before, or at least practiced explaining it.

Rae reached over to the coffee table and closed the computer, silencing the bald man's warning midsentence.

"What're you doing?" Dustin asked.

"Dustin," she whispered. "Please look at me."

Slowly, as if the movement required fighting a lateral type of gravity, he turned his face toward her. His eyes were as clenched as his jaw.

She held his hand very tightly, or perhaps extremely loosely. Her sense of perspective had gone, making way for more important things. "Did you mean to do it?"

"It was the dog. I told you."

Her heart crumpled in on itself. "Dustin. Why did you cut yourself?"

He sighed, like he was too tired to keep up the lie. "I just wanted to see if it made me feel better."

Ellen had told her to cut her losses, but here was Dustin, physically cutting his. For so many months now, she'd been looking at every bright side, bright spot, and bright sliver, trying to tell herself that Dustin was improving and that he'd beat the depression soon. But now, reading the story written in the dark-red ink of his own blood, she was forced to see everything she'd tried to close her eyes to—how Dustin wasn't any better now than he'd been two and a half years ago when she'd started trying to be his friend, how the upward path she'd attempted to steer him toward had turned out to be nothing but an upside-down roller coaster ride, how she'd reached a dead end on how to help him but had kept going anyway, banging her own head against his steely walls in an attempt to break through, but the only break had been in her own bones.

She'd justified so much in the name of love. But if she overlooked his cutting too, she'd be complicit in his pain, an ally to his illness.

Rae stood up from the couch. "Come on," she said. "We're going to the hospital."

"What's a hospital going to do?" His tone was scornful, but a faraway part sounded curious too.

"I don't know. But we need to get help."

"You're overreacting. It's hardly even a scratch."

"They're cuts," Rae said, gulping on the plural. "You cut yourself."

"I told you I was broken. You knew what you were signing up for."

The words sliced her with the blade she pictured Dustin pressing into his wrist. She searched his face and tried to find the man she loved more than anyone in the world. All her imagination still left her short.

Dustin didn't budge.

"I'm calling an Uber." Her voice sounded muffled, like she was talking into a coffee mug. She took out her phone and ordered a car to the Mount Sinai Emergency Room in the East Village, just on the other side of the Williamsburg Bridge.

"Let's get up," Rae said, though she was already standing.

"No."

"Please. Meet me halfway."

"I don't like halves."

There was a poem in there somewhere, too dark to spot.

Her phone buzzed, announcing the Uber was arriving. If she didn't leave now, she'd have to pay the $5 cancellation fee. It sounded small, but the metaphor felt large—the price she'd pay to cancel on this car waiting to take them to get help.

The thought of leaving was impossible, but she realized she'd already lost him. Whether she was directly beside him or many miles away, she'd miss Dustin just the same.

She tried to picture their wedding day, her favorite image to seek shelter in when things got bad. It felt like a memory now from all the times she'd conjured it up to help her keep hope. But this time the vision was so smoky that she couldn't discern Dustin and she couldn't even discern herself.

It took that image of her own invisibility for her to start to see herself again.

Ellen's voice echoed in her head, only now the words sounded almost like her own thoughts. She hadn't just changed for Dustin; she'd bent herself in every direction, rearranging her present to fit the version she'd hoped would heal him—neglecting her friendships, her work, her own health. But when that hadn't worked, she'd gone two steps further, shifting around all her future plans too, telling herself she didn't care about getting married or even having kids, all so she could continue to defend her decision to stay.

But now, all the bending was finally about to break her, if it hadn't broken her already. It was hard to tell, but she knew it was time to stop making excuses for Dustin. She couldn't help him until he wanted to be helped, and she had to respect herself enough not to let him take her down with him.

She was finally strong enough, or perhaps just exhausted enough, to do what she had to do.

Jamming her feet into her still-tied sneakers, she walked back to the couch once more. "Come with me?"

Dustin looked like he might say yes. He looked like he might apologize. He looked like he might even thank her for helping save him from himself.

"I'm staying," he said instead, tone implying she was the one who was choosing to go.

But this wasn't walking away. This was limping toward safety. Maybe that was a Wall Street–like loophole to lessen the guilt, or maybe it was the honest distinction that would keep her upright.

She took two handfuls of messy curly hair and kissed the top of his head. "I'll always love you," she said, despising the future tense, the *always*. The best way to always love someone was to never actually use the word *always*. Ordinary *I love you*s just stacked into an elegant forever, one present-tense, adverb-free line at a time.

Dustin opened the computer back up and resumed the documentary.

Walking mechanically around the apartment, Rae collected only what seemed imperative—the Stall Street Journal, her work computer and charger, the yoga mat she hadn't used in months, the skillet she'd contributed from the penthouse.

Then, leaving her toothbrush in the bathroom, leaving her blazer on the peg, leaving Phyllis and the sunflowers in the window, leaving her key on the counter, leaving Dustin lying on the couch listening to the sound of a man's voice warning that it would take only thirty-nine minutes and twenty-two seconds for a North Korean nuclear missile to reach New York, Rae left the Lorimer Loft, let the door close behind her, and walked alone to the stairs, out of time to wait for the elevator.

It wasn't until later, at Ellen and Aaron's apartment, that she'd look in the mirror and see how much of herself she'd left behind too, all the parts that had ever felt whole, as indivisible from Dustin as he was from depression.

PART 3

775 DAYS TO GO

CHAPTER THIRTY-FIVE
RECOUPING LOSSES

"This one's a gorgeous, fully furnished studio, below market price," the landlord told Rae as he showed her a dorm room–sized apartment on the corner of Wall Street and William. "A real steal."

It was a couple weeks after the breakup, and Rae was looking for somewhere to live so she wouldn't have to keep crashing on Ellen and Aaron's couch. It was the first apartment she'd toured, on the twelfth floor of an elevator building. The apartment's only window faced the sleek glass of Rae's office.

The separation Rae had once insisted on keeping between where she worked and where she slept now seemed like little more than an impractical ideal. It wasn't like she was ever able to unplug anyway, and living next door would prevent the subway from snatching more hours from her life than it already had.

"Fully furnished" in this case consisted of a double bed, a desk that doubled as the kitchen table, and an armchair barely more comfortable than Rae's office chair.

Rae could now afford something nicer than this three-hundred-square-foot sliver, but she'd made herself calculate what else she could put that money toward—her grandpa's health care bills, a Caribbean cruise for her mom and Mr. Non-Right, her 401k. She didn't like thinking about her Poet's Fund anymore—it just reinforced the feeling that she was deluding herself into thinking she'd ever have the guts to trade in a corporate life for a creative one.

And what did she need the extra space for? It wasn't like she'd be hosting the Scramblettes or bringing guys back here. She tried to tell herself that, once more time had gone by, once her heart had healed or at least once the fresh bleeding had stopped, she'd be open to meeting someone new, but it was impossible to picture that now, maybe because her imagination had quit working, or maybe because it was just too farfetched a fantasy. This apartment didn't have to be home, just a place for her to lie low in while recouping her emotional losses.

"And look at this *dishwasher*," the landlord went on, as if pointing out a private swimming pool. "Very unusual amenities for something at this price."

The discounted price was because this was a lease takeover, likely from a brave, lost soul who'd bailed on Wall Street after one too many all-nighters. Rae preferred the six-month commitment to the standard twelve months, as it fit with her timeline of working hard through year-end, getting promoted, and then quitting after January bonuses to move back to Indiana.

She'd been tempted to return to the Midwest right after the Dustin Divestment, as she mentally called the breakup, but if she moved now, she'd be running away. If she moved in six months, she'd be walking *toward*.

She hadn't heard from Dustin since the breakup, not that she'd expected to. As the Uber had brought her back across the Williamsburg Bridge, she'd left a voice mail for Dustin's mom, whose number she had from exchanging the occasional photo. Rae knew the message would be enough for his mom to intervene, just as she knew it would be enough for Dustin to never speak to her again.

She hadn't deleted or blocked his number or even been tempted to, so numb was she with closure. His birthday had come and gone without a single twitch to text him. She ached to know how he was doing, but it was the type of ache that inhibited action. It seemed she'd finally given up on trying to crack open cracked doors.

Even my tears are too stuck to flow, was the Bellini line that resonated most right now, not that she was trying to think about Bellini at all.

"And did you see the tub?" the landlord asked. "Jacuzzi sized!"

Rae walked the one and a half steps into the bathroom. The tub was as shallow as a sink, and she'd have to bend her short legs to fit. Kindly, she stayed quiet.

She hadn't been using her voice much lately, grinding at work to block out the hurt and returning to Ellen and Aaron's after they'd gone to bed so she felt like less of a bad houseguest for not wanting to chat.

"It's available for immediate move-in," the landlord said, making it sound like a fantastic deal for Rae rather than his own money going down the drain every night it went empty.

Rae scanned the place once more, quickly so her eyes wouldn't have to linger. "I'll take it."

She recalled the first apartment she'd rented after college, how she and her traitorous ex-roommate had looked at twenty-seven spots, holding out for the one. Now she was ready to sign at the first option. She tried not to extrapolate it as a symbol of how she was on track to settle in life and love.

"I haven't even shown you the roof!" the landlord said, after shoving the fat lease application into her hand. "Even more impressive than the tub."

"That's all right," Rae said, anticipating how cluttered Manhattan would appear from the Financial District's skyscraper vantage point compared to Williamsburg's river-rimmed panoramic. "I don't need to see the roof."

*　　*　　*

249

"Whatcha working on?" Rae's new colleague asked, spying on her from the desk next to hers.

It was a weekday at the end of September, and TB's old seat had finally been filled by a bland white man, whom Rae thought of as her co-wannabe boss.

Co-wannabe had been assigned to a window seat but decided it had too much of a glare so had moved himself to this desk instead, cluttering up the space with Nerf footballs and trophies called "tombstones" to commemorate deals they'd worked on. The men in the office collected and compared tombstones with *Did you know I was varsity captain in high school?* energy.

"I'm doing a WAAC sensitivity analysis for a DCF," Rae answered, fingers darting across the keyboard in a winless race.

"Damn," Co-wannabe said, as he set about rearranging his tombstones from a V formation to a horseshoe. "Never seen a girl crunch numbers like that before."

Rae shot him a scowl, but Co-wannabe was too busy lusting over his trophies. "I have more tombstones than you, though," he said.

It wasn't true. Rae had counted as he'd lined them up his first day. She just kept most of hers in her bottom drawer, so her peripheral vision wouldn't snag on them and start associating them with success.

"Congratulations," she deadpanned, then stood up to seek refuge in her banker bunker.

Her stall was occupied, and laughter leaked from under the gap in the door—that attempted muffling sound that only doubled the output.

It must be the junior analyst Kelly, catching up on a group text with friends, venting about wannabe bosses or sharing screenshots of dating app prospects for collective analysis.

Rae's prick of annoyance directed at Kelly was trailed by another prick, directed at herself, for being one of those people who was annoyed by the sound of joy.

Locking herself two doors down, Rae took out the Stall Street Journal from her blazer pocket. She'd decided to keep the journal—a visible symbol of emotional growth—to show that she no longer needed to discard the past in dramatic tantrums.

She'd hoped a creative surge might be the breakup's silver lining, but the numbness had left her infuriatingly unproductive, refusing to let pain be harvested for poetic profits. Now she tried again to summon a creative phrase to describe heartbreak, but the page remained blank and smug.

Kelly's toilet flushed, followed by another giggle that haunted Rae like her own early-twenties ghost.

Closing her eyes, she tried to take a nap, but she wasn't tired. Her body had finally figured out how to function normally on reduced rest. She wondered if this might imply that love, like sleep, was something you could train yourself not to need.

* * *

"Cell C43 should link to B256, not 255," Rae said, standing over Kelly's desk as she reviewed a full-screen Excel model Kelly had put together for a deal they were working on.

The company was an HR software platform, and Rae was having Kelly prepare a pitch book to show why the company should acquire a project management business to diversify its products—and more importantly, bring in more revenue. Having only received the financial statements earlier today, they were scrambling for a client meeting tomorrow.

They were the only two left in the office at ten P.M. on an October Tuesday, which happened to be Rae's twenty-eighth birthday. No one at the office knew, and Rae hadn't wanted them to. She didn't need more reasons to analyze why she felt even more lost at twenty-eight than she had at twenty-five, or admit that she didn't have any plans to celebrate other than taking a bubble bath in her small but spotless tub across the street.

Ellen had abruptly flown back to be with her family in Washington, DC, over the weekend after her dad had sustained a minor heart attack. He was recovering, but it had deeply shaken Ellen, and Rae too.

When Rae's dad had texted her happy birthday today—before noon—Rae had included *I love you, Dad!* in her response and even asked when he was planning to be in New York next. He hadn't replied yet, but Rae let herself acknowledge how much she wanted him to.

Her dad had iced her out for a bit after she hadn't been able to connect him with anyone at her bank after all because it was a perceived conflict of interest. She was glad he'd reappeared.

With Ellen's dad's health scare, Rae had started picturing her own dad's funeral and the speech she'd give, if she was asked to give a speech at all. The words were soft and nostalgic, and she didn't want to wait until he was gone to share them.

"Sorry about that," Kelly said, relinking the formula in the massive grid.

Rae brought her attention back to the computer screen in front of them. "Save 'sorry' for when you knock over someone's coffee," she said, recalling how often she used to apologize to her wannabe bosses, and how none of the guys ever had. "For work stuff, just say, 'Thanks for explaining' or 'I'll incorporate that going forward.'"

"I'll incorporate that going forward," Kelly said, nodding with a sternness that didn't come naturally.

Rae felt a punch of remorse as she realized she was telling this girl to harden herself, but the best way—the only way—to survive Wall Street with your soul intact was by playing a rigid character, the armor so thick that none of the criticism or shallow values corrupted the core. That's how Rae had done it, though increasingly she wondered how much had seeped through the shell. The lines weren't as clear as they'd once been.

The motion-sensitive overhead lights turned off. The office was dark except for the false glow of the computers and the skyline lights right outside the window—worlds away.

Rae waved her hands until the bulbs lurched alert, then continued coaching Kelly. "And for the EBITDA calculation in row thirty-two, add back the marketing costs in row eighty-four."

"But those are recurring expenses, right?" Kelly asked, with timid courage. "So wouldn't that overstate the available cash flow?"

"Technically, yes," Rae said. "But that's how they want us to show it."

Kelly nodded with the *I'm just the cog who needs to do what she's told* look Rae knew too well. "Can I ask you something?" Kelly asked.

"I know, the run-rate revenue calculation seems like an exaggeration too," Rae said. "But that's just industry standard for software companies."

"It's not about this," Kelly said. "It's . . ." She paused, adjusting her messy bun. In the months Kelly had been here, her hairstyle had devolved from sleek curls to messy buns. Rae had found her feelings toward Kelly become more friendly once her hair became as flyaway filled as her own.

"How do you have time to date?" Kelly asked. Her face pinched as she said it, like it went against all the things she'd heard about how women shouldn't bring up their personal lives at work.

"I don't." Hearing how the syllables slapped the air, Rae added, "I had a boyfriend for a while. But not now."

"Did you break up because your hours were so bad?"

"No," Rae said, though she'd wondered many times if they'd still be together if she'd had more time to devote to him, to physically be there on his bad days. "Other reasons."

"Oh." Kelly stared back at the grid on the screen.

"Are you dating someone?" Rae guessed.

Kelly nodded glumly. "But it's wrong to prioritize a relationship over a job."

"Not necessarily," Rae said, recalling Ellen's insight that it was easier to find a good job than a good man. "Don't get so lost in the weeds of work that you miss out on the trees of life."

Kelly jotted down the advice in her notebook, and it gave Rae a melancholy sense of accomplishment.

"It's my birthday today," Rae heard herself announce.

Kelly's eyes widened with that look that Rae saw around here only when people learned they'd just beaten out a competitor for a high-profile deal. "Why're you still at the office?"

"I'm not a big birthday person," Rae said, and it didn't even feel like lying. "What's your boyfriend up to tonight?"

"He cooked omelets for us. And toast!" Proudly, Kelly showed Rae a photo on her phone of scrambled eggs and charred bread, as if presenting a Michelin-star meal.

Rae smiled and flipped her tone. "Go eat with him. I'll finish the pitch book."

"No," Kelly said. "I'm more junior than you, so I stay later than you. It's the hierarchy."

"Fuck the hierarchy. And fuck the patriarchy."

Kelly blinked, then beamed.

"Get out of here," Rae said. "Stale eggs are gross. Believe me, I know."

Color surged back into Kelly's face. "You're the coolest boss ever."

"I'm not technically your boss," Rae said, though she sponged up the praise and hoped Kelly might share it with the girls in her group chat.

On her way out, Kelly stopped by Rae's desk with a half-eaten pack of chocolate-covered espresso beans, adorned with a yellow sticky note that said *HAPPY BIRTHDAY!!!*

Kelly skip-sprinted out of the office, and Rae was alone on her twenty-eighth birthday in a graveyard of tombstone trophies.

CHAPTER THIRTY-SIX

STAGNATION

"Stagnation. My life is in stagnation," Rae told Ellen on a Thursday night in mid-November, in Rae's apartment, which was tidy only because it was so bare. No dishes in the sink, no books on the desk, no art on the walls. "No growth."

She was sprawled on her bed, dressed only in a black camisole and black tights, having yanked off her stiff work dress the moment she'd gotten home. Staring up at the ceiling, she clutched a wine bottle to her chest.

Ellen was on the armchair, cross-legged in yoga clothes as she sipped water. She'd recently introduced a no-drinking-before-Friday rule for her and Aaron.

Rae was drunk enough not to scold herself for gulping straight from the bottle or using economic jargon to describe her life—both habits she'd thought she'd shed.

"You're definitely growing," Ellen declared. "Just at a *slightly* lower growth rate in your career than you projected."

Rae grunted her best contrarian grunt.

"And anyway," Ellen went on, "stagnation is better than a recession."

"False," Rae said. "At least after a crash you know there's going to be a bounce back up. Stagnation's a perpetual standstill."

All notions of *forward* and *upward* had been exposed as a cruel hoax earlier today when she'd received her performance review at work.

She'd been ranked "outstanding" in every category, but when she'd asked about her career trajectory (she was too timid to use the word *promotion*), her boss had told her there weren't enough slots for her to be promoted this year due to factors outside his control, but that if she continued to demonstrate meaningful value-add to the firm, it would be on the table next year.

She'd asked if Co-wannabe, who'd been there only a few months, was getting promoted, and her boss's cagey response had told Rae all she needed to know.

When Rae had pressed for areas for improvement, her boss had said, "A little more presence, maybe—you know, commanding a room with real authority."

Afterward, Rae had locked herself in her toilet stall, flinging irate texts at Ellen, and this evening Ellen had scurried over to talk it out in person.

"They want presence?" Rae growled. "I'll give them *presence*." She stood up on her mattress, stumbling to keep from falling over, and held the half-empty wine bottle as a microphone.

"Attention, ladies and gentlemen," she belted to the wall, not caring if her neighbors heard. None of them knew her name or even made eye contact in the elevator. "I need you all to put your head up your butts. Even farther down—no half-assing it! Now hold your breath and close your eyes. Just like that! Good work, everyone! Now just keep wasting your whole fucking lives like this."

Ellen stood up and took the wine bottle away as Rae collapsed onto her comforter with a defeated sense of victory.

"It's sexist bullshit," Ellen said. "You've worked so hard for this."

"It's not about how hard I've worked," Rae said, though it partly was. "It's that I objectively deserved it. I got a top fucking performance review."

"You'd have gotten the promotion if you were a man," Ellen said.

A car horn from the street below punctuated the truth of the sentence.

"Fuck my boss," Rae said.

She knew it wasn't his decision—it was his boss's boss's boss's decision—but she also would bet her bonus that her boss had fought for Co-wannabe, who'd been in his same college fraternity, and not for her.

"And fuck Dustin," Rae said, angry at him for the first time since the breakup—a sudden but overdue surge. "I was a fucking angel to him."

"A fucking angel," Ellen repeated, nodding solemnly.

"I would've done anything for him."

"You *did* do anything for him," Ellen said. "You gave him so many chances."

"Like, I get it, he was hurting," Rae said, syllables slurring into one another, craving connection. "But guess what? I was hurting too."

She wondered if she'd caught depression from Dustin through emotional contagion. Or maybe she'd always had it in her, the dark but necessary flip side of her own depth, but she hadn't felt entitled to acknowledge it, given its relative mildness. Or maybe she wasn't depressed at all, she was just being overdramatic from a bad day at work and too much wine and it would look better in the morning.

"It'll look better in the morning," Ellen said.

"No it won't," Rae said.

She was heading back to Indiana for Thanksgiving next week and had hoped a promotion would cancel out the lack of a proposal. It was one thing for her high school classmates to all be married or engaged, but with Ellen now in that category too, Rae felt the smack of something she wanted to call betrayal but couldn't.

"I'm going back on the dating apps," Rae announced. It felt very firmly like the only logical next step. "I've got under two years to lock in a husband." She hadn't thought much about the marriage deal since she and Dustin had ended. It was too impossible to picture going on a single date with someone else, let alone spending her whole life with them. After Dustin, settling down could only mean settling. She'd told herself that she didn't care about getting married or having kids anymore, that she'd dumped her marriage and motherhood goals into some Brooklyn dumpster, but here it was, her most primal desires—or at least fears—exposed in this drunk speech.

Her window to get her life back on track was closing. She turned thirty in just under seven hundred days. The clock was ticking, counting down to her irrelevance and undesirability as a woman, and she had to act fast.

She downloaded a dating app right there—the app the guys at work talked about as having the highest return on investment—and even paid forty-three dollars for the premium version to get unlimited daily swipes.

"Do you really think this will make you feel better?" Ellen asked softly.

"Yes," Rae said, hurriedly filtering photos as she built her profile. "I do."

She began swiping, one profile every 0.75 seconds—double her pace from two years ago. It was a perverse kind of satisfaction, how she'd at least improved at something.

Within six minutes, she already had twenty-two matches, boosting her ego a few percentage points.

Two of her matches messaged her.

Heyy! How's it goin?

Yo how's ur week been

"What uncreative openers," Rae said. She reviewed their profiles again, finding glaring red flags—the peace sign, the backwards hat, the dead fish in hand. These were the same Peter Pans who'd been in the love market back when she'd tried out online dating after her quarter-century crisis.

While there was a doomed-but-amusing feeling to sifting through New York's weasel-infested dating pool in her midtwenties, in her late twenties it just felt doomed and depressing, a loop that never ended except in the wrong ways.

She deleted the app, resenting how she could've bought an entrée with that money instead, or half a massage. She'd have to meet someone in real life instead, linger in the ice cream aisle of the grocery store until a guy without a wedding ring walked by or go to one of those speed-dating events that were synonymous with desperation. The thoughts made her feel like she was about to throw up.

Taking a swig of Ellen's water, Rae slurred, "I'm sorry I never listened to you. About Dustin."

"It's okay," Ellen said. "Love makes people crazy."

Rather than resenting this mantra, Rae found it newly inspirational. Leaping up, she rummaged through her work bag and took out the Stall Street Journal, which, after the nonpromotion, she'd decided she would drop down the garbage chute. The chute now felt like a very cheap form of disposal compared to a fire.

Walking the three short steps into the corner kitchen, she lit one of the burners on the gas stove.

"Rae—" Ellen warned.

"I won't set off the fire alarm." Holding out the journal's opening page, she willed the thick paper to catch fire.

Ellen appeared beside her, turning off the burner.

The flame wasn't big enough to require them to blow it out. It curled up into itself, but not before singeing Dustin's inscription.

It wasn't the sensational combustion Rae would've liked, but it achieved its symbolic effect. She didn't have it in her heart to burn the whole journal. Not that she was sure she had much left in her heart anymore.

"Fuck them," she said, and it was more than just Dustin and her boss now. It was her dad, too, for ghosting her after the long, heartfelt email she'd had the guts to send him a few weeks ago, expressing how she wanted to work on their relationship. And the *Fuck you* was also for her cheating college boyfriend and those dating app frat bros who'd never texted her back, and all the subway man-sprawlers, and all the pressure to conform to antiquated gender norms, and all the myths or nonmyths that single women over thirty are societal deadweight, and the whole implicitly anti-women world.

Hurling the journal under her bed, she spread out on the armchair, head on Ellen's lap, feet draped on the armrest. She noticed a fresh run in her tights, or maybe it was an old one.

Ellen stroked her hair, tucking sections behind her ear in even increments.

Rae's anger deflated, like a balloon popped on a windy rooftop. She was just tired. So tired.

"Ellen?" she mumbled.

"Rae-bae?"

"Do you think it'll ever happen?"

The *it* was all encompassing—the *it* of Rae ever falling in love again and getting married, the *it* of rebuilding something real with her dad, the *it* of Dustin recovering, the *it* of having a career that didn't crush her.

"Of course it will," Ellen said. "I feel it right here." She pointed to her gut.

"That probably just means you're hungry," Rae grumbled, but it made her feel better anyway.

CHAPTER THIRTY-SEVEN
CIRCLING BACK

"Has it really been a whole year since the Scramblettes were last together?" Ellen asked Rae, Mina, and Sarah one night a few days before Christmas.

They were sitting around Ellen and Aaron's circular kitchen table in matching bamboo chairs, eating vegan Santa Claus omelets (bean-based egg replacements stuffed fat with veggies and cashew cheese), cooked by Aaron, who was now doing the dishes and pretending not to listen as the Scramblettes pretended having a guy around didn't disrupt the dynamic.

Rae had been scheduled to fly back to Indiana today, but she was on a deal that was closing December 23, so her departure date had been pushed back to Christmas Eve.

She'd had no excuse, then, not to attend the Scramblette reunion, so here she sat, still in her suit, with her old Santa hat draped on her lap like a napkin. She'd planned on wearing it, but none of the others were dressed in theme, and it felt like a metaphor for forcing something on that no longer fit.

"Feels like it's only been three weeks," Mina said, scooping faux eggs with one hand and swiping dating app profiles on her phone with the other. She was fresh off another surge-then-crash relationship.

"I think it feels like three *years*," Sarah said, back from Austin for winter break with short hair and an extra shot of confidence. "Business school is just so busy. A classmate invites you on their yacht in Croatia, and you can't really say no, since it's a networking opportunity. So hard to balance with studying."

"I can only imagine," Rae said, only half trying to keep her eyes from rolling out of their sockets.

"Sounds exhausting," Ellen agreed, nudging Rae's foot under the table in a symbolic chortle.

"Not as exhausting as this summer will be," Sarah said, missing the sarcasm. "During my venture capital internship."

"I thought you didn't want to go back into finance," Rae said. What she thought, but didn't add, was, *Wasn't that the whole point of business school? To pivot careers?*

"Venture cap is so much different than investment banking," Sarah said. "You can't even compare the two."

Deeper than Rae's resentment was a sad kind of pity. Sarah, too, was stuck on the hamster wheel that was the financial industry. Even those who tried to leave ultimately sprinted back into the cage of their own volition, addicted to life's riches and indifferent to its richness.

Rae poked her omelet with her fork until it more closely resembled a scramblette. "Got it," she said.

"How about you?" Sarah asked. "Still plotting your Wall Street escape plan?"

"No," Rae lied. "I'm pretty happy with how things are going."

"Rae's crushing it," Ellen said. "Putting all the guys in their place." Ellen had been more supportive of, or at least more sympathetic to, Rae's masochistic attachment to Wall Street after she'd been passed up for the promotion.

"How's the wedding planning going?" Mina asked Ellen without looking up from her phone.

"The planning is pretty much done," Ellen said. "Just finalizing the cupcake lineup." She grinned at Rae.

"I'm iterating based on learnings from the beta batches," Rae said. She'd been filling her Saturdays testing recipes, having decided to make them all from scratch rather than outsource to a bakery.

"It's too bad the wedding is in June," Mina lamented. "Since it's in DC. Because I'll be out in San Diego by then, so I'll have to fly all the way back."

Rae didn't even try to disguise her eye roll at Mina's self-centered approach to Ellen's big day.

"You're not actually moving to San Diego, are you?" Sarah asked.

"Of course I am," Mina said. "I'm interviewing for jobs, and I've already changed my dating app geography settings. Hot surfer guys are the SoCal equivalent of New York's boring finance bros. Massive upgrade."

She tilted her phone toward them so they could see her pipeline of long-haired, bare-chested, surfboard-holding prospects.

"What happens when these guys find out you actually live in New York?" Sarah asked.

"We'll FaceTime for our first few dates, obviously," Mina said. "Then once I know he's my true love, I'll move out there."

"Failproof," Ellen deadpanned.

"Rae, what's the Dustin update?" Sarah asked.

Ellen had filled Sarah and Mina in, separately, after the breakup so Rae hadn't had to write it in the group text or endure the *You're better off without him!* clichés that would have ensued.

"No update," Rae said, hating how truncated the truth sounded—and felt. "We don't keep in touch."

"I'm sure he'll circle back at some point," Mina said, as if this were a helpful thing to say.

Rae's phone rang from her lap, underneath the Santa hat.

Her first thought was that the universe had heard Mina and it was Dustin. But another unexpected name appeared on her screen—Dad.

As she rushed into the bathroom, Rae's stomach twisted at the prospect he might be calling from the hospital.

"Dad?" she said, tongue tapping the roof of her mouth to the unfamiliar syllable. "Everything okay?"

"Hey there, kiddo," he said, and Rae relaxed at his upbeat tone. "Just realized we haven't caught up in a while."

There was a lot Rae could pick apart in his words, but she found herself wanting to pick things up off the ground instead. "Guess we haven't," she said. "What's new?"

She regretted the question instantly, how childish it sounded, but he started talking about the outdoor patio they'd put in, big enough to fit two grills and a fire pit, and how he'd joined a new golf course, top ten in the state of Florida. "We'll have to play there together sometime," he said.

"Sure," Rae said vaguely, trying not to race ahead and think about who from work she could ask for golf lessons, trying to remind herself that the trip, of course, would never happen.

"I'm sorry I never replied to that email of yours," he said, as if Rae had sent him a news article rather than ten paragraphs of bleeding prose pouring forth her deepest hopes that they might grow closer again. "Just been so busy with work recently and helping the twins on their college applications."

Rae felt a stab in her stomach, more sad than sharp. It didn't seem fair that these random girls got her dad when he hadn't been around to help Rae with her college applications. But it wasn't about what was fair, she reminded herself. It was about finding a way to receive and appreciate what her dad was able to give rather than judging him against her old and idealistic expectations of what a father should be. And here he was, giving an apology. She couldn't remember the last time she'd heard him say he was sorry for something, however small it was. "No worries," she said, trying to keep from putting him on the defense.

"I'm glad you're finally starting to realize your old man's not so evil after all," her dad went on, seeming to interpret this as the convenient punch line of her letter. "Karen and I would be happy to have you out here sometime."

Many conflicting emotions stretched and contorted within Rae. He was making her feel like she'd done something wrong, but maybe the only way to make things right was to let him be right. "Okay," Rae said. "A trip down there could be nice." She doubted it would actually happen. It was probably just an empty offer so her dad could check the box of his fatherly duties for the day and head to the golf course guilt-free.

"Martin Luther King Day weekend?" her dad asked. "Markets are closed that Monday, so you get the day off, right?"

"That could work," Rae said. *Low expectations, high standards,* she recited, that old dating mantra that doubled for deadweight dads.

"Great. I already booked your ticket. Just didn't want you to come if you didn't want to."

Something leapt inside Rae, something she hadn't even realized still had a way, or will, to get off the ground. She wanted to take this olive branch and rock it against her chest to the bedtime lullabies her dad used to sing to her when she was little.

"Just forwarded you the itinerary," her dad said. "Karen's already planning some activities."

Rae wanted to ask if they could have some one-on-one time, just her and her dad, but she didn't want him to accuse her of being immature and retract the offer altogether. She could take the deal as presented to her, or decline. She had no bargaining power for negotiation.

After saying good-bye—*I love you*s and all—she soaked her hands with scalding water and rejoined the Scramblettes at the table.

"Who was that?" Mina asked.

"My dad."

"You guys talk now?" Sarah asked.

"Sometimes," Rae said, feeling Ellen looking at her curiously.

"Told you time heals all wounds," Mina said, though she never had. "Now let's get some holiday karaoke going."

"I have to get back to FaceTime the girlfriend," Sarah said. She'd fallen for a business school classmate and had already called dibs on the next wedding after Ellen's.

"I have to pack," Rae added.

"Come on," Ellen said. "One song."

Ellen put on "Jingle Bell Rock," and in the warmth of the reliable radiator, with snow falling outside the curtained windows, the four of them passed around the wine bottle microphone, singing into it one at a time rather than huddling close enough to share it like they used to.

CHAPTER THIRTY-EIGHT
EMOTIONAL BANKRUPTCY

"You're a hundred times more fun with a couple drinks in you," Co-wannabe told Rae as they danced on the crescent-shaped couch of 1 Oak, an exclusive West Chelsea club that was known for turning nearly everyone away at the door except A-list celebrities and half-clothed, full-cleavage girls. The partner in Rae's group had bought their way in with a several-thousand-dollar cover charge along with bottle service at a private table to celebrate Bonus Day after a year of record-high fee income. It was a Thursday night in late January.

Sometime after midnight, inebriated bodies had swarmed the narrow dance floor, swaying to the blare of electronic tunes being spun by the DJ, a gold-chain-dripping guy whose name everyone seemed to know except Rae. The space was dark except for circular light beams on the ceiling that looked like halos, almost like angels had grown bored in heaven and decided to crash a party in hell for a night. Psychedelic patterns on the black-and-white floor were making Rae dizzy, or maybe that was just the $600 prosecco.

She'd never been to 1 Oak before, but the energy was nearly identical to that of the other clubs in the city that she'd gone to back in her college days. She'd forgotten just how sweaty and oppressive the scene was, packed above capacity with potbellied men in Italian-wool suits and ties and underage girls in leather miniskirts and crop tops. Her coworkers were draped over these bare-legged prospects, pouring drink after drink as the girls flirted in the usual opportunistic way.

"I'm always fun," Rae shouted back to Co-wannabe, propelled by a desire to be a past self tonight—or maybe just a different self altogether. "You're just too busy polishing your tombstones to notice."

"Nineteen and counting," Co-wannabe whooped.

Someone handed them tequila shots, and Rae drank hers in one determined gulp, the first shot she'd had in years. Co-wannabe offered her a lime, but Rae declined, craving the burn, how it cut through the numbness of the last five months.

Rae saw Kelly push her way toward the exit, dodging a drunk man who'd been getting too close. She knew she should go make sure Kelly was okay but stayed exactly where she was.

"Rae?" Co-wannabe shouted.

"Twenty-three," Rae shouted back, "is how many tombstones I have in total."

"That's not what I was asking," he said, though he looked even more impressed than when she'd downed tequila without a chaser. "How do you know if you're ready to get married?" He asked it as if soliciting advice on signing a deal with a new client.

"I'm not exactly the industry expert on marriage," she said, wagging her bare ring finger.

"My girlfriend doesn't know what EBITDA stands for," Co-wannabe said. "How the hell are we supposed to spend the rest of our lives together if she doesn't understand half of what I'm saying?"

Rae felt very bonded to Co-wannabe in this moment, the person on the planet she far and away spent the largest proportion of her life with.

"It's less about whether she knows the acronyms," Rae advised, "and more about if she's interested in learning the concepts behind them."

"She's not," Co-wannabe sulked. "She makes me put a dollar in a jar every time I use a finance term in a conversation. Says the money is going towards her engagement ring."

Rae privately thought this sounded very savvy and anticipated the girlfriend would be receiving a three-karat diamond in short order.

"How can I spend *the rest of my life* with someone who doesn't know *EBITDA*? Or even ROI." He wrapped a white-cuffed arm around Rae's waist to keep from tipping over but brought them both down onto the couch cushions instead.

"Rae," he said, looking at her as if for the first time. "You understand EBITDA. And ROI and COGS and ARR and FCCR and—"

"Unfortunately," Rae muttered, but then Co-wannabe was kissing her and she was letting him kiss her, and his hands were sliding over her ass and she was letting them slide.

She felt nothing, but in spite of that, or perhaps because of it, she let it continue for a few more beats of the overweighted bass.

Then she managed to roll off the couch, pick up her purse, and slide through the crowd—away, away, *away*.

Refusing to wait in line for the coat check, she stumbled outside in just her sleeveless dress, too drunk for the cold air to cut her arms like she wanted. A long line snaked down the block, full of 1 Oak hopefuls who seemed convinced that they would finally be somebody if they could just make it to the other side of the gatekeeper bouncers.

Flagging down a cab, she got into the back seat, leaving her seat belt undone. "Wall Street and William," she mumbled to the driver.

Rae rested her head on the window, full of emptiness, or empty of fullness, too tired to ponder the paradox. Emotional bankruptcy best described her condition.

She missed Dustin, or maybe she was just uninhibited enough to admit how much she always missed him, but she felt no desire to call him. She felt no desire for anything other than resting her forehead on the window as the cab lurched from red light to red light—and even that couldn't be called a *desire*, more a *default*, the path of least resistance.

Her phone buzzed. Where the fuck did u go?? Co-wannabe texted. Rae didn't reply.

Numbness was less about feeling nothing and more about feeling everything so much that it froze you. Numbness blocked everything while shielding you from nothing. She wanted to jot the insights down on her phone notepad, but the paralysis prohibited her.

The numbness had dominated her trip to Florida to visit her dad a couple weeks ago too. Rae had braced herself for fresh heartbreak upon seeing him with his new family, but everything had passed over her in a detached sort of way, as if all the rain had been wrung out of the storm clouds and only a gray haze remained. As she'd sat at the dinner table making small talk with her dad's wife and stepdaughters as if it were an awkward first date, Rae had almost felt like she was looking down at her body, observing someone else.

The trip could best be described as fine—an adjective Rae deemed worse than *awful* or *combative* in how emotionless it was.

Once or twice she'd caught herself wondering what Dustin would think if he found out she had visited her dad, but she didn't linger on it. Both her head and heart seemed to know that wasn't safe territory anymore.

Her phone buzzed again from the back of the cab. U fucking kissed me first.

Rae knew this was the version of the story Co-wannabe would stick to if Rae dared report him.

The old thoughts returned. *One day* I'll quit my job. *One day* I'll leave New York.

One day I'll start writing.

The cab braked as a U-Haul truck cut in front. Rae let physics whip her body forward and back again, numbly cursing whatever fool was driving a U-Haul at two in the morning—probably some kid who'd driven fifteen hours straight from her Midwest hometown and was now blinking in awe at the sheer number of *lights* in this city, naïve enough to think she might become someone here rather than be swallowed up and spit out as an unbecoming number in the denominator of New York's makes it/dreams it ratio.

But from the numb bitterness and bitter numbness, a new thought coalesced.

One day had arrived.

Her bonus had safely hit her bank account, and tomorrow—*today*, technically—she'd walk into her boss's office and quit. It was a two A.M. thought, but the kind she knew would stick in daylight, if only because she didn't have the energy to brush it off any longer.

The cab driver sped past the U-Haul truck and beat it to the next red light.

$*$ $*$ $*$

I did it, Rae texted Ellen from the office bathroom the next afternoon.

Earlier, hungover in the Starbucks line, she'd filled Ellen in on the club incident and how she was quitting her job today.

"Report Co-wannabe to HR and threaten a lawsuit if they don't give you a damn good severance package," Ellen had coached.

Ellen was adamant that Co-wannabe had committed sexual assault. When Rae had protested that she was as much to blame because she'd gotten too drunk and hadn't done anything to stop him, Ellen had accused her of missing the whole point of the #MeToo movement. Rae had come around to agreeing that Co-wannabe was the sole culprit, but she found it easier to encourage other women to speak up than to speak up herself.

Her main focus today had been to break up with Wall Street. She'd procrastinated the "It's not you, it's me" conversation with her boss all morning, until Co-wannabe had swaggered in at noon, slouching down at his desk without glancing or even grunting Rae's way.

Slurping a sixteen-ounce Red Bull through a plastic straw, he flipped back and forth on his computer browser from a blog post titled "Three Steps for Exiting a Long-Term Relationship" to an engagement ring website, then to a valuation analysis for a new deal.

Rae felt nauseous seeing him, something that had nothing to do with the alcohol. It had been the motivation Rae needed to stand up and march—or at least *walk*—into her boss's office. She'd dressed in her crispest suit, hair pulled into a neat bun and makeup masking the under-eye shadows.

And then, after years of fantasizing about this day, she'd quit. Or at least, she'd tried to.

How'd it go?!?! Ellen replied now.

Unexpectedly well, Rae answered, still trying to process what had just happened.

YAY!!!! You're finally free of the decimal point dungeon!!!!

Not exactly . . . I didn't end up quitting after all.

WHAT???

Rae pictured Ellen hopping out of whatever meeting she was in. Sure enough, Rae's phone rang, and she picked up, not caring if Kelly or women from other groups at the bank eavesdropped. There was a sacred kind of sisterhood formed by using bathroom stalls as bunkers, a sisterhood Rae hadn't appreciated until now, in the wake of her failed escape.

"What happened to the plan!" Ellen said.

"I told my boss I quit," Rae assured her. "I really did." She hadn't managed to say the actual words *I quit*, or write them on a Post-it note, but she'd told him that after careful consideration, she'd decided to put in her two weeks' notice and take her career in another direction.

"So what the hell went wrong?" Ellen asked.

"He asked what it would take for me to stay. So I don't know, I threw out a few ridiculous things—that I'd need a promotion, a 20 percent raise, and to work from Indiana."

"And—" Ellen pressed.

"And he said that all sounded very reasonable and he'd talk to his boss and his boss's boss and his boss's boss's boss to see if they could make it happen."

"And—"

"And half an hour later, he called me back in and said they'd been wanting to build out their Midwest client coverage and had decided to make me a vice president in our Indianapolis office, with a 10 percent raise. It's actually a 40 percent raise if you factor in cost-of-living adjustments."

"Damn. Do you think someone told them about Co-wannabe's assault?"

Rae felt very exposed all of a sudden, even though she was safely within the confines of her stall. Her body burned, raw and shamed, in places he hadn't touched directly but would have if he'd had his way. "I don't think so," she told Ellen. "Everyone was too drunk last night to notice, and Co-wannabe seems set on pretending it never happened." Still, now she wondered if the reason they'd agreed to her terms wasn't because they didn't want to lose her but because they didn't want to be sued by her.

"Doesn't matter," Ellen said quickly. "You earned this."

"I told him I had to think about the offer," Rae said. "But I'm going to take it."

"You're leaving me?"

Ellen's whimper scraped.

"I didn't mean it like that," Ellen said quickly. "I just—shit, I'm going to miss you."

Rae nodded, which was a silly thing to do, given it was an audio call, but she knew Ellen could feel the motion, just as she could feel

Ellen nodding in acknowledgment that it was the right decision for Rae, not just for her career path but for her life path.

"I'm taking you to Per Se tonight to celebrate," Ellen said.

Per Se had been on Rae's bucket list for so many years now, but she'd still never gone. There were so many things like that—restaurants, museums, shows—all deferred and now, in a couple weeks, dead. She felt an odd peace at the thought, at how she'd no longer be deceiving herself that these things might, and could, happen next week.

"Per Se books up months in advance," Rae said.

"You're forgetting Aaron's culinary connections," Ellen said. "It's why I'm marrying him, remember?"

"I thought it was because he folds your laundry," Rae said.

"That's a close second," Ellen admitted.

They said good-bye, but before leaving the banker bunker, Rae called her mom.

Her grandpa picked up. "Who's this? If you're another political survey, I haven't changed my mind about my right to own a damn rifle—"

"It's Rae," she said, and then corrected herself. "Raelynn."

"Raelynn? What the hell're you calling in the middle of the day for? Did those white-collar sharks fire you?"

Rae let out a laugh, and for the first time in a while, it sounded like her own. "Not quite."

"Hold on," her grandpa said. "Let me call your mother in—she's just out shoveling the driveway. Five inches last night and the plows still haven't come round."

Rae pictured her mom, over sixty now, lifting heavy shovels of snow. She was glad she'd be closer again to help out with things like that.

"Raelynn?" her mom said a moment later. "Everything all right?"

"Everything's fine," Rae said. "More than fine. I got a promotion. And a raise. And they're transferring me to Indy."

"No!" her mom exclaimed.

"'Bout damn time," her grandpa muttered, poorly disguising pride.

"When?" her mom asked, excitement nearly contagious enough for Rae to catch it.

"Six weeks. I'm coming home in six weeks."

The word *home* didn't fit anymore, but she figured it would again, with enough practice.

CHAPTER THIRTY-NINE

SELLING ASSETS

"Sell or hold?" Ellen asked, standing at Rae's dresser on a Friday night and holding up a black, leather-ish miniskirt, a staple of their early-twenties days.

Rae was moving to Indianapolis on Sunday, shipping just the essentials and selling the rest at a secondhand store.

Rae glanced up from the kitchen, where she was kneeling in front of the oven, clearing scuffed black pumps from the oven rack storage. She'd been eating all her dinners at the office and had found a more practical use for the oven than cooking.

"Sell," she said, physically cold thinking about all those times she'd worn the tiny piece of fabric in the dead of winter, waiting in line for irrationally exclusive bars and clubs.

"How about this?" Ellen asked, pointing to a pilled black sweater that Rae had worn relentlessly over the years, creatively pairing it with different scarves and necklaces to create the illusion of a diverse wardrobe.

"Sell," Rae said, as she added her bathrobe and Santa hat to the giveaway pile. "Sell it all."

"For such a sentimental person, you're not fazed by parting with all of your belongings," Ellen said.

It was true. She ached at leaving Ellen but otherwise felt eerily little attachment to any part of her life here. "Guess I left my heart on Perry Street," she said. "Even if Wall Street took my soul."

"You still have your full heart *and* soul," Ellen said, but they both knew this was an exaggeration and Lorimer Street had been where the real emotional carnage occurred.

She was leaving the apartment furnished for the next tenant, just as the tenant before her had done. Rae wondered if New York's kindest acts weren't acts of kindness at all but acts of fatigue—too tired to move furniture across the country, you left it for the next person. Too tired to carve out personal space on the subway, you let someone cram in next to you. Too tired to wait for the barista to make you a new latte with oat milk instead of almond milk, you told him not to worry about it.

Clearing out beneath her bed, she encountered the bag of golf clubs her dad had sent her for college graduation in lieu of attending the ceremony. She put the whole bag in the sell pile but one by one extracted clubs that might come in handy for corporate golf outings—just the driver and putter, and then the seven iron, then the nine iron too. In the end, she kept every club except the sand wedge, which gave her the feeling of being stuck.

She also came across the Stall Street Journal, which had been untouched under her bed where she had tossed it after her stovetop bonfire. Odds were slim that the store would give her anything for a half-used pocket-sized journal, but maybe Ellen could persuade them to take it for free. There was a certain comfort in considering that someone else might fill the rest of the pages with real poems, even if hers had never gotten past the bullet-point phase.

"You can't toss this one," Ellen said, from the kitchenette now. She was holding up the signature scramblette spatula. "I'm not allowing it."

"You take it," Rae said. "I bequest it."

"But you'll have a bigger kitchen in your Midwest mansion."

Rae was moving into a two-bedroom Indianapolis apartment, and Ellen had been getting a thrill at the notion that Rae would have a *spare* bedroom—the adultness, the elegance of it!

"Please," Rae said quietly. "Take it." She didn't want to picture herself all alone in her too-big apartment, still failing at flipping omelets. The point of moving was to move on.

"Fine," Ellen said, and stashed the spatula in her bag, along with the card Rae had given her, which she'd instructed her not to open until she got home. "We'll use it together when you visit."

They let themselves picture it—Rae would fly back every other month and they'd walk along the Hudson River arm in arm and stay up late drinking just enough wine to get them giggling like they had in their midtwenties, but not so much wine that they'd fall victim to late-twenties hangovers, and in the morning they'd cook flawless omelets and praise themselves for how far they'd come.

"Three boxes," Rae said, when they were done sorting. "That's all I'm taking away from New York."

What had she been doing for the past ten years—sprinting down a well-lit, poorly understood path, amassing nothing she cared to keep? She'd come here for college, so sure she'd reach her big literary dreams in this city, so sure she'd meet her husband here and live out her own Broadway-worthy love story. Instead, all her diamond-clad dreams had dissolved into dust. She was leaving the city all alone, waving her flimsy white flag that no one would even look up from their phones to notice.

"And a best friend you're stuck with for life," Ellen said.

"Yes," Rae said with a begrudging smile. "That too."

*　*　*

Rae, this is Ellen, your hospital charity case. I was going to text you but it's hard to type with my arm in this cast, so I decided to call.

Unable to sleep on her last night in New York, Rae had gone to the rooftop of her FiDi apartment building for the first and final time.

Standing at the railing, overlooking the volatile city that hadn't *watched* her grow up (too passive) but *forced* her to, she recalled that half-poem she'd written long ago about her love-hate relationship with Manhattan, asserting that all subway lows were forgiven on that next rooftop high.

But she wasn't susceptible to renewal tonight, or even resentment.

Wrapped in numbness, or stripped of feeling, she assessed the scene objectively—how there were too many lights per square foot, too many horns per traffic jam, too many ambitions per open slot.

Acutely glad to be alone but absently craving company, she'd scrolled through old voice mails until she'd found the first one she'd ever gotten from Ellen, after the car accident the day they'd met.

Very old-fashioned, isn't it, leaving a voice mail? Ellen's voice bounced on, disconcertingly clear through the speakerphone. *Can't remember the last time I did this, and now I feel like I'm doing it wrong, rambling too much. Anyway, just wanted to thank you for the bagels. The food here is straight plubber—plastic and rubber—and you completely saved the day. And if you wanted to bring more bagels tomorrow, I'm craving egg. Kidding! Though I do love egg bagels . . . Anyway, I know I'm going to see you again once I break out of this room—just a joke, I'm not breaking out!* She was probably talking to a hovering nurse. *But actually, Rae, the universe is telling me that we're going to be splendid friends. Love you!*

Her voice stopped as abruptly as it had started. Ellen, the girl who'd loved Rae right away, for a simple bagel, and the woman who still loved her today, for all her complicated holes in the middle.

Rae wanted to laugh or cry, but she just stood there blankly, blinking at the jagged skyline that no longer smiled or even scowled but just saw straight through her.

She would have played a voice mail from her college boyfriend, too, just to acknowledge that time in her life, but she'd long since deleted them, if he'd ever left any at all. Texting with punctuation had been effort enough for him.

She played a message from her wannabe boss, from back when Rae was a junior analyst.

Rae, are you there? Fuck, this is why I told you to sleep with your ringer on. Wendell needs a round of edits ASAP before we send the pitch book to Jared—

Rae paused the message midrant. It triggered PTSD.

The next voice mail was from Dustin, picked at random from that hot-and-cold stretch when they'd been attempting friendship. He spoke in a soft volume, and she had to hold the phone closer to her ear.

Sorry I've been off the grid. I'm walking home and just got splashed with puddle water by a speeding cab and wanted to see if you could make a poem out of it. Come to Brooklyn tomorrow? Or I'll even venture into Manhattan if you want . . . that's how much I want to see you . . .

His voice faded out, and Rae tried to resurrect angst but just found herself nodding slightly—nodding that it had happened, nodding that it was no more.

The last voice mail she played was from a month ago, from Dustin's mom. Rae's stomach had plummeted when she'd gotten the call at work, anticipating the news she'd been fearing since that day in Washington Square Park when Dustin had told her about his depression, and every day and night and dawn and twilight since. She'd stumbled into the bathroom to listen, preparing to pass out on the tile floor.

But the message had brought good news, not bad, and she played it again now.

Rae—it's Debra here, Dustin's mom. This is an overdue thank-you for reaching out to me over the summer about Dustin's . . . issue. He's been in treatment, and things are looking . . . up. I know we're not in the clear—we never really will be, will we? But I feel—I feel like I have my son back. And I know it couldn't have been easy putting up with everything when you were together, but you've been a gift to us, and I just needed you to know that. I'm sorry I didn't reach out sooner, I've just been . . . processing everything. Thank you, Rae. Take care now.

In that secondhand way Rae experienced emotions these days, she'd felt relief, trailed by consolation or maybe curiosity—she couldn't separate them and didn't try to. Maybe that was why Dustin had been in her life, not so they could spot poems side by side all their lives but so she could spot warning signs to help keep him alive. Maybe that was how she was supposed to love people—leave them better than she found them, but leave them nonetheless. Maybe she wasn't supposed to tie the knot after all but just help people untie their own knots.

As she listened to the message again tonight, she felt nothing but bland envy that someone else had managed to help him where she hadn't, bland annoyance that Dustin's mom called him someone to "put up with," and an equally bland, though not dull, pain because Dustin hadn't reached out himself.

Rae had planned to call his mom back, but she'd kept procrastinating, and now she knew that the window had passed and she'd never return the message.

Fire truck sirens blared urgently from below while ambulance sirens arced through the avenues and drawn-out car horns punctured the air with impatient periods, splicing floating fantasies into fallen fragments. Rae missed the seclusion of the Lorimer Loft rooftop just long enough to remember that she wasn't supposed to miss it. In just a few hours, she'd be going somewhere much quieter than Brooklyn, somewhere that she could look up and see the stars rather than a murky fog of light pollution.

A decade ago, New York had lured her with its lofty valuation that had turned out to be built on nothing but dazzling delusion, and now she was finally executing her exit strategy before the city split up the rest of her heart to sell it for parts.

Thoughts stuck to the ground, eyes stuck to the spire of the Empire State Building, lit up red tonight, Rae wished that one day she'd feel like wishing again. Then she turned her back and walked inside, writing the last sentence of her New York chapter with all the words left unsaid.

CHAPTER FORTY

REINVESTING

"I've told you, Mom, my interest rate in men is zero right now. I just don't have the emotional capacity to make any new investments," Rae said, as she and her mom sat at the kitchen table of her Indianapolis apartment, eating homemade pecan pie her mom had brought over. "I'm still getting settled."

"You've been here two months now," her mom said. "I call that settled enough."

In many ways, Rae felt like she'd been back two years already, the slow pace light years away from Manhattan's rat race. The dinner had turned into a bid for Rae to hurry up and settle down with a local boy.

"I'm busy at work," Rae said, though her schedule was gloriously flexible. Her boss was usually out courting clients, and when he was in the office, he left by six to get home to his family—"I'm not like those New Yorkers with fucked-up priorities," he often bragged.

Rae still worked into the night sometimes, but she did so from the comfort of her apartment, after trying out a new recipe for dinner. Her oven was shoeless, and she hadn't set off the smoke detector yet.

She hadn't named her apartment, located on the second floor of an all-amenities building on Wilcox Street in west downtown Indianapolis. She was still working on not discounting "downtown" by using quotation marks.

If she *had* named the apartment, she would have selected the Wilcox Box. The boxy kitchen branched into the boxy living room with a boxy gas-burning fireplace, attached to two boxy bedrooms that faced the apartment complex's boxy courtyard, complete with a boxy pool.

Initially, the nine hundred square feet had felt cripplingly large for one person, but now she couldn't fathom how she'd ever survived with less.

Her mom had helped furnish it with warm knickknacks from the past—a knitted quilt draped over the L-shaped couch, shineless but sturdy copper pans in the cabinets, and four-by-six photos from pre-divorce days dotting the coffee table "to remember how happy your childhood was." Seeming mostly relieved and only slightly stung that Rae had visited her dad's new family, her mom was convinced that a father-daughter reconciliation would clear Rae's emotional arteries and help her feel ready to walk down the aisle. Any lingering bitterness over the divorce was apparently very small next to the horrific prospect of Rae still being single as she approached thirty.

Rae hadn't removed or even rearranged the family pictures yet. The bag of golf clubs was in her bedroom, filling the gap between bedside dresser and desk. A Manhattan snow globe sat on the desk, a gift from Kenny the security guard on Rae's last day in the New York office.

The emotional numbness hadn't lifted with the change in scenery, though it had settled into a calming numbness versus a crunching one. She still had writer's block, but she'd been reading more and binge-watching Netflix, which she justified as her storytelling diligence process.

"You're not getting any younger," her mom said.

"Am I not?" Rae deadpanned. "I thought that's how aging worked."

"Don't talk back to me, Raelynn. You've turned into a hermit, and I'm just trying to help."

"I'm not a hermit," Rae said. "I see you and Grandpa all the time. Chris, too." She'd been making more of an effort to bond with Mr. Non-Right and refer to him by his real name. Ever since the Dustin Divestment, she'd had more appreciation for what her mom saw in his stability.

Her mom raised her eyebrows, asking Rae to listen to herself.

"And Brianna," Rae added. Brianna was her best friend from high school, married and pregnant with her second child. They hadn't seen each other nearly as much as Rae had thought they would since she'd been back.

"I hear Stu is single again," her mom said knowingly, as she covered the rest of the pie with Saran wrap and stashed it in the luxuriously large refrigerator. "I still don't understand why it didn't work with you two that summer."

"Because I lived in New York," Rae said, preferring to use that line over delving into the whole drama with Dustin and how she just hadn't been able to keep from playing with matches.

"Well, now you live here," her mom pointed out, very pointedly.

Rae sat there with her thoughts. She'd like to see Stu, but she didn't want to reach out, didn't want to lead him on when she wasn't sure how much, if anything, she had left to give. And more than that, it felt like she'd be stuck in a backward loop, trying to relive an expired phase of her life. "Too much time has gone by."

"You're overweighting the downside risk," her mom said.

Rae smiled in spite of herself. "Where'd you learn that term?"

"I've overheard enough of your work calls," her mom said, looking rather pleased with herself as she slipped on her shoes and straightened the *Home Sweet Home* welcome mat she'd gifted Rae. "Just be open to the upside."

"I am open," Rae said, kissing her mom's crinkled cheek and closing the door behind her.

*   *   *

"I'll send the revised document in a few minutes," Rae said, as she slowed to a walk and answered her phone on a post-work trot along the charmless but crowdless White River on Indy's western edge. She hoped her wannabe boss on the line would mistake her panting for being winded from a negotiation with a lawyer. "Just wrapping up another work stream."

It had been a good day. She'd presented at a client meeting and left the office while there was still daylight. Big wins, by New York standards. But now the old East Coast villains were chasing her about updating forecasts of pro forma depreciation expenses in an asset-light acquisition, as they were all "stretched beyond capacity."

"What document?" the voice on the other end said with Midwest ease, not Manhattan speed. "If you're referring to our prenup, I don't want us to have one, if that's all right. They're so unromantic, don't you think?"

Rae came to a full stop, watching the sunset's bronze and blues bleed together in the river's reflection, the current too weak to distort the watercolor creation. "Stu?"

"Guilty as charged," the voice said, light with laughter.

"Shit," Rae said, then realized she'd said it aloud.

"That wasn't exactly the reaction I was hoping for," Stu said. "Why didn't you tell me you were back?"

Rae felt a jab of delayed remorse at how poorly she'd treated him. She tried to keep her tone as upbeat as his. "I figured some pageant queen would've snatched you up by now," she said.

"They've tried. But unfortunately I'm still hung up on the girl next door who ditched me for the New York lights." He said it cheerfully, with none of the bitterness that Rae thought her actions merited. "Pretty lame, huh?"

"Very lame," Rae agreed. "Sounds like that girl doesn't deserve you."

"Oh, but she does," Stu said. "She's got a good head on her shoulders, she'll come back begging for me sooner or later."

"Our breakup didn't shake your confidence, I see."

"Not much," Stu agreed. "So, you free tomorrow night?"

Free implied a spiritual state more than a physical one, but Rae didn't go down a philosophical rabbit hole. She just let bad habit beat good humor and said, "I'm not really dating."

"Think of it less as a date," Stu said, "and more of a guided tour of Indy with an old friend."

"I grew up near here," Rae said. "I don't need a tour."

"Things have changed," Stu said. "Have you seen the new poetry museum?"

"What poetry museum?"

"It's a new thing only the locals know about. I can show you if you'd like."

Rae was nearly certain Stu was pulling her leg, but she was intrigued enough to agree, with the appropriate terms. "I can't stay out late. I have work the next day."

"I'll have you home by a-love-in."

Rae tried to roll her eyes, but the corners of her mouth rolled up instead. "Bad pun."

"Better than 'I'll pick you up at sex.'"

"Your pickup lines have gotten worse. And that's saying something."

"Sorry. I'm much more refined when I'm not sweating."

"You're sweating?"

"Profusely. And you're smiling."

"No," Rae lied, kicking a stray pebble forward on the gravel running path.

"Well, we've gotta change that tomorrow. Good night, Raelynn."

"Good-bye, Stu."

"Thanks for not adding *-pid* to my name this time."

"I considered it."

She hung up and kept running, feeling stuck. Not the familiar stuck of latching on to the past or freezing up when she thought about the future, but the fresh stuck of staying firmly planted in the accessible now, kicking herself for defaulting to her disagreeable banker defense mechanism.

Beneath the analytical regrets, though, something else was stuck, too—a childlike smile that she tried once or twice to wipe away but decided it was easier to just let stay as she watched the day fade over the western plains and the first stars freckle the sky with humble light.

*   *   *

"That was the best poetry I've read in ages," Rae told Stu, standing outside her apartment complex the next night, sometime before eleven, somewhere between buzzed and drunk. "Have you ever heard of a verse as elegant as the Forget-Me-Not Lager?"

Stu had taken her to a beer garden, apparently the city's newest must-see establishment. Rae had audibly scoffed ("*This* is the poetry museum?"), but Stu had insisted she'd understand once she saw the creative menu. And to her surprise, she had.

The notion of beer being poetry was very Bellini-esque, but the date had gratefully ditched Bellini's dark edges, staying light but not shallow—a pairing Rae would have once called paradoxical.

Being back in Stu's buoyant presence had made Rae realize on a whole new level just how sick Dustin had been during their relationship. He'd taken so much from her, and worse than that, she'd willingly given it to him. She would still be force-feeding him her love if she hadn't had that agonizing, essential moment of knowing that enough was enough.

Being with Stu tonight hadn't made her miss Dustin any more or any less than she always did and, in a way, always had. And the date had made her miss Stu a lot more and the way warmth physically radiated out from his body.

"The Hoppily Ever After still gets my vote," Stu said.

It felt different being with Stu in downtown Indy than it had up on Elmer Lake. Indy wasn't New York, but it was still a city, and though it didn't quite bustle, it had a hum to it and that was something. It was a little too big for Stu and a little too small for Rae, and she caught herself wondering if it might be just the right size for the two of them together. Not that they were together by any means, but they weren't apart any more at least.

They were both in denim. Rae was wearing a jean jacket, and Stu was in a button-down shirt, one of those soft fabrics that didn't require ironing. Rae had on hardly any makeup, just a dusting of powder to lessen the sheen on her nose and a heavy coat of ChapStick.

"Next date, I'll up my game and take you to Vivida," he said. "It's Indy's only restaurant that might impress a New Yorker."

Rae smiled in the wake of the phrase *Next date*. She caught herself pondering, just in the abstract, if perhaps this was the setting and the timing that would make the stars finally align for them. "You've been impressing me since we were eight years old when I saw your water gun aim," Rae said. "And I'm not a New Yorker, I just *lived* in New York."

"Just like you're not an investment banker," Stu said, dark eyes dancing. "You just *work* in investment banking."

Earlier, Rae had struggled to describe her job to Stu. He'd never asked much about it two summers back, and Rae hadn't volunteered much. But tonight it seemed important that he understand that side of her, so one empty stein later (she'd made herself drink every time she'd caught herself using an acronym, like she knew the Scramblettes would do if they were here), Stu had summed it up as "helping companies gobble up their competitors." Rae had started defending herself by saying she hadn't let her capitalistic career twist her morals, but Stu had cut her off. "Raelynn, we drank the same well water growing up. I know you've got good values."

As for his updates, Stu had recently taken over his dad's auto dealership business. He didn't care for the managerial part of it, but he liked working with the customers. "Think about it," he'd told her, as they'd sat across from each other on the beer garden's outdoor picnic bench. "People name their kids, their dogs, and their cars."

Rae had thought about adding "and plants," but she'd stayed quiet.

"It's pretty cool to help people find cars that become part of their families like that," he'd gone on, and told the story of a woman in her early seventies who, after her husband and lifelong chauffeur died, had come in looking for a "no-frills sedan" and had driven home in a red Mercedes convertible, hooting like a teenager.

Rae had enjoyed the metaphor so much she'd agreed to stay for another round, not that she'd been thinking about heading out.

Now, standing with Stu on the quiet street outside the Wilcox Box (her tipsy thoughts couldn't resist the endearing name), she impulsively buried her head in his shoulder. It smelled deliciously familiar.

"You still like me," Stu said, arms around her.

"I don't *not* still like you."

"Double negatives hurt my head."

"Better than hurting your heart," Rae mumbled.

"What'd you say?"

"Nothing." Rae stopped herself before she went down a melodramatic path of the past.

Alcohol usually packed the numbness tighter, but tonight it was having a loosening effect, as if she had been wanting to unclench for a while now.

"Don't you hate how our moms are gonna gloat over this?" she asked.

"You know," Stu said, stroking her back in soothing circles. "In this case, I really don't mind at all."

Rae's body was suddenly raw but also burning for someone to wrap her up and hold her through the night, skin to skin.

"I have a full-sized refrigerator," she said. "Want to come up and see?"

"Not tonight," Stu said.

Rae stepped back and folded her arms in front of her, processing the rejection.

"I want to," he added quickly. "Believe me, I'm sure it's an incredible refrigerator." He paused for a grin. "It's just—I don't know much about stock markets, but the one tip my dad gave me was to always focus on the long term, not the short term. And it's always been about the long game with you, Raelynn."

Rae humphed, but the semisober part of her knew it was the right decision. "Fine," she said. "But at least kiss me good-night?"

He did, and it reminded her of past memories, plus ones she hadn't made yet.

"Your breath smells like poetry," she said.

"Yeah, I get that a lot."

They kissed again with limerick lips, and then Rae walked inside by herself but less alone, all the feelings back in her bones.

CHAPTER FORTY-ONE
MARRIAGE MERGER JITTERS

"I don't know if I'm ready to get married," Ellen moaned to Rae in the cozy bathroom of a Savannah rental house where they were celebrating Ellen's over-the-top-but-stripper-free bachelorette party during the last weekend of May.

Ellen was perched on the toilet in a skimpy black dress, eyes caked with smearing makeup, dark hair thick with southern humidity and adorned with a bedazzled tiara. It was nearly midnight, and they'd been drinking since noon, when they'd overpaid for one of those pedal-while-you-drink bars on wheels, their glutes burning without the Perry Street staircase training regimen. The weekend was turning into a throwback to early-twenties glory days, which they both now remembered hadn't been glorious in the least.

"I can never hedge or diversify or call my romantic options ever again in *my whole life*," Ellen moaned. "My man market size has shrunk to one."

"Less finance, more dancing," Rae said, quoting Stu, who had no problem calling her out on her banker talk on their dates, of which there had been quite a few in the three weeks since they'd reconnected. "You're crazy about Aaron."

"I know I am," Ellen said. "But what if I'm crazy in general and go on a dating app spree like I just did out there?"

The bachelorette party attendees—the four Scramblettes plus a few of Ellen's college and work friends—had been playing Pin the Veil on the Bride's Ass in the living room when Mina had missed her turn, too busy swiping through a dating app. She hadn't moved to San Diego yet, deciding surfer bros were commitment-phobic, but she'd been surfing through the Savannah dating pool instead, as her apparent dream man was "a Southern gentleman who's also a feminist."

Ellen had reached for Mina's phone, and Rae thought she was going to rightly throw it across the room, but she'd just started swiping through the profiles with the expression of a ravenous racoon.

"What the fuck are you doing?" Sarah had asked, yanking the phone from Ellen's grip.

"I'm the bride!" Ellen had screeched, clawing for it back. "I can do whatever I want."

Rae had herded Ellen into the bathroom and locked the door. They hadn't been together in the same small bathroom since Perry Street, and Rae had forgotten what a bonding experience it was.

"I don't even *want* to look at anyone else," Ellen said now. "My thumb just gets this *need* to swipe, and I can't stop myself and I'm going to completely ruin the best thing that's ever happened to me."

Rae removed Ellen's tiara, which looked to be poking uncomfortably into her head. "You're not going to ruin anything," she said, trying to project presence.

Ellen buried her face in her hands again. "I'm an app addict."

On Ellen's phone, Rae pulled up the photo album titled *Aaron & Ellen* ♥, with 837 pictures, about 90 percent of them selfies taken by Ellen.

Gently, Rae pulled Ellen's hands away from her face and gave her the phone. "Swipe through these instead of the app until your thumb gets tired."

"That's not going to work," Ellen grumbled, but she started swiping anyway, as if on a mission to give her thumb arthritis. Gradually her pace slackened, and several hundred photos later, she announced, "It's better." She looked momentarily relieved before adding, "But what if *Aaron's* thumb gets a need to swipe?"

"Has he ever given you reason to believe that would happen?"

"Well no, but it *could* happen. And the divorce data—"

"Don't pay attention to the data," Rae said, surprised but not surprised to hear herself saying this. "What does your heart say? Do you trust Aaron? Do you want to spend your life with him?"

Ellen looked back from the photos to Rae, back to the photos again. "I really do. But I—I don't want to lose myself, you know?"

"You won't lose yourself," Rae said. "Marriage is a merger, not an acquisition." She wasn't entirely sure she believed this, but it was nice to hear the words out loud.

"I'm keeping my last name," Ellen said.

"That's my girl," Rae said. "Now let's get back out there and dig into the ice cream." They'd loaded up on Ben & Jerry's, delighted by how perfectly the Chubby Hubby flavor fit the bachelorette theme.

The living room music was pushing its way under the slit of the bathroom door. It was too loud, all pop and sugar.

"Or," Rae offered, "we could stay in our bachelorette bunker a little longer."

Ellen nodded. "I need a toilet nap. Still my best invention to date."

"I remain partial to the Rae-bae scramblette."

But Ellen was already dozing off, head propped against the tile wall.

Sitting down on the shower mat, Rae hoped that she wouldn't have a meltdown at her own bachelorette party, but she was oddly comforted nonetheless, that even as they entered a more grown-up life stage, she and Ellen still needed one another to bail each other out of bathroom stall crises.

CHAPTER FORTY-TWO

RELATIONSHIP VALUE APPRECIATION

"Spot a poem," Rae said, lying next to Stu in the bed of his pickup truck, named Marlene, one Friday night in late July, on the side of a cornfield-straddled back road. The engine light and taillights were off, the scene snug in a darkness that set off the stars, which were starting to pop out of the earth's navy-black roof, two by two.

Wishing on New York lights seemed far away and futile. Rae once again preferred the reliability of stars, how no one could turn them off. Crickets chirped rhythmically, noisy but not imposing.

"What do you mean?" Stu asked. He fixed a blanket over her, tucking the fabric around her arms to protect her from mosquitoes, which were outnumbering the fireflies four to one. Rae was a little too warm but didn't mind.

They'd gone to a bonfire at Stu's married friends' house outside the city (all his friends were married) and were taking the scenic route back. Rae hadn't even critiqued him for driving under the speed limit.

"It's a game Ellen and I used to play," Rae half lied, with a pang she attributed to natural nostalgia. "You look around and find something ordinary that reminds you of poetry."

"That's easy," Stu said. "The stars."

Rae tilted her head on Stu's sweatshirt-turned-pillow and looked at him, his face so close that it was exempt from the surrounding shadows. She kissed his scruffy cheek, which never scratched. "And what about them makes them poetry?"

"How bright they are."

Rae stopped herself before she pressed for something deeper. Her version of poetry didn't have to match his. "I spot that wispy cloud over there," Rae said. "It looks like a wedding veil. Maybe that star right next to it is getting married to that one over there." She pointed across an imaginary aisle. "And she's racing to meet her fiancé, even though their parents"—she indicated a cluster of four stern-looking stars—"think their love is just going to burn out. But intergalaxy gravity is pulling the starry-eyed couple together, and nothing can stop them."

Stu let out a sound between a whistle and a laugh. "That's a bit of a stretch to me. But is this your way of asking me to marry you?"

"You know me so well," Rae deadpanned.

"I do, don't I?" Stu said, grinning his glow-in-the-dark smile. He kissed her forehead, then her lips, then her collarbone, where T-shirt met blanket. "Well, I'm ready when you are."

Rae had the feeling he was one-third kidding, two-thirds not, and she liked how he wasn't afraid to show how firmly committed he was. She wasn't going to abuse the security he gave her, but it was nice not to have to walk on eggshells worrying she might say the wrong thing and poke the bear.

They'd been back together only a couple months, but they'd picked up right where they'd left off, and Rae noticed how the slow pace of life here accelerated relationships. They got to spend most evenings together—sunsets and happy hours, not just midnights and late-night pizzas—and given how close both their families lived, they traded off Sunday night dinners (as expected, their moms were over the moon with smug satisfaction).

Last week Rae and Stu had even gotten together with her dad, who'd had a layover at the Indianapolis airport and taken them out to dinner at the Terminal A bistro. Stu knew her dad from years back, of course, but he'd told Rae it felt like meeting a stranger. Rae had half hoped for some kind of fatherly interrogation from her dad—asking about Stu's intentions or threatening to show up with a shotgun if he ever broke her heart—but they'd just talked about cars and football and swapped burger-grilling advice as Stu "played nice" (his words) and Rae had crammed in a few words about the deals she was working on, unable to keep from seeking her dad's approval despite telling herself she didn't care. His flight had started boarding before the entrées arrived, cutting the evening short, but he'd picked up the tab and texted Rae afterward—Love Stu!! Great u reconnected. See u soon kiddo.

"I'll never forgive him for what he did to you and your mom," Stu had fumed on their drive back, as Rae sat in the passenger seat, hugging the takeout boxes on her lap so they wouldn't jostle. "Wish I'd pissed in his boat when I'd had the chance."

Her relationship with her dad seemed to have stalled out in a place where he thought it was pretty good and she thought it was pretty grim. It felt like they were going through the right motions but not actually moving forward.

Now under the blanket in the back of the truck, Rae nudged Stu's bare feet with her socks. "Your turn again," she said. "Spot another poem."

Stu stared at the sky, concentrating hard, and then turned to look at Rae. "Your eyes," he said triumphantly. "Prettier than any star."

Rae felt a letdown at the cliché, but it quickly fell away at the feeling of his hands running under her shirt, needing no lantern to find their way. Her body folded gratefully into his, determined not to pick a fight over a compliment.

Maybe love was always cliché, and anything too original just meant you were overcomplicating some knockoff to convince yourself it was true.

She'd already attempted to sabotage the relationship multiple times, first by forcing the "What are we?" conversation after the third date (he'd responded by asking if she'd be his girlfriend, to which she'd said no but then changed her mind the next day). Then there had been the time he hadn't replied to her text in eight hours, and convinced he was ghosting her, she'd deleted all their messages, only to receive a call from a different number saying his phone had broken and he was at the store getting a new one. Stu had felt so badly for making her question his feelings that he'd shown up at her apartment that night with two dozen roses.

"Raelynn?" Stu said now. He always called her Raelynn, like everyone out here did, and it felt like getting some part of her back, a part of her she hadn't wanted but now saw she needed.

"Yeah?" Her nose was itchy with leftover bonfire smoke.

"I love you, if you haven't figured that out by now."

Rae sneezed into the blanket. She accidentally remembered what Dustin had said, that one day she'd sneeze out poems.

"I love you too, Stu."

The *too* didn't strike her as a tack-on, as it used to. It reminded her of the number two, so much better than one, ironic because it sounded like *won* but was really a loss.

And *I love you too, Stu* rhymed, and though she'd once preferred free verse, she was newly attracted to the levity of rhyme scheme and the way the predictable patterns worked as a team.

Stu patted the floorboards of his truck. "Hear that, Marlene? I tricked my dream girl into falling in love with me."

"You didn't trick me," Rae said, thinking she'd never fallen in love with anyone as intentionally as she'd fallen back in love with him. It was true, what people said about love not just being a feeling but a choice.

Relationships weren't only a checklist, but they were *also* a checklist—making sure you were picking someone who was happy within himself and didn't disappear or shut down when you asked questions.

For so long, she'd clung to the hope that Dustin would beat his depression, that one day he'd wake up and be over it. But she finally understood now, looking back at the jagged patterns of their relationship, that depression wasn't something that was ever fully beaten, ever conquered. It never surrendered and it never disappeared. Even if Dustin felt like himself again for days or even years, it would always be in him, mutating like a virus, plotting new strains, new ways to grip him again. It was so clear now that Dustin would never be in the clear. Rae had done what she'd had to do to keep her own life from getting taken over by it too.

Stu was marriage material in all the ways Dustin would never be. Though Rae had persuaded herself into believing she didn't care about finding a husband anymore, that she was perfectly fine if that never happened for her, being back in Indy around all the contented couples made her feel like she'd just been telling herself that to justify staying with Dustin on their *Titanic*, and then to justify why she'd kept clinging to the sunken shipboards at the bottom of the ocean.

She'd learned her lesson by going for the high-risk, high-reward option and winding up both broke and broken. Now it was time to choose the reliable investment, the emotionally stable man who wouldn't let her down. Before now, she hadn't had the maturity to value this kind of steady return profile, but she valued it now, and that was what mattered. She'd woken up and adjusted her portfolio strategy before it was too late.

She'd never admit it to her mom, but she was starting to find herself daydreaming about an outdoor wedding featuring Stu, a live country band, and spiked-lemonade pitchers. The images elicited a certain kind of pride deep within herself, like they were proof that she was the type of person who made good decisions.

"After a robust diligence process," Rae said to Stu now, "I choose to loan you my heart."

They rolled their eyes in tandem about how she just couldn't help making bad finance puns when they were professing their love.

"Hope you're not expecting me to give it back," Stu said.

"I'll accept back rubs as your interest payments."

"I suppose we can work with that," Stu said with a wink as fireflies blinked. Scooping her into his lap, he began massaging her shoulders.

Eyes half closed but never more open, Rae located the lovestruck stars from her story, now abandoned by the veil, which had swept far across the sky though not out of sight, and she wished on the faraway suns that her relationship with Stu would keep appreciating in value against the Midwest market backdrop of cricket-chimed bedtime rhymes.

CHAPTER FORTY-THREE
THE POETRY IPO

"The Post-it Poet, in print!" Stu said, jiggling open Rae's apartment door with his spare key. He walked inside, balancing a stack of newspapers up to his nose.

It was a Wednesday night in late August. Rae was in the kitchen, drying the dishes after making a tomato-and-basil quiche. Omelet-to-quiche was her latest egg evolution.

Stu set the newspapers on the kitchen table with a thud. "I stopped at every gas station on my way here to buy out the copies. There are more in Marlene, but we'll take those to your mom so she can frame them."

Rae's first-ever piece of writing had been published today, under the Post-it Poet pseudonym.

With her improved work-life balance, she'd been feeling increasingly guilty about not using her free time productively, and so a few weekends ago she'd shut herself in her apartment for a fourteen-hour write-a-thon. It had been cut short when Stu had shown up to take her on a double date with his friend and her wife, which he'd forgotten to tell her about.

She hadn't quite reached her twenty-poem goal, but it was progress at least. After looking up the top literary journals to submit to, she'd decided she wasn't ready for that kind of reception yet—or that kind of rejection. Instead, she emailed the top eleven poems to the Arts & Culture editor at the local *IndyStar*, and one had been deemed decent enough for the paper's shrinking circulation.

From the bathroom at work today, Rae had read the online version, but she'd waited for Stu to arrive before looking at the physical copy.

Picking up one of the flimsy papers, she flipped to the Arts section. There it was, on the bottom of page F7, wedged between a review of a local high school play and an article about how the city's main bookstore was closing down.

"A Note to New York, from a Flyover State" by the Post-it Poet

Keep your volatile skyline,
I'll take the mellow sweet pines.
Keep your jaded scowls,
I'll take the awe-struck owls.
Keep your Italian-made suits,
I'll take the Timberland boots.
Keep your 3AM 'open' signs,
I'll take the well-rested sunrise.
Keep your steel-rung rat race (and all the rats)
I'll take the unstrung pace and summer gnats.
Keep your millions of scared-to-grow-up Peter Pans,
and I'll take my one proudly grounded Midwest man.

She didn't like the space-efficient way the editors had typed the poem, or how they'd cut her favorite couplet, rhyming *bedroom half-walls* with *roomy bathroom stalls*. She wished her name was there but was glad it wasn't. The piece wasn't good enough for her to claim it, and the last thing she needed was people at work finding out she wrote love poems for the local paper. It would threaten all the work she'd put in over the years to prove she was a serious businesswoman, not a cute little girl.

Still, there was a certain comfort in knowing that if she died today, she'd have put a few words out into the world beyond scraps and drafts and halves.

Earlier today, Ellen, from her Hawaii honeymoon, had texted the link to the Scramblettes.

LOOK RAE IS FAMOUS (though I do have to take credit for the Post-it Poet name . . .)

I need your autograph!! Sarah had replied a few hours later.

It's so amazing, Mina had added. I'm going to write a poem like this for Ryan!!! Ryan was Mina's latest obsession. She'd collided with him in the stairwell of her apartment building, presumably because her nose had been buried in her phone.

The Scramblette bond had surged to old highs at Ellen's picture-perfect wedding last week. Ellen had convinced Rae to bring Stu, whom the Scramblettes had deemed as scrumptious as the cupcakes.

"Proudly grounded Midwest man," Stu said now, wrapping Rae from behind as they reread the poem together. "That's me."

Rae tried to smile, but it got stuck halfway, and she was glad Stu didn't have a view of her face. Her emotions were twisting around themselves in some kind of difficult knot. "That's you," she said.

"Ready to head out? You can give me and Marlene a private reading on the way over."

Rae's mom was hosting a celebratory dinner party, which her grandpa had agreed to attend so long as Rae promised not to quit her job to become a starving artist.

Her chest felt like it was being stepped on, and she ached for a gulp of fresh air from an eighth-story rooftop. "I have to water the plant first," she heard herself say.

She filled a glass of water and walked into the living room, where a houseplant with heart-shaped leaves was sprawling in the window, in a spot that collected indirect sunlight.

After Stu had discovered Rae's aversion to cut flowers, he'd asked what her favorite potted flower was. She'd accidentally responded "Philodendrons," which wasn't even a flower, and Stu had brought one over the next day.

Now Rae dumped water on the dried-out soil, watching it seep through the bottom of the green pot, which had more holes than she'd realized. She took one of the newspapers and rested it underneath. The runoff smudged the poem in a way that added the literary character it had been lacking.

A fidget appeared, or rather reappeared, to text the poem to Dustin.

She still hadn't heard from him once since the breakup—a year ago yesterday. Not even one drunk text.

He rarely entered her thoughts anymore, but he never left them. It was so much easier to keep someone out of your conscious thoughts than it was to kick them out of your subconscious, she was learning. He remained a stubborn hum in her heart, never fully in focus but never out of focus either.

He wouldn't like the poem, of course, but she wanted to show that at least she'd done *something*, that her writing had IPO'd in the public markets and all those days poem spotting at Brooklyn cafés hadn't completely gone to waste. She wanted to thank him for keeping her creative muscles alive and argue with him about why rhymes weren't cheap. And above everything, but below it, too, she needed to know how he was doing.

"What's wrong?" Stu asked, from across the room.

"Nothing," she said quickly, sweating despite the central air-conditioning vents. She'd filled Stu in broadly about how she'd dated a guy with depression back in New York and how it had helped her understand what she wanted in a relationship, but she'd never mentioned him by name, never revealed anything that might give Stu any reason to think she hadn't fully moved on, when she had.

Dustin wasn't on her mind, or even if he was on her mind, he wasn't on her heart, which was what mattered. The only thing dragging her heart down right now was her own self-doubt about her writing, and by extension, her purpose in the world, the legacy she'd be leaving behind when time catapulted her to the end of her life.

Looking into Stu's eyes, the same unwavering brown as always, she whispered, "What if this is the only thing I ever publish?"

For so long, she'd been worried about dead or deferred dreams, but what if living, breathing dreams were the real risk? What if she tried as hard as she could and never got there, and no longer had the *Oh, I never really focused on it* excuse? Or what if she did get there, but actual success fell short of imagined success, and she could no longer comfort herself with the wondrous wonderings of *one day*?

Stu walked across the carpet and met her at the window. "First of all," he said. "I know you're going to publish more, if you want to."

He said it with such nonchalant confidence that Rae nearly believed him. "But if I don't?"

"Then I'm glad I bought a hundred and twenty-three copies of this one. Low supply makes it more valuable, right?"

A smile squeezed its way out. Rae left the overwatered plant in the window to collect the overcooked quiche from the kitchen.

"Just promise you won't forget me?" Stu asked, as he opened the front door and held it for her. "When you're a big-shot poet?"

"I think *big-shot poet* is an oxymoron," Rae said, trying to laugh though her lungs felt squeezed by the impossibly large gap between local paper and international best seller. "And," she added, more to herself than to Stu, more of a regret than a rebuttal, "I don't know how to forget people I love."

Fighting off one fidget by surrendering to another, Rae balanced the quiche in one hand and texted the poem to her dad with the other, explaining that she'd gotten published under a pseudonym.

Then she put on her shoes and led her new, blueless muse down the single flight of stairs, reminding herself that this was *up*.

CHAPTER FORTY-FOUR

STEADY EMOTIONAL CASH FLOWS

"There it is," Rae said, pointing to the top floor of a grime-splotched apartment building with a precarious-looking fire escape on the fringes of the West Village. "The Perry Street Penthouse."

She and Stu were half a step behind Ellen and Aaron, both couples hand in hand as they walked on a sunny sliver of sidewalk. The October air was quintessentially crisp. Rae had forgotten how an autumn day could reform Manhattan, and in the next gust of wind, tinged with yellow cab exhaust and mismatched restaurant kitchen scents, Rae caught a whiff of missing listing New York as her city of residence.

They were celebrating Rae's twenty-ninth birthday weekend. She hadn't freaked out nearly as much as she'd anticipated she might upon entering the last year of her twenties. She liked to think it was because of how secure in herself she'd become, but something told her it was mostly because of how secure she was in her relationship with Stu, how on track she felt to getting engaged and perhaps even married in the next 365 days before reaching the dreaded cliff of thirty.

It was Stu's first time in New York, so they'd been checking off the obligatory items—Times Square, dollar pizza, the Statue of Liberty, Wall Street (they'd gone in her old office, where Stu had refused to stand anywhere near the forty-second floor windows), and more pizza. They hadn't made it to Brooklyn. Now in the late Sunday afternoon, they were at their final tour stop.

"Ninety-six steps to get up there," Ellen said. "One hundred and twelve if you count the full trek from the laundry in the basement."

"Which is why we only did laundry once every five weeks," Rae explained. "We had it down to a science."

"Called bulk-buying underwear," Ellen said.

"And rewearing socks whose stench levels fell below the 'repulsive' threshold," Rae added.

Stu paused to take it in as passing pedestrians glared and huffed at his audacity to stop in the middle of a sidewalk. "It's not as shabby as I pictured from the stories."

"You'd have to see the inside to understand," Rae said, cringing at cockroach memories but also craving the coziness of being curled up on that love seat couch with Ellen, tossing popcorn in the air, squealing if they caught it in their mouth and squealing if they didn't.

"Should we buzz up and see if someone's home?" Aaron asked.

"Let's not bother them," Rae said. "They're probably busy waiting for their shower to warm up."

"Or waving dish towels in front of the smoke detector after a kitchen fiasco," Ellen added.

"Raelynn's still never cooked me a scramblette, you know," Stu said, feigning offense. "Says it belongs to a 'prior era.'"

"You haven't lived if you haven't tasted a scramblette!" Ellen exclaimed, at the same time Aaron coughed, "Count your blessings."

Rae looked at her old bedroom window—that skinny, sorry little thing dripping with condensation from a window air-conditioning unit—and wondered if the half wall still existed or if the new tenant had torn it down and turned it back into a real one-bedroom apartment.

She hoped whoever lived there now felt the Elle-Rae ghost in the giggling of the pipes, or perhaps in loopy heart drawings that reappeared in the steamy bathroom mirror no matter how many times the glass was scrubbed.

More pedestrians pushed by. Ellen linked her arm through Rae's, and they kept walking, setting a brisk pace while the guys lagged back in a dutiful attempt to bond.

"Stu is even greater than I remembered," Ellen said. There was no risk of being overheard thanks to the urban mash-up of horns, garbage trucks, construction cranes, and helicopter traffic.

"So great," Rae agreed.

They'd spent most of the weekend double dating, though she and Stu had opted to stay in a hotel, where they'd taken off the bathrobes nearly as fast as they'd put them on.

"He's easygoing," Ellen went on, "but still has a strong personality. Very good balance for you. Do you *ever* fight?"

"I picked a fight last week about how we never fight," Rae said. "Does that count?"

Ellen pinched Rae's arm. "Let yourself be happy."

"I know," she said, as they passed their old coffee shop on the corner of Perry and Bleeker. "I've decided I value steady emotional cash flows over the highs and lows of risky investments."

"Very mature of you."

"Well, I am twenty-nine now," Rae said, her tongue still getting used to the number. According to the fertility data, 90 percent of her eggs were now dead. The stat hung over her head, polluting her birthday with a sense of dread.

"I can feel a proposal coming soon," Ellen said. "And I'm never wrong about these things."

Rae felt something in her stomach that she figured must be butterflies. "Don't be one of those people," she said, "who gets married and then starts evangelizing the whole world that they should get married too."

"Not the whole world," Ellen said. "Just you and Stu."

"We'll see," Rae said, not wanting to divulge too much to Ellen since the guys weren't far away, or at least that was how she chose to explain her secrecy, a more palatable reason than the truthful alternative, which was just how much she and Ellen had grown apart after her marriage and Rae's move.

Privately, Rae had decided she'd only need to date Stu a year before getting engaged.

It was a significantly condensed timeline, but she and Stu went back so far that she felt fully confident in her vetting process. His roots were so entwined with her own that she knew, with a kind of calm she hadn't thought possible after watching her parents' marriage snap apart, that she wasn't going to uncover any surprises or skeletons in Stu's closet. And she was old enough now, too, that she didn't need as much time to make up her mind.

Ellen beamed triumphantly, like she'd heard all of the words Rae had just thought to herself, and said, "Remember all those nights we stumbled out of cabs at this corner at two A.M., crying our eyes out because some guy didn't text us back?"

"Us, overdramatic about guys?" Rae said with mock incredulity. "Never."

Ellen laughed, flinging the sound freely so that it soared above the millions of competing noises. "The universe had a plan the whole time."

"Maybe it did," Rae said, as her feet led her along the cracked sidewalk toward Washington Square Park, where she figured they could sit on a bench and rest for a while. "Maybe it did."

*   *   *

"Nice job in there," Rae's boss told her one Thursday morning in early November as they rode an empty elevator down from a three-story office building in downtown Indy. "You really have a knack for telling the story of corporate synergies. I think we'll win that deal no question."

Rae had just finished her first solo-ish acquisition pitch, with her boss there to add the stamp of middle-aged masculinity that clients seemed to correlate with credibility.

"Thanks," Rae said, feeling crunched because her storytelling skills were being wasted on such dry plots, but also feeling pumped up by her accomplishment and the independence she was earning.

"And you hardly even used any numbers from the projection model," he said.

Rae fought the urge to apologize.

"That was a compliment," her boss clarified as the elevator doors opened and he let her out first. "Can't tell you how many guys I've seen read from their spreadsheets and completely miss the body language in the room."

"I don't bow down to decimal points," Rae said with a grin. She'd been letting her personality seep out more at work recently, appreciating the more casual vibe of Midwest corporate life. And unlike the guys back in Manhattan, she trusted her current boss in Indy wouldn't dismiss her as a ditzy blond if she let out a bubbly laugh.

Her boss chuckled appreciatively, a deep, resonant sound that Rae found herself envying. "You'll be taking over for me soon enough," he said.

"Maybe one day," Rae said, trying not to analyze how "one day" had gone from meaning *one day* she'd be a free-spirit poet whose words changed the world, one soul at a time, to *one day* she'd be a midlevel banker whose work propagated capitalism's status quo.

When she'd started out in finance, she'd thought inching up the ladder would take decades of grit-your-teeth-and-be-the-bitch blood, sweat, and pain. But the volatility of the early years—the low lows of three A.M. ASAP emails and being chewed out by wannabe bosses for accidentally printing a document double sided; the high highs of sneaking out of the office for a ten-minute walk with TB or GQ or unexpectedly getting Sunday off—had mellowed into a steady routine of ten-hour days ranging from *not great* to *halfway decent*.

On the middle rung she'd reached, she could coast along. It would be hard to rise up much farther, but even harder to fall off completely.

In a resurgence of ambition after her New York trip with Stu, she'd drafted a multipage outline for what taking the plunge to full-time writer would look like. But as one predictable pay period settled into the next, she'd decided there was nothing wrong with keeping writing on the side. She'd written a poem about it—"On the Side Like Fries"—contemplating: If French fries were entrées, would their taste still amaze?

She and her boss walked into the parking lot, which had dozens of open spots and no car horns polluting the air. Eight months after her move to Indy, Rae was still getting used to these luxuries.

The afternoon was translucently overcast and warm enough to forgo a coat. Fall stretched longer here.

"I'm playing golf with a couple big clients on Saturday," her boss said. "Want to join, if the weather holds?"

Rae had never been asked to join a golf business meeting. She started to say that she didn't play but stopped short. She'd been hitting balls at the driving range and had even sent videos of her swing to her dad for him to provide feedback, which he had, down to the angle of how her left thumb should grip the club. She still wasn't good enough to impress anyone, but she was decent enough not to embarrass herself, and she owed it to herself and women everywhere to say yes.

"I'd love to," Rae said.

"Great," her boss said. "We'll play a scramble format."

Rae smiled and mentally added the suffix *ette*, deciding late-twenties scramblettes would be made on the golf course rather than in the kitchen. It seemed like a fitting metaphor for growing up and holding her own in a male-dominated industry.

Reaching his BMW, her boss fist-bumped Rae good-bye. "Nine o'clock tee time too early?" he asked.

Rae winced at the phrase *tee time*, habitually hearing it as *tea time*, accompanied by the ambience of a Brooklyn café.

"That's fine," she said, opening the sticky door to old Fordable Francine. She still refused to trade in the truck, though Stu must've shown her a hundred options that were objectively better. "See you at nine."

*　*　*

"So this is it," Rae said, one night a couple weeks later, feet dangling from the back of Marlene.

The tailgate was down, and they were sitting side by side, looking out at Elmer Lake. Stu had picked her up and driven north to show her the plot of land he was thinking of buying, opposite the cottages where they'd spent their summers. She'd made a picnic of "chilled cheese" sandwiches that they were eating from an old, blue cooler.

"This is it," Stu affirmed, eyes twinkling. "What do you think?"

It was a wooded lot, the trees reaching right down to the water. A single boat zigzagged across the surface, out for an end-of-season cruise, the motor the only man-made sound in earshot. The sun wouldn't be setting for another hour or two, as the sky tried to hold on to fall even as the air was forfeiting to winter. The trees had dropped their leaves, making the lake look cold and naked. Rae had only ever been here in summer.

"The view looks different from this side of the lake," she said, wrapping Stu's jacket around her. She hadn't worn a warm enough jacket, so he'd lent her a layer. She couldn't pick out Our Little Yellow House from across the way, and it made her feel a little dizzy.

"The house'll go there," Stu said, pointing behind them. "And then we'll put the dock there, and a bonfire pit over there and maybe a trampoline for the kids right there."

"Kids?" Rae said, feeling a little nauseous from the windy back roads they'd taken.

"Well, yeah, I'm not trying to build a bachelor mansion here," Stu said. "I know you've got your whole *We need to date for a year before getting engaged thing* going on." He mimicked her voice, and Rae couldn't help but laugh along. "But in your words, I'm 'bullish not bearish' on us and just wanted to make sure you liked it before I made an offer on the land," he said.

Rae had hoped that their trip to New York might've whet Stu's appetite to explore the world, but it had only proven to him what he'd known all along—big-city people were living life backwards, upside down, and inside out. He'd literally kissed the ground when they'd gotten back to Indiana and doubled down on his decision to build a house on Elmer Lake, which had "all the food groups of a real good life," as he said.

"It's your dream place," Rae commented.

"*Our* dream place," Stu corrected. He kissed her, and it tasted like iced tea with extra lemon.

Rae smiled, but she was finding it difficult to swallow, like the cheese from her sandwich was getting wedged in her throat. *Was* this her dream house? She couldn't remember now. She'd never been one to dwell too much on a physical structure. Her dream home was more of a feeling than a place.

Stu put a hand on the ripped knee of her jeans and gave it a loving squeeze. "What's it called when a movie starts and ends with the same scene?" he asked.

"A full-circle ending?"

"That's it!" Stu said, looking at Rae like she was very brilliant for knowing this. "That'd kind of be like us on this lake, huh?"

She nodded. It felt like she was living out a feel-good, full-circle ending, but all the character development in the middle had fallen out. "It would be a crowd-pleaser movie for sure," was all she could say.

"Don't you think we'd be happy here, Raelynn?"

Rae answered without thinking, and that's how she knew it was the truth. "Yeah, I do." She wondered, very briefly and very rashly, if maybe what she craved most wasn't happiness but wholeness. Stu knew all the different parts of her, but they were only that—parts.

He never looked at her and made her feel like he was holding her entire soul and all its ugly overflow in the orbs of his own two eyes.

But that wasn't a fair bar to judge love by, Rae reasoned. She couldn't expect one person to fill all her needs and wants. She could join a book club or a writing group or watch old romantic movies to touch those deeper parts of her. For a life partner, she was prioritizing traits of a good husband and a good dad, and Stu was off the charts in both. He'd never cheat or leave her like her dad had, and he'd never stop finding little ways to make her smile. He'd be the kind of husband whose friends made fun of him for how much he bragged about his wife, and the kind of dad who left work early to coach his kids' soccer teams.

Rae tried to picture herself writing in the blare of toddler sirens. She suspected, shamefully, that she'd be the type of mom to neglect her kid's diaper to finish a stanza.

Stu seemed to sense her fear, and Rae read it as a sign that he was more in touch with her emotions than she gave him credit for. "We'd build a separate writing workshop for you," he said, pointing to a clearing in the trees. "So you can have all the peace and quiet you need to keep churning out love poems for me."

Rae had gotten two more poems published in the *IndyStar* in the past month—"Gravel Road Romance" and "Bull Frog Prince," both of which Stu had interpreted to be about him. In reality, they'd been about fifty percent about him, twenty-five percent about no one in particular, and twenty-five percent about everyone in particular, but she hadn't corrected him. She liked the feeling of making him smile like that.

Rae took a sip of iced tea, and the lump in her throat floated away with the flavor. Maybe it was the way the sun was drizzling a tangy orange glaze over the mirror-clear water, or maybe it was how Stu was reaching into the cooler to fetch her a fresh iced tea before she'd even noticed her can was empty. Whatever the reason, Rae began to see it too, Stu's ten-year forecast unfolding before them.

She saw the oak-leaf-lined aisle where they'd get married in a small, no-suits-allowed ceremony. She saw the wood-shingled house with its yellow front door and elegant porch and garage attached to the house so they wouldn't have to walk outside in the winter. She saw the dock where they'd watch the stars at night, and in the daytime, where the dogs—a golden retriever and two rescue mutts—would try to prove who was bravest in the water. She saw the lake-facing bay window, lined with healthy plants that weren't philodendrons. And she saw the kitchen table, set for more than two, with triangular paper napkins asymmetrically folded by small fingers.

It was everything she wanted to want. The only thing standing in her way was herself, overanalyzing everything until there was nothing left to dissect. But she wasn't going to indulge those tendencies tonight. She had agency over her own destiny.

A sleepy kind of relief seeped into Rae's bones. Here it was, her end goal materializing right before her eyes. She'd gotten her life back on track, letting go of the city that was sucking her life, letting go of the guy that was sucking her love, and now she was with someone who gave so much more than he took, someone who was the steady shore to all her waves.

She reached for Stu's hand and held it extra tightly, almost like she was trying to help herself hold on to him. "Could the workshop have a roof deck?" she asked, as the first of the crickets began to sing.

"Absolutely," Stu said. "And a full-sized fridge."

"Stocked with whipped cream?"

"Is that even a question? I plan to interrupt your creative flow with a helluva lot of dessert coffee deliveries."

"You're officially the perfect man," Rae said, chastising herself for saying *the*, not *my*, but not wanting to mar the moment with a minor revision.

CHAPTER FORTY-FIVE
VOLATILITY RETURNS

"The *New York Times*!" Ellen yelped through the phone one Friday in January. "You're in the fucking *New York Times*! I've already taped five copies of the poem to the bathroom stalls at work."

"Everyone's just going to flush it down the toilet," Rae said. "Or use it as toilet paper." Rather than being locked in a bathroom banker bunker, she was taking the call from her new private office, the size of her Perry Street bedroom, with a floor-to-ceiling glass wall.

To make up for that fact he couldn't give Rae a salary raise due to "senior leadership's concerns about a vulnerable macro outlook," her boss had given her an office, the most conspicuous symbol to date that she was rising in the world. She paced the perimeter now, liking how the carpet muffled her heels, occasionally glancing at her reflection in the glare of the glass. Her skin was fair and freckleless from winter, but her face was bright and spotted with life.

"Stop that," Ellen said. "It's the best piece of social commentary of the century, and the fucking *New York Times* agrees."

Rae had written a poem published this morning, titled "Presence," about a Wall Street woman denied a promotion because of systemic sexism. She'd tried to make it rhyme, but the words had clawed their way out of couplet cages.

The poem had been rejected by the *IndyStar*. From her online stalking of the editorial team, Rae had found that old white men were calling the shots. This had spurred her to submit it to the *New York Times* and a few other liberal publications. Months later, long after Rae had assumed it had been rejected or, more likely, lost, she'd gotten an email saying the *Times* wanted to print it.

"I'm still mad you didn't give me a heads-up this was happening," Ellen said. "I know we're in a long-distance friendship, but don't I deserve to know when you're about to get famous?"

"I didn't tell anyone," Rae said. "Even Stu or my mom. Didn't want to jinx it."

It had been more than that, too. She'd liked the notion that a stranger somewhere, likely in the relative stillness of Manhattan's predawn yawn, would be the first to stumble across the poem while flipping through the paper over green tea or a sugary cappuccino, and form their own opinion before the universe had been biased by anyone else's input.

"You're annoyingly nonchalant about the whole thing," Ellen said. "I'm physically bouncing on the toilet." Ellen had her own office now, too, but still took their calls from the bathroom.

"I'm still processing it, I guess."

"Well, process faster. How should we celebrate? Couples' retreat in the Bahamas?"

Rae looked at a framed photo beside her computer, of her sitting on Stu's lap on Christmas morning at her mom's house. Her grandpa had insisted on taking the picture, and it was endearingly off-center. The photo made her feel safe but in a constrictive sort of way.

"Stu doesn't like the poem," she told Ellen. "He thinks it's a disrespectful exposé."

"Wall Street deserves an exposé," Ellen said. A toilet flushed through the line, and Rae had a feeling Ellen had deliberately waved her hand in front of the sensor to punctuate her point. "But it's not like you mentioned any names, and no one knows you're the Post-it Poet. And the whole point is that the poem isn't just your story, it's millions of women's stories."

"I know," Rae said, feeling closer to Ellen than she had in a long time. "But Stu said one poem isn't going to fix sexism and it's just stirring up trouble."

"That doesn't sound like Stu, getting upset."

"Well, we've only been texting about it," Rae said. "I'm sure we'll work it out when we talk tonight." He was at Elmer Lake today, overseeing the construction of the new house. He'd bought the property, and everything was on track to be done by the end of summer. The idea was that he'd move in first, and then she'd join him when they got engaged (he didn't like saying *if,* so Rae had stopped using that word too, and found herself happier for it).

"He's probably just hurt he didn't know about it first," Ellen said.

Rae bristled. "I don't need his permission to submit my poetry."

"Of course you don't. But this is a big deal. When we look back on your literary career, we'll say this was the first big break."

"Not my *IndyStar* acclaim?" Rae deadpanned.

Her phone buzzed with a new text. She checked it, expecting it to be Stu, responding to her last passive-aggressive message.

The name on the screen registered naturally at first, then backtracked to the appropriate shock.

Dustin.

Something inside her stopped by starting again.

"I have to go," she told Ellen, and hung up.

Sitting down at her swiveling desk chair, she absorbed the text with a single drink of her eyes and then went back to individually imbibe each word.

Congratulations on the poem. Always knew it would happen. Heard you moved to Indiana. Keep shining and sneezing.

It was only four short fragments, but it felt like an encyclopedia after a year and a half of complete silence.

Her heart skipped, a lurchy forward motion that felt like reverse.

Had he recognized the pseudonym and looked up her LinkedIn profile and seen she was in Indianapolis now? Or maybe he'd run into Ellen at some point on a subway platform and Ellen had hidden the encounter from Rae? Were the women at his office talking about today's poem? Did they like it? Did he like it?

His text hadn't included a question, but she began drafting a reply anyway.

As she was revising draft number six in her phone notepad (she was finding it infuriatingly difficult to capture the *Happy to hear from you but even happier without you and genuinely hoping you're happy too* tone), her phone rang.

It was Stu.

In the fraction of a second that she felt disappointed at seeing her boyfriend's name, she loathed her emotions, tempting her to ride the love market's bubble until it burst and left her with nothing.

Perhaps it had been too optimistic an assumption to think she'd fully divested Dustin, but she was in control of her forward-looking investments, at least. And she chose the one with the steady track record.

She deleted all six text drafts, then called Stu back to smooth things over with the guy who might not pull her heart to a record-breaking high, but never sent it spiraling into a recession.

PART 4

135 DAYS TO GO

CHAPTER FORTY-SIX

CLOSING THE DEAL

"To Raelynn," her boss said, holding up his champagne flute. "For closing the biggest deal of the year."

It was late spring now, and Rae and Stu were seated outdoors at Moynihan's Steakhouse in downtown Indy. Her boss and his wife were there too. They were celebrating the firm's latest deal—a large tech company had acquired a Chicago-based cybersecurity firm, and Rae had led the whole process, from the pitch several months ago to the valuation analysis to negotiating the term sheets to overseeing the wiring of the $5.41 billion dollars to the correct bank accounts at three A.M. this morning.

After work today, she'd just wanted to go back to the Wilcox Box and get some sleep, but her boss had insisted on a double date to soak in the accomplishment. It was a much tamer closing dinner than the open-bar iniquity back in New York, and Rae was glad for this.

Stu let out a whistle. "That's my girl," he said, as they all clinked glasses.

"It was a team effort," Rae said, though it wasn't really true.

"None of this modesty bullshit," her boss said. "Take credit where you deserve it, otherwise someone else will take it for you."

"Now there's some good advice," Stu said, thumping Rae's boss on the back. Her boss had taken an immediate liking to Stu, declaring him a breath of fresh air from the usual corporate crowd.

"Keep it up at this rate, and you'll be the youngest woman partner in the firm's history," her boss said.

Rae didn't like how he used "woman" as a qualifier—an adjective rather than a noun. It felt like it diminished the accomplishment, but she didn't point that out, just let herself take it as the compliment she knew it was intended as.

"I'm going to make sure Harold knows how much the clients lean on you," her boss went on. Harold was his boss, one of the head honchos based back in the Manhattan headquarters.

"Thanks, Bill," Rae replied. She had a throbbing impulse to record the conversation so she could send a voice memo to her dad. Though she told herself she'd stopped trying to impress him, she knew she'd never stop hoping he was proud of her.

Her boss's wife, Linda, spoke. They'd met briefly at a couple of work events, and Rae liked her down-to-earth demeanor and how she and Bill had been married thirty-five years. "I've just got to tell you, Raelynn, it's an encouraging thing to see a young woman like you holding your own in this industry," she said. "I worked on Wall Street after college but didn't even last two years. I married Bill and stayed home to raise the kids, and I don't regret those things for one second, but I just wish I'd felt like I could've made it in the finance world if I'd wanted to. Like it had been a real option."

Rae had never known any of this. She'd foolishly assumed Linda hadn't had big career aspirations, that being a full-time wife and mom had always been her goal.

"And there was this poem in the *New York Times* earlier this year," Linda continued. "Not sure if you saw it, but it was all about sexism in finance, and I told Bill—didn't I, Bill? I said now this is the

truest thing I've read in years, so you make sure you look out for Raelynn, because she's got to be feeling some of that herself. It's impossible for men to ever understand how women feel like the 'other,' but
you've at least got to try to understand, put yourself in her shoes and
feel how damn difficult it is to walk in heels."

Rae sat there, stunned in the very best way. This woman she
hardly knew, a generation older than her, had seen herself in Rae's
words. And she'd seen Rae in them too. It was an exquisite type of
power, knowing her own writing had enabled this anonymous-but-
intimate type of human connection.

She wanted to excuse herself to the bathroom and start in on a
new poem now, something else that might shift even one person's
perspective, but her brain was so deadened by deals that the creative
valve was sealed shut.

From beside her, she could feel Stu bursting to reveal that Rae
was the poet behind that very piece. She gave his shin a firm kick
under the table, and he managed to stay quiet by stuffing an entire
bread roll in his mouth.

"Your husband is the best boss I've ever had," was all Rae ended
up saying, with genuine gratitude. "He could teach a thing or two
to the guys in New York." She didn't go into any details, but she felt
Linda's understanding in the way she gave Rae's hand a maternal
squeeze.

The conversation continued, but Rae was wrapped up in her own
cocoon, mulling more over Linda's truncated Wall Street career and
all the times she herself had nearly quit. During her first few years as
an investment banker, Rae had thought she hated the job because the
hours were bad and the work was pointless. But perhaps the biggest
reason she'd struggled as a junior member of the team was because
she didn't actually feel like part of the team—and certainly not
someone who might lead that team one day.

There were no women in the senior ranks, no one above her who
looked like her, and how could you be what you couldn't see? In

hindsight, she could observe how she'd nearly self-selected out of the boys' club not because she couldn't put in the long hours but because she didn't think she'd ever truly belong. She thought, too, of how TB and GQ hadn't seen themselves either, and so they'd left.

She'd reflected on these things before, but they'd never crystallized in this way, never allowed her to recognize corporate prejudice on such a macro and a micro level.

Now, for the first time in her whole life, she let herself picture herself as CEO of an investment bank, a role model for young girls to look up to. Maybe then her scraping fear would go away, her fear that nothing she did mattered at all, that it was all just noise so she wouldn't have to sit in the silence and observe how her own hopes, her own heart, had stopped making any sound.

But if she was being honest with herself, she didn't know if she could genuinely encourage those little girls to follow in her footsteps. She didn't want any child with bright, splatter-paint dreams to have her spirit broken in the kind of way required to grind to the top of a profit-obsessed bureaucracy, to end up like this, clinking champagne flutes for something as meaningless as shifting money around, siphoning fees for profits. If she really wanted to be a role model, she should insist they cling to their passions at all costs. And she should take her own advice and break out of the golden handcuffs that kept her chained to this joyless job year after year.

But it wasn't that simple, not for her. She'd already made it this high, so she might as well keep going and break the glass ceiling, or at least put a few cracks in it. And it wasn't like she was that passionate about her passions anymore, even writing. Aside from the *New York Times* piece, all the poems she wrote came from deliberate planning, not zealous abandonment. She hadn't managed to write anything new since that one had been published, and she was certain she was a one-hit wonder.

She had the time to write now but not the inspiration. Everything in her life was even keeled and comfortable. There was none of

324

the drama or emotional extremes that had compelled her to heave the words off of her chest, scrawl them with the ink of her own bleeding heart before they suffocated her. That's why the best poets always had messed-up lives, she'd decided. They channeled their angst into art. If she had to choose between writing well and living well, she chose living. But there was a restless feeling deep inside that made her wonder if there was another world, a parallel universe that she'd nearly been born into, where those two objectives might align.

Bill and Linda headed out after the main course so they could stop by to see their grandchildren before the kids went to bed, but Rae, alert from her new-yet-old revelation, said that she and Stu would stay for dessert.

"How wild was that?" Stu said, once they were alone. "I guess you were right about that poem after all."

Stu had quickly apologized for his poor reaction to Rae's sexism poem, but she'd felt he'd still never quite believed it was doing much good.

"Who would've thought?" Rae said dryly, and they both laughed at themselves.

"I wonder if Linda has read your love poems too," Stu said.

"Maybe," Rae said, not particularly interested in knowing the answer. Those poems didn't stir much within her own heart, and she knew by that barometer that they didn't stir much in other people's hearts either.

"I still think romantic rhymes change the world more than political rants," Stu said.

"The Wall Street poem wasn't political," Rae said, trying to keep the edge out of her voice. "It was personal."

"Well, I'm just saying, all your *IndyStar* fans would be wanting my autograph if they only knew I was your muse. Your pseudonym is really keeping me from being a household name, I'm not sure I like it anymore."

"Har, har. You could always submit your own poems."

Stu snorted. "You know I don't speak that language," he said, and Rae felt a sad kind of truth in his words. "I leave that up to my multitalented girlfriend. Wheeling and dealing deals one day, publishing poems the next. She's unstoppable."

"Hardly," Rae said. She had a foot in both worlds, but it felt like her soul had stopped being in either one.

They ordered two desserts and split them both. Stu took the bigger halves for himself, but he made fun of himself as he did it so Rae couldn't get annoyed. She charged the meal to her corporate credit card and left a 50 percent tip, wondering how the waiter would do with the unexpected cash, remembering back to how an extra hundred dollars had once left giddy.

"You know," Stu said, looking at Rae with his open adoration. "Some guys might have their masculinity threatened knowing their girlfriend makes way more money than them, but not me. I know I'm dating a rock star and I'm perfectly happy being your trophy husband."

"Is that so?" Rae said with a sly smile that made her forget that he'd offended her at all. It was impossible to resist Stu's uplifting aura, and she'd stopped trying to. Life with Stu had a golden hue cast over it, like it was always summer. His optimism was an inflatable tube she could sit on to keep from sinking into the murky seaweed water of her own overly deep contemplations. "Well, if you play your cards right, that just might come true," she teased.

"I like my odds," Stu said. "But for real, I'm proud of you. I know you've been grinding and you don't exactly love your job, but who does, honestly? And all things considered, you have it pretty good."

Rae felt ashamed of how she hesitated to agree with him. Here she was, with all the privilege in the world, making a grotesque salary, and yet she still felt like she was coming up short, like her destiny was something bigger, something more vibrant than this black-and-white-suit reality.

If someone had told her, back when she was an intern, that she'd be closing a multi-billion-dollar deal before she was thirty, she would've looked at her future self with total awe. Now the awe was directed at her past self, all the youth and innocence she'd had back then, the spunk in her step that made her so sure she wasn't going to get sucked into something that didn't light her on fire.

But she *had* gotten sucked in. She didn't regret the decision to stay at her firm—she was proud of how she'd proven herself, in a strong-jawed kind of way—but she did regret the dreams she'd never truly let fly in the daylight, and now it seemed it was too late. Even if she set them free now, their wings wouldn't work right. They'd flop right onto the pavement and get run over by greasy tires.

"Yeah," Rae finally replied, willing herself to feel the satisfaction that she knew she should. "I have it pretty good."

She'd closed a high-profile deal at work, one that had the potential to accelerate her whole career. Now, as she and Stu walked out of the restaurant together, his arm draped over her shoulder, she tried to turn her thoughts to the other deal that had been on her mind, a far more meaningful one that would impact the rest of her life.

* * *

You used to leave dandelions at my door,
now I want you as my husband forevermore.

Rae scribbled the rhyme on a sticky note as she lay in the spacious bathtub of the Wilcox Box. Immediately, she balled up the pale yellow paper square and tossed it onto the tile floor, along with a dozen other rejected opening lines.

She'd been in the tub so long that the hot water had lapsed to lukewarm and the suds had fizzled into nothing. The dusky sun sloped through the bathroom's single skylight. A wine glass, empty with just the residue of a red ring, was propped beside the tub. Rae's prune-like fingers gripped a blue pen as she reached for a fresh note from her dwindling pad.

It was a couple weeks after the big deal at work had closed, and Rae was trying to write a proposal poem for Stu. They'd been dating a year now, and her grandpa had spilled the beans that Stu had asked him for Rae's hand. When Rae found out, she'd made Stu go back and ask her mom too. She was annoyed he hadn't thought of doing that in the first place, but she supposed that was just how things were done around here. It wasn't exactly Stu's fault for breathing in the inequality tinged air.

Rae had decided she'd say yes, of course. They'd have a short engagement and a small autumn wedding on Elmer Lake shortly before her thirtieth birthday, just over a hundred days from now. She'd walk down the foliage-lined aisle and they'd exchange short, humorous vows that got the guests laughing, and then they'd take a cruise around the lake, the pontoon adorned with a homemade *Just Married* sign. It was all coming together, as if it had been planned out for her whole life, which perhaps it had been. After so many years of her life veering off course throughout her twenties, Rae found this very soothing, like she could simply go along for the ride and be led in the right direction.

Still, it made her jumpy not knowing when Stu might pop the question, if she'd be having a frizzy hair day or wearing a dress that photographed like a parachute, so she'd decided to preempt the process and close the deal early. She liked the idea of subverting the gender norms of a typical proposal, and she was sure Stu would like it too, once he got over that initial jolt of masculine conditioning that said the man should be the one to get down on one knee. It would set their marriage off on the right note, a note that proved she wasn't just going to become like every other Midwest housewife.

She'd never quite had that when-you-know-you-know moment that told her Stu was the one, but she figured that most people just embellished their own love stories to get more likes on social media. Or maybe Rae had too much of an analytical side to ever make such an important decision without turning it over in her head a hundred and ten times.

She chalked any lingering hesitations up to scar tissue from her parents' divorce. It was natural that she'd have fears about getting married, and caution wasn't correlated with poor decision-making. If anything, it was the opposite.

In emotional markets, just like in financial markets, trade-offs had to be made. It was impossible to get sky-high returns without the risk of crater-deep lows. For a lifetime investment horizon, she wanted a more reliable return. DSMB was the acronym she'd half facetiously patented—*Date Stocks, Marry Bonds.*

And logic aside, she loved Stu, with a love that was easier than anything she'd experienced in her life. It was a simple kind of love, but Rae now had the perspective to understand that didn't mean it was simplistic. It just meant their relationship wasn't weighed down with irrational anchors or ornamented with unimportant things. It was sewn from a single strand of golden thread from the local hardware store, the same thread that had tied them together as kids and back together as adults.

She thought about putting all of this into the proposal poem, but she was determined to come up with catchier couplets for Stu, since he preferred rhymes to free-verse rambling. She wanted him to know that she always heard him, even if she didn't always agree with him.

She racked her brain, willing a worthy rhyme to appear, even wiggling her nose to try to work up a sneeze. She didn't sneeze, but she did get a tickling sensation that made its way into her chest, then down her legs.

She ignored it until she couldn't. Getting out of the tub, she pulled on the *Team Bride* bathrobe she'd had made for Ellen's wedding. Traipsing wet footed into the kitchen, she refilled her wine glass, taking a few sips to keep it from sloshing as she walked.

Then, following the fidget that had a heart of its own, she went into her bedroom and opened the desk drawer, where she picked up a palm-sized notebook.

It was the Stall Street Journal, recently sent by mail from Ellen, who'd apparently snagged it from the "sell" pile, along with Rae's old Santa hat, before Rae had left New York. Ellen had refound them when she and Aaron were packing up to move apartments (they were looking for a bigger place to start a family) and decided it was time to return them to their owner.

The Stall Street Journal now seemed to be whining, crying even, to be written in, and so she brought it with her back into the bathroom, hoping it might catalyze her creativity. She liked, also, the notion that she was old enough to appreciate the symbiotic relationship between past and present, how her yesterdays helped write her tomorrows.

Slipping back into the tub, she leafed through the parchment-like pages, too quickly to make out any individual words, until she landed on a blank one. In her best cursive, she wrote the proposal poem's title—*Hoppily Ever After?*—an ode to the beer from their date in Indy, the night she'd realized that their love story might have a lot more life left in it.

Rae took another sip of wine, and then a gulp, waiting for inspiration to strike.

The sun shifted down, casting a lone ray on top of the cabinets, turning dust into glitter.

She turned to the very last page in the journal, deciding it might help if she started at the end and worked her way up. But the last page was already written on, in alarming red pen:

> Some hearts never start;
> Some hearts never stop;
> But all of ours are beating tonight.
> —Bellini

Vein by vein, coldness cut through Rae. She turned on the hot water but quickly turned it off again. She was craving the cold, the alertness of her senses, taking in the world one frozen frame at a time.

The red pen matched the ink on the very first page, half burned, where Dustin had inscribed that other Bellini quote about how if the world feels cold to you, then at least you know you're still warm inside. And Rae realized how Dustin had known, back when he first gave her the journal, that she'd write her way to the end, even when she hadn't had a drop of faith in it herself.

Submerging her head in the tub, she held her breath as long as she could, and then a little longer.

For a while now, she'd been trying to block out the darker, complicated emotions that might threaten her contentment. She'd been keeping her feet on the path she wanted them to follow, keeping her head down and burying herself in Stu's smooth-water optimism so she wouldn't feel her own storms. But in trying to keep the peace, she now realized she'd lost so many other pieces of herself. She was living the life she thought she should, not the life she thought she could.

Her lungs stretched, and her eyes blinked water in and then out again.

The forecast for the future was dissolving into hazy clouds, but she saw hazel clarity for tonight.

She couldn't hold her breath any longer.

Coming to the surface, she dried her hands on the sleeve of the bathrobe and opened the Stall Street Journal to its second-to-last page, completely blank, and wrote four rhymeless words.

PART 5

ELEVEN DAYS AFTER THE DEADLINE

CHAPTER FORTY-SEVEN
A NEW CYCLE BEGINS

"I've missed you," Rae gritted out, finally guiltless as she stood on the Lorimer Loft rooftop in late October. "God, I've missed you."

She was staring into the bright eyes of the volatile skyline that had wrapped her back into its urban folds as spectacularly as it had elbowed her out.

From across the East River, Manhattan pulsed to an electric hypnosis that made Rae forget that she'd ever left, or why she'd wanted to.

An ambitious wind gust tugged her newly chopped hair, poking out from the Santa hat she was wearing. The hat's pom-pom bobbed against her cheek to the changed-but-still-the-same Brooklyn beat.

On her walk over, no one had looked twice at her for wearing a Santa hat in October, and though she once might've been miffed that no one had even looked *once*, the blanket acceptance now made her love this city with fresh intensity.

She'd moved back on her thirtieth birthday, eleven days ago. It had felt like a very satisfying symbol of rejecting the rigid married-by-thirty timeline that she'd built up for years and years, ballooning it into the ultimate delusion of success.

The plane ride had physically lifted her, freeing her from the weight of other people's expectations, and more importantly, freeing her from her own. Contrary to what she'd made herself believe, and what society had made her believe, she had not shriveled up into a withered old maid now that she was single at thirty. Paradoxically, or perhaps not paradoxically at all, she felt younger than ever, a new-born child in this vast, vast world that asked nothing from her except that she might pause and breathe in its miracle.

This was her first time on this rooftop in over two years. She'd sneaked into the building in the drunken wake of a group of baby-faced midtwenties. Too energized for the elevator, she'd walked up all eight flights of stairs and emerged onto the empty roof.

Back in Indiana, the breakup with Stu had gone as smoothly as she could've hoped, but it still left her feeling frayed. He'd asked if she'd change her mind if he agreed to move to New York with her, but she'd said no, she still didn't think they were the right fit, and he'd said okay, there was no way he'd move there anyway. During their final hug, she'd slipped that horribly insufficient *I'm so sorry, Stu* note into his jeans pocket, liking the idea that he might keep it for a while and remember her handwriting, before he found someone else whose cursive was easier to read.

She hadn't wanted the hug to end, but she'd been relieved when it had. Stu, too, seemed to acknowledge that this good-bye was going to stick in a way their prior ones hadn't. He had seen it in the way Rae's eyes stayed fixed even as they dripped tears: the two of them came from the same place, but they were branching toward vastly different futures. Or rather, she was branching off and he was staying put.

Sitting there in the hot tub of the Wilcox Box, Rae had finally started to admit to herself how a comfortable life with Stu in that comfortable house on the lake gave her the feeling of being caged in, like a cheetah who'd been taken to a zoo before she'd ever had a chance to sprint full-speed across the savannah and feel the raw power of her own legs.

Rae wasn't done with her wild yet. It was starting to feel like she'd never be done with her wild, that maybe that was the whole point of womanhood after all, to break out of all the self-made or man-made cages, to run unleashed down the paths that you can't stay away from, not to obediently walk down the ones you think you ought to.

Leveraging the momentum, she'd broken up with her job, too. It was finally time to work as hard for herself as she'd been working for someone else—no more distractions or excuses justifying why her dreams still had no mass. She'd saved up enough money to take a gamble at the writing life for a while. Otherwise, she'd never know. As she explained in a poem she'd jotted down in the cab ride from the airport, *I'd rather be haunted by failure than by not knowing if I would've failed.*

The decision to move to New York hadn't felt like a decision at all. The same holy force that had drawn her to New York for college had drawn her back now. There was no other setting in which she could picture herself being a real writer, no other place bursting at the skyscraper-and-subway seams with so many stories.

She'd told her boss that she was moving back east to be a writer so she could look herself in the eyes before she died and say, *Yes, I tried.* He'd listed off all the reasons she should stay until she made partner, but when she'd come into his office for a last good-bye, his computer had been open to an article titled "10 Reasons to Retire ASAP and Travel the World in a Van."

Rae hadn't second-guessed the decisions to leave her steady partner or steady paycheck, and it left her with a peculiar sense of melancholy that she wasn't the type of person who was content being content. But more than that, it had given her a new kind of adoration for herself, that she was finally making decisions based on how they felt inside her, not how they looked on paper.

Intuition was her new portfolio manager, exposing the grave-shaped holes in emotional investment strategies that focused on minimizing loss over a hundred-year time horizon rather than maximizing gains during each twenty-four-hour period.

Her mom hadn't said much about Rae's high-risk career switch, too busy mourning not getting Stu as a son-in-law (the moms had evidently already planned the wedding, down to the peony bouquets). Rae had told her mom to use the flowers at her own wedding to Chris, scheduled for the fall. As unfeminist as it felt, picturing her mom having a husband made it easier for Rae to move away again.

Her grandpa had ridiculed Rae's decision, but at the airport he'd grumbled lovingly in her ear, "You've got your grandma's spirit."

Her dad had been the most enthusiastic fan of the pivot. "Life's short," he'd told her, during one of their biweekly catch-ups that they now had scheduled in their calendars—consistent baby steps in what had been an inconsistent rebuilding process. "Might as well go for it."

Rae had finally felt like her dad understood her in that moment. He knew what it was like to do irrational things to avoid the haunting *What if?* Though Rae hadn't left her family to chase after a new life, she'd still let people down in the process. Perhaps this might be the deep connection point they'd been lacking to really get to know one another as the adults they'd become.

Ellen had been surprisingly unsurprised when Rae delivered the newly-single, newly-jobless news. "The universe was pulling you back," Ellen had said as Rae set down her suitcase in the future nursery of Ellen and Aaron's new Tribeca apartment, where she'd stayed while apartment hunting.

Rae had been set against ending up in Williamsburg but ultimately caved to the creative energy. She was subletting a scrunched third bedroom from two off-Broadway actors she'd met on a roommate-matching app. The women had resisted accepting "tainted money" from an ex–Wall Streeter until Rae had shown them the *New York Times* poem, which proved "decent insurgent potential."

Having roommates again was somewhat of a step backward, but she felt propelled forward with a freedom she'd thought she'd find only in fiction.

"And so begins a new cycle," Rae said, gripping the rooftop railing with clammy palms. Nothing had ever inspired her quite like this view.

Since being back in New York, she'd had two coffee chats with literary agents, the only ones who'd gotten back to her from the long list she'd cold-called. She hadn't shown them her writing—she was still experimenting with voices and styles and wanted to play a while longer before being judged on a full manuscript—but she thought it would be helpful to learn about the industry from insiders. During both coffees, Rae had ordered tea, and both agents had explained that poetry books were extremely hard to sell. They didn't want her to be disillusioned, they'd said, though that seemed very much their intent.

Instead, Rae had walked away more determined than ever to beat the odds.

Last night, in her thin-walled bedroom, as her roommates belted lines in the living room, she'd sneezed out six pages of half-prose, half-poetry that felt like it might take her somewhere, or perhaps nowhere, but she was going to find out.

All four Scramblettes were back in New York, with Sarah having returned after business school with her girlfriend-turned-fiancée. Mina had never managed to move away and was now living with the guy she'd bumped into on the staircase. Perhaps they'd all scramble back together, or maybe they'd just flip memories from time to time, smiling as the yellow yolks broke over a city that wore too much black.

As for Dustin, Rae hadn't told him she was here. She'd moved back here for her own personal goals, not any expired romantic hopes. Sure, she'd thought about him while sitting in the bathtub trying to write that proposal poem for Stu—and more than a few other times since—but that didn't mean he was the right person for her. It just meant Stu was the wrong one.

She wasn't even halfway sure anymore that she wanted to end up with anyone. Maybe she'd never get married or have children, maybe she'd adopt kids on her own or have a sperm donor, or maybe she'd become a wife after all, but on her own timeline. She had no idea what the future held, but this didn't make her feel blind or behind. It made her feel like she was bursting with life.

The only deal she wanted to close was the one that freed her from all of her archaic obligations and expectations.

She and Dustin would always be tied together at a spiritual level, but in a concrete sense, they were destined to unravel. She'd matured enough over the years to see that and respect it. Gone were the days of trying to force fate to conform to her own imagination.

She wasn't exactly sure how she'd ended up back on this roof tonight. She would've liked to blame the judgment call on alcohol, but she hadn't been drinking. She'd just been taking a nighttime stroll through the graffiti-streaked streets of Williamsburg, sponging up the vibrancy so she could wring it out onto the page later, and she'd somehow wound up here.

Now she found herself scrolling through her phone to find Dustin's number. Perhaps it wouldn't be the worst thing to just let him know she was here, she decided. It would be a pleasing and poetic proof of her evolution as an independent woman, how she could stand right beside him on this memory-haunted rooftop and not fall back into his arms.

He picked up in the gap between the third and fourth ring.

Her voice escaped, a raw, scraping sound. "Dustin."

A pause stretched, then condensed. "Rae?"

She willed herself to think of something poetic or witty, or better yet wittily poetic or poetically witty, but nothing came.

"Where are you?" Dustin asked, betraying no emotion.

"On the roof."

He might have moved apartments, but she knew he hadn't, with as much certainty as she'd known she had to return.

"Lorimer Street?"

"Lorimer Street," she repeated, the name back on her lips like it had never left.

Silence stretched until Rae knew he'd hung up. Her heart began to plummet, and she cursed how much she still cared, but she exalted in it, too, the ability to feel so much.

He reappeared in her ear. "I'll be right there."

Hanging up, Rae stared across the river, at Manhattan's manic magnetism, the ups and downs of the architecture, the complete naïveté of ever thinking a formula could predict tomorrow.

The lights were illuminating, not blinding, tonight. Rae wished on them, diversifying her single ask across many potential listeners—the spire of the Empire State Building, lit up green; the silver beads of the Williamsburg Bridge dancing once on steel and twice on water; the golden glow of a penthouse in a gravity-defying building; the red tail of an airplane taking off, or maybe landing, it didn't matter.

She didn't wish for a white-dress ending, or even for a single kiss. She just wished that Dustin would see her, down to every smudge on her soul, the way he'd always seen her, impossibly so, ever since that dating app algorithm had shown him her filtered photo through his phone screen. And she wished, too, an add-on request that she hoped the universe wouldn't find greedy, that he would let her see him as well, and all his smudges, old and new.

Rae didn't hear the door, but when she turned, he was there, walking toward her in the baggy shadows of their sleepless city.

He was still a little too thin and still moved a little too heavily. She didn't register these as flaws, just facts that bookended the *I love him* refrain that popped into her thoughts, as beautifully intrusive as ever. She repressed it the best she could, but by the time he was halfway to her, her defenses had all but surrendered to the wild beating of her heart.

Rae didn't know if Dustin would push her away or pull her under his chin. She didn't know if the scars on his arms had faded or if new ones had appeared, or if his thoughts had lightened or lifted or just drifted and darkened again. She didn't know if they'd rally together to a new peak or crash again into a trough, or if there would even be a "they" at all.

All she knew was that if she died tomorrow, she'd be glad she'd spent her final night alive.

Pulling the Santa hat higher on her forehead so it wouldn't impede her view, Rae watched Dustin cross the rooftop until he was standing right in front of her, so close that she could tuck her hands into his coat pocket if she wanted.

"You're back," he stated, like it had always been a matter of when, not if.

"Yes," she said, her balance as unsteady as her breath. "I'm back."

Dustin's parenthesis smile deepened the creases around his eyes, one free-verse line and then the next.

ACKNOWLEDGMENTS

I have so many people and places to thank for helping me reach my lifelong dream of being a published author.

My superhero literary agent, Abby Saul of The Lark Group. Not only do you provide incredible editorial feedback, but you continually lift me up just when I need it with your contagious confidence and kindness. I can't tell you how grateful I am to have you on my team for this magical, manic adventure.

My amazing editor, Faith Black Ross of Alcove Press. Thank you for understanding this story so well and for helping me elevate the manuscript into its final form. And a huge thanks to the rest of the Alcove team for all of your hard work.

My mom, Amy, for being my biggest cheerleader since day one. I've inherited so much of my creativity from you, and you even came up with the book's title. This is dedicated to you, of course.

My dad, Steve, for raising me to believe I could do anything so long as I put my mind to it. From you, I've learned how to dream big and challenge the status quo.

Acknowledgments

My brother, Jeff, for always being there to look out for your little sister and for sharing in my wins as if they were your own.

My aunt, Dr. Valerie Vullo, for reading so much of my writing over the years and helping me believe that I would be published.

My grandparents—Bill and Rita Vullo, and Jeanne and Rod Galloway—for being ridiculously proud of me no matter what. Granddad, I'm so happy you were able to learn about my book deal before you passed on, and I still feel you smiling over me now.

This book also wouldn't be here without my marvelous friends who provided so much sisterly love and creative fodder during our tumultuous twenty something years.

Lydia Moynihan, for all the nights we laughed, cried, and danced in your sixth-floor walk-up that inspired Rae and Ellen's penthouse. Amy Chang and Sophie Hoffman, for the coffee breaks and giggly hugs in the office that kept me smiling through the grind. Sarah Wood, for the joy and selfless support you've brought as a friend and fellow writer.

My characters—Rae, Ellen, and Dustin—for leading me through the plot when I couldn't see more than a chapter ahead, and for pushing back when I tried to pull you in directions that weren't authentic. I'm so grateful that you exist.

Charles Salzberg, whose writing conference lit my publishing dreams on fire when I attended as a college student. Thank you for all of your encouragement over the years. Kate Prosswimmer, for helping me write my first query letter at age nineteen, and for all of the guidance since. Beth Bauman, for workshopping the first couple chapters of this manuscript in your writing class and helping the story stand on a firm foundation.

New York City itself, for inspiring me with your exhilarating energy. You're a main character in this book, and I'll always feel a romantic attachment to you.

The dozens of coffee shops and indie bookstores around the city where I wrote and learned about the publishing world. Special shout

out goes to Books Are Magic in Brooklyn, which was kind enough to partner with me for preorders.

The strangers I met, and the ones I simply observed from afar, at those coffee shops and literary events and random street corners. You helped lift me into the creative power of the collective and kept me going in a way I couldn't have in isolation.

Dartmouth College and the Creative Writing Department, for changing my life when I discovered freshman year that I could get course credit for writing make-believe stories. A big thanks to Catherine Tudish, my writing adviser for the manuscripts I wrote during college. I know I wouldn't have been able to write this book without that process of trial and error and relentless revision.

My Michigan hometown, for grounding me in the simple joys of small-town life, and my teachers and sports coaches at Mattawan Public Schools, for the time and interest you took in helping me reach my potential. The way you still check in to see what I'm up to means so very much, and I hope to always make you proud.

God, my creator, for gifting me with this exquisite existence and the ability to create. I pray that my words can touch a few hearts and help people know they are not alone.

And the love of my life, Aaron. Thank you for filling my world with so much sunshine, support, and (most importantly) ice cream. Meeting you was the golden lining of the pandemic, and life with you is sweeter than fiction.